To Anne & Kev
With love &
John

22-12-05

CW01080765

DREAM BOY

John Lalor

authorHOUSE™

1663 LIBERTY DRIVE, SUITE 200
BLOOMINGTON, INDIANA 47403
(800) 839-8640
WWW.AUTHORHOUSE.COM

First published by AuthorHouse 12/01/05

ISBN: 1-4208-8117-5 (sc)

Printed in the United States of America
Bloomington, Indiana

This book is printed on acid-free paper.

To

the Memory of

Doris Lalor

TABLE OF CONTENTS

My Grandparents	1
Grandma and Auntie Joan	5
Amanda Pringle	13
The Bus Journey and Hilda, alias Bert	19
Uncle Jack and Auntie Ida and The Storm	37
Bill and the Policeman	51
Frog Farm	63
Harry Postlethwaite and Miss Ethel Weatherspoon	85
Clare, The Old Man, The Nun and The Parrott	111
Crazy Shoes	137
The Shoplifter	143
Home Again	153
The Dream	167
Church, Father Ignatius and Julie	177
The Bird	195
Father Ignatius - An Irish Childhood and the Bishop	203
Father Ignatius - Man and Priest	211
Julie	215
School	221

The Man in the Fawn Raincoat 239

The Gang 247

Exit Miss Weatherspoon 261

Grammar School Scholarship 271

Six Months Later St Thomas More's Grammar School 283

The Park 305

Mortal Sin 311

Manhood Revealed 319

The Surgery and The Undertaker 325

Five Years Later The School's Demise 331

Wash Day 337

School Cricket - The Herbert Sutcliffe Memorial Cricket
Trophy 341

Prize Giving and Leaving School 359

Port and Lemon 367

The Bank 371

Hazel 383

One year later The Robbery 391

Ted and Eric 397

The Funeral 401

ACKNOWLEDGEMENTS

The following people merit my thanks for their advice, expert opinions, suggestions, encouragement, and much more. In particular, my family:

Sabina	Artwork, layout, and advice.
Roger and Thomas	Cricket rectification.
Simon	Second proof-reading and suggestions.
Matthew	Copyright permissions and technical support.

and

Anne Wright	First proof-reading, and amendments.
Neil Kendrick	Cricket advice.
Maureen Hallam	Typing up, and retyping.

In addition to the above I would like to thank the following people, agents and publishers for their kind permission to use quotations and poems as epigraphs which head each chapter. They are an integral part of each chapter content.

The quotations and poems for Chapters 1 to 8, 10 to 15, 18, 19, 21 to 23, 26 to 29, 31 to 35, 37, 38 and 'All Things

Bright and Beautiful' in Chapter 19 are accredited to Oxford University Press.

Chapter 16. 'Angela's Ashes' by Frank McCourt accredited to Harper Collins Publishers Ltd. (1996) and Aaron Priest (USA Agency).

Chapters 20 and 30. 'Under Milk Wood' by Dylan Thomas accredited to David Higham Associates and J M Dent & Sons Limited (Publishers).

Chapter 25. 'Men Talk (Rap)' by Liz Lockhead accredited to Polygon Publishers.

Extracts in Chapter 3 from 'The Sea Nymph' alias 'The Sea Princess and Other Poems', are attributed to Doris Hughes of Huntingdon, and The Cowper Press.

CHAPTER 1

My Grandparents

"In a hole in the ground there lived
a hobbit. Not a nasty, dirty,
wet hole, filled with the ends of
worms, and an oozy smell, nor
yet a dry, bare sandy hole with
nothing in it to sit down on, or to
eat; it was a hobbit hole, and
that means comfort."

The Hobbit or There and Back Again.
by J R R Tolkien 1892-1973.

CHAPTER 1

"Go on, have a feel!"

I was gobsmacked.

"Should I, or shouldn't I?"

Decisions! Decisions! Panic! Panic!

"What should I do?" raced through my mind.

I went weak at the knees and red as a beetroot. Sorry! I'm ahead of myself. I must retrace the steps of my early childhood.

Let me introduce myself.

My name is Derek, without a 'c'. Derek James Albert Postlethwaite, born July 14th AD. My great grandfather, Albert James Postlethwaite, hence my name, was a drum major. He had commanded the corps of drums in the military band of the Flockton West Yorks Fusiliers. We had a sepia picture of him, which had become faded and spotted with age. This hung on the parlour wall, together with other relations. They had all since met their demise. Great Grandfather's photograph always impressed me as a boy, despite never meeting him. He was blown up by a German bomb in London at King's Cross railway station during the Great War. It was dropped by a Zeppelin. I wasn't even born then.

His photograph portrays him as a tall, slim, stiff-backed, upright man with a sturdy military bearing. He seemed to be at least 6′6″. His photograph had been taken against a contrived ruined wall, one end of which had an embroidered cloth loosely draped over it. His left leg with knee-length, spurred boots is lodged on a rough looking lump of rock, his left arm is resting on the top of the wall. His large hand, and right arm almost akimbo, clutches the curved handle of his long-bladed sheathed sword. His tunic is embellished with chunky brass buttons down the centre. The sleeves have white cuffs with roped embroidery almost to the elbow. The right sleeve has the crown of the realm nestling at the intersection of two crossed swords. Whilst the other sleeve has emblems, which are undistinguishable. High up across his chest is a white sash, below which hangs a row of medals.

His face is large and oval. A big Roman nose, with penetrating eyes set very closely together, his small ears, and kidney shaped short hair, gave him an imperious look. A white helmet with a rounded peak, and a pointed bulbous spike at its apex sits proudly on the wall next to a pair of white long-cuffed gloves. I really couldn't imagine him as an infantryman charging into battle firing a musket dressed so elegantly, nevertheless he was my family hero. Great Grandfather Postlethwaite was my father's grandfather.

Next to him hung a picture of my mother's parents, Grandad and Grandma Pilkington, Fred and Bertha. They were sitting astride a tandem, with Grandad at the front, wearing a checked, peaked, flat cap, coarse tweedy jacket and plus fours, knee length socks and very large pointed boots. He must have had unusually large feet. A cigarette hung between his walrus-moustached lips. Like my Great Grandfather Postlethwaite, his nose was long, straight and very Roman looking. Grandma sat at the back of the tandem, wearing a long sleeveless black dress, possibly distended by a framework of steel hoops. She too, had a Roman nose. They both had kind faces, and looked very serious. I would think they were in their early thirties. I never knew Grandad. He was the illegitimate son of Lord Rothershyde, who had lived somewhere in Yorkshire, and died at sea, shipwrecked, having fathered 15 children.

These two photographs became the bedrock of my family history. Although very faded they represented a past which still existed in my mind. There was a great deal of empathy between us - the dead and the living. They symbolised my parentage, and gave me comfort.

CHAPTER 2

Grandma and Auntie Joan

---

*"I mourned, and yet shall mourn
with ever-returning spring."*

Walt Whitman 1819-1892.

CHAPTER 2

"Derek, I want you to hurry home as quickly as you can after school to say goodbye to Ma before I take her to hospital for a few days," said my father.

I ran home after school, falling down on the way, and badly grazing my knees. Both were bleeding, and my shirt was torn, hair dishevelled, a muddy face and out of breath, but I saw her just as the taxi was about to leave. My father was sitting by her side.

"You've left it a bit late, lad," he said.

My mother hugged me tightly. We both cried.

I never saw her again.

Ma was only 33 years when she died. I was only nine, nearly ten. I was never told what had happened. She disappeared from my life, became extinct, vanished, and lost forever without any explanation.

I had a younger brother, Brian. He was four years my junior and quite oblivious to the changes that were taking place in our lives.

This was a turning point in my young life. I was not aware of what had happened. Yet resulting from this inextricable dilemma I have grieved for a large part of my life. I felt I had been cheated, not because my mother had died, but because I was not told. I only found out as I grew older, and worked it out for myself.

I was sent to my widowed Grandma in London. The one on the tandem. She was a lovely lady, who had a penchant for Shakespeare. Grandma had a large Victorian house and garden with an orchard full of apple, pear and plum trees. I spent many happy hours climbing trees with my aunt. My Aunt Joan was only five years older than me. She was my mother's younger sister. Joan was a real tomboy and led me into a lot of mischief, which has stayed with me most of my life.

She was a very mature 14 year old girl with breasts like young ripe lemons, topped with pink nipples resembling newly developed rosebuds. They hung loose from her bra as she climbed through the branches. I would follow her closely as we climbed together, my eyes glued to her knicker-clad thighs, hoping to see what girls had between their legs. My aunt was my first experience of a woman's body, and all things sexual. Girls had become a mystery to me. They were sensuous, unknown, and curious. They excited me. I wanted to know more about them. I developed an indescribable fascination for breasts.

Joan often caught me gazing fixedly at her breasts. She would tease me by undoing the top two buttons of her blouse, bending forward to show me her rounded bosoms as they fell almost unfettered out of her bra. On one occasion she left off her bra and wore a low-cut, see-through, pale lemon, chiffon kaftan. I saw her nippled, firm, rounded breasts, and right down to her ankles. I was not sure if she was trying to tease me, or impress the young Air Force pilot on leave next door. Grandma hastily told her to put something decent on.

"What do you imagine Derek will think? You're immodest dressed like that. You've got nothing on underneath. And where did you get that dreadful dress from? Your older wayward sister I suppose," she said - another aunt.

Little did she know I loved it, especially the breasts.

Joan turned round in anger and stamped up the stairs to change, her pear-shaped bottom oscillating as she moved. I gazed at her tramping up the stairs captivated by her moving bottom swaying from her hips. The kaftan clung to her body emphasising its nuances. I had discovered a new dimension to a girl's sexuality.

I longed to touch Joan's breasts or rub up against them. I tried many times to get close to Joan, but she always shied away. Once I nearly asked her if I could feel them.

"Joan would you mind if I touched your breasts, just one with my finger? They're so lovely. I wish I had breasts. I would let you touch mine." I never did ask her. I was too shy. Joan was my first love, although, in theory, she was my auntie. This experience was the precursor to my compelling interest in breasts, which has intrigued me all my life.

I had been in London for most of the school summer holidays - about four weeks I suppose. Apart from Joan's breasts there were not many other incidents, though I do remember one. Whilst climbing trees with Joan in the orchard, swinging on ropes and generally fooling around, she suddenly said,

"Fancy a fag, Del?"

She always called me Del which annoyed me.

I wasn't sure what she meant, but I said,

"Yes, please."

"Follow me", she said.

We went through the long grass, nettles, a large patch of overgrown rhubarb and brambles towards a dilapidated wooden shed. The door was hanging from its hinges, the window panes smashed, but the roof seemed in reasonable condition. I found out later that this part of the orchard had been a vegetable garden.

"Come on, Del, don't hang about."

I followed Joan into the shed.

"Make yourself comfy on that straw. I'll get the fags."

I went to sit down, and as I did a monster thing shot out of the damp straw and disappeared somewhere in the shed. It was like a long brown rabbit, but savage and bloodthirsty-looking with yellowish teeth. I yelled out in fright and started to cry. I expected to be torn from limb to limb at any moment.

"What's up?" she said. "It's only a rat. It won't hurt. There's lots about. The smoke will scare them off when we get the fags going."

I stood still, frozen to the floorboards of the shed desperately trying to hold back my tears. Joan eased up a plank of wood and lifted out a biscuit tin. I knew it was a biscuit tin because written on the top was 'Old Blacksmith's Shop. Gretna Green'. Underneath in faded letters it read, 'Petticoat Tails Shortbread Biscuits'. The coloured paint was beginning to wear off leaving flaking rust. There was a blacksmith with his hair tied with a ribbon holding an open book. He faced a smartly dressed man and woman. Joan prized the lid off and pulled out another tin, a smaller one this time, opened it up and inside were the fags which I now realised were cigarettes, together with a small bundle of silver paper.

She sat down on the straw with her legs apart. Her skirt was riding high above her knees showing her green elasticated school knickers, and her scratched, chunky thighs. She handed me a cigarette, and put one between her own lips. Next she unfolded the silver paper which held the matches and a piece of rough sandpaper. The first match fizzled out after a sputter of sparks as she scratched it across the sandpaper. The second match frothed and bubbled, but it too didn't light.

"Sod, sod and bugger!" she said.

She held the third match firmly between her fingers and nervously dragged it over the sandpaper. Still nothing happened.

"The bloody, bloody sandpaper is damp, and bloody well bloody wet!" she said in exasperation, the cigarette still dangling from her lips.

I still held mine between my middle two fingers just like my dad. Outside the shed I remembered seeing some bricks because I'd stubbed my toe on one, and it was still throbbing.

"Joan, I know what to do. I'll get a brick, that should do it. Hold my fag."

"Put it in your mouth silly", she said.

Cautiously I put the cigarette into my mouth, too much of it at first. I had to carefully pull it out so it rested on my bottom lip. It was now held firm and in place by both lips. I fetched the brick, and we were in business once again. The brick and match in unison gave way to sparks, effervesced, and burst into flames.

"Bloody good," she said.

The match well alight now, was put to the cigarette. She sucked hard. The cigarette lit, and smoke belched out of her mouth making her cough and splutter. The match dropped onto the shed floor, and ignited the straw. We both trampled on the flames, and soon put out the fire.

"Del, light your fag."

"How?" I said.

"Put your fag end on the glowing tip of my fag, and suck hard."

I drew near to her face and our cigarettes touched, like mating couples.

"Suck, suck you fool!" she said.

I was more interested in getting close to her, looking into her blue eyes, and peering down the top of her blouse. I sucked hard, and soon smoke was drawn into my mouth, down my throat and into my lungs. I coughed, choked, and my respiratory organs became garrotted. I ceased to breathe momentarily. I pulled the cigarette from my lips, but it had stuck. I tried again, harder. It came away, and so did the skin from both lips.

They bled relentlessly.

"Haven't you smoked before?" said Joan puffing away between coughs.

"Not fags", I said. "I usually smoke my dad's pipe."

"You're a bloody liar," Joan said.

"Honest I do."

"Don't believe you, you're a bloody fibber."

The smoking episode taught me a lesson because I never smoked a cigarette again. Grandma was worried about me. My bleeding skinless lips took a great deal of explaining. I was sure she knew what we had been doing. I learnt much later that Joan, at 16, had been expelled from St Hilda's Public School in Brighton for smoking and drinking alcohol.

CHAPTER 3

Amanda Pringle

"When amatory poets sing their loves
In liquid lines mellifluously bland,
And pair their rhymes as Venus yokes her doves.
They little think what mischief is in hand."

Don Juan canto 5, st.1.
Lord Byron 1788-1824.

CHAPTER 3

Whilst staying with Grandma, I was taken out by a lady who had been my mother's friend. She was a poetess, known as Amanda Pringle of Paddock Wood. I understand she was well known within literary circles, having had several books of poetry published. She had given me one of her books. It was green with a hard cover and called 'The Sea Nymph, and other Poems', illuminated in gold letters. It was not the poems which captured my imagination, but the illustrations.

The Sea Nymph lives beneath the sea, in a palace guarded by strange sea-monsters. Flashing fishes great and small bring her news of the world above the sea. Her robes are made of seaweed, and pearls adorn her naked breasts and hair. Mermen sit and pine for her. They sing of their love, but in vain. The Sea Nymph is hungry for a mortal's kiss. She lures her mortal love from the shore, lulls him to sleep, and bears him down beneath the sea. He lays cold, and resting on her bare bosom. She says,

"Belov'd awake, awake my love!"

He neither stirs nor speaks, but only sleeps. Through a million, million years he lies in ageless sleep. Whilst she in immortal life lives on in endless longing that she might sleep with him.

Several poems had exciting illustrations, thrilling me with their sexual undertones. These were realistic drawings in black and white reminiscent of Aubrey Beardsley. The Sea Nymph stands with proud nippled breasts supported by a garment flowing to her slender ankles. She has a grief-stricken look on her face as she gazes unhappily at her sleeping lover, prostrate on a carpet of flowers. His body is canopied with ornamental silks.

> *"Where my love untroubled lies,*
> *Sleeping with soft-shuttered eyes;*
> *While the silver fountain rise,*
> *Singing solemn melodies:*
> *Would that I might sleep with him!"*

My first understanding of the loveliness of the female figure was the book's illustrations to Amanda Pringle's poems, 'Song of the Spirits'. The spirits were of ethereal beauty in all kinds of poses, hovering in flight with arms outstretched, their long hair flowing, pert breasts sitting proud as their bodies lean back in retreat, explicitly rounded bottoms - a tour de derriere. The provocative images explored the limits of extreme sexuality, and invited the viewer to share in forbidden fantasies, as well as the poem's substance.

> *"Where loveliness is naked unashamed and free,*
> *We are the Song of the Spirits*
> *beyond an opal sea."*

I have treasured this book, not because of its titillating drawings, and in some cases prurient verse, but because of its association with my mother. One poem in particular called 'Friendship', was dedicated to her. The poetess writes,

"My days were happy for I found a friend."

The friend of course was my mother. Through the poem I found I was nearer to her, not in flesh, but in spirit. We had become closer through Amanda's poetry.

Amanda Pringle took me to Buckingham Palace to see the Changing of the Guard, to museums, galleries, parks, the Tower of London, the Planetarium, Madam Tussaud's Waxworks, and many more famous and interesting places. We always finished the day with a visit to a Lyons Corner House Café for tea. One day I had a ham salad, and being hungry I ate the lot including a raw, red chilli pepper. The pod was almost 2″ long and pointed at one end. I looked at it, not having seen one before, or knowing what it was. Should I cut it up and eat it? I cut it in half and popped the largest portion into my mouth. The first bite breaking the skin was hot, so I chewed vigorously and swallowed. My mouth and throat became hotter and hotter, like a burning furnace. Without thinking I spat out what was left of the chilli, but missed my plate.

I splattered the white tablecloth with chewed bits of red pepper and seeds, some of which went in Amanda's tea. My mouth seemed to be on fire, hot and smoking.

Amanda called the waitress for some cold water. I drank copious amounts, which seemed initially to make my mouth hotter. After about an hour my mouth and throat began to cool down. I was still badly shaken, and tears were still trickling down my cheeks from swollen red eyes. Amanda held my hand tightly as we made our way to the bus stop, back to Grandma. We told Grandma what had happened, and I started to cry again. Amanda clasped me tightly to her bosom to comfort me. What joy that was. I could feel her firm pointed breasts beneath my thin cotton shirt. I relaxed at the unusually soft touch of her warm kiss on my forehead, at the same time she pressed me closer and tighter against her swelling bosoms. This was my first known contact with breasts, and a warm moist sensuous kiss. I was transported, blissfully happy. The heat from my body was no longer the chilli, but the effects of Amanda's warm embrace. I was in love again, but this time with a 30 year old woman, not a 14 year old schoolgirl.

Amanda took me out once more, then it was time to go home to Dad. I never saw nor heard of Amanda again. I have her book of poems, and her spirit and kindness lives on through her words.

> *"Love still remains! Ah, on my tender breast*
> *Pillow your head!*
> *There let your tortured soul awhile find rest*
> *For your heart to make,*
> *There let its throbbing and its anguish cease*
> *There let it break!"*

I packed my case and said goodbye to Joan, who smelt very strongly of tobacco. We separated from the impulsive hug she gave me, she winked, and said,

"I'll miss you Del, don't do anything I wouldn't do."

She winked again and ran off. I remember the embrace she gave me, it was warm and comforting. Though I didn't feel her breasts there was a real bond between us. I learnt later that she went to her room and cried. I, too, felt tearful.

CHAPTER 4

The Bus Journey and Hilda, alias Bert

"What is this that roareth thus?
Can it be a Motor Bus?
Yes, the smell and hideous hum
Indicat Motorem Bum!....
How shall wretches live like us
Cincti Bis Motoribus?
Domine, defende nos
Contra hos Motores Bos!"

A D Godley 1856-1925

CHAPTER 4

"You're going to stay with your Auntie Ida and Uncle Jack until it's time for school. Then you'll go home to your Dad and Brian. They'll meet you at Royston and take you to Cambridge," said Grandma.

Grandma put me on the bus and gave me a big bar of chocolate and a bottle of lemonade. She smothered me with hugs and kisses. We both cried and waved frantically to each other as the bus pulled out of the station.

"Sit down lad, and don't bloody move," hailed the driver through his cab microphone. There were very few people on the bus, and I knew he was speaking to me. His aggressive manner made me cry even more.

A lady, dressed in black trousers and jacket with red piping around the cuffs and collar, wearing a red peaked cap came up to me.

"Never mind love. He's a nasty bastard. I'll look after you. Your Grandma told me all about you, so don't worry love. What's yer name? Mine's 'Hilda'.

"Don't know! I mean Derek! I said.

"Well, Derek, if yer want anything just you say. And take no notice of the bloody driver. He drives the bus, I look after the passengers. OK, love!"

"Yes Miss, sorry, Hilda. Thank you," I said.

The bus shook, and rattled as it trundled along. It had a pungent smell, rather like a urinal. The bus's vibration and stench made me feel sick. I nearly threw up several times. It started to rain, and the sky turned black. I noticed the roof was leaking just above the seat in front of me. There were more leaks in other parts of the bus. Passengers had to keep moving from their seats to avoid the drips from the leaking roof. Hilda came up to me.

"Are yer alright me duck? This bleeding bus ought to 'ave been scrapped long back since. One day I'll set the bloody thing afire."

"What time do we get to Royston?" I asked.

"As long as it takes me duck, no set time, anything up to ten hours. One day the bloody bus broke down, and we 'ad to sleep in the damn thing whilst it was mended. Don't worry love, I'll see you alright."

The rain had stopped but it still looked very gloomy outside. The bus lights were glimmering on and off.

"Do yer want a pee, Derek, we'll be stopping soon at Hertford. The bus driver has to stop for a pee, and a fag. Nasty bugger 'e is."

"Don't know," I said.

"Wait and see 'eh," Hilda replied.

The bus pulled into the bus station. Most people got out to go to the loo. I went but couldn't pee. As soon as I got back into the bus, and the driver started the engine, I wanted to pee like mad. I got up, and Hilda took me to the loo. She even went inside the Gents with me, and almost stood over me whilst I peed.

"Give it a good shake, Derek. I allus do," she said.

Bit odd, I thought, but then I didn't understand how ladies peed. Back in the bus again, the driver shouted through his mike …..

"Why didn't you leave the daft bugger behind?"

"Never mind 'im," said Hilda.

We were on our way again. The heavens opened, the sky became blacker and blacker, lightning streaked ahead and thunder clapped above. The approaching traffic had their lights on, which dazzled me. I shut my eyes to keep out the glare, and within a very short time I was asleep.

The bus came to a grinding halt. I was thrown forward, my body thrust against the back of the seat in front, recoiling back to my original sitting position as the bus noisily came to a standstill. Waking up from my deep sleep suddenly, not realising where I was, nor what was happening, I felt disturbed and isolated. It was gloomy outside.

"Where am I? What am I doing here?" I thought.

"All orff, don't leave any stuff behind. Yer gerin' orff 'ere," barked the driver through the mike.

The bus had pulled into a bus station of sorts. It had stopped raining and was almost dark. The bus clock said 9.50pm. The lights were dim, and the few passengers hurried off the bus with their plastic bags, cases and umbrellas. One old man was dragging a small tree wrapped up in some old sacking down the bus gangway.

I was not big enough to pull my small brown leather attaché case from the overhead rack. I stood on the seat, but still couldn't quite reach it. Standing on tiptoe and straining upwards with my sinews almost at snapping point the case still eluded me.

"'Ang on, luv. I'll gerr it," said Hilda.

My case firmly in my hand, and the half-melted, untouched chocolate bar in my pocket, we both alighted from the bus.

"Good night, Fred," shouted Hilda, as the driver locked up the bus and rushed off, his head bent down, coat collar turned up. His peaked cap was angled tightly on his head and an unlit cigarette dangled from his mouth.

"Tarrah! See yer, Bert," called the driver.

"Odd," I thought, "she's called Hilda."

"We must find your aunt and uncle," said Hilda.

We spent at least an hour looking for them, making enquiries at the office, but they had not been seen nor heard of. I was becoming panicky, wondering what was going to happen to me.

It was now almost 11 o'clock, and the bus station was deserted, only me and Hilda left. The office was closed. Suddenly the bus station lights went out. We were left alone in total darkness, and an eerie silence hung in the damp air. The distant sound of a car horn broke the silence, making us both jump.

"You'd better spend the night with me," said Hilda. "What do you think?"

"Don't know," I said.

"Can't leave yer here," she said. "I've got tomorrow off. We can sort things out then."

"Thank you," I said.

"I only live about five miles off, in a caravan just by Kneesworth Woods. Hang on here. I've to get me bike. It's just behind the offices, unless someone's nicked it."

We collected the bike, tied my case to the parcel carrier behind the seat, and set off with me sitting on the crossbar. At first we moved unsteadily from side to side. I nearly fell off several times, but we were soon cycling along at a steady pace, until we got to our first hill. It was not very steep, but it was too much for Hilda with me sitting on the crossbar.

"I'm knackered," she said as we alighted. "Are you alright, Derek?" she added.

"Don't worry, you're alright with me. We'll sort it out, Derek."

By now we had left the town behind, and were well into the country. Soon we were flying down the other side of the hill at breakneck speed racing into the black night, our lungs almost bursting with the rush of air as we went headlong into the moonless emptiness below. We both shouted as loud as we could in frenzied guffawing. Hilda peddled faster and faster, so fast that her feet could not keep up with the speed of the bike. We slowed down gradually and stopped, both falling off with the bike on top of us. We lay still for a few moments and then burst into uncontrollable laughter. Covered in mud and feeling slightly bruised I got up and tried to wipe the blood from my knees. They were cut and bleeding. The blood and mud mixture reminded me of black puddings.

My friend Eddie's father was a butcher, and I sometimes helped him, with Eddie, to make the puddings. We mixed pig's blood, suet and pork fat in a big vat with other secret ingredients, turned a handle, something like the handle on Grandma's mangle, and the mixture was fed into one continuous long black skin. The black sausage was cut into lengths of about 8". Some were tied end to end to make a round pudding, whilst others were left in sausage strips. He also made meat puddings, sausages and pork pies. Eddie used to smuggle out a pork pie for both of us to eat.

I was shaken out of my reverie by Hilda fussing over my knee with her dirty handkerchief.

"Are you alright Derek?" she said.

"Don't know," I said.

We'll soon clean that up," said Hilda.

Hilda looked dishevelled. Her cap was one-sided, her hair askew, her face muddy, and the knees of her trousers wet and torn. She straightened her cap, but her hair remained awry, as though it had moved off her scalp. She looked very funny. I had a job trying hard not to giggle at her.

"Come on, we're nearly home, just down the track, beyond the gate, through the woods. Ten minutes away, about," she said.

Hilda opened the double wooden farm gate, and pushed the bike through. We were now on a wide rutted mud track, with fields on one side, and a row of trees on the other. It was impossible to cycle because of the uneven muddy track. We just had to trudge along. I was feeling exhausted and hungry. In a short time we came to a dilapidated barn, where the track narrowed, and went into the wood.

"This is Kneesworth Woods," said Hilda. "My caravan is just through the trees ahead. It's not mine really. It belongs to Bill Wragg. He keeps the Bull Inn. His pub backs onto these woods. I do odd jobs for 'im, get plenty of free ale, and a place to kip. I only work on the buses four days a week, suits me a treat."

We soon reached the caravan. It was a pale, washed-out green with the paint peeling off. Hilda leaned her bike against the caravan side, and unlocked the door with a key she took from under a large piece of concrete.

"Follow me, don't forget yer case,' she said.

She fumbled about inside the caravan, struck a match, which went out, struck another and lit a lamp. The inside of the caravan glowed with a dingy light, and a damp musty smell lingered in the air.

"I know it smells mouldy, but it soon goes, you'll get used to it in a bit,' said Hilda.

An unmade double bed was at one end, and a small table and bench in the middle. Near the door was the sink and tap, a stove littered with unwashed pots and pans. A brush and shot gun stood leaning against the caravan wall in the corner.

"Tinker! Tinker! Tinker!" shrieked Hilda. "Tinker! Tinker!"

Within a few seconds a mangy, scruffy three-legged cat came slouching through the door. Hilda opened a tin of cat food and spooned half of it onto the caravan floor. Tinker went at it as though it was his last meal. The cat food eaten, and the floor licked clean, Tinker jumped awkwardly onto the bed, curled up and went to sleep.

"Must get this lot orff'" said Hilda.

She unbuttoned her tunic, exposing her chest and bra.

"Bit flat-chested," I thought.

She slung her tunic on the bed. Next, her bra came off, revealing a bare, flat hairy chest. I noticed that the bra cups were padded.

"That's better," she said, scratching her chest and arm pits.

She now took off her cap, her hair, which seemed to be part of the cap, and threw them on the bed. The cap and hair separated, and both landed on the cat. Hilda's head, without the hairpiece, had short cropped spikey hair, which reminded me of a hedgehog. I was astonished at Hilda's transformation. Her secret persona was revealed for all to see. Well, only me as it happened.

"Are you a man?" I asked.

"I'm a fella," said Hilda, "with a willy too!"

She undid her trouser flies, pulled out her willy, gave it a wiggle, and put it away again.

"I'm a gel when I'm working, only way I could get the job. They wanted a woman see. Off duty I'm a bloke. Call me Bert when I'm out of them poncey clothes. Yer don't mind, do yer Derek? I don't want yer to think I'm kinky. I'm dead straight, straight as a ramrod, in fact I'm ramrod straight. Bill'll tell yer."

"Don't know," I said, feeling distressed by Hilda's dual personality. "I mean, it's fine with me, Hilda, I mean, Bert, sorry! I'll get used to your new name," I said.

"Yer do talk posh," she said.

By now the cat's head was in Bert's hairpiece. I noticed the bra cups had pieces of shaped foam in them. I felt cheated, and wondered if all bras were padded out, instead of housing two warm soft nippled breasts. I had grown very fond of breasts during the last month.

Perhaps I had been deceived, and ladies' breasts were not as I had imagined. I had not seen them completely naked. I mentally made a note to pursue the nature of ladies' breasts and discover their real identity. Are they round and fleshy, soft and firm, comforting and cosy, or just lumps of foam hidden in a brassiere cup?

"Well Derek," Bert said, "want a drink before we turn in? I'm knackered."

"Don't know," I said.

"Ow about tea, coffee, Bovril. Oh! I've got some drinking chocolate, and chocky bickies," said Bert.

"Yes please," I said.

"What then?"

"Drinking chocolate and bickies please."

"Ginger or chocky bickies?"

"Don't know."

"Only got chocky biscuits, now I come to think. Tinker ate the ginger nuts."

The stove was lit. The kettle filled from the tap, which shuddered and rattled when it was turned on. At first brown water flowed but after a short time the water cleared. Two mugs were rinsed, and half filled with powdered drinking chocolate. The kettle vibrated and hissed, let out an agitated whistle as the top blew off, and hot steaming water gushed out of the spout. Bert filled the mugs, whilst I stirred the chocolate.

"Now for the bickies," said Bert. Bert started to move things about, old newspapers, cereal packets, clothes, books and pans in his attempt to find the biscuits.

"Where's the bleeding bicky tin?" he said.

"Don't know," I said. "Is that it?"

I could see a round red tin just peeping out from under a blanket on the bed.

"Good lad, that's it," said Bert, retrieving the tin, and prizing off the lid. Inside was an assortment of chocolate biscuits.

"Help yerself."

I looked inside the tin to choose a biscuit, and saw an enormous black hairy spider crawling over them. It looked like a tarantula. I gave out a gasp, and decided against a biscuit. Bert thought nothing of it, and ate about six biscuits, dismissing the spider as if it lived in the tin, and had a right to be there.

"Live and let live, I say," said Bert.

I felt too tired to eat, and just wanted to sleep. It was well past midnight. Within minutes of drinking my chocolate, and moving onto the bed, I was soundly asleep.

Slivers of sunlight penetrated through the faded thin flimsy curtains as dawn approached. A chorus of birds saluted the day with their morning song. A distant cockerel let out a throaty screech disturbing the relaxed start to the day. I woke up suddenly, realising I was in a strange place. I was frightened and coiled myself up into a ball underneath the blanket. The cockerel did not let up, and soon Bert was awake.

"Morning Derek, did yer sleep OK?" asked Bert.

"Don't know," I said. "Sorry I mean, Yes! Thank you!"

Bert sat up, stretched his arms, nearly poking me in the eye. He started to yawn. His breath was foul.

"Like his armpits," I thought.

"Could do with a fag," said Bert. "Can't 'ave one though, stopped smoking two days ago. May 'ave one later though for a treat. Do you smoke Derek?"

"Not now. I've stopped too," I said, feeling grown up at being asked the question.

Bert started to cough uncontrollably. He got out of bed, still coughing, kicked the caravan door open with his foot, yelling out, "Me bleeding toe!"

I followed him out, desperately wanting a pee.

"Where's the toilet, Bert?" I asked.

"Pee anywhere yer like, don't pee on the cat, 'e don't like it," said Bert.

"Fancy a fry up? Allus 'ave a fry up on me days orff," said Bert, grinning all over his face, his lips drawn back revealing his blackened teeth.

He went back inside the caravan, folded the bed and blankets, and set the table for breakfast with a bottle of tomato sauce and two forks.

"Bert! Where do I wash?" I asked.

"If yer want a proper wesh, 'ang on a bit, and we'll go to the pub. Yer can get some 'ot water there. If yer want a splash, use the bucket outside, as long as yer didn't pee in it. I'm going to the pub when we've had brecky," said Bert.

I rubbed my eyes and decided to go to the pub with Bert for a proper wash.

Bert soon had bacon, beans, sausages, mushrooms and tomatoes all frying together in a large pan, which took up most of the stove.

"Fancy an egg or two?" said Bert.

"Yes please, only one will be enough," I said.

"I allus reckon on two or three mesenn," mumbled Bert, with an unlit cigarette hanging from his mouth. He cracked four eggs into the pan's contents, the runny part of the eggs invading the mixture. The yolks seemed to sit on top of the medley, which was now looking like a pastiche of liquefied liquorice allsorts. Despite the unappetising mixture I ate with great enjoyment, mopping up my plate with two slices of pappy white bread, all swigged down with a mugful of stewed sweet brown tea. I was hungry, and despite the hotchpotch of foods, it tasted good. We both finished about the same time. Suddenly Bert let out a noise, which seemed to shake the caravan.

"Manners," he said. He belched again. "It's only stomach wind, least it don't smell like a good old fart, eh Derek! That's better," he said, giving out more noises. He dribbled from his mouth onto the back of his hand, which he wiped across his shirt front.

"Ah, that's better, where's me fag? Can yer see it Derek? Put it down I'm sure, might have fell in't pan," laughed Bert.

I had visions of Bert's cigarette dropping into the pan and blending with the mixture. It wouldn't be noticed, all stirred, up, and I'm sure it wouldn't be tasted either. It was never found.

"Do yer know where your auntie and uncle live Derek?" asked Bert.

"Don't know," I said. "But there is a label on my case, with an address on it."

"Let's have a look, see," said Bert.

Written on the label in Grandma's handwriting was:

Master D. J. A POSTLETHWAITE
C/O MR & MRS J. HOGG
FROG FARM
FROG END
CAMBS.

"Bill Wragg at the pub will know Frog End. He's born and bred in these parts. He knows all there is to know, does Bill. We can have a proper wesh at the same time. A towel for you, one for me. Orff we go," said Bert.

Bert gave me a towel, which had seen better days. It was greyish white, more grey than white, almost threadbare with a red splash of something on it, which looked like paint.

"My Grandma wouldn't use it as a floor cloth," I thought, but didn't mind. I was beginning to feel more confident. I was on a real adventure, now that my hunger pangs had gone.

We washed in the pub's toilets with cold water. The hot only came on at lunchtime. I felt better after a good wash with soap and after cleaning my teeth.

"Hang about, Derek. I need a crap," said Bert.

Bert took his time, and then we had to find Bill - the landlord. I followed Bert into the front of the pub. Bill was wiping down the beer pumps and bar top.

"Ay up," said Bert.

"You're an early bird, Bert," said Bill.

"Gotta a problem, Bill. Need yer help," said Bert.

"See what I can do," said Bill. "Let's sit down. Who's this young man Bert?"

"Derek, mate of mine," came the reply.

This made me feel really grown up. In a pub, and being called a mate. I stuck my chest out and tried to appear taller.

Bill held out his dinner plate hand and shook mine. My little hand crumpled up, my bones cracked, and I let out a silent wince of pain.

"Ow do, pleased to meet yer Derek, I'm sure," said Bill, known as Big Bill.

"Hello," I said.

Bill Wragg was all of 6'10" and at least 20 stone. His belly distended over his trouser belt in rolls. His hairless head, unshaven stubbled face, tattooed arms, and black finger-nailed hands were the colour of seasoned oak. He wore dirty brown corduroy trousers, which were too small. A short sleeved red check shirt undone by at least three buttons revealed a tightly curled brown pepper and salt hairy chest. His muddy boots were as big as snow shoes with hob nails and steel toe caps. No wonder he was known as 'Big Bill'.

"Sit yer sen down," said Bill. "Fancy a beer Bert? A coke for you lad?"

"Ah don't mind if I do," laughed Bert. "Bit early. It's me day off, so to 'ell w' it. Derek'll 'av a coke I'm sure. What yer say Derek?"

"Yes please," I said, feeling very grown up.

"Two pints and a coke Eth!" yelled out Bill at the top of his voice.

A tabloid newspaper lay flat on the table top. Bill nudged Bert with his elbow, and said, grinning all over his face, "Fancy yours as busty as these mate?"

Bert looked at the newspaper. "Make me top 'eavy with tits that big, but I'd like to get me molars round them chunky bits."

The newspaper was upside down which made it difficult for me to see what they were talking about, but it was something to do with the top half of a naked lady. I tried by twisting my head sideways to get a better look.

"Don't snap yer neck lad," grinned Bert, turning the paper round for me to see it full frontal.

At the same time he yelled, "Where's our bleeding beer Eth?"

Now I could see all. Two lovely welcoming voluminous breasts, pear shaped and pendulous, complemented with erect unrelenting nipples. I wanted to touch them with my hands, my face, and feel their soft warmth against my skin.

"Yer like tits lad!" said Bill.

"Don't know. Well 'err! They're alright, never thought about it," I said.

Knowing what a liar I was I could feel my face going red. I loved breasts, but I couldn't tell Bill about my obsession with girls' and ladies' breasts, and my fantasies.

"Yer wait 'til yer see the real thing. Can't get the feel of a good tit from a picture," muttered Bill.

"Give over," said Bert. "Don't fill the lad up wi' yer mucky talk, e's too young for that sort of rude prattle."

Bill was puffing away at his bent meerschaum pipe sending clouds of sweet-scented smoke into the air, a satisfied smirk on his face. Ethel arrived with two large beers and a coke. She gave Bill the coke, me and Bert a beer each.

"Eh, what yer doing, Eth? The coke's for the lad!" said Bill.

"No it ain't," came the reply. "Yer too fat, and yer beer belly will burst. I'm not clearing up no more mess."

Ethel turned her back on us and went wobbling out of the tap room. Her laddered lisle stockings just stopping short at the hem of her blue floral dress, which barely covered her large bottom. She disappeared before Bill had time to reply.

"Cheeky sod," he said, swapping my beer for his coke.

"Let's see. Frog End, yer said, Bert?"

"Ah! Frog Farm at Frog End, or is it Frog End at Frog Farm?" replied Bert.

"Yer daft bogger! One pint, and yer can't think proper."

"The farm's at Frog End, 'bout 50 miles yonder. Tell yer what, I'll get Eth to see to the bar, and we'll go in 't truck and get it sorted. 'Ang on, I'll ave a word with Eth."

Bill got up, grabbed his newspaper and ambled out of the tap room, stopping midway to light his pipe, heaving clouds of pipe smoke in his tracks, he disappeared.

CHAPTER 5

Uncle Jack and Auntie Ida and The Storm

'His rash fierce blaze of riot cannot last,
For violent fires soon burn out themselves
Small showers last long, but
sudden storms are short,
He tires betimes that spurs too fast betimes'

Richard II. Act 2 sc 1, 1.33
William Shakespeare 1564-1616

CHAPTER 5

The night that Uncle Jack and Auntie Ida were supposed to meet me, an almighty storm broke loose at Frog End, which caused my Uncle to give way to his little weakness - once again.

"Jack," shouted Ida. "I've got one of my bad heads. I don't feel too good. I'm going to lie down for a bit. You'll have to meet Derek without me. I'm sorry, but I'm no good till my head's gone."

"Trust you. Yer daft bat," grumbled Jack, out of earshot.

"Please don't leave it too late. The bus gets into Royston about nine. You be nice to our Derek. You know his Mam's just died."

Auntie Ida was my mother's elder sister. I had met her a few times when she came to see us, but I'd never met Uncle Jack. Uncle Jack was disliked by all the family. He had a reputation for getting blown out of his mind with drink, and pinching girls' bottoms, or anyone wearing a skirt. He avoided anyone wearing trousers, just in case they were not female. He once pinched a very shapely trousered bottom thinking it was a woman he knew, but it turned out to be a stranger. The stranger felt the pinch, turned round, saw Jack, and head butted him. Jack over-balanced and landed flat on the pavement.

"You dirty pervert," yelled the bearded man. "You ought to be locked up".

After several attempts Jack nervously managed to get back onto his feet. Suddenly he was hit again, this time on the nose. The blow split both his top and bottom lips, splashing blood everywhere.

"What's all this about then?" said a helmeted policeman.

"I see this as an instance of two people fighting in a public place. That's disturbing the peace mate. I'm afraid I'll have to charge you both with causing an affray. You'd better come to the station with me."

"Bollocks!" bawled the assailant, and walked off in the opposite direction.

Jack, his face covered in blood, sped down a narrow passageway between two buildings. The policeman, about 6'6" tall, stood legs apart, fuming that his authority had been usurped. He pulled out his whistle and blew, his cheeks puffed out as though blowing a trumpet, but no sound was made. He blew again, harder and harder, his cheeks getting redder and redder, but still nothing.

"I've lost my pea," he said. "Sod it! You win some, you lose some."

He adjusted his helmet, mopped his brow with his unused white handkerchief, straightened his jacket, looked to the left and to the right and crossed the road. He was last seen trundling down the street as if nothing had happened, and soon disappeared round a bend at the end of the road.

"Haven't you gone yet?" Ida shouted out in a high pitched cry of pain.

"Can't find the van's keys," yelled Jack. "I'll have to take the tractor."

"It'll take ten hours by tractor, and it's six now. Get a move on. You've only got three hours to meet the bus. Find the keys and get off," Ida cried out.

"Got 'em. The bloody cat's sleeping on 'em. I'll feed yer to the pigs if yer don't get out of my way," shouted Jack trying to kick the cat through the door, but missing and kicking the table leg instead. The table shook and the tea-pot fell off shattering on the stone floor.

"I'm off," yelled Jack, up the stairs.

"Bye," came a tormented cry from above.

Outside it was getting dark. The sky was black and thundery. Heavy clouds hung low and looked angry. A few large spots of rain splashed onto the van. In the distance, just beyond Hagg's Wood, streaks of lightning flashed across the sky. Claps of thunder, like gunfire, broke the stillness of the early evening. Jack turned up his coat collar and shuddered at the thought of driving to Royston in his clapped out old van. The van, when new, had been white, but when Jack bought it at auction five years ago, it was greyish white. Now it was a drab leaden colour with large blotches of rust breaking through the shabby paintwork. The honeycombed metal roof was so thin that shafts of daylight penetrated the inside from its perforations. One windscreen wiper, and the nearside headlamp, were inoperative. The tyres had no tread. The van was never taxed or insured with the excuse that it never went on the roads, and it was only used to house chickens. The van always started with the second or third turn of the key, usually with a bang, emitting noxious black diesel fumes. After a few minutes it would settle down. The engine was very noisy, and repeatedly backfired. It was not the sort of vehicle for a round trip of nearly 100 miles.

It was now 6.30pm, and Jack was on his way with about 50 miles to go before reaching Royston. The van would not go very fast, because the fourth gear had seized up, and the footbrake assisted by the handbrake, would only stop the vehicle if it was going 20 miles an hour. Any faster then fate took over. Jack felt all was well and he was in control, two and a half hours to get to Royston, and roughly 50 miles to go. The two nesting chickens in the back of the van didn't seem to bother him.

"I've got time for a quickie," he muttered to himself, pulling up and stopping abruptly against some chain link fencing outside 'The Dirty Duck.'

He retrieved three hen eggs from the back of the van and put them on the front passenger seat. The hens screeched, and tried to escape.

"Get in yer daft boggers," he shouted, slamming the van door shut followed with a kick to make sure it was secure.

Jack had only driven about five miles, but felt he was well justified in having a rest.

"Plenty of time to get to the bus station," he thought.

With head and shoulders bent forward against the impending storm he went into the pub's smoke room.

"Ow do Jack!" greeted the barman.

"Ay up mate," said Jack. Pint of Best in a jar. I'll have a chaser too whilst I'm at it."

The barman pulled a pint, filled a small glass with scotch from the optic, and pushed them across the bar top towards Jack.

"On the slate, mate, bit short, if yer don't mind."

"I don't mind, but Harry does. He says you owe him 40 quid. You've got to settle up he says. No more credit Jack. Orders is orders."

"Tel 'Arry I'll see 'im right with interest next week. Spud cheque due in any day now, and 'Arry 'as first call. OK mate!"

"If you say so, Jack, don't let me down, or I'm in the shit again."

"Good on yer mate."

Jack sat on a bar stool at the end of the counter with his back leaning against the wall. With one swallow the whisky disappeared, and with another half the beer. He took off his cap and dirty old raincoat, and dropped them onto the floor. From his grubby tweed jacket pocket he pulled out the 'Horse and Hounds' and started to read avidly. Looking up from the paper and eyeballing the barman, he said, "Fancy a win 2-30 tomorrow at Newmarket mate?"

"Good on yer, Jack," said the barman.

"I'll give yer a dead cert for a pint of Best and ten cigarillos, but don't put 'em on the slate."

"Sorry, Jack. If Harry finds out I'm finished."

"'E won't find out, there's no-one to tell 'im, only me and thee, and thee won't tell 'im. I'll not tell 'im, so what's the bother mate. Yer could be a few hundred quid better off tomorrow. I've got insider information for a dead cert win. Straight up! I tell yer it's KOSHER."

"You've twisted my arm, Jack, "said the barman.

Another pint was pulled, and cigarillos appeared with a box of matches.

"Ave a drink yerself," said Jack. "On the house mate."

Two pints of Harry's Best bitter were held high, and glasses clinked.

"Cheers, Jack."

"Good 'ealth mate."

Jack lit his small Spanish cigar, looked at his watch, comparing it with the clock on the wall.

"Yer clock's an hour fast mate."

The barman looked at his watch and the wall clock and said, "It's right by me, 'bout 8.30 I reckon Jack."

"Bloody hell, I'd better 'ave a quick one quick, and a chaser, large one if yer please mate."

The intimidated barman pulled another pint, and with a large scotch grudgingly slid them across the bar top towards Jack.

"Thanks mate."

The beer and scotch were quickly drunk, between noisy belching. Jack stood up, picked up his raincoat and cap, stuffed his paper into his pocket, and unsteadily walked out of the pub.

"Night Jack, safe journey," shouted the barman.

"Tarrah," returned Jack as he banged into the door pushing it open with his shoulders.

Once outside in the cool damp night air his body began to sway out of control. He stopped abruptly against the rear van doors pushing them inwards. Jack fell flat on his stomach onto the van floor leaving his legs dangling over the edge. The disturbed chickens gave out an ear-splitting squawk, and with feathers flying in all directions took off into the night. Jack lay in the filth of the van floor. Wet straw soaked in chicken droppings, broken eggs and farm muck which had cushioned his fall. He managed to extricate himself from the stinking filth of the van, and gingerly got to his feet. His dishevelled figure resembled a scarecrow.

The barman realised he didn't know the winner of the 2.30 at Newmarket, and rushed outside to find Jack.

"Bloody hell, Jack! What's happened?" he exclaimed in surprise.

"Just a likkle mis'ap, tripped over me foot I reckon, berra 'ave a drinkie to get me sekkled," stuttered Jack in a slurred voice.

"What's the winner of the 2.30 Newmarket race tomorrow? Yer said you 'ad a dead cert. A deal's a deal, Jack."

"It's KOSHER mate. I tole yer," gabbled Jack.

Jack fumbled at his trousers trying to find his fly fronts. He found the zip and hastily unzipped his flies, clumsily groping inside for his penis.

"Ah! Gorr it, yer likkle boggar," he said, pulling it out.

Soon a steaming jet of strong-smelling urine splashed against the van's side, making a twangy noise as it hit the metal sides.

"That's berra, needed a leak, real bad," said Jack, putting his penis away, but forgetting to zip up his flies.

"Thanks, Jack," said the barman. "Don't forget to zip up yer flies."

He rushed back into the pub at the onset of rain and a blackening sky. Within seconds the rain tumbled down like stair-rods, thunder rolled, and lightning blazed across the sky with an intense brilliance. Jack let out a cry of pain catching his pubic hairs which tugged against the zip as he pulled it upwards.

"Bloody 'ell," he yelled.

Slowly he released the zip, adjusted himself, and very carefully without force positioned the zip to its resting place.

"That's berra," he mumbled.

By now Jack was soaked, dirty, and not too sure where he was, or what he was supposed to be doing. He dragged himself to the front of the van, missing his footing, and saved himself from tripping over the chain fencing by holding onto the passenger door. Luckily the window was down, which saved him from further disaster. Opening the door he sat down, sitting on the hen eggs he'd put there earlier. His trouser pocket caught in the gear lever, ripping his trousers as he slid across into the driver's seat. He fumbled in his jacket pocket for the van keys, but couldn't find them. Within seconds he was snoring loudly, oblivious to what had happened, where he was going, and the thunderstorm raging outside the van.

Ida woke up suddenly to the incessant crowing of the farm's two cocks. Opening the curtains she peered out of the bedroom window to a damp grey day. She looked up at the clock on the cheerless, faded-blue, peeling wallpapered wall, but couldn't see the time. The clock hands were blurred. Her spectacles were not to hand. Where had she put them? Somewhere safe, but where? Eventually she found them in her slippers. The clock said 6.30, but was it morning or evening? After taking the doctor's remedy for her migraine headaches she always felt drowsy, sick, and far from with it the next day. The tablets really knocked her out, and sent her into a long, deep, unconscious sleep. It usually took a few hours after waking to recover and to feel her normal self again.

Ida groped her way down the narrow stairs into the kitchen, put the kettle on the hob, and made some tea. After two cups of strong, sweet tea she began to feel much better. She heard the postman push the mail through the letterbox, as the metal flap rattled onto the stone floor. She had given up asking Jack to fix the letterbox which came adrift each time letters were pushed through the door. The clatter alerted Ida to the reality that she'd been in bed around 12 hours, and a new day had dawned.

"Where's Jack?" she mumbled, "and Derek?"

"Jack," she shouted.

Ida's adrenalin now took over. She dashed round the house, looked in Jack's bedroom. His bed had not been slept in. The room she had prepared for Derek was empty. She ran outside shouting, "Jack! Derek!" but there was no response to her cries.

Jack was the bane of Ida's life. He was lazy and continuously the worse for drink. The farm was an excuse not to work. It had not paid for itself for years, and they were always in debt. The telephone had been disconnected. The electricity was more often than not cut off. Ida had a job at the local shop in the afternoons which kept them in food, and the bare necessities to keep their heads above water. Jack sometimes made a killing on the horses, but then he'd blow it on his drinking debts, and more drink.

Their two boys, Roy and Graham, now in their twenties, had left home a few years before. They had tried very hard to work the farm and make it pay, but Jack was stubborn and insensitive to their efforts. He had no respect for his sons. The boys gave up and left when 40 acres of land was sold off for next to nothing. Jack owed them each a year's wages which he refused to pay. He maintained they should work for their keep only, as it was a family farm. Ida had threatened to divorce Jack many times, and her two sons had urged her to leave him, but she always thought things would get better. They never did improve, but only got worse with time.

This was the last straw for Ida. She was worried about Derek. What on earth had happened to him.

A police car pulled up outside the farm gate, and two uniformed policemen got out, made their way through the oppressive animal dung yard to the house, scattering hens, and goats in their path.

Ida saw them coming and anxiously waited at the door. Her feminine instinct told her something was wrong. She went hot and cold and her left eye started to twitch, beads of perspiration hung on her forehead. The salty sweat trickled into her eyes, ran down her nose and dripped onto her lips. She nervously fumbled in her apron pocket for a handkerchief to wipe her face, but couldn't find one.

"Good morning, Mrs Hogg," greeted the tall moustached policeman offering her his spotless white handkerchief.

"Thank you …. thanks ….sorry," said Ida.

"Keep it, I've got another. We'd better go inside and sit down, if you don't mind," said the policeman.

They all went into the large warm kitchen, and sat around the white scrubbed pine table. The kettle on the hob was spluttering with steam as the water boiled. The other, shorter policeman quietly removed the kettle to avoid it boiling dry. He joined the other two at the table.

"We've had to lock your husband up, Mrs Hogg, drunk-in-charge, no road tax, no insurance, and the van not roadworthy. When he's sobered up we'll see what the magistrate has to say, but we'll keep him locked up for the present. It's not the first time, and he's still on probation. It's for his own good. Sorry, Mrs Hogg," said the tall policeman.

"Where's Derek? Jack went to Royston to meet my nephew off the bus. Was Derek with him? What's happened to Derek?" sobbed Ida.

"We'll have to make enquiries about Derek. Don't you worry, Mrs Hogg. We'll find him. He won't be far away. We'll bring him to you shortly." said the short policeman.

"I bet he's still at the bus station," said the tall policeman, turning to his colleague. "Put a call through to the station, quick as you can."

The two policemen left, leaving Ida with her head in her hands sobbing and muttering between sobs, "I'll kill that bastard when I see him, I will, I will, as God's my judge. Can't trust the good-for-nothing bastard out of my sight."

CHAPTER 6

Bill and the Policeman

"When constabulary duty's to be done,
A policeman's lot is not a happy one."

The Pirates of Penzance Act 2.
W. S. Gilbert 1836-1911.

CHAPTER 6

Bill came sauntering back shrouded in clouds of greyish black pipe smoke, smelling like burning stooks of newly harvested barley straw.

"It's sorted, see yer outside in 15 minutes," said Bill, overjoyed at being let off for a few hours. Stocking up, cleaning and pulling pints for a few lunchtime customers. They were never worth the mess they made, just passing trade, who only stopped for a pee, half a pint and a fruit juice for the Mrs. "A few crisps if you're lucky," thought Bill."Come on Derek, we'll get yer case and get yer to Frog End, as fast as a frog's fishy fart," said Bert, laughing.

Soon they were on their way. Derek sitting between Bill driving, and Bert on the outside. The truck had seen better days, but motored well. It had difficulty in getting up steep hills, and would often roll backwards when changing down into lower gears.

The overnight storm had barely touched Kneesworth. The roads and puddles were beginning to dry up, and a feeble sun was trying to break through watery clouds. The road out of Kneesworth was narrow, and not wide enough to allow for passing traffic. Coming towards them was a tractor. The truck stopped, but the tractor came moving towards them.

"Bloody 'ell," grunted Bill.

The tractor stopped as its front touched the truck's bumper, and buckled it slightly. The tractor driver climbed down from his seat, and approached Bill angrily yelling.

"Yer can goowonn gerroff uss road. Yoal etta mekkit ga bakkuds."

"Balls," Bill shouted back.

The tractor driver got back into his cab, and slowly started to push the truck backwards down the road. The truck bumper split into two parts, and fell off. Bill got out of the truck, stood his full height of 6'10", expanded his chest, and menacingly scowled at the tractor driver. This was sufficient to put the fear of God into him. The tractor reversed about 20 yards, stopped, came forward, swerved to the right, and ploughed into the hedge, and overtook the truck, leaving a flattened hedgerow in its tracks. The nearside tractor wheels sank into an invisible deep ditch. They spun round, throwing mud and water in all directions, as the engine desperately revved in an effort to free the wheels. The tractor was stuck in the chewed-up hedge, and a mass of slimy sludge from the ditch.

"That'll teach the leary bogger," smiled Bill, throwing the broken bumper into the back of the truck.

Bill, Derek and Bert, with infectious laughter, raced down the road with Bill's foot pressed hard down on the accelerator. The horn was intermittently pressed in joyous rapture, leaving the indignant tractor driver behind. At the main road they turned right and headed towards

Cambridge. A fanfare of police sirens, and an overtaking police car directed them onto the hard shoulder.

"What's up now," grumbled Bill

He wound down the window and greeted the capped policeman in his best English voice.

"Good morning, officer. What can I do you for?"

"Morning, sir," replied the policeman.

"Nice day," said Bill.

"Tell me, sir! Do you know what speed you were doing?"

"As a matter of fact I do. I always keep my speed to well within 70 mph. I observed the 50 sign way back. I've made sure I haven't exceeded 70 mph. I'm a keen observer of the law, officer. You chaps are doing a grand job," smiled Bill.

The policeman looked dumbfounded at Bill.

"Are you taking the piss? Sir!"

"Certainly not!" came the reply.

"Well, sir! If you see a 50 sign, you keep your speed to within 50 mph, not 70 mph. Got it. Sir! Read the Highway Code, and get familiar with it,. Can I see your driving licence, sir? If you've got one, that is."

"Yes, of course officer, but it's back at the Bull."

"What do you mean? Back at the Bull'. The Bull what?"

" 'The Bull Inn', I'm the landlord," said Bill.

"That's my dad's local. You must be Bill Wragg then," said the policeman.

"That's right. I reckon you're Syd's lad," said Bill.

The two greeted each other like long lost friends, and shook hands.

"Forget the bloody Highway Code, Bill. It's a load of old cobblers. I'm sorry to have bothered you," said Syd's lad, the policeman. "Better get off and catch some speed maniacs."

"Before yer go, Ken. 'Tis Ken in't it?" said Bill, reverting to his local dialect.

"Ah! tis and all," said Ken - the policeman.

"Where's Frog End, Ken?"

"Funny thing. We're looking for a lad who's supposed to be at Frog Farm at the 'End, but he ain't turned up. Name of Derek, Derek Postle, Postle-something."

"Postlethwaite. Derek Postlethwaite," shouted Derek. "That's me, that's my name."

"Well, tickle me arse with a feather," said Ken, the policeman. "Follow me, Bill.

I'll soon get yer to Frog Farm. Mind yer, the ole farmer's in the nick, but 'is Mrs 'll be at 'ome. She's nice, she is."

Bert nudged Derek and gave him a wink as they turned and smiled at each other. Derek wasn't sure if he wanted to go and stay with his Auntie now. He'd been having such an exciting time with grown-ups, drinking in the pub, seeing pictures of breasts, hearing and learning swear words, and rude talk.

"Wish I was a grown up man and didn't have to smoke my pipe in private," he said to himself.

"Did yer say summat?" said Bert.

"Just thinking aloud," replied Derek.

Bill could hardly keep up with the police car, which was going well over the speed limit. He chased after the car, overtaking any traffic that was in his way. Derek thought this was great fun. It was like playing cops and robbers for real, but the robbers were chasing the cops. Bill started to fill his pipe with one hand, and steer the truck with the other. He managed to fill it, spilling tobacco all over his lap, but his attempts to light it were not very successful. He nearly swerved off the road onto the grass verge when both hands were briefly holding and lighting his pipe at the same time. Bert just managed to get the truck under control and on a straight course again. We all felt shell-shocked and clammy from the near miss accident. Bill said he always filled and lit his pipe when driving.

"The bloody policeman's going too fast, and you're taking up all the room. Can't move me bleeding arm. Move over, 'utch up a bit, Derek," said Bill angrily.

"Sorry," said Bert, trying to make more room.

"Light it for me, Derek," said Bill, handing it to him with the matches. "Don't tamp the bogger down too much when you've gorr'it lit."

For a split second Derek was taken aback, but realised it was a grown up thing to do. He must light Bill's pipe at all costs. Bill was treating him as a grown-up mate with Bert, and as an equal. "I must not let him down" he thought, sticking the pipe in his mouth, and holding the stem firmly between his teeth. He sucked vigorously taking in a mouthful of dottle, which caused him to choke. He swallowed hard, trying to be manly and confident.

"Are yer orryte, Derek? I'll do't for thee."

"I'm OK, Bert, used to it. Light me dad's," he said.

The pipe was heavy and hung down from his mouth. With his left hand he held the bowl gently to take the weight, but found he needed both hands to strike a match. He took his hand away, and the pipe nearly fell out of his mouth, it was so heavy. He took out a match and tried to light it. It gave out a few sparks but spluttered out without igniting. He tried another match, which ignited, but the end dropped off, fell onto his trousers alight, and burnt a small hole. He took the pipe out of his mouth repeatedly. His jaw bones cracked, and his ears popped. He stuck the pipe back into his mouth for another attempt.

"Gorr'it lit yet, Derek?" said Bill anxiously.

The next match ignited. Derek dropped the box of matches, grabbed the pipe bowl with his left hand and cautiously lit the overflowing tobacco. He puffed frantically, sucking in and swallowing bitter smoke. Soon the front of the cab was filled with a pungent choking smell. His eyes started to smart and run, his mouth tasted foul.

"Good lad," said Bill, grabbing the pipe from his mouth,. He shoved it into his own mouth and puffed away, tamping down the red embers with his index finger.

"Thanks mate," he said. "Smoke yer sen do you? You've got this going a treat, Derek."

"Smoke me dad's," he said.

"Better than fags, Derek, cleaner, more satisfying, helps yer think straight," said Bill.

Bert chipped in. "Didn't keep yer straight on the road though, did it? I reckon it's a filthy mangy mess, what with all that baccy dottle juice yer suck up the stem. It's like drinking parrot pee."

"Never drunk parrot pee me'sen. 'ave you, Derek?" snickered Bill.

"I'd sooner 'ave a fag any day, good for yer heart and lungs, cleans them out, that's what the doctors say," grunted Bert.

"You're a bloody liar. Doctors reckon fag smoking's no good for yer. They fancy fags are homicidal," replied Bill.

"What's homicidal yer daft bogger?" said Bert.

"They'll kill yer, yer ignorant fairy," laughed Bill.

"I'll 'ave a fag any road," said Bert, lighting a bent cigarette hanging from his mouth.

Derek looked from one to the other, grinning all over his face at the exchange of joking language between the two of them.

"What de yer say, Derek?" said Bill.

"Ah! What de yer reckon?" added Bert.

"Don't know," Derek replied, not wishing to take sides.

By this time they'd lost sight of the police car, but saw a sign to Frog End. Once again on a narrow country lane they passed 'The Dirty Duck' the scene of Uncle Jack's undoing. They soon reached the village square at Frog End. Bert got out of the truck, popped into the Post Office, and got directions to Frog Farm.

"Turn right at 'The Horse and Feathers', about two miles down on the right," said Bert. "They say it's the farm with the shitty smelly yard full of goats, hens, ducks and geese wandering about."

They soon found Frog Farm with a police car outside the gated yard. Bill sounded his horn to announce their arrival. Ken, the policeman, stood in the house doorway with a mug of tea in his hand.

"What took yer s'long, couldn't yer keep up with me?"

"We observe the speed limit, Ken," said Bill.

Ken laughed and came to greet them. Bill, Bert and Derek walked round the edge of the yard to avoid six to ten inches of wet stinking animal muck.

An aproned Auntie Ida appeared smiling with relief to see Derek, dashed towards him with open arms, and gave him a smothered hug.

"Oh, my poor darling," she said. "I was so worried. Are you alright? Where have you been?"

"I've been with my two friends, Bill and Bert," said Derek.

They all exchanged greetings and handshakes and went into the kitchen.

"Sit down. I'll make a fresh pot of tea, and bring out my special chocolate fudge cake I've made for Derek," smiled Ida, who was now beginning to feel more relaxed.

Sitting with good-humoured company around the table, drinking tea, eating cake and laughing made Ida content and really happy. She was not happy with Jack around, and this made a real change. After about 25 minutes, Ken heard his car radio. He dashed out across the yard to answer the call. Within a couple of minutes he was back for his cap, his trousers covered in wet animal shit, and dirty specks on his white shirt and face.

"Gotta go, herd of cows on't main road. Brought the traffic to a standstill. See yer. Tarrah then!" and off he went.

"Bye!"

"Cheers!"

"Thanks!"

" See yer!" Came a mixed chorus, as Ken disappeared out of earshot.

"Bogger off," bawled Ken, as he nearly fell over a brown hen, and stumbled into a goat's flank.

Oh well, we'd better be orff too," said Bill.

"All's well that ends well," replied Bert.

"Very true, mate," came the reply.

"Very true indeed," giggled Bert

"Shurrup and get yer'sen moving," replied Bill, looking at Bert and Derek.

Bert got up from the table, spitting on his right hand fingers, and mopped up his plate of cake crumbs.

"Bloody good cake this," he said. "I'll get yer case, Derek," and disappeared into the yard.

Screeching, squawks and shrieks were heard as farm birds and animals freaked out in all directions, causing a shiver of alarm to run through Bert's body as he trudged across the yard. Ida cut two huge pieces of cake for Bert and Bill, and gave them each a box of new laid eggs.

"Thanks for looking after our Derek, and bringing him back. I was very worried," said Ida.

"Our pleasure. He's a good lad is Derek. Thanks for the eggs and cake," said Bert.

"'e can light a good pipe, can your Derek. Them eggs will go down a treat with a pound of barn bacon, some of 'Arry's 'erb sausages and fresh mushrooms, and stiff fried bread. Can't wait to get me molars round that lot," piped in Bill.

"Tarrah! Tarrah then! Tarrah, Derek, lad!" they shouted as they tried to avoid going through the muck in the yard.

"Sod it! Gorra bootful!" said Bert.

"Yer daft bogga," said Bill. "Yer want to be more careful."

They both turned round at the gate and waved. Derek with his case at his feet was feeling distraught and heartbroken as Bert and Bill stood at the gate waving.

"Tarrah then! Tarrah then!" they simultaneously shouted again as they climbed into the truck.

Tears welled up in Derek's eyes as the truck disappeared from sight. Would he ever see again these kind men who'd looked after him, and treated him as their equal. He could still taste the smoke in his mouth, but not as strong, and this gave him some comfort.

"I think I'll take up smoking a pipe seriously," he muttered to himself.

CHAPTER 7

Frog Farm

"Curse the blasted, jelly-boned swines,
the slimy, the belly-wriggling
invertebrates, the miserable sodding
rotters, the flaming sods, the
snivelling, dribbling, slithering,
palsied, pulse-less lot that make up
England today. They've got white of
egg in their veins, and their spunk
is that watery it's a marvel they can
breed. They can nothing but frogspawn - the gibberers! God, how I hate them."

Letter to Edward Garnett, 3 July 1912.
D. H. Lawrence 1885-1930.

CHAPTER 7

Ida wanted to hear all the news of Derek's overnight disappearance.

"Where have you been?" asked Ida.

"Don't know," said Derek, who was not eager to give away any information. "It was secret," he thought.

"Where did you meet Bert and Bill?" said Ida.

"Don't know," said Derek.

In the end Ida gave up the cross examination. She was so relieved to have him safely in her care. Derek never thought to ask why he'd never been met at the bus station. He was so preoccupied with his recent adventures.

Ida took Derek to his bedroom, which was small. It had a black, wrought iron fireplace on one wall and against the opposite wall was an iron single bed. Resting on the bed pillow was a tatty one-eyed, one-eared teddy bear by the name of Rufus. His leg had been hurriedly stitched back onto his trunk, and hung shorter than the other leg. Apparently, Scamp, the Golden Labrador, played with it, but Ida thought it would be nice for Derek to have it on his bed. It was chewed, looked dirty and smelt strongly of dewy dog. Ida had tried to restore the bear to its former glory, but her efforts had been far from successful. She had tied a lavender mauve ribbon around the bear's neck to make it smell sweeter, but it still gave off the dog's odour.

Opposite the cracked pane of the sash window stood a tallboy with lots of drawers, half of which would not open. They had seized up with damp, and lack of use. On the top of the tallboy stood an 18th century ormolu clock. Its hands were stuck at 12.25. They had been stuck at the same time for the past 30 years. Just poking out from under the bed was a large porcelain blue and white chamber pot, which Ida referred to as the piss-pot. A faded homemade patchwork rag rug filled the area between   the bed and the fireplace. A splintered split cane chair stood against the window, complementing the Spartan layout of the room. Over the bed hung a silk embroidered framed picture with the words,

'Behold the end is near,
says the Lord.'

On the fireplace mantelshelf stood a bowl of faded-blue, artificial, dusty flowers, their washed out green leafless stems limp and bending with time. Derek soon found that the overhead bed light pull switch would switch the light on, but not off, and would occasionally part company with the ceiling rose.

"Is the room alright, Derek?" asked Ida.

"Don't know," said Derek. "I mean, yes, thank you."

Derek was too polite to say he didn't like it, and wished he was back with Bill and Bert. He had a sudden urge to wee, and started to screw his face up with the tension of squeezing his anal muscles.

Ida looked at him, saying, "Are you alright, Derek?"

"Don't know. I mean, I want to wee. Where's the bathroom?"

"Follow me, that's downstairs, and the lav's in the yard. I'll show you."

Down the dark twisting stairs they cautiously trod. Ida in front. The staircase was narrow with only a handrail fixed to the wall.

"Don't hold onto the handrail, it's loose. You may do yourself a mischief, just tread carefully, and mind the loose stair-rod at the bottom."

The bathroom had once been half-tiled, but at least half the tiles had dropped off leaving bare patches. The grimy white-enamelled iron bath was badly chipped and rusty. A lonely shadeless grey light of mean wattage hung low over the bath. It gave out very little light. When the bath was filled with hot water, the steam would blot out most of the light, making the room dingy and airless. In the corner was a cracked, plugless wash basin with dripping taps.

The outside toilet, built by Jack, which he referred to as 'the shit-house', was equally as sordid. The loo pan was only about 10" off the ground, which did not make it user-friendly. If you had long legs you could sit on the pan with legs stretched out either side of it. If you had short legs it meant sitting with your knees up to your chin, or stretched out in front of you. Either way it was very uncomfortable. The pan was an old shallow stone sink with part of its base knocked out. It was inadequately flushed by tugging at a piece of rope dangling from a water-filled iron cistern loosely fixed to the wall. Too much strain on the rope would wrench the contraption off the wall, and not enough would fail to flush the toilet. Written on the wall it said, 'Pull at your peril'. Another written message on the door said, 'Have a nice shit.' Ida had unsuccessfully tried to remove the graffiti.

The flushing system looked dangerous and insecure. Ida would flush the pan daily with a bucket of cold water. The cesspit was never emptied. Jack had been known in his more active days to spread the contents on his vegetable garden. There was a constant lack of proper loo paper, only old newsprint and magazines. Fork-tailed swallows ceaselessly flew in and out over the loo door to their dried mud nests cemented to the high walled ceiling, sucking up insects in their flight. Derek was not impressed with the tour of the house, and felt very uneasy about staying with Auntie Ida and Uncle Jack.

"Let me carry your case upstairs for you, Derek," said Auntie Ida. "I can manage. It's not heavy. Thank you, Auntie Ida," said Derek.

I went to my room and unpacked. The drawer I tried in the tallboy was stuck. It wouldn't open. I pulled hard, and the brass knob came away, causing me to jerk backwards. I crashed down on the floor bruising my bottom. The brass knob spun in the air, and disappeared somewhere in the room. I never did find it. I tried another drawer, which opened with ease. Two big black spiders glared up at me and darted about frantically trying to escape. I closed the drawer quickly, squashing one spider as it snapped shut with an explosive slam. It disturbed a mouse, which scurried across the bedroom floor, and disappeared under a gap in the floor skirting. I decided to keep my few things in the case, rather than trying to open any more drawers.

"Where's Uncle Jack?" I asked.

"Oh! Eh! He's away at the moment - on business, yes, on farm business. He'll be back shortly," said Auntie Ida.

I asked Auntie Ida about my mother, but she would not talk about her. My Grandma, Joan, Amanda, and now Ida, would not talk about the person most dear to me. My mother had overnight disappeared from my life. She had died and was gone. She didn't physically exist anymore but her memory did. So why was she now a taboo subject? Even my father wouldn't talk to me about her. Brian was too young anyway, and perhaps hadn't noticed that our mother was missing. We had all been affected, so why wouldn't anyone tell me what had happened, and talk about it. I deliberately tried to include my mother in conversations, but the subject was conveniently set aside and hushed up. To talk about my mother was a forbidden subject. The matter had been innocently disapproved of. Because of the imposed silence and secrecy, I became unhappy, depressed, mystified and was soon to develop a complex leading to abnormal states of behaviour.

Auntie Ida's kitchen was the best place in the house. It was always warm, heated by a large Aga cooker. Things were not falling apart like the rest of the house. It was the hub of activity, where decisions were made, rabbits skinned, hens plucked, pigs jointed, hams boiled and roasted, jams boiled, and jarred, meals prepared, cooked and eaten at the time-worn pine table.

The long bench-like refectory table was a symbol of activity, wholesome cooking, cleanliness and good living. It stood scrubbed clean down the length of the large kitchen. The kitchen was Auntie Ida's sacred and private place - her sanctum sanctorum. Two winged grandfather rocking chairs stood at each end of the table. A sturdy oak Welsh dresser leant against the wall displaying a collection of plates, bric-a-brac, and cookery books. Located over the Aga was an airer of four slatted bleached wood strips slotted into, and supported by, an iron bracket at each end. They were pulled up and down by a thin rope pulley system. The rope was wrapped round a large hook anchored to the wall. Hanging from the airer was my Uncle's tatty, almost worn out long-johns, two short-sleeved button-fronted vests, and three collarless shirts. These occupied two of the wooden slats. On the other two hung my Auntie's directoire elasticised knickers in sky blue and peach, and what I assumed to be three brassieres. The two cups of each bra were as big as small pudding basins.

I began to fantasize about the contents of the bra cups. Were Ida's breasts like the ones I saw in Bill's newspaper, or like Joan's? Did they have nipples? I wasn't sure if all breasts had nipples. My auntie seemed to have moderately large breasts. They hung quite low, and seemed to wobble as she moved about. I wondered sometimes if she wore a bra. If she did, then her breasts ought to have been held tight against her and in theory shouldn't sway to and fro when she walked. The breasts I had come across recently seemed to vary in shape and size, and it was becoming apparent that sizing varied considerably. Women's breasts, whilst being an interesting feature of the female body, appeared to be very complex things. Were they just ornamental, or did they have a practical use? The more I became acquainted with things associated with breasts the more interested I became in them. It was now a burning ambition to feel one, preferably two, as they came in pairs. Do men grow breasts? Will I grow them? I seem to have a type of nipple on my chest. "Will it grow into a breast," I thought? Some older, fatter men, seemed to have small breasts which showed through their shirts. Who can I ask about these things? I would have asked my mother without any fear of bashfulness, and she would have known all the answers, but to ask anyone else would cause me a great deal of embarrassment.

It was early evening and Auntie served supper of homemade soup and bread, a chicken leg with pickle, and apple and blackberry pie with custard. After supper we had games of Snap and Dominoes sitting at the kitchen table. It was time for bed, almost nine o'clock, and I was feeling tired after a busy and exciting day.

"Ready for bed, Derek?" said Auntie.

"Don't know," I said, not wishing to admit my tiredness.

"Off you go upstairs now. I think you ought to go to bed. You look tired to me," she said, smiling.

"I'll bring you a drink of hot chocolate, and some biscuits to have in bed."

"Thank you very much."

I groped for the light switch at the foot of the stairs, clicked it on and off several times, but the light refused to go on. I fumbled my way upstairs to my bedroom, cleaned my teeth, and got into bed. The bed felt cold and damp.

"Sod! Sod! Sod! You bastard, Jack," mumbled Ida, as she struggled up the stairs in the dark carrying a tray of hot chocolate and biscuits.

"Nice and comfy, Derek?" said Ida, trying to remain calm, and smiling as she handed me the tray.

"Don't know," I said, pulling the blanket up.

I was cold and miserable and wanted to go home to dad and Brian. I often wondered about Brian. "Was he with relations too?" I did miss them both. "What was going to happen next?" I wondered.

"Yes. I'm alright," I added. "Thank you." It was a lie. I wasn't comfy, and it wasn't nice.

"Where's Rufus?" asked Ida. "He belonged to our Roy, but he grew out of it, and gave it to our Graham. I thought you'd like it now." She picked up the bear, still smelling of wet dog, and tucked it next to me in bed. "What a stink," I thought, "I'll throw it out when she's gone."

"If you want to go for a pee-pee use the piss-pot," said Auntie, pulling the pot out from under the bed. She took a torch out of her pinafore pocket and slipped it under my pillow.

"Just in case you have trouble with the light pull."

She kissed me goodnight, tickling me with her long straggly chin whiskers. I couldn't understand why she didn't shave them off, or pull them out. There were only about ten of them, an inch long and silver. Ida's hair was a dark grey, turning to silver, and swept back into a large bun, which nestled in the nape of her neck. She wore silver framed round lens spectacles, which sometimes hung on a cord from her neck. They were my Uncle's army issue glasses, which he'd discarded long ago.

I woke to the noise of cockerels crowing continuously, yapping dogs and sheep bleating. I pulled the curtains apart to a dismal day, and peered into the yard. Two goats were mating and adding to the cacophonous babble and general pandemonium. The postman was walking round the edge of the yard, trying to keep his shoes clean. He was carrying a large parcel and letters. Within a few minutes he was sitting down in Ida's kitchen eating porridge and two freshly boiled hen's eggs. He sat at the top of the table with a mug of tea at his elbow, and a plate of hot buttered toast.

"Good morning, Derek" said Ida. "Sam here has a parcel for you, specially delivered by Royal Mail addressed to:

> Master Derek J A Postlethwaite
> c/o Frog Farm
> Frog End
> Cambs."

I looked at the parcel on the table, not knowing what I should do.

"Go on, open it, let's see what's in it," said Ida, cheerfully.

The parcel was heavy, and very well wrapped. Inside was a pair of long bottle green corduroy trousers, a brown and green check shirt, two books, 'Alice in Wonderland' and 'The Wind in the Willows' and two Mars bars. I tucked into my breakfast eagerly before trying on my new clothes. Ida seemed more excited than me, hardly letting me finish my toast.

"Try them on, Derek. Hurry up! Let's see you in them."

They fitted perfectly. I was wearing my first pair of long trousers. I felt very proud and grown up. Auntie Ida gave me a big hug, squashing me into her floppy, hanging bosoms. The postman started to clap! "Well, best be off. Thanks for breakfast. Same time tomorrow, Ida," said the postman.

"Bye, Sam. See yer then." replied Ida.

In the shirt pocket was a letter from Grandma and Amanda and a £5 note. Between them they had sent me this wonderful present. I was beginning to feel happier now at Frog Farm - until the arrival of Uncle Jack.

Shortly after breakfast, a police car arrived and dropped Uncle Jack at the farm gate. He came into the kitchen scowling, ignored me, turned to face Ida and forcefully demanded breakfast. He sat down and glared at me hypnotically, as though I was an intruder. He picked his nose and grunting said, "Who are you?"

"It's my sister's boy, Derek. You set off to meet him at Royston bus station, remember," said Ida.

"No, I bloody don't," said Jack.

In the next ten minutes whilst Ida fried bacon, sausage and eggs they argued. It was all to do with meeting me at Royston, and Jack failing to turn up. He insisted I wasn't at the bus station when he arrived. Ida slammed the plate down in front of him, angrily saying, "If you want anything else, get it yourself."

She gave me an embarrassing look saying, "Come on, Derek, let's go and feed the pigs. Keep away from him. He's not a nice man. I'm sorry he's so nasty - just keep him at arm's length. Don't talk to him, just ignore him."

Ida grasped my hand, and stormed out of the kitchen, glaring at Jack on the way out. He said nothing, being too involved in ravenously tucking into his breakfast.

"He eats like a pig. Ought to be living with 'em", sighed Ida.

Ida took me into a dilapidated building, full of empty plastic sacks, bales of straw, farm tools and machinery. A small cart, like a wheelbarrow but with a wheel and a supporting leg missing, housed a litter of kittens. The place was a rubbish dump full of debris with barely room to move. Chickens, and a variety of feathered birds found refuge in the rubbish. Rats and mice scurried across what little floor space there was, and disappeared into gaps between the garbage. Two mangy looking cats, one black and white, and the other ginger, lay in a pile of loose straw purring as they slept.

"Derek, you'd better put these wellies on. Our Graham wore these when he was about your age, I think they'll fit," said Ida, still distraught. She looked at me, burst into tears, and squeezed me into her large soft warm melting bosoms. My face seemed to nestle in the hollow between her breasts. She hugged me tighter. My breathing became difficult, until she released her grip, allowing me to breath again. The close contact between us helped to lessen the hurtful ordeal we'd earlier experienced with Jack. It enabled us to communicate our tacit feelings and awareness of each other. We shared the same chemistry and were blood-related. Auntie Ida was my mother's older sister, about in her early fifties. My mother must have been 20 years younger. There were four other sisters, and one brother. Joan was the youngest of Grandma's seven children.

"Auntie Ida. What did my mother do when she was a little girl? Did she climb trees, like Auntie Joan? Please tell me."

Ida ignored my questions.

"Come on, Derek. Let's feed those hungry pigs. Grab those two buckets and follow me."

We trudged through the muck and slush to the back of the yard. In the corner stood a large metal bin with a hinged lid. I was not tall enough to see inside. Near the bin was a wobbly wooden box, which Ida pushed with her foot towards the bin. She stood on the box and lifted up the hinged lid.

"Give me a bucket, Derek," she said.

Ida lowered the bucket into the bin, and with great difficulty, almost falling off the rickety box, lifted it out dripping with pigswill. The bucket crashed onto the floor with Ida nearly plunging into it, the milky contents spilling over its sides.

"What's that?" I said.

"It's pigswill."

"What's pigswill?"

Ida had not yet composed herself. She was still feeling distressed and anxious. In a quivering voice, she said, "It's food for the pigs."

"What's it made of?" I asked.

Kitchen scraps, boiled spuds, grain, anything we don't eat, the pigs will," she replied.

"Is that why it's called pigswill?" I said, giggling.

Ida didn't seem to hear. She picked up the bucket, and staggered with bent body towards the pigsty. Stopping in her tracks suddenly, she roared out with hysterical laughter, shaking the bucket and losing most of its contents. Tears came to her eyes as she laughed uncontrollably. It was some time before she calmed down.

"What's the matter?" I said.

"Pigswill, pigs-will, pigswill, swill, pigs, swilling pigs," guffawed Ida, weeping with emotional laughter.

"You do make me laugh, Derek," said Ida, still chortling to herself.

I didn't think my comments were all that funny, but understood her high spirits. I started to laugh, just to reinforce the double meaning of pigswill. Ida mopped her face with the front of her apron, lifting up her dress at the same time, displaying her baggy peach bloomers. Ida grabbed the bucket again, and made towards the pigsty.

There were several pigsties next to each other. They each had a chute on the outside wall, which channelled food into a trough on the inside wall. The trough was long and narrow and built into the wall. It was about twelve inches from the ground allowing the pigs to reach into it to drink and eat. The piglets, after weaning, did have difficulty getting their snouts over and into the trough. Occasionally they had to be fed individually out of a bucket. I fed them once and finished up flat on my back in the filth and slush of the sty. The sow thought she had priority over the food rather than her offspring, and aggressively pushed me out of the way, bucket and all. Ida emptied the bucket into the chute, and the swill slopped into the trough. The pigs stampeded, pushing each other out of the way. In the corner of the sty was a mammoth sow with ten piglets greedily sucking away at her teats.

"What are those tiny pigs doing, Auntie?" I asked.

Ida, happy to show off her farming knowledge, exclaimed, "the sow has farrowed, and she's feeding them!"

"What does 'farrow' mean," I said.

"Well, the pig, called the sow, has given birth to a litter of pigs. They're called piglets and they're sucking milk from their mother's teats," she said.

We carried on the conversation, and I soon realised that the teats were the nipples of the sow's breasts, but the sow had lots of breasts, not just two. She seemed to have a breast for each piglet.

"Interesting!" I thought. Pigs' breasts were not quite the same as ladies' breasts, but I saw there was a connection. I just couldn't work it out. Pigs' breasts did not have the same fascination as ladies' breasts. I had no desire to lick a pig's teat, or caress its breast, but a woman's breast provoked a stirring of libidinous, yet strange, innocent pleasure. Ladies' breasts when sheathed in a brassiere of black lace on white silk, and cloaked in a glamorous dress gave way to wanton joy and excitement. More to the point, erect nipples are not like pig's teats. They are designed for some higher purpose, other than a mother breast-feeding her baby. Even at my tender age my quest for, and love of bosoms, was seductively scintillating, and thought provoking. I had worked out that breasts with teats or nipples were designed for suckling piglets and babies. Pigs' breasts did nothing for me, there were far too many for a start, but the two bosoms of a lady were just the right number. They were comforting, exciting and desirable. The more I thought about bosoms the more they tantalised me.

From the next pigsty came noisy grunts and gasps from two very large long-backed pigs - a sow and a boar. The boar was trying desperately hard to mount the rear of the sow by rearing up on its back legs and anchoring its front legs on either side of the sow's flanks. The sow let the boar ease himself into her, and just as the boar thought he'd found the ideal mate, and dovetail fit, she'd move forward leaving the boar collapsed, and squealing on the ground. The boar made four attempts at mating, but the same thing happened. On the fifth he seemed to be happy that all was well, and the sow was agreeable to his lovemaking. The spirited sea-saw thrusting of the boar, gathering more and more momentum, startled the sow who, terror stricken in her submission leaped forward leaving the boar in mid-air. At this precise moment the boar ejaculated an abundant creamy hot steamy fluid into the air, some of which landed on the sow's back. The air was filled with an aromatic odour like the patchouli shrub, leaving the atmosphere with a heavy suffocating evocative smell, herby and musky. Both pigs screeched out with piercing thunderous screams; the sow in terror, and the boar with frustration.

The two pigs captivated my imagination. I had a vague suspicion they were mating. I had seen dogs doing a similar thing, and once saw a bull on top of a cow.

"Auntie, what were those pigs doing to each other?" I asked.

From behind a gruff voice bellowed, "They're having a bloody good fuck, or trying to."

We turned round quickly and faced Uncle Jack. He was standing with gaited booted legs apart, both arms akimbo. His shabby tweed cap was at the back of his head, and a simpering smile was spreading from ear to ear.

"Language in front of Derek. Go wash your mouth out with carbolic, Jack," said Ida angrily.

She grabbed me by the hand saying, "Lets collect the eggs, and get some goat's milk."

Ida ushered me towards some hen houses mumbling under her breath.

"The bastard. I'll leave him. I'll go to our Graham's. I'll kill the bastard. I will. I bloody will one of these days. The drunken bastard."

I collected ten eggs, some brown and some white.

"Auntie, why are some eggs brown and some white?"

"The brown eggs come from brown hens, and white eggs come from white hens" she replied.

I didn't say anything but I could only see brown hens. There was not a white one anywhere. Ida was still bottled up with anger at Jack's remark. The matter became far worse when I asked her, "What does 'fuck' mean?"

In exasperation and shaking, she said, "It's a dirty, nasty, wicked, horrid, swear word, and don't let me ever hear you say it, Derek. Do you understand?"

"Don't know," I said.

"What do you mean? Don't know." she replied.

"No, I won't, but what were the pigs doing?"

"Trying to make babies. You'll know about these things when you grow up."

'Fuck' was now a taboo word, just like talking about my mother. Both were to be disregarded, and were to be passed over, not mentioned, or talked about. It was like many questions I asked, which I thought were quite normal. They were either ignored, brushed aside, not heard, dismissed or strictly disapproved.

I was to spend a further five days at the farm, but these were not without drama involving my Uncle. The following day after breakfast, Auntie gave me a bucket of kitchen scraps with instructions to throw them into the pigsty containing the segregated piglets. Happily, wearing Graham's green wellies, I splashed through the wet mud in the yard, and threw the kitchen scraps amongst the pigs. They were ravenous, and greedily ate the lot, the bigger pigs getting most of the food. Uncle Jack appeared from nowhere.

"What de yer think yer doing, laddy?" he grunted.

"Don't know," I said, in fear.

"Feeding the fucking pigs are yer?" he said, and he went for me trying to hit me across the head with his large fisted hand. I ducked. Uncle Jack lost his balance, crashed into the sty wall and fell into the mud smacking his right shoulder and side against the stone wall of the pigsty. He let out a shout of pain as his knuckles scraped across the rough stone surface leaving blood in their wake. I ran and hid behind some bales of hay, disturbing a gaggle of gabbling geese. Uncle Jack lay in the mud overcome with anger. Slowly, treading his cap into the mud, he got to his feet. The right side of his body and face were covered in mud; his hand and forehead were bleeding. He leaned against the sty wall recovering his balance and yelled out as loud as he could, "I'll have yer, yer bogger!"

I stood in fear, trembling, and feeling very insecure.

I didn't see Uncle Jack until the next day. He had a plaster above his right eye, his right hand swathed in a bloodied white bandage, and an arm held tight across his chest in a sling. He eyeballed me, but said nothing. I'd just finished my breakfast with Auntie. Uncle Jack never ate with us. The rest of the day went without further incident until the evening.

In the afternoon I helped Ida stock up the shelves in the local shop where she worked. Later we had tea in her warm kitchen, two boiled speckled brown hen eggs, which I'd collected earlier, and hot toast made from freshly baked bread we'd made together. Tea ended with two big slices of chocolate fudge cake and a mug of hot chocolate. We played cards until bedtime. Ida took me to bed, read me a story, and tucked me up, and kissed me goodnight. Within seconds, an almighty row broke loose between Jack and Ida.

"When's that little bastard going 'om?" Jack bawled out.

I didn't hear Ida reply, but I heard things crashing about in the kitchen. I curled up into a tight ball in fear of what might happen next. The back door crashed shut as Jack stormed out into the yard. I peeped through the closed curtains to see Jack rampaging down the road in anger. I could hear Ida sobbing downstairs. I crept back into bed, fearful of what might happen when Jack returned. Within minutes I was sound asleep.

The backdoor smashing against the house woke me up suddenly. The house shook as if an earth tremor had bolted through the building. The window frames rattled. The roosting birds, pigs and goats woke, disturbed by Jack's thunderous return. Within a short time all was quiet again, and silence and sleep returned.

Ida found Jack the next morning collapsed on the kitchen floor. He was lying flat on his back in a pool of blood. His unshaven face was grey, his blue eyes gaped wide open peering up at the ceiling, and his frothy cavernous mouth was wide open with salivated foam and vomit dried up in the channels of his chin.

He was dead.

Within half an hour he had been taken away, covered by a grey white sheet. Ida, red-eyed and bruised, not from grief, but from the beating Jack had given her the previous evening, sat with me having breakfast, and calmly told me Uncle Jack had died in his sleep. The Coroner's verdict was 'death due to concussion from falling, asphyxiation from swallowing his own vomit resulting from drinking excessive amounts of alcohol.'

"More toast, Derek" Ida said, in a lively voice, smiling at me.

Although Ida would not admit it, she instantly became more bubbly, and a much happier woman. Jack's demise was a happy release for her and the family.

The next morning we went by taxi to Cambridge train station. Ida gave me a big hug, and put me on the train with fresh eggs I'd collected, and a big wedge of chocolate fudge cake. We waved goodbye to each other. I was on my way home, comforted with the thought that I would shortly be seeing my dad and Brian. I thought about my mother. She would not be there, but I knew I would be aware of her presence in other ways.

CHAPTER 8

Harry Postlethwaite and Miss Ethel Weatherspoon

*"Oh, Mrs Corney, what a prospect this opens!
What a opportunity for jining of hearts, and
house-keepings!"*

Oliver Twist ch 27 (Bumble)
Charles Dickens 1812-1870

CHAPTER 8

Harry Postlethwaite, coat collar turned up, brown trilby hat pulled well down on his head, his staring eyes peering ahead through the driving rain, his smouldering pipe dangling from his drooping mouth, was depressed, and miserable. It was his first day back at work after two weeks sick leave following his wife's death. Harry had a well paid job as chief clerk at a large prestigious building and construction works, Shotesham Bros. Ltd. He was responsible for wages, invoicing, purchasing and general administration, with six junior clerks to assist him. His wife, Phyllis, had gone into hospital for a routine appendix operation, but peritonitis had developed and proved fatal. His thoughts turned to his two sons. Derek was with his Auntie, and would be home in a few days, and Brian was being looked after by a friendly neighbour. His whole life had been turned upside down by recent events, and he just didn't know how to cope.

Harry was a good Catholic, attending Mass each Sunday with his family. Derek was a server on the altar, and this made Harry very proud. He could not understand why God should do this to him, nor could he come to terms with the situation. It didn't make sense. Fr Ignatius, the parish priest, was not able to give a satisfactory explanation as to why God should allow this to happen. His answer to Harry's misfortune was, "You must have faith, God will provide, keep praying and be God-fearing."

Platitudes of this nature did not help Harry to accept that his wife's death was God's will. He became resentful of the Catholic Church, and angry with God. Fr Ignatius was no longer welcome on his frequent visits. Harry stopped going to church, and ceased to pray.

The rain became torrential with a gusting wind. Harry reached his local newspaper shop and went inside to avoid the worsening weather.

"Evening, Harry," said the man behind the counter.

"Hello," he muttered, a little put out at being greeted. In the window, standing out amongst the many advertisements was a large pink card which read:

Refined middle-aged lady, seeks position as Housekeeper in respectable home. The care of children and pets (no cats) welcome. Excellent references available. Apply to Miss E Weatherspoon at 'Sea View', Beach Road, Morecombe, Lancs.

Within the hour Harry had written and posted a letter to Miss Weatherspoon. Would she be interested in looking after his two well-behaved boys and the house, subject, of course, to mutual agreement?

Two days later, early evening, a loud knock shook the normally unused front door. The impatient knocking was repeated getting louder at each knock. Harry had not been home very long. He'd just made a pot of tea before collecting Brian from his neighbour, two doors down the road.

"Damn! Who could this be?" he muttered to himself, hurrying to the front door.

Through the leaded thick opaque glass he could just pick out a large figure.

"Just a second," he shouted. "I've got to find the key".

For a moment Harry couldn't remember where he had put it. After what seemed ages he found it in a small drawer in the hat and umbrella stand. The door was unlocked, and two very stiff rusty bolts were withdrawn from their sockets. Harry pulled hard on the door knob, but the door held firm. Paint held the door stuck to the frame.

"Bloody painters," thought Harry.

After several more attempts the door was wrenched open, flinging him against the opposite wall.

"Sorry!" he said, eyeing a woman of disproportionate size standing in the now open doorway, holding a big brown leather Gladstone bag in her large ring-fingered hand.

"Weatherspoon at your service, Sir," came the reply, in a polished contralto voice.

"Oh! Do come in," said Harry.

"Thank you. Please collect my bags and pay the taxi," said Miss Weatherspoon.

Harry didn't know what to say. He was dumbstruck, and meekly went down the long front garden path, paid the taxi driver £5, and returned carrying two large heavy cases, one in each hand, and a smaller third case tucked between his left side and arm. Arriving back at the front door completely drained, he found that Miss Weatherspoon had vanished. Harry carried the cases into the hall and in not too loud a voice softly called, "Miss Weatherspoon, Miss Weatherspoon. Where are you?"

No reply was heard. Louder this time. Harry shouted, "Miss Weatherspoon, where are you?"

"There you are," came the reply. "Which is my room? I don't like sleeping with my head facing south, east or west, and I don't like to overlook the main road."

Harry was taken aback by Miss Weatherspoon's presumptuousness, but didn't know how to handle her.

"I could do with a nice cup of tea, one sugar, and a little milk," she said.

Harry, now overwrought by Miss Weatherspoon's arrogant attitude, ignored her request, picked up his pipe, nervously filled it, lit it, and puffed away until the small kitchen was filled with clouds of sweet smelling tobacco smoke.

"Sorry, Mr Postlethwaite, you'll have to put it out, or go outside to smoke. I have a respiratory condition, and smoke upsets my breathing. I suffer with chronic asthma."

Harry went into the back garden, puffing in and out as fast as he could leaving clouds of smoke behind him. Miss Weatherspoon started to cough and breathed with violent thrusts of her chest. He was convinced that the outburst and heaving bosom was nothing more than theatrical exhibitionism. She returned to normality within seconds of Harry leaving the kitchen.

"I must collect Brian," he thought, having been side tracked by the arrival of his visitor.

He returned with Brian within ten minutes of the incident to find Miss Weatherspoon sitting in the kitchen drinking a cup of tea and smoking a black Russian cigarette. How was he to deal with this brazen impudent gargantuan woman? She had taken up residence in his house, forbade him to smoke his pipe, demanded a room in the back with her bed head pointing north - "What next?" he thought.

"What a lovely, lovely little boy. What's your name, my darling?" she said, in a sickly honeyed singing voice.

Brian looked at her with a confused expression on his face, not sure if he should say anything.

"Brian," said Harry.

"What a lovely, lovely name. You may call me 'Auntie', Brian. I bet you like sweets and ice cream, Brian. We can go shopping tomorrow when daddy is at work, but now it's time for bed. Come with Auntie. We'll have a bath, clean our teeth, and I'll read you a lovely, lovely story. I've brought my special books with me, and I'm going to look after you. Say goodnight to Daddy, Brian."

Brian blew Harry a kiss, and waved goodnight. They both disappeared holding hands through the kitchen door, and up the stairs.

Overwhelmed, exhausted and feeling helpless, Harry sat with his head in his hands and cried. Phyllis, his wife, who only a few weeks ago had sat opposite him, was dead. They had talked about a seaside holiday next year. That night they had made love for the last time. In place of Phyllis, this crazy woman, whom he disliked intensely, had taken over his family and his life in a matter of only a few hours. What should he do? He reluctantly, but with conviction, asked for God's help, but then he reminded himself that it was God who had taken Phyllis away from him, and his two sons. It never occurred to him that perhaps they were missing their mother, and were unhappy too.

Miss Weatherspoon was making a considerable amount of noise upstairs, moving furniture about, singing in a loud-pitched voice, when suddenly she shouted from the top of the stairs, "Harry, bring my cases up. I need to unpack my things."

Harry came to from his melancholy state, disturbed to hear Miss Weatherspoon's demands, and the use of his Christian name. He didn't move, but sat paralysed, riveted to his chair. Again the same voice, shouting, and louder.

"Bring my cases up, Harry, don't hang about. I'm waiting to unpack."

"The bloody woman, damn, damn, damn!" muttered Harry to himself.

Slowly and unwillingly he eased himself out of his chair, wiped his damp brow with a crisp white handkerchief, dragged himself into the hall, picked up two large heavy cases, and grudgingly, climbed the stairs. Standing at the top of the stairs, looking down at Harry with an intimidating stare, she said, "Thought you were never coming. Put them in Derek's room. I'm sleeping there. The bed points north. Derek can sleep with Brian.

"But there's only one bed in Brian's room," Harry said, in alarm.

"I know, I'm not blind. I can either sleep with you, in your double bed, or we buy another single bed for Derek," she replied aggressively.

Harry didn't say anything out loud, but thought, "You're not sleeping with me, you fat cow."

Harry went into Brian's room to find him sound asleep, kissed him goodnight, and went downstairs. He was feeling thirsty and hungry. "A pint and some fish and chips wouldn't go amiss," he thought.

Harry shouted up the stairs, "I'll be back in an hour."

"Make it half an hour. We need to talk business," came the reply.

"Bollocks!" he said, in a soft voice.

"I heard that, Harry. I'll expect you back at eight o'clock precisely."

"Bollocks!" he said again, but not loud enough to be heard.

A distraught Harry, pipe clenched between his teeth, almost ran down the street to the 'Blue Goddess'. The swinging sign of the female deity was visibly naked from the waist upwards. Her small round-nippled breasts audaciously lustful and mocking, looked down, welcoming Harry. He in turn looked up at her with relief as if she were his mother Goddess. He dashed under the sign, through the door into the bar and, almost breathless and panting, said to the barman, "Double scotch, and a pint, please."

"In a hurry, are we?" came the reply.

Harry spluttered, showering the bar top with spittle.

"I've had a terrible experience, I need a quick fix."

"OK, mate," said the barman, pushing a scotch towards Harry.

The scotch disappeared in one gulp. Crash went the empty glass on the bar.

"Same again, please," said Harry.

"Thirsty are we?" said the barman, sliding a second scotch across the bar.

The scotch disappeared in the same way - in one gulp. Harry relaxed, took a handkerchief from his breast jacket pocket, and mopped his sweating brow.

"That's better, thanks!" he said, picking up his pint, and taking a slower gentle slurp. He licked his lips, making his way to a table by the window, where his friend, Ron, was sitting.

"Hello, Harry, fancy seeing you here midweek. Don't blame you, mate, with all your rotten luck. Alice was only saying at tea she ought to pop round and see you, see if you needed any help. How's things? Any better? Good to get back to work, I expect?"

Harry nodded, gulping down a large mouthful of beer, leaving a frothy ring around his mouth. He wiped it off with the back of his hand, and said, "That's good, feel better already."

The rest of the pint disappeared almost as quickly as the scotch.

"Same again?" said Ron.

"Don't mind if I do. Thanks!" came the reply.

The next pint was drunk more leisurely. The conversation turned to the new housekeeper, who'd tricked her way into Harry's life in the space of only a few hours. They had another pint, without resolving the problem. Harry, very unsteady on his feet, stood up, and sat down. He had another attempt at getting up; leaning on the table, and nearly upsetting the glasses, he said, slurring his words, "I'm gerring off for some 'ish and fips for me tea. Goo' night, Ron, ole chap."

Ron bade him goodnight adding, "Mind how you go, Harry. Take care."

Harry swayed from side to side as he left the pub. He stopped outside the front entrance, looked up at the swinging sign of the 'Blue Goddess', giving her a glassy-eyed wink, and stammered, "Goo night, ole thing. You want to get a jumper on sweetie. Night's getting a bit chilly. See yer."

He started to walk away, stopped in his tracks, turned round, and blew a kiss to the swinging sign. Just behind Harry was a young couple, who thought his amorous signal was intended for them, or rather the man thought the kiss was meant for his lady friend clinging to his arm. The man raised his arm with clenched fist, and shouted, "Piss off, yer bloody pervert!"

"Harry stopped, turned round, looked at the couple, and said, "Pardon. Can't hear welly wel."

The lady dragged the man to the other side of the road, and was heard to say, "Cum on puddin, let's gerroff an 'av a bit. Take no notice of 'im."

They disappeared down a narrow passageway on the other side of the road, and were soon out of sight.

It was almost ten o'clock and dark. Harry, without looking either way attempted to cross the road. A car going far too fast swerved to avoid Harry, and finished up in the front entrance of the pub. The 'Blue Goddess' sign fell upon the car's impact, and embedded itself in the car roof. Harry, quite unperturbed, carried on crossing the road, muttering to himself, "Bloody fool! Pissed I shouldn't wonder."

Just round the corner was the 'Cod and Haddock' fish and chip shop. Harry joined the small queue and waited his turn leaning on the counter to support himself. The fresh air had marginally sobered him up, but he was still feeling happy-go-lucky. Two policemen peered through the shop window, looking at each punter in turn. They rested their eyes on Harry, who, guilt-ridden, came out in a hot sweat. The taller of the policemen poked his head through the door, still looking intently at the line of people, and suddenly blurted out, "Evening all" - no response from the queue - "Seen any drunks about? Anyone seen the car crash into the 'Blue Goddess' pub? Driver's got concussion, broken nose, blood everywhere, broken leg an' all, looking for witnesses."

The queue remained silent, apart from the odd cough, and a fat lady in front of Harry blowing her nose.

"Are you alright sir?" said the policeman, looking at Harry.

"Fine, never felt berra," replied Harry, wiping his brow once more.

The policeman glared at Harry with a penetrating stare, which seemed to go on forever. Suddenly, the policeman clicked his heavy boots together, breaking the silence, stood to attention, and said, "Good night all."

He turned about, and with big strides marched out of the shop in military style. The queue, still silent, turned to look at Harry. Harry's face went fiery red and inflamed.

"Who's next?" shouted the white-aproned lady behind the counter.

"It was Harry's turn.

"Caddock and fips please," said Harry, straightening himself up.

"Wrapped or open?" came the reply.

"Yes please," said Harry.

"Salt and vinegar," the lady bawled back.

"Yes please," garbled Harry.

A hot putty-coloured, wrapped-up package slid across the counter and came to an abrupt halt against Harry's chest. Harry paid, and nervously walked out of the shop. He felt the eyes of the queue follow him with each unsteady step, as he fumbled his way to the shop door. The fresh night air was cool, refreshing and sobering on his face. He felt like a fugitive, free at last, walking up the road, hungrily munching at his fish and chips.

Miss Weatherspoon was very put out by Harry's disappearance. She wanted to organise the business side of her engagement as Harry's housekeeper. She had of course employed herself. Harry had had no part in the appointment. It was now up to him to confirm to Miss Weatherspoon's conditions of work. She sat down at the kitchen table with pen and paper, and wrote down her own ground rules.

Housekeeper's Conditions

Wages	£25 (cash only) per 6 hour day, 5 days a week, payable in advance, all found.
	Weekends £5 per day extra. Bank holidays double time.
Duties	Light cleaning only, toilets, sinks, bath, windows not included.
	No outside work.
	Washing and ironing - shirts and hankies only.
	No darning, mending, or shoe cleaning.
Meals.	Evening meals only - no puddings
Housekeeping	£45 cash weekly for general expenses and food. Payable in advance.
Employment	No notice required by employee.
Termination	Six months notice by the employer effective from the 1st of each month.
General	Housekeeper's bedroom out of bounds, unless by invitation. Punctuality must be observed.

The reading of the above is considered acceptance and agreement of the aforementioned conditions.

Two copies were written out, one for Harry, and one for Miss Weatherspoon. Harry's copy was left on the kitchen table pending his return. The newly self-appointed housekeeper spent the next two hours searching the house. She went through every room, sifting through drawers and cupboards, reading all Harry's private correspondence. She had moved Derek's clothes from his wardrobe and chest of drawers, including his books and toys. They all lay in an untidy heap in Brian's room. Her own things were put in place, including making her bed with her own bed linen.

Miss Weatherspoon was becoming indignant by now. Harry had not returned as instructed. It was well gone eight o'clock. She poured herself a very large gin - Harry's gin, and sat down in his favourite chair. By ten o'clock she gave up on Harry, locked all the doors, shut all the windows, poured out another large gin, and went upstairs to bed. Two very large gins had made her angry at Harry's disobedience. "He can damn well spend the night outside if he hasn't got a house key with him. I'll get him into line. He won't cross me again. Who the hell does he think he is?" she said, talking to herself.

She stripped down to her bra and knickers, exposing mounds of fatty pink flesh, and removed her teeth, popping them into a glass of pink water. They went plop, water spilling over the side and wetting her own set of instructions for Harry. With a splitting head she crashed out on top of the bed in only bra and pants, quite unaware of her whereabouts. She was soon unconscious and snoring loudly. At the onset of each gasp of expelled air a fine spray of spittle spewed from her toothless jaws. Her mouth opening and closing as she breathed in and out with her pouting lips vibrating a tuneless jingle.

Harry screwed up his empty fish and chip wrapping pounding it into a ball between his big leathery hands. He threw it high in the air, and attempted to kick it, but he missed. He had three more goes, but his foot just wouldn't make contact with the paper ball. The fifth attempt was more successful. His foot kicked the paper ball with such venom that his shoe rocketed into the air. Harry saw the shoe and paper ball spiral upwards, and the ball plummet to the ground. He lost sight of his shoe, which just seemed to vanish literally into thin air. He searched all about him, but it had completely disappeared.

"Where's my bloody shoe?" said Harry to himself, almost scuffing his face on the pavement and road searching for it.

"It's bloody well evaporated. I don't believe it!"

Coming towards him was a hooded figure wearing a dirty camel-coloured duffle coat. The figure looked at Harry as he came alongside him, saying, "Gorra fag, and price of a cuppa mate?"

Harry eyeballed him and said, "Have yer seen a shoe on yer travels mate?"

"Left or right, mate?" said the figure.

"Right, mate," said Harry.

"Black or brown, mate?" said the figure.

"Brown, mate," said Harry.

"What size, mate?"

"Nine, mate."

"No, sorry, mate. Seen a left black size eight though."

The figure laughed, walked on, saying, "See yer, best of luck wi yer shoe, mate."

"Bloody old fool, "said Harry to himself.

Harry, one foot shoeless, limped down the road kicking the paper ball with his left foot. He reached his house, walked down the front path and tried the front door. It was locked.

"Sod," he said, feeling in his pockets for a key, but no key. He went round to the back door, which was locked too. He tried the windows, but these were shut. He banged on the door with his fist, but nothing would waken Miss Weatherspoon. She was sleeping off a good half bottle of gin.

Harry sat down on his back doorstep, feeling more in control of himself. The alcohol was beginning to wear off. He rummaged in his pocket for his pipe, found it, knocked out the old burnt ash, refilled it with fresh moist sweet smelling tobacco, tapped it down lightly, and lit up, puffing away slowly with deep satisfaction. He looked up into the starlit, canopied sky and thought of Phyllis, his dead wife, and his two sons. Drawing in deeper draughts of tobacco and exhaling, he gazed at the swirling grey smoke as it curled like a corkscrew into the air, and out of sight. He took deeper and longer puffs, breathing out thicker clouds of greyish white smoke. Soon he was shrouded in a fog of thick tobacco vapour. He coughed, unable to breathe freely. Unsuccessfully, Harry tried to wave away the smoke.

He stood up gasping for air, and moved out of the fumes. In doing so, Harry stubbed his big toe, still shoeless, on the large plant pot of Bear's Breeches. He lost his balance and fell headlong into a bush of prickly pyracantha. His pipe flew out of his mouth with its red embers exploding in the air, like detonated fireworks sending showers of electrified fine stardust cascading to the ground. The firethorne tore into his flesh; painfully he untangled himself from the bush. His bloody face was stinging in agony. His hands, covered in blood, were throbbing pins and needles. His knees felt bruised underneath his torn trousers, and his shoeless foot felt punctured with thorns.

He sat recovering on the doorstep. His thoughts turned again to Phyllis. What was happening to him, and his two sons? Why had God let this happen? Everything was out of control. He prayed silently, his head in his hands, asking God for help. He remembered one of his best-loved poems - an Anglo-Saxon religious poem - *'The Dream of the Rood'*. Harry felt like the dreamer in the poem, oppressed by his own misfortune, conscious of his sins, and falling out with God. He saw a vision of the bleeding Christ on the cross, a crown of thorns, nails through his hands and felt brought to life by the poem he knew so well, which mirrored his own grief and distress. The poem began to speak to him as he sat in the still night.

"Hear while I tell about the best of dreams" …..
"And I with sins was stained, wounded with guilt"…
"They pierced me with dark nails;
The scars can still be clearly seen on me,
The open wounds of malice" …..
"I was made wet all over with the blood
Which poured out from His side" …..

Harry must have dozed off briefly. He woke suddenly feeling shaken and confused.

"Had God been speaking to him?" he wondered.

Instantly he realised he was locked out of his own house by that bitch, Miss Weatherspoon. It suddenly dawned on him that a spare back door key lay hidden under the large pot of Bear's Breeches. Phyllis had put it there for emergencies. Harry groped in the dark, and found a plastic packet under the pot. He could feel the hard shape of the key in the wrapping.

"Thank you, God," he said, with relief.

The packet was fastened with sellotape, and the two plastics had fused together. Releasing the key from the packet became a major task. The plastic would not tear, and at each failed attempt to free the key Harry became more frustrated. He finally got hold of the key by chewing through the plastic with his teeth, and biting his bottom lip in the process. His jaws ached as he carefully positioned the key into the lock mechanism. He turned the key, but it held fast.

"Fuck!" he said, in anger.

Harry had to be really at the end of his tether to use the word 'fuck' out of its proper context. To fuck was to have fun, and this was no fun he thought, but it was a male and female dilemma. He took the key out of the lock, wiped it clean on the front of his shirt, which was now torn and hanging out of his trousers. He held it in line with his eyes to determine which way to put it in. He breathed on the key and carefully reinserted it in the opening. Once again the key would not turn.

"Fuck! Fuck! Fuck!" Harry said, in a loud voice.

He pushed the key hard into the lock. It moved forward and clicked. He turned it and the lock mechanism made a healthy grinding noise, moved, and snapped into place. Anxiously he turned the door knob, and the door squeaked open. Harry turned on the light, closing the door behind him, and made his way into the kitchen. He saw Miss Weatherspoon's written condition on the table, but didn't bother to read them.

"Silly bitch!" he muttered to himself.

He looked up at the clock. It said 1.30am. Silently he crawled up the stairs to the bathroom. He ran a hot bath, putting in a handful of salt to heal his cuts and bruises.

"Better see if Brian's in bed, he said to himself.

The door of Derek's room was open, and the light still on. Miss Weatherspoon in see-through bra and knickers lay snoring like a wild pig stretched out on Derek's bed. She looked obese, inflated pink flesh hung over her baggy elasticated knickers, her beefy breasts lay squashed like flattened molehills, each pinnacled with spiralled worm casts. Frothy white saliva bubbled at the corners of her mouth   to her   thunderous snoring. A strong smell of alcohol hung in the room like a damp dawn mist.

Harry thought, "What a sight! Enough to put you off sex for life. Bet she's still a virgin with a body like that. Put a blind man off she would."

Harry grinned to himself, and quietly shut the door. In doing so she made a tuneful gurgle, and continued snoring, a semi-tone higher.

"Very musical," thought Harry.

Brian was sound asleep. Harry drew the covers up to his shoulders and kissed him goodnight.

"God Bless! Derek's home at the weekend. We'll have some fun together. Lots of ice cream and sweets. Your favourite, a choc ice-lolly. Goodnight, Brian," said Harry, quietly.

Harry lay in the hot, salty, soapy bath feeling more relaxed, and ready to face Miss Weatherspoon in the morning. His cuts were smarting from the salt, but after a while the pain eased. With his big toe he manipulated the hot water tap for more water. For a minute or two he nodded off luxuriantly, soaking in hot foamy water. He woke up suddenly hearing the toilet in the WC being flushed. Looking towards the bathroom door he saw the door handle move, first up, and then down. Slowly the door opened. Miss Weatherspoon, now only in pants, stood in the doorway looking daggers at Harry in the bath, as if he was an intruder. She looked more bizarre than before. Her enormous pendulous breasts hung like large purple veined aubergines down to her waist.

"You're back, are you? You dirty stop out! We'll talk about this in the morning," grimaced Miss Weatherspoon.

She shut the door with a bang. A second slam echoed as Derek's door was shut.

Harry quickly got out of the bath and locked the door. Drying himself, wrapping the towel round his waist, he silently made his way to his own bedroom. He locked the door, set his alarm for 7am, and got into bed. Within minutes he was asleep.

The alarm sounded and shook Harry from out of his deep sleep. He felt stiff and had difficulty getting out of bed. His bruised legs and stiff joints pained him at each step. Washed, shaved, and ready for work he went downstairs for breakfast. Miss Weatherspoon sat at the kitchen table drinking tea, and eating toast.

"Ah!" There you are. Read this. I want £25 wages in advance, and £45 housekeeping, all cash, before you go to work," she said, thrusting her written conditions in front of him.

"Good morning," said Harry, ignoring the paper."I've only got £20 until I go to the bank at lunch time. In any case £45 is too much for housekeeping. £30 is plenty."

Harry laid four £5 notes on the table. She quickly picked the notes up thrusting them down into her cleavage. Harry made himself some fresh tea. He still felt shell-shocked from the previous night's events, and now further bombardment from Miss Weatherspoon put him off his normal breakfast of cereal and toast. He sipped two cups of sweet tea.

"Mrs Brown will pick Brian up at 8.30," said Harry.

"I'll look after Brian, take him shopping, don't you worry. I'll have a meal prompt at six o'clock tonight, but I don't do puddings," came the reply.

Harry felt too harassed to argue. He got up, saying, "I'm off now. Say hello to Brian for me, and take good care of him. I'll be home around 5.30. Bye!"

"We'll talk tonight, Harry. Good morning!", came the brusque reply.

Harry went out through the back door, and found his pipe in the pyracantha bush.

He felt relieved to be out of his house leaving Miss 'Fat Cow' behind. He called at Mrs Brown's to say Brian was with his new housekeeper and wouldn't need collecting.

Mrs Brown waved him goodbye calling after him, "Any time Harry, anything yer want, give me a shout. Have a nice day. I'm here if yer want me. Bye! Harry."

Harry disappeared down the road leaving his problems behind. His thoughts turned once more to his complete family, as it had been a month ago.

"Please God, help me today," he said, silently.

The prospect of Derek coming home tomorrow put an extra spring in his step. "Life wasn't too bad after all," he thought, as he whistled his way to work.

Next morning: Harry lay in bed considering getting up. It was almost seven o'clock, dawn was breaking with a watery sun seeping through his curtains, and casting scattered shadows on his bed covers. He was feeling much happier this morning. It was Saturday, and Derek was due home late afternoon. He heard a rattle of cups, and a faint tap on his bedroom door. Perhaps it was his imagination but the tap became a knock. In a slow melodious voice he heard, "Good morning, Harry. Nice cuppa tea, Harry. Wakey, wakey, Harry."

This was real. He was awake, and not mistaken. Should he disappear under the bedclothes? He saw the door handle turn, and the door slowly open, as Miss Weatherspoon's foot nudged it ajar. In the doorway, holding a tray of cups and teapot, stood the purple-veined breasted Amazon in a pink transparent negligee. Extraneous flesh hung loose everywhere. The bottom edge of the tray rested on her girdled misshapen stomach, below which was spread nestling at the top of her thick fat thighs a black, hairy monster. It lay snugly dormant as if comatose in hibernation. As she moved towards the bed it seemed to bristle like a hedgehog.

"Your nice cuppa tea, Harry," she said, smirking.

Her smudged lipsticked lips opened wide, her false eyelashes fluttered as she spoke, and forced a smile at Harry.

"The horror! The horror!" he thought. "What am I to do?"

She put Harry's tea on a small table at his bedside. On the other side of the bed she placed a second cup. She sat on the bed, lifting her legs up and onto the bedcovers with her back leaning against the bed wall.

"Please, Miss Weatherspoon, it's not right for you to get into bed with me. Please go!" said Harry.

"Call me Ethel," came the reply. "I know that we got off to a bad start, Harry. Let's kiss and make up." she said, smiling at him.

She moved her arm so her hand rested on his body, which lay like a corpse under the covers.

"I'll do puddings, baking, ironing, anything you want, if only you'd …"

She didn't have time to finish. Harry jumped out of bed, knocking his tea over, grabbed his clothes, and ran into the bathroom, locking the door after him.

"Harry, Harry, come back! I'm only trying to be friendly," he heard her shout.

Harry mentally said, "You're trying to seduce me you fat tart. You're nothing but a fast pot-bellied flabby fucking whore!"

Dousing himself with cold water he added, "Cow! Bitch! Just clear off and leave us alone."

He shaved, dressed, and nervously went downstairs, clenching his fists with tension.

Brian was sitting at the kitchen table reading a book, still in his pyjamas. Miss Weatherspoon appeared as if from nowhere, properly dressed, sans lipstick and eyelashes. She looked more the housekeeper than the tart who had earlier climbed into his bed.

"Sorry for the misunderstanding. I'm only trying to be friendly. Call me Ethel. Please Harry! Will you, Harry?" she said.

"Yes, Miss Weatherspoon. I mean Ethel," said Harry.

She looked at Brian, smiling, "You can call me Auntie Ethel."

"Yes, Auntie Ethel," said Brian.

"We're one big happy family," she sang out in a high pitched voice.

"Who's for bacon, eggs, mushrooms and stiff fried bread?" she asked, in a boisterous voice.

Harry and Brian looked at her in surprise.

"Yes please, Ethel, Auntie Ethel," they both exclaimed simultaneously.

"Give me ten minutes. Off we go," she sang out.

Ethel was in high spirits, despite Harry's earlier rejection of her impassioned advances. Harry and Brian went into the garden to check out a nesting thrush in the hedge. Harry lifted Brian up to peep into the nest.

"Four eggs! Can I have one?" said Brian.

"Better not," said Harry. "It's not fair to take a bird's eggs. I wouldn't like it if someone came along and took you away, Brian."

"I'm not an egg, Dad," said Brian, in high dudgeon,

"Bit late in the year for laying eggs," thought Harry. "Bet she's deserted the nest."

"Breakfast ready, Harry, Brian, come and get it," came an ear-splitting shout from the top of the garden.

Harry had to admit to himself that Ethel was a good cook. Last night's dinner of steak and kidney pie, cabbage and spuds, even without a pudding, was terrific, and now the breakfast.

"I'll get fat like big arse Weatherspoon at this rate," he thought to himself, looking up at the kitchen clock.

"I've just time to do some gardening. Coming, Brian? Then we'll meet Derek at the train station."

Harry and Brian, hand in hand, walked happily into the garden.

Miss Weatherspoon started to clear up the breakfast pots, singing in her melodious contralto voice.

> "You made me love you.
> I didn't want to do it.
> You made me love you,
> And all the time you knew it.
> I guess you always knew it.
> You made me happy sometimes
> You made me sad.
> And there were times when you made me feel so glad.
> You made me cry …."

CHAPTER 9

Clare, The Old Man, The Nun and The Parrott

*"One gets the greatest joy of
all out of really lovely
stockings," said Ursula.
"One does," replied Gudrun;
"the greatest joy of all."*

Women in Love.
D. H. Lawrence 1885-1930.

CHAPTER 9

The whistle blew. The train slowly chuffed out of the station. Sitting opposite me was a lady, who perhaps was between 18 and 28 years old. I was not very good at people's ages so I couldn't be really sure. She was mature, anyway, with long blonde hair. It parted in the middle and hung loosely down each side of her head and face, curling very slightly at the ends. She had sparkling blue eyes with long lashes which seemed to flutter when her eyes changed direction. Her nose turned up at the tip in an attractive way, which later I discovered was called a retrousse' nose. Each time her lips moved they seemed to have a playful sensuous kissing action. They were shiny and a brilliant red colour. Her neck was long and slender. She held herself like a majestic swan leading her cygnets down the river.

What really caught my close attention and adulation was her cleavage. My eyes were lured and provoked in such a way that I became transfixed and tantalised. The lady leaned forward, perhaps unwittingly, which gave me a full view of her cleavage. I focussed into a dusky gap which contrasted with the creamy flesh of her bosoms. The vision was wonderful, and magical. It was like a magnet drawing me into its field. I felt myself going red. My body was getting hotter, and becoming damp with perspiration.

"Are you alright?" she said, in a soft, husky voice, still leaning forward.

I could not turn away. I was hypnotized by her breasts, which seemed to tease me.

"What's the matter?" she said, bending forward still more, and getting closer.

A whiff of intoxicating perfume seemed to drift towards me as she moved. I hoped her movements were for my benefit, and a happy exchange of mutual admiration - for my part, because I couldn't take my eyes off her, and she in turn was flattered by my interest in her bosoms. Perhaps I was deluding myself, and this was not the case. I did enjoy the experience, and hoped she did too. I was reminded of Auntie Joan, and a tremor of excitement ran through my body.

The train jerked with a sudden screeching of brakes throwing me forward into the arms of the lady. She instinctively opened her arms to catch me as we collided. My body was cushioned against her soft breasts. Our heads cracked against each other as the train suddenly came to a grinding halt. For what was only fleeting seconds she held me tight as if to protect me. The sudden jolt of the train stopping so dramatically was frightening, but the ensuing clinch filled me with gratuitous excitement. Our bodies locked together. It felt warm and safe.

"Are you alright?" she said again, smiling.

"Yes, thank you. Are you?" I replied.

"I'm fine," she said. "Where are you going?"

"I'm going home. I've been away. Staying with my Grandma and Auntie for the school summer holidays."

"All by yourself. Didn't your mum and dad go too?"

"My mum died. Dad thought it would be a good idea to go away. I don't know why. I wanted to stay at home with dad and Brian, but dad just sent me away," I said, tearfully.

Whenever I thought about my mother I cried. It made me sad thinking I wouldn't see her again. I suppose I looked unhappy with big salty tears rolling down my cheeks. She leaned forward and took both my hands. Once more her tantalising cleavage came into full view inviting me again to share her sensuality.

"What's your name?" came her husky voice.

"Derek. Derek James Albert Postlethwaite," I said.

"Mines Clare. Clare English. I am going to Grantham."

"Where do you live, Derek?"

"I live just outside Doncaster. A place called Armthorpe. My father will be at the station to meet me, but not my mother, though," I said, bursting into tears again.

She squeezed my hands, released them and said, "Would you like some chocolate, Derek?"

"Yes, please. I love chocolate."

She fumbled in her handbag, and gave me a big bar of thick milk chocolate.

"Thank you," I said, breaking it into two pieces, and offering half to Clare.

"No thank you, Derek. You can have it all."

"I've got some very special chocolate fudge cake my Auntie made. Please have some, it's very special."

"What a good idea, but only a very small piece."

The fudge cake had been put into a small faded blue tin box, and wrapped in greaseproof paper. Clare took a small portion between her long red-nailed finger tips, broke off a tiny piece, and delicately put it into her mouth. A thick piece of fudge didn't quite make it, and dropped down into her cleavage, resting innocently on the silk ribbon joining the two bra cups. I noticed the cups only half covered her blush breasts, but held them compact, in shape and secure. The ribbon seemed to be elasticised and stretched to about two inches between each cup. It had a small daintily tied pink bow in the middle. The fudge, the size of a pea, lay nestled in the knot of the bow, and was held, securely lodged, by the two wings of the bow.

"Oh, Derek, look what I've done," said Clare, peering down into her cleavage. I bent forward and looked down into the gap between her breasts.

"Can you see it? The piece of fudge, I mean. It's down there," she said, trying to retrieve it with her two fingers.

"Damn! It will melt, Derek. Please get it out for me. Hurry!"

I felt myself blushing, my body getting sweaty. I was nervous and anxious. It was not the thought of retrieving the fudge, but the idea of putting my fingers between her breasts. What if I should accidentally touch them? I must be adult about this - pretend I'm removing a fuse from a time bomb. The breasts after all are quite harmless, not at all like a time bomb. They won't explode. All I've got to do is to remove the fuse to deactivate the bomb, but in this case it's just a matter of removing the fudge. With these thoughts in mind, I was ready to tackle the problem. The longer I waited, the greater the danger. The fudge would melt. The bomb would tick away.

"Please hurry, Derek. I can see the fudge is beginning to melt," said Clare, anxiously.

I looked into Clare's eyes, lifted my right arm and with all fingers delicately poised, refocused my eyes into the gap. Slowly, but firmly, I poised my thumb and forefinger for entry. We both took deep breaths - the fudge moved, but settled again, and remained in situ. There was no serious danger involved, but I began to tremble.

"Please hurry, Derek," said Clare, again.

I clenched my teeth, and closed the fingers of my left hand into a tight ball, my knuckles turning white with stress. My whole body became tense and rigid. I removed the fudge without any problem, but as soon as I held it between my fingers it became squashy and began to liquefy. Withdrawing the fudge in this state meant I had to relax my hand to avoid the fudge dripping onto the ribbon. My middle and remaining fingers felt the soft warm flesh of Clare's breast, as I slowly withdrew my hand from her cleavage. I held my thumb and finger in the air covered in softened fudge. Clare took my hand by the wrist and bending forward slowly sucked the fudge from my thumb, sending a warm glow and shivers of excitement through my body.

"Suck your finger, Derek, don't waste it," she said, relieved.

She wiped my thumb and fingers with a moist handkerchief from her handbag.

"Thank you, Derek. You're a real gentleman. Look, clean as a whistle," she said, peering down between her breasts.

She bent forward again for me to have a look.

"Yes, clean as a whistle," I said, not really understanding what 'clean as a whistle' meant.

The train meanwhile was speeding north, leaving memories behind, but heading towards an unknown future. The memories, although in the past, were still real to me. Memories of my mother, but she, like the past, was irretrievably lost. She was dead and gone for ever. Without warning the train was sucked into the black unknown of a tunnel, the past, present and future like time, seemed to stand still. We were in no-man's land. I felt sad and tearful in the dark. My mother was too young to die. I thought only old people died. I was not prepared for her to die. I thought I was safe, without really understanding why. I began to realise, we are not safe, no-one's safe. Perhaps it's all a dream, but it was not. The train catapulted into the light, and into the rush of air, as it thundered against the train. Startled, and alone, I was back in the real world, and its future.

We both sat back in our seats. Clare smiled at me, noticing my melancholy.

"Are you alright, Derek?" she said.

"Don't know," I said.

Clare leaned forward, giving me yet another glimpse of her bosoms. She took my hands in hers and squeezed them, saying, "Cheer up, Derek. You'll soon be home."

I felt comforted. We sat back in our seats, Clare still smiling at me. More shivers of excitement ran through my body from yet another look at her breasts. They made me feel protected and safe, as if mother nature were assuaging my fears for the loss of my mother.

I couldn't help notice that Clare was constantly moving one leg over the other. Each time they made a swishing sound as they glided over and touched. Her shapely legs were clad in very fine, almost invisible stockings. Each time she crossed and uncrossed her legs her skirt seemed to get shorter by riding up her thighs. As soon as the stocking welt became visible she would lift herself up from the seat, and pull her skirt down. I noticed that the stocking welt was attached to a hanging pink ribbon strap, which was secured by a keyhole-shaped metal ring sitting over the welt. It seemed to be held in place by a rubber button which pushed part of the welt through the ring, and held the strap and stocking top in place. It was a mystery to me. Where did the strap come from, and were there more straps the other side of the leg?

Her crossed legs made a chafing noise with the gentle sway of the train, as they rubbed against each other in their caress. The chafing, loud then soft, with each vibration of the train as it hurtled headlong over the trucks, gathering more and more speed,

"diddle-de-dee, diddle-de-dee, diddle-de-dee, did-le-de, did-le-de, did-le-de, did-le-de."

The chafing sound from Clare's legs were like crickets whispering in the grass, or the faint rustle of satin. I felt a sensuous delight in the sounds her legs made rubbing against each other. It had an hypnotic effect on me. I wanted it to go on for ever.

My enthusiastic interest in bosoms, now, included female hosiery - stockings and their accoutrements. I was not sure if my curiosity was normal for someone of my age, or if my friends had the same interest. It was not something we discussed. Maybe I was guilty of sinning. Perhaps I should talk to Fr Ignatius, my parish priest, about my secret desires and longings. I had touched Clare's breast, but only brushed one of them with the backs of my three fingers. "Was this a sin?" I wondered. Perhaps only half a sin for one breast. I had longed to hold both breasts in the palms of my hands. I would have loved to have slid my open palms over her silk clad legs. Longingly, with enjoyment, I looked at her. She reminded me of my mother. They were both beautiful, comforting and reassuring.

I remember my mother putting on her stockings, but I don't recall getting excited about it. Her stockings were so small and lifeless as they lay crumpled on her chair. But as soon as she inserted her outstretched fingers into the foot, spreading it open, the stocking took on a new dimension. She would always wear a pair of fine delicate cotton gloves to avoid snagging them with her fingernails. The stocking would be pulled over her foot until it fitted snug and wrinkle free, then slowly, but quite deliberately pulled upwards so it glided up the leg, expanding and contracting as it hugged the contours of the limb. I would help my mother smooth the stocking up the leg to even out the wrinkles until it fitted intimately in place. The whole process had a mysterious ending, because I never knew where the stocking top finished, and what held it in place. I just assumed it disappeared under my mother's skirt or dress, and stopped somewhere at the top of her leg, until it was later removed to lie crumpled and insignificant on the chair again. My mother always put her stockings on after she dressed, but before she applied her make-up. I remember her as tall, with high cheek bones and a retrousse' nose. Her lips were sensitive and bestowed a warm and gentle smile, with eyes a greenish brown which seemed to complement her soft brown hair, cut short and always tidy. She was a very elegant lady.

"Did-le-dee. Did-le-dee. Did-le-dee." The train's hooter blew repeated blasts like shrill cornet sounds as we entered another long dark tunnel. We were in total darkness, and time seemed to stand still. Only the sound of the train drumming along the tracks gave an eerie feeling of loneliness and gloom. Clare was barely visible, only her dark shape silhouetted against the background of the carriage. She leaned forward taking my hands in hers, giving them a squeeze.

"Are you alright, Derek? The lights seem to have failed. It's a bit frightening in the dark. We'll be out of the tunnel very soon," she said, anxiously.

"Don't know. I mean, I think so. Thank you."

"I can't hear you," came the reply.

In a louder voice I repeated myself. The grip on my hands loosened as the darkness faded, and the train boomed out of the tunnel into the bright sunlight. Her hands relaxed, as she let mine resume their random position resting on my knees. We both sat smiling at each other.

"How old are you, Derek?" she said.

"I'm nearly ten," I said.

"If you were older you could be my boyfriend."

"How old would I have to be?" I said, in my best grown up voice.

"I'm 24, so you'd have to be at least 20. Perhaps 18 would do."

"Oh! I'll never catch you up, but we can pretend. You could be my girl friend then."

"What a good idea. I'd like that," Clare said.

The train pulled into Peterborough station, stopping with a jolt. A loud hiss of steam erupted from the engine, and slowly died away. An old man came into the carriage wearing a worn ginger brown and mustard flecked suit, a bottle green shirt, and a yellow wool tie. A big yellow silk handkerchief tumbled out of his breast pocket. He was carrying a straw coloured canvas bag. The stiff hind legs of a rabbit stuck out of the top with stalks of rhubarb and a bunch of dried flowers. He took his cap off by its threadbare peak, and hung it on a rhubarb stalk sticking out of his bag.

"Ow do," he said, in a pleasant voice, placing his bag next to him, as he sat down next to Clare.

"Good morning."

"Morning." We both responded simultaneously.

"Want an apple lad, young lady?" he said.

"Yes please."

"No thank you." We both said at once.

He pulled out the rabbit and rummaged around in the bag. After a few seconds he produced an apple, spat on it, and polished it on his jacket lapel. He did this several times until it was clean and shiny.

"Nice 'un, this 'un," he said, handing me the apple. "It's a Grantham Crispen, sweet as honey, crisp as me Dad's starched collars. Grew it me sen."

"Thank you very much," I said, taking the apple and munching into it.

The old man's head rolled from side to side with the motion of the train. Within a few minutes he was snoring loudly and sound asleep.

"I get off at Grantham in a few minutes," Clare said. "Here's my address if you ever come to Grantham. I live with my mum and dad. You are very welcome to come and see us." She handed me a piece of paper with the address written on it.

"It's been lovely meeting you, and thank you for removing the fudge. I'll always think of you when I eat fudge, Derek," she said, smiling.

I felt very sad she was leaving. Tears welled up in my eyes. The train pulled into Grantham station. Clare stood up, smoothed down her skirt, bent over and kissed my cheek. One last look as my tearful eyes focussed into the gap between her breasts. Quite spontaneously I bent forward and gently kissed the bare flesh above where her low cut blouse revealed her breasts. She held me tight, pressing me into her warm soft body.

"Bye," she said, releasing me.

I was too distraught to say anything.

The old man was still asleep, quite oblivious to both of us. I looked out of the carriage window. Clare walked down the platform. Her tall trim swaying figure gradually leaving the train behind. The whistle blew, steam hissed, the train moved forward. Soon I was alongside Clare, level with her. We looked into each other's eyes as I lifted my arm, and waved my hand, rolling my fingers to and fro. Tears rolled down my cheeks. We looked intently at each other. She blew me a kiss, and the train sped on, leaving her behind. She was soon out of sight, as the train rounded a bend. Like my mother, she was gone for ever. I never saw her again.

"Diddle-de-dee. Diddle-de-dee. Diddle-de-dee."

The train took on another note as it hurtled between two high banks with overgrown trees.

"Didgeridoo. Didgeridoo. Didgeridoo. Didgeridoo," leaving another love of my life behind.

I had become carried away with Clare in the short train journey we had experienced. My infatuation was twofold. Her breasts and silken legs made me feel warm, sometimes hot and sweaty. I wanted to be intimately close to Clare, feel her flesh against mine. She aroused my senses mentally and physically. It was not a sexual arousal, but a bonding and comforting between two people who could identify with each other. My relationship with Clare - albeit very brief - brought back strong memories of my mother. I remember my mother holding me tight against her bosom to comfort any distress I might have. It was an embrace of love which had no equal. It cured my pain, troubles and misery. Her love was unique. We bonded in our loving maternal relationship - mother and son. Clare and my mother had gone, and were now only a memory.

The old man was still sound asleep. I moved to where Clare had been sitting thinking I might feel her warmth and presence. I closed my eyes and for a brief moment I experienced a closeness, and the scent of her perfume. It was as if we had a spiritual intimacy. Sitting in her seat made me feel happy and confident.

The old man's big round belly heaved as he let out each gasp of air. Each breath, in and out, pushed his trousers up and down, over and under his hips. His faded red braces were now only a fashion statement. They had lost their elasticity. The two front parched worn leather straps anchored to the waistband were held by one button only. Each trouser leg rode high above his polished boot tops, and yellow socks, showing off his creamy white long legged underpants. His bushy eyebrows and thick military moustache bristled and shone with the glancing sun caught by the speeding train. His sideburns were thick and gingery grey in colour. Deep lines ran across his forehead, and disappeared under his wispy fast-thinning hair. Crows feet radiated from the corners of his closed eyes. His face was red and puckered. Wiry whiskers, like tufts of couch grass sprouted from his ears and nose. With his mouth ajar he spluttered and splashed, dribbling down the front of his chin. The train slowed down and jolted, screeching metal on metal, and came to a halt, throwing the old man forward. He woke with a start clutching his canvas bag.

"Bloody 'ell," he said, alarmingly. "What's up? Good Heavens! What's 'appened? Where are we?"

He stood up, adjusting his trousers by pulling them down over his hips, so they settled on his boots. He let go.

They shot up over his hips again, once more displaying his long-johns tucked into his yellow socks. I thought he must have very short trousers, or telescopic braces.

"Fancy another apple, lad?" he said.

"Yes, please," I said.

He took the rabbit out of his bag again, found an apple and cleaned it as before.

"Try this, lad, crisp as a nice bit of crumpet," he said, winking at me, and handing me the apple.

"Thank you very much," I said.

"Been crying lad?" he said, looking straight into my eyes.

"A little. I'm a bit sad," I said, holding back my tears.

"Soon put that right, lad," he said, feeling in his jacket pocket. He pulled out a small ball of garden twine, a box of matches, a pipe and a penknife. Holding the penknife in his right hand with the blade poised, he lifted the rabbit by its short furry tail, and slashed it off. The rabbit fell to the floor leaving the tail held fast in his strong steely grip. His knuckle bones shone white through his thin worn skin.

"This'll bring yer luck, make yer 'appy. If yer ever feel down, feel the soft fur, woks a treat. I allus 'ave one in my pocket," he said.

He handed me the rabbit's tail, at the same time taking another tail from his pocket.

"'Ad this long as I remember, never failed me yet. Gypsy's trick," he said, putting it back into his pocket.

The train came into Newark station. The old man collected his things, put on his cap, saying, "Bye, lad, stroke the tail and wish. It allus woks."

He walked down the platform with bent shoulders, head thrust forwards with the peak of his cap set straight above his eyes. I noticed his trousers were at least six inches above his boots.

"Another friend gone," I thought, as he disappeared over the bridge linking the platforms.

A nun came and sat opposite, almost in the same place as the old man. She wore a long black habit tied with a thick black leather belt around her waist, clasped with a large silver buckle. Her head and neck were covered in a black headdress, a white cloth covered her forehead and the sides of her face, which was tied off under her chin. A wooden crucifix hung from her neck on a thin white rope. She glared at me with a forbidding look, so much so I felt intimidated. She took a pair of black horn-rimmed spectacles, which she settled on her nose, and a black leather bound book from out of a large well-worn black leather valise. She opened the book, which turned out to be a breviary, thumbed through a few pages, and crossed herself saying.

"In nomine Patris, et Fillii, et Spiritus Sancti."

"Amen," I said, quite involuntarily.

"Are you taking the mickey, boy?" she said.

"Don't know," I said, and added, "Don't know what a mickey is."

Without thinking, and not knowing what I was saying, I said, "Do you mean taking the piss?"

I'd heard the expression used by grown ups, and thought it was the right thing to say in the present circumstances.

"Wash your mouth out with carbolic, and may God forgive you. You nasty little boy," she said, in a high and mighty voice. "Wherever did you learn that sort of talk boy?"

"Don't know," I said.

She resumed reading, occasionally crossing herself, and muttering various Latin phases, "Laudamus te, Deo Gratias, Benedicamus Domino."

She would close her eyes for a few moments as if in prayer, and then would continue reading.

I looked out of the carriage window trying not to gaze at the nun, but found it hard to divert my stare. Each time I looked at her, she seemed to be peering over her spectacles looking intently at me. Our eyes would meet. I would look away, but her overbearing manner made me feel embarrassed and inferior. I felt I had no right to be in her presence.

Suddenly we found ourselves in total darkness as the train bolted into another tunnel. It was black, damp, cold and eerie. The noise of the train speeding underground was thunderous and deafening. The carriage rattled, swaying from side to side, making a metallic cracking sound with each sway, as though it would derail as it tottered in all directions. The air became colder and clammy as we seemed to burrow deeper into the Stygian gloom. I felt threatened by the black-cloaked invisible nun sitting opposite. I heard her utter, "Benedictus Deus."

Her voice sounded menacing. I was frightened. If only Clare was in the carriage to hold my hand. For a moment her captivating scent and presence seemed to charge the air, and then it was gone. The pitch-black, jet-black, coal-black ambience took charge again. The train gave a sudden lurch, the wheels screeched against the rail tracks - steel against steel. The squealing brakes slowed the train down as it juddered to an unexpected halt.

"My God, Lord have mercy on us. What's happening, boy?" she said.

"Don't know," I said, frightened.

"We must pray. Put your hands together. Repeat after me," she said.

I ignored her, pretending not to hear. I felt in my pocket for the rabbit's tail, found it, and feverishly stroked the soft fur. Immediately the train sprang into life. It started, stopped, started, stopped and slowly eased its way forward without stopping again. The forward thrust of the train was comforting and lifted my dampened spirits. I felt relieved and overwhelmed that the rabbit's tail really worked.

"It must be magic," I thought.

Between us we had made the train go. We were on our way again, but still in the tunnel. Some shafts of daylight coloured with sun broke the gloom of the tunnel causing my eyes to blink and water.

"Prayer works boy, even without your help. Do you say your prayers, boy?" asked the nun.

I ignored her comments, shielding my eyes against the glare of the approaching light, still clutching my rabbit's tail. We were soon in broad daylight again, back to normal with the train rumbling on. It was as though the train had lost all its inhibitions and was now quietly murmuring along without a care in the world. The clammy cold air evaporated and became close and sultry. The nun's head bent in her breviary continued to mumble her prayer reading.

I looked through the windows watching the fields, trees and cows rush by. The train slowed down, and so did everything else. The cows stopped munching the grass. They stood lined up staring over the fence, still chewing as the train now idled along. They looked like the china ornaments my Auntie Ida had lined up along the shelf in her kitchen. They gawped, almost in a trance, munching and drooling. Their big brown eyes followed me as I stared back at them. A big chestnut brown horse galloped across the field towards the fence, and joined the cows in their vigilance. A tiny hamlet of grey slate roofed houses came into view, with a winding road threading its way through, like a needle and thread, trailing and ending its way into a rough track. You could see it twisting, unhurried, down towards, and disappearing into a small copse of trees. The powder blue clouds were high in the sky, lightened by the sun and slowly sinking in the west. Long paint strokes of sunlight cleaved apart by trees, lay across the fields, broken by hedges and scattered farm buildings. A river snaked its way into a thin strip, and faded into nothing. Soon the train ran into driving rain coming from the east. Heavy dark clouds bounded over the low hills, leaving the sun behind, at rest for another day.

My daydreaming was disturbed by the needle-sharp voice of the nun.

"What's that in your hand, boy?"

"It's my lucky rabbit's tail," I said.

"No such thing as luck. It's God's will. Nothing to do with luck. You stupid boy," she replied.

Her aggressive reply made me annoyed.

"I got the train started again in the tunnel with my rabbit's tail - it's magic. God made it magic."

"You profane blasphemous heathen!" came her bad tempered reply. She looked at me with hate in her eyes.

"No, I'm not. I'm a Catholic."

"Anglo, or Roman?"

"Don't know."

"Well you jolly well ought to. God only likes Roman Catholics anyway."

"I'll ask Fr Ignatius when I see him," I said, in frustration.

The nun said, all smiling with a smarmy look on her face, I'm Roman. A Sister of Charity, and I asked God to start the train. He did start the train. So there, boy!"

"No, He didn't. My magic rabbit's tail got it going first, before you started praying. I know, I know," I said, defiantly.

Easing my bottom off the seat I released a long soft silent plop of wind. Slowly it infested the air, like an uninvited guest. You could almost see the air thickening and changing colour. I willed the air to become a poisonous gas, and destroy the nun. Taking in a deep breath, and straining myself I pushed hard again but nothing happened. After several attempts I gave up. I just couldn't manage another plop. The nun looked at me with some alarm, no doubt wondering what I was trying to do. She sniffed the air, and said, looking me straight in the eyes, "Have you broken wind, boy?"

"Don't know."

"You have. I can smell it," she replied.

"I've farted, if that's what you mean."

"You foul dirty boy," she said, getting up and trying to open the window.

The window was stuck. I offered no assistance. I enjoyed the smell, even if the nun didn't. She pushed one way and then the other. She stopped her efforts, made the sign of the cross, and tried again. Suddenly it opened throwing her backwards into the seat. The unexpected rush of air lifted off her black headdress, leaving behind her naked shaved head. The white band across her forehead, and the sides of her face remained in place as if sutured to her face. She sat as though she had been struck by lightning, not daring to move. Her cropped head bristled with short black tufts of shiny bristles, her white polished scalp shining through. I picked up the headdress and handed it to her saying, "I'm sorry, Sister."

She gave me an embarrassed look and said, "Thank you, child."

Nervously she replaced the headdress, and closed her eyes. The breviary lay unopened on her knees, covered with her hands, as though she was deep in meditation. She soon fell asleep. I got up silently and closed the window. The air was much sweeter now. I tried very hard to suppress further plops of wind. Those that did exude were not as odious as the first one.

Looking at a ledge below the window there were two lines of ants, each going in opposite directions. The line moving towards the nun were carrying white crumbs of something, and disappearing into a gap at the end of the ledge. The other line of ants coming towards me were empty-handed. They too vanished into a crack. The two unbroken lines moved continuously up and down the ledge. A buzzing fly landed on the nun's nose. She unconsciously flicked it off, but back it came, again and again. Finally it gave up, and disappeared, only its buzzing remained.

The train pulled into Retford station. The nun gave out a snort like a piglet, as if gasping for air, licked her thin pale lips, moved her body to a new resting position, yawned, and continued her deep unbroken God-fearing slumbers.

The station was thronged with people getting on and off the train, some with dogs or live and dead chickens. One man was holding a goat straining against its leash. Some had shopping bags bulging with market produce. Others were struggling with garden pots, shrubs and plants. Market day in Retford was a beehive of activity - a day for buying and selling.

A middle aged lady came into the carriage, looked around and sat down in the opposite corner to me. Perched on her right shoulder was a large long-tailed parrot with bright green and yellow plumage. Below its short hooked bill hung a small brass bell, which jingled at each movement the parrot or lady made. The parrot's pointed pincer-like curved claws dug like nails into the lady's coat, holding it firm against the moving train. The lady wore a coarse green and yellow-flecked tweed coat over an ankle length bright red silky dress. A felt red close-fitting flattish brimless hat complemented her outfit. The strange lady removed the parrot from her shoulder, and seated it next to her. It stood, with claws stabbed into the seating looking around, first at me, and then the nun. Occasionally its beak opened as if trying to say something. The lady sliced up an apple, which the parrot ate greedily. It then seemed to go to sleep, still standing on the seat.

"Tickets, please," said a stern looking uniformed official wearing a peaked cap, and holding a metal ticket punch.

The nun, very put out at being woken up, said, "Hmmm."

She fumbled about, looking for her ticket.

"Got it somewhere," she said, emptying her bag on the seat.

"Ticket, young man," he said, looking at me.

I felt grown up at being addressed as 'young man', not like the nun, who called me 'boy' and 'child'. I produced my ticket, saying, "Here you are, sir!"

He gave me a funny look, punched my ticket, saying, "Thank you, sir!"

We obviously respected each other, and I responded with, "Thank you very much, sir!"

He gave me another curious look as if to say, "You're not taking the mickey, are you, sonny?"

He turned to the nun, who had now found her ticket. She had been using it as a bookmark.

"Thank you, miss," the ticket man said, handing back the ticket.

"I'm not a Miss! I'm a Sister! A Sister of Charity," said the nun, indignantly.

"You don't look like a nurse to me, sorry, miss," he said

"Hmmm," said the nun, in high dudgeon.

The parrot lady held out her ticket.

"Where's the bird's ticket?" the man said.

"He doesn't need a ticket," she said.

"It's occupying a seat. Rules and regulations stipulate anyone occupying a seat on a train journey must have the appropriate ticket, for the appropriate fare, for the appropriate train journey in question. 'Regulation Passenger Conveyance by train 1939. Sec 5, Rule 7C.' I don't make the rules, madam. I only apply them as the case may be," said the ticket man.

"Bugger off! Bugger off!" said the parrot, in a loud raucous voice.

The parrot kept repeating, "Bugger off," until the lady picked him up, put a cloth over his head, and put him in a stiff leather bag. She closed the bag with a forceful crash, almost decapitating the parrot, as the two halves of the bag snapped together. The bag was then thrown onto the overhead luggage rack.

"Will that do?" she said, irritatingly.

"Providing he says up there, and doesn't occupy a seat," said the ticket man, walking away muttering to himself.

As soon as the ticket man was out of sight she released the parrot from her portmanteau, and perched him on the seat again.

"Stupid man!" she said.

The parrot in turn repeated, "Stupid man! Bugger off! Stupid man! Bugger off!"

He only stopped when he was fed with more apple. Still upright he seemed to resume his sleeping again.

The remaining journey to Doncaster went without further incident. I was getting very excited. Soon I'd be home with Dad and Brian. It was late afternoon. The sun was getting low in a still powder blue sky, with the dark clouds and rain left behind. The fields were slowly fading away, and being replaced with tall smoking chimneys, and rows of dull red-bricked terraced houses. Cars, lorries, buses and cyclists diligently moved along the roads, appearing and disappearing like gliding river trout. Leaving all this behind the train pulled into the station. Collecting my belongings I looked at the sleeping nun, and said, "Goodbye, sister."

She stirred, and grunted, "Hmmm."

The parrot lady said, "Bye," and smiled at me.

The parrot, not to be outdone, squeaked in a high-pitched cry, "Bugger off! Bugger off! Bugger off!"

Its cry became weaker as I left it behind, stepping onto the platform, and walking away.

CHAPTER 10

Crazy Shoes

"I said to this monk, here, I said,
look here, mister .... you
haven't got a pair of shoes, have
you, a pair of shoes, I said,
enough to help me on my way. Look
at these, they're nearly
out, I said, they're no good to me. I
heard you got a stock of
shoes here. Piss off, he said to me.

The Caretaker Act 1.
Harold Pinter 1930-

CHAPTER 10

"What time's the train, Harry?" said a smiling Miss Weatherspoon, trying to be pleasant.

She soon realised she'd overstepped the mark by preening herself, and almost getting into Harry's bed earlier in the day. Miss Weatherspoon, now in her late fifties, was getting desperate for a male suitor. Earlier in her life she'd had lovers, and enjoyed the experience. She was now obsessed with men, feeling her youth was ebbing away rapidly. She still had strong sensuous feelings, and wished to satisfy them. Her working life had been as companions, housekeepers, and matron at three boarding schools. She had masqueraded as a titled lady, married to an English diplomat abroad, which had only lasted six months. Miss Weatherspoon never held down a job for very long. She was always on the move under different names, and disguises. She was a lady of many parts.

"Harry did you hear me? What time's Derek's train?" shouted Miss Weatherspoon.

"About four o'clock. We'll be leaving soon and look round Doncaster until the train's due. I'll get some fish and chips tonight from the chippy. Don't bother to cook,

Miss Weatherspoon …. sorry! I mean Ethel," stuttered Harry.

"No we won't! I'll cook you some fish and chips, mushy peas, rhubarb pie with custard. No lumps or skin either," said Ethel, in a very assertive voice.

"Didn't think you cooked at the weekends. Can't afford to pay extra, Ethel," said Harry, now feeling more confident with himself.

Ethel shouted back aggressively, "Special day today. Derek's home. One big happy family, me, you Harry, and the boys. Won't cost you any extra. My cod, chips and peas are the best in town. You'll see, Harry. It'll be on the table seven o'clock sharp.

Right, Harry! OK, Harry! Don't be late, Harry!"

Harry just didn't want to remonstrate with Miss Weatherspoon, and shouted back confidently.

"Fine, we'll be sitting down at seven o'clock. Thanks! We're off now."

Harry felt once more put down by the overbearing, dictatorial, Miss Weatherspoon. He didn't have the courage to tell her he *liked* skin and lumps in his custard.

"You've got shiny shoes, Brian. I've never seen them so clean," said Harry.

"Auntie Ethel cleaned them. She's done yours too. Your best brown ones that Mummy bought you," said Brian.

Miss Weatherspoon, feeling superior, and completely in charge, appeared as if from nowhere with Harry's best brown brogue shoes. Harry had very large feet, hence his shoes were big and heavy. She held both shoes between thumb and index finger, clasped tightly together. The shoes were thrust right under his nose, so much he could smell them …. sweaty feet, leather and paint.

"You know what they say about men with large feet, Harry," said Ethel, grinning from ear to ear.

"No," said Harry, feeling uncomfortable.

"They wear big shoes," said Ethel, still grinning.

They were polished, and shone like glass, enhanced by the sun. The leather's patterned perforations had disappeared under the gloss. Harry was not pleased. He liked to clean his own shoes, his way, with his own wax polish. Ethel appeared to have coated them in a hard glossy transparent shoe paint, like clear varnish. Harry thought his shoes looked ruined.

"Put them on, Harry. I'll clean the ones you're wearing ready for work Monday," said Ethel.

Harry swopped over his shoes saying, "Please don't clean them. I'd rather do my own, but thanks anyway."

"Alright with me, Harry. A job less to do. Only trying to be helpful. Now off you go, and be back by seven. Give Auntie Ethel a kiss, Brian."

Kisses were exchanged. Brian didn't mind the fuss and attention.

Harry mumbled under his breath, "Sod off! You fat cow."

He gave Ethel a sarcastic smile, grabbed Brian's hand, and dashed out of the house relieved to get away.

The bus for once was on time. Harry, with Brian at his side, felt liberated from his autocratic housekeeper. What was he to do though? He felt constantly threatened into submission by her demands. He was not in control. She was. He looked down at his shoes. Their gloss had gone, and what was left was an opaque, dull surface with very fine cracks, like microscopic crazy paving. She had painted them with clear varnish, not once, but several times over. Just walking a few hundred yards had crazed the gloss. Harry took pride in his shoes, especially his new brogues, which were a birthday present from Phyllis, worn for church and special occasions only, and now ruined, only fit for the garden.

CHAPTER 11

The Shoplifter

"Fish got to swim and birds got to fly
I got to love one man till I die,
Can't help lovin' dat man of mine."

"Can't Help Lovin' Dat Man of Mine."

From Showboat 1927.
Oscar Hammerstein II 1895-1960.

CHAPTER 11

With Harry and Brian out of the way, Miss Weatherspoon stomped around the house, not in anger, but jubilant, knowing she was in control, and in charge. Her footfalls were heavy and noisy. She was asserting her power, making her presence known, and felt in the house. She looked at the photographs on the wall, and stared at the picture of Drum Major Albert James Postlethwaite.

"Hmmm, I'm in charge now, and take that look off your face," she said.

With her large bosom pushed out, and standing tall, she glared at the couple on the tandem.

"On yer bike," she said. I'm the boss now."

She went into Harry's room, and once more opened drawers, looked into cupboards. Under the bed were two leather cases. Inside were Phyllis's clothes, shoes, personal things and jewellery. Unfortunately for Miss Weatherspoon nothing fitted, only the jewellery was of use. This she took to her own room, hiding it under her mattress.

"A large stiff gin now, before I go shopping," she said, speaking quietly to herself.

With three large gins under her belt she looked at herself in the mirror.

"Not a bad looking lass", she said, aloud. "I'll improve with some lippy," she added.

The bright red lipstick was smeared across her mouth, half on and half off her lips. She rubbed her lips together in an effort to even out the colour, but not very successfully. She tried again with the lipstick. The colour this time went above and below her lips. Above her upper lip was a red uneven line stretching from the corners of her mouth like a thin ragged moustache. The only saving grace was that the existing growth of ugly facial hair on her upper lip was now red instead of a fuzzy brown. Red powder was then applied to both cheeks, and a smear of rouge to her cheek bones. False eyelashes were stuck above each eye, with the left eyelash a different colour to the right, and all askew. It seemed that Miss Weatherspoon was colour blind. Her burning cheeks now flushed a bright crimson and shone with an alcoholic glow. The slapped-on make-up applied, in an inebriated fashion, emphasized by her large pointed jug ears, resembled a circus clown's face. To complete her outfit she put on a wide- brimmed, green and blue flecked-tweed hat, with a squashed indented crown, sporting three very big greenish blue feathers. Looking very peacockish, she picked up her large shopping bag, slammed the front door with an almighty crash, and swaggered down the garden path into the street humming,

> *"You made me love you,*
> *I didn't want to do it,*

You made me love you."

Two neighbours on the opposite side of the street were chatting away as Miss Weatherspoon walked by with head held high. They stopped their gossip, and stared across the road, dumbstruck at what they saw. Miss Weatherspoon eyeballed them smugly, and retaliated with, "Never seen a fine lady before?"

In her superior manner she carried on walking down the road leaving the ladies stunned.

"I'nt that 'Arry's fancy woman?" said one.

"And Phyllis not co'd in 'er grave," said the other.

"She looks a tart that's seen berra days," came the reply.

"Takes all sorts yer know. Can't be 'Arrys bit on the side. 'Es got berra taste."

"Yer right, Maggi, anyway 'Arry's not like that. 'Es a Cathlick, and Cathlicks don't do that sort of thing."

"They're no different to anyone else, ge's urges, like your Ted," said Maggie.

"Worra about your Eric then? 'Es randy all the time. If that's norra bun in't oven I'll eat me 'at," came the reply.

"It's wind I tell yer, a good clear out, me best corsets in place, and I'm flat as a pancake. Anyway 'es got brewer's droop most of't time."

"My Ted's the same. Too much ale, I reckon. Berra gerron. Can't gas allus day. Bye!"

"See yer, Beth."

Both neighbours disappeared into their front doors, turning round for one last look into the street. They each banged their door shut. The windows shivered and rattled as if upset at being disturbed. The street resumed its stillness.

Miss Weatherspoon walked, unruffled, into the small town feeling haughty, and a cut above the rest. The gin was beginning to wear off. She felt confident, glamorous, and in control. She nodded at people, smiling, saying in her put-on refined, formal voice to passers by,

"Good afternoon!"

"How are you?"

"Have a nice day!"

"Lovely day!"

Most nodded back and grunted, feeling that their privacy had been invaded by an eccentric strange woman. She could have been walking a goat down the street, and the effect would have been the same. She cut a very unusual image, striding down the main street of a sleepy conventional country town. Walter's Wet Fish shop was her first assignment.

"Some nice cod fillets," she thought. She looked into the shop, and waited until it was empty before she walked in.

"Good afternoon, Walter," she said, as if she'd known him all her life.

"Morning," came the reply. "What can I get yer Madam?"

"Just having a look for the moment," she said, scrutinizing the fish on the slab.

"Hmmn! Hmmn! All fresh?" she said.

"In the sea, six hours back," came the reply.

She spotted a display of cod fillets, labelled, 'Best Atlantic Cod'.

"Excuse me," she said. "Someone at the back of the shop, sounds like a break-in, glass breaking"

"D'int 'ear 'ote," said Walter, rushing into the back of the shop.

Miss Weatherspoon calmly picked up three large cod fillets, slipped them into some newspaper, and popped them into her large canvas shopping bag. The sleight of hand took seconds only. Walter returned looking put out.

"Nowt at back," he said.

Miss Weatherspoon looked him straight in the eyes and said, "Fancied a lobster, but you don't seem to have any."

She turned her back on Walter and marched out of the shop.

"Good day," she said.

Walter grunted in reply, "We 'aint got none, silly bitch."

"I heard that," said Miss Weatherspoon, turning round to eyeball him once more.

"G'day, Walter," she said again gleefully, with a smirk on her face.

The next stop was the grocers. Added to her bag with the cod were two large tins of mushy peas, a large bottle of dandelion and burdock, two bottles of brown ale, four bars of chocolate, small cigars, a tin of pipe tobacco, and a box of matches. Miss Weatherspoon had only paid grudgingly for the matches. She was on her way home through the park, having swapped her tweed feathered hat for a brown beret, and was now wearing thick, dark brown sunglasses. The weight of the shopping bag made her stoop as she walked. Miss Weatherspoon accentuated her slouch in an effort to conceal her earlier appearance. Tired, she sat down on a park bench, and soon dozed off.

Startled, she woke up, feeling something between her ankles. Looking down she saw a poodle with white curly hair, which was clipped from his ribs to his tail. His legs and tail were shorn, apart from two inches of white curly hair on each leg at the paw base, and the end of his tail. Its red tongue hung out, dry, and frantically panting for a drink. A leash attached to a black-studded collar trailed behind the dog. A nub of carefully groomed curly hair sat proudly on his head between very short ears. Miss Weatherspoon liked dogs, and bent down to pat it. Immediately they were friends. They had bonded.

"Must get you a drink," she said.

The dog looked up dolefully, sniffed, and desperately panted, wagging its tail excitedly. Behind the bench was a tap with a short hose for watering the flower beds. The hose dripped, but when Miss Weatherspoon turned the tap on fully, water splashed up from the ground like a fountain. The poodle lost no time in lapping up a drink from the creation of small puddles. The dog's thirst quenched, tail dancing with yaps of approval, it followed Miss Weatherspoon back to the bench, curled up on the ground, and went to sleep. The dog's collar read 'Mitzi' with a phone number. Miss Weatherspoon collected herself together, picked up the leash, pulling the sleeping dog reluctantly to its feet, saying, "Come on, Mitzi, let's go."

The dog's ears pricked up. It wagged its tail, panted, and looked up knowingly, as if to say, "I'm ready. Let's go. I'm hungry."

They both walked off together through the park, Mitzi stopping at every lamppost, and cocking up a leg for a wee.

Miss Weatherspoon called in at the corner shop for a tin of dog meat, paid for one tin, but managed to conceal four more tins in her bag without paying.

Back in the house with Mitzi running around at her feet she opened a tin of rabbit meat, with the dog sniffing, wagging its tail and moving from side to side in expectation of a meal. Mitzi looked up at Miss Weatherspoon with his head cocked to one side, jaws open, and gasping in frenzied suspense. Before the bowl of food reached the ground Mitzi reached up and nuzzled into the rabbit. The bowl was licked clean, again and again, until it shone spotless as if sterilized. Water, slurped in eager gulps, left an empty bowl as dry as earth parched by an unrelenting sun. Mitzi, exhausted with food and drink, now silent and content, curled up in Harry's chair, and went to sleep. Dog spit dribbled, saliva foamed from Mitzi's jaws onto the chair's cushion leaving white frothy stains.

Miss Weatherspoon felt very pleased with her day's work. Spread out on the table were fresh Atlantic cod fillets, mushy peas, tobacco, chocolate, drink, dog food, and in Harry's chair, a French poodle, all for the cost of a box of matches, and a tin of dog food.

"Think I deserve a strong gin," she said to Mitzi, looking down at him, and rubbing his bristly tummy.

Gin in hand, she started to sing,

> *"You made me love you,*
> *I didn't want to do it,*
> *You made me love you,*
> *And all the time I knew it."*

She sat down, and was soon gently snoring in time with Mitzi, who occasionally let out satisfied burps, and bursts of wind. Two large meat flies were buzzing mischievously around the room intent on annoying both sleepers. They landed on Mitzi's damp nose, walking up and down. One tried to penetrate Mitzi's nostril, but was rudely sneezed out. The dog's head in anger would rear up and shake off the flies. The flies soon got fed up. They flew over to Miss Weatherspoon, hovering above her face, like humming birds, drinking nectar.

Her perspiring face and forehead exuded tiny droplets of salty body moisture. The smudged lipstick glowed moist with thin sparse red hairs shining through. The excited buzzing flies circulated above her deciding where to land first. One went for her wet chin, whilst the other landed on her nose. She waved them away in anger, annoyed at being disturbed. Back they came, buzzing a few inches above her face.

"Bugger off!" she shouted.

They persisted and continued their efforts to irritate - circling and landing, circling and landing. Each time they were beaten off. The flies would not give up. Miss

Weatherspoon sat up, opened her eyes. One eyelash fell off. She looked up at the clock. It said five o'clock.

"Better get the supper ready - two hours, plenty of time though," she muttered to herself.

A good wash followed. The remains of the lipstick and eyelash removed, a change of clothes, and she looked remarkably normal again. Trying to impress Harry, she put on a wire support uplift bra, and see-through cream silk blouse. It was cut low with buttons, collar and short sleeves. Nestling in the hollow of her cleavage was the loop of a string of pearls hanging from her neck. She sported a large ruby ring on one finger, and a diamond ring on the other. Ruby earrings hung from her jug ears. Cheap sweet-smelling scent, sprayed between her squeezed up breasts, completed her attempt to court Harry.

Gin in hand, she madly attacked the preparation of fish, chips, mushy peas, rhubarb pie and custard.

Relaxed and happy she burst into song again,

> *"What'll I do when you are far away?*
> *And I am blue?*
> *What'll I do?*
> *With just a photograph,*
> *To tell my troubles to.*
> *What'll I do?*
> *With only dreams of you,*
> *That won't come true,*
> *What'll I do?"*

CHAPTER 12

Home Again

The bird forlorn,
That singeth with his breast against a thorn.

'The Plea of the Midsummer Fairies', st 30.
Thomas Hood 1799-1845.

CHAPTER 12

The bus to Armthorpe trundled along. It seemed to stop every few yards for no apparent reason. Occasionally, bundles of newspapers were thrown out, some went into the hedge bottoms, or onto pavements. They were thrown out at random. The last bundle landed in a large puddle of water, splashing a lady wheeling a pushchair. The wheeled baby let out a high-pitched cry as muddy water ran off its white woollen bonnet, and down its face. Dirty water soaked into the baby's white cardigan leaving large discoloured splash marks. In fright the baby flung her toy doll into the air, which landed in an adjacent bottomless muddy puddle. The doll floated, soaked up water and slowly submerged. It sank out of view.

An elderly man saw what was happening and ran to the rescue of the pushchair lady, baby and doll, his shoes covered in water, treading hastily to retrieve the doll. He disappeared. The puddle at this point had no bottom. A manhole cover had been removed leaving an umplumbable void. The man with arms flailing sank out of sight, his trilby hat left floating on the water. Bubbles broke the water's surface, and the man's face appeared above the water line. Fire engines' sirens added to the existing excitement. The incident soon drew a small crowd of onlookers. The man, squirting a jet of water from his mouth, disappeared again. Several times he bobbed up and down, until he managed to gain control using his arms stretched out either side of the hole. A fireman pulled him out. The local policeman arrived, wanting to take charge.

"Hello! Hello!" he said.

The onlookers hurried away at the sight of the law.

"Please yerself," said the policeman, to himself.

The bus carried on, the driver, with a smoking cigarette hanging from his mouth, quite oblivious to the trouble he had caused.

Harry, Derek and Brian sat on the bench seat at the rear of the bus. Harry was sound asleep. Derek and Brian were reading comics.

"We've got a new Auntie at home, Derek," said Brian. "She gets our meals. Her name's Auntie Ethel. She gives me extra pocket money, and tons of sweets. She's going to buy me a dog. You'll like her. We're having fish and chips tonight, Derek. You're sleeping in my room now. Auntie Ethel's in yours."

I was angered and troubled by Brian's news, that a strange lady had wormed herself into my house, and established herself as a mother figure. She was even sleeping in my bed in my room. Although I was yet to meet her I had a gut feeling I'd hate her. I was not ready for a new Auntie, or whatever she called herself. I wanted my mother, and the embracing comforts she offered. I had been half expecting to see my Mother when I got home. The reality now was she would not be there, but instead an impostor, a cheat, fraudster and a swindler. My sixth sense was all too foreboding. If only I could speak to Clare, or just be in her company. I needed reassuring and the comfort of being close to her, to hold her hand, look into her eyes, and breathe her fragrance, to rest my head within her bosoms, and to feel the warmth and love of her body. I felt alone again. My eyes swelled with tears, and my face flushed red and burnt. A lump came to my throat. Why did I feel this way?

Brian seemed insensible to our plight. He seemed to be only interested in having more pocket money, sweets, comics, and the prospect of a dog.

"Brian, do you miss Mummy?" I said.

"What?" came the reply.

I repeated myself.

"No, not really. We've got Auntie Ethel. She's fab, dead fablus," Brian said.

"I miss her all the time, Brian," I said.

"You're a baby, Derek, anyway you'll like Auntie Ethel a big lot, Dad likes her. I think she'll sleep with Dad. Then you can have your room back," said Brian.

I started to sob again.

"Cry baby! Cry baby! Our Derek's a cry baby," sang Brian.

At this point dad appeared to wake up. He'd been listening to our conversation and had not really been asleep. He said he'd been resting his eyes. In rather a snappy voice, he said, looking at Brian, "Miss Weatherspoon will not sleep with me. She stays in Derek's room until I make other arrangements. Don't let me ever hear you talk like that again."

Brian not to be outdone said, "Well, anyway, dad, I saw Auntie Ethel come out of your bedroom with hardly any clothes on."

"How dare you talk like that, Brian? And don't call Derek a cry baby. He misses Mummy, and I miss her too," said dad.

"Mummy's not your mummy. She's your Missis," said Brian, with a cheeky look on his face.

"Enough of all this, let's play 'I spy," said dad.

We played 'I spy' until the bus pulled into the market place at Armthorpe. The church clock said six fifteen. Most of the market stall holders had left, leaving a few workmen clearing up the rubbish.

Dogs and cats nosed around in the rubbish looking for scraps to eat. A long brown rat scurried across the rough cobbled market square into a grating. A brick thrown by one of the workmen followed the rat. It missed, skidded across the cobbles, and hit a car parked on the kerbside. The irate driver got out, stood with feet apart, hands on hips, looked around and shouted,

"Oo's pleein silly-boggers?" looking at the workmen.

The man who threw the brick walked over and said,

"Wottsup wiyyo serri?"

"Oo throde tha brick?" The driver angrily replied.

"Teent me," said the guilty workman.

The driver getting red in the face said,

"Assal purrim on tha nose."

The workman turning his back on the driver said, walking away,

"Yoal etta, Tarrah serri!"

The sun had sunk below the church spire, leaving a vivid orange-coloured sky, streaked with fiery red and electric-blue layers. A flock of birds, chatter, chatter, chatter, they seemed to sing, hovered high in the heavens. The noise became deafening, as more birds joined the flock. The sky was peppered with black moving specks. Thousands of shifting dots darkened the firmament moving higher into the heavens - the noise became fainter. Suddenly they flew eastwards. The feathered convoy soon vanished into emptiness.

A lone bird, perched high on the clock tower cried out, "cheep cheep, cheep, chee, chee, acheep, acheep," it's yellow beak pointing upwards. The crying stopped, his beak and head fell slowly into sadness. He had been abandoned.

I empathized with this lone bird. Like me, he had been deserted, jilted by his kith and kin, and left to fend for himself. Maybe his mother was miles away by now.

"Did he have a mother like me?" I thought.

I wanted to take the bird in my hands and comfort it, in the same way I had been comforted by my own mother, and latterly by Clare.

The metal frames which supported the wooden planks for the market stalls, rattled and crashed, as the workman clumsily piled them onto the lorry. The lone bird frightened by the noise flew to a nearby house, and rested on the ridge tiles. He carefully walked along the ridge on his thin, thinner than matchstick legs to the chimney breast, and squatted into a fluffy feathered ball against the pots for warmth, folding his head into his feathers.

The dogs and cats still rummaged through the rubbish, unconcerned by the disturbance around them. The occasional brown rat was seen scurrying about in a quest for food.

The car driver swearing to himself, drove off with acrid black fumes gusting from the car's exhaust. It misfired, backfired, stopped, let off explosions, and finally got underway, fitfully leaping up the road like a firecracker.

Harry and the boys walked home, Derek, not feeling at all happy at the prospect of meeting Auntie Ethel. Harry opened the door to the smell of fish and chips. "Just like the chippy," he thought.

Mitzi jumped off the chair, barking as he ran round in circles, sniffing at Harry, Derek and Brian. After accepting their right to be in the house, he went for Harry, and frantically sniffing at his trousers, jumped up and made for his crotch. Harry, taken in surprise, jumped backwards hitting a chair, and fell over flat on his back. Mitzi now had him where he wanted. He gave out high pitched yaps and pushed his wet nose into his genital area, pushing, yapping, sniffing excitedly. Harry was overcome with alarm. He was pinned down by a dog.

"My testicles! She'll eat my balls! I'm being raped by a dog!" he thought.

His back was hurt with the fall, and he couldn't move with the dog on top of his lower body. The boys looked on, and laughed.

An aproned Miss Weatherspoon heard the rumpus, saw what was happening, rushed into the kitchen, grabbed a bowl of cold water, and threw the water over Harry and the dog. Most of the water went over Harry. The dog eased off, wagged its tail, and skulked off into the kitchen. Harry lay on his back, wet through, unable to move. He finally got to his feet with Miss Weatherspoon's help and went upstairs to his bedroom, still accompanied by her.

"Harry, let me help you change your trousers," she said, trying to undo his belt and buttons.

"No thank you! I can manage. Please go!" Harry replied, feeling intimidated, and threatened again.

"Only trying to help, Harry," came the reply. "Supper on the table in five minutes," and off she walked, feeling miffed.

"Sod off," said Harry, to himself.

"Come on, Derek, give Auntie Ethel a big hug," she said, grasping me savagely to her chest.

My face was pressed into her cleavage, hard against her big floppy bosoms. The wires in her bra were cold and unyielding, pressing rock-like into my chin. She smelt sweaty and of cheap sweet scent. I managed to recoil from her strong hold, but she pulled me forward again. A little higher up her chest this time. I could see blue veins, and brown spots. I looked up to where her neck joined her crazed chest. It was not like Clare's, young and smooth, but wrinkled and spotted. I could hear her heart beating, and the blood surging impatiently through her veins. I managed to free myself from her tight grip, almost falling in reverse as I sprang back. Miss Weatherspoon glared at me with hatred in her eyes. I stared back feeling intimidated. We were sworn enemies and at war with each other.

She turned to Brian, saying, "You'll give a cuddle, wont' you?"

Brian rushed towards her with open arms.

"Yes, Auntie Ethel. I love you a big lot."

They crashed intimately together like long lost lovers.

"Love you too," she said, as they continued their love sick embrace.

The sight of Brian and Miss Weatherspoon, coupled with my own experience, left me nauseated and in a state of shock.

I felt Brian was renouncing the memory of our mother. He seemed to have forgotten that she had ever existed. It was only a matter of weeks since we had been together as a family. We were happy, laughing, loving, warm and secure. For my part my security was gone. Miss Weatherspoon was a replacement for Brian, or seemed to be, but for me, she was like a bad dream. I was alone without the essential bodily love, warmth, and kindness of my mother. I wanted to see her infectious smile, and hear her voice and laughter again. I craved to touch her, feel her warm flesh against mine, hold her, feel her soft warm breasts tightly embracing against my thin frail empty shell, smell her balmy body. Although Clare was far away now, she radiated what I had lost, and what I wanted and needed. My mother's love was being replaced by a cheap impersonator, who only gave out shabby false affection.

I felt as if I'd been dropped into the ocean, I was left alone, treading water and swimming to save my life. I could see the shore line, people and lights, but was unable to make it to safety. I was getting tired, my legs and arms were becoming weaker. There was no help, no boat, nothing to cling onto to ease the fatigue. I must keep afloat whatever happened.

My dad loved me, he would put his arms around me, but his body love was different. He smelt of tobacco, and body sweat, his face was prickly with beard stubble. His clothes were uneven and coarse. My mother's were soft and silky. His skin was rough and tough. My mother's was smooth and gentle. His voice was deep and loud. My mother's was soft, and tuneful. My father had a flat hairy chest. My mother had smooth soft breasts. The extreme contrasts between my father and mother were such that there was no substitute for my mother's death. My father loved and cared for me, but his affection lacked the bonding of a mother's love.

We all sat around the table. Miss Weatherspoon sitting in dad's usual place at the head of the table, giving out instructions like a Sergeant Major, and serving the fish and chips. Dad and she drank beer, me and Brian, dandelion and burdock.

"Too many bones in my fish," said Brian.

"Let me take them out for you, dear," said Auntie Ethel.

She flaked the white fish, removing any bones she found, which were only four. "There you are, dear," she said, passing the plate back to Brian.

"Eat up, Brian," said Dad.

I had to admit to myself that the fish and chips were mouth-watering.

"May I have some more, please, Miss Weatherspoon?" I said.

"Call me Auntie Ethel," came back the reply.

"You're not my Auntie, I can't call you Auntie, Miss Weatherspoon," I snapped back.

"Please yourself," she replied, ignoring my request for a second helping.

"More fish, Harry? I'll do you some fresh chips," said Miss Weatherspoon, in a condescending voice as sweet as honey.

"Yes, please," said Harry, gulping down a mouthful of beer. "Derek, would you like some too?" he added.

"No thank you, Dad," I said, feeling put down by the dragon.

"Thought you wanted seconds, Derek?" said Dad.

"I'm not hungry anymore," I said, as cheerfully as I could under the circumstances.

Back came Miss Weatherspoon with fresh chips and cod for Dad.

"Some more fresh chips for you, Brian, dear?" said the monster, smiling at Brian.

"Please, Auntie," said Brian.

"Here you are, dear. Nice and crispy. Done especially for a good boy," she said.

The rhubarb pie and custard looked wonderful, but I wouldn't eat it, on the pretext of not being hungry. Upon reflection, I was stubborn in refusing any pudding. Dad had three helpings, Brian had two, and Miss Weatherspoon ate two large portions, which she gobbled down like Uncle Jack's pigs gulping down their swill.

"My late Uncle Jack. He's dead too," I thought.

I was rather hoping there would be some pie left which I could eat later unobserved. But Miss Weatherspoon had other ideas. She gathered up all the pie remains, including the custard, and put them into a large tin bowl.

"Mitzi will enjoy the pudding. He's eaten the remains of the fish and chips. He loves the skin," said Ethel.

I felt miserable, but tried very hard to be cheerful. I was still hungry, and realised I'd made a big mistake in turning down second helpings of fish and chips, and rhubarb pie. I'd cut off my nose to spite my face.

"Ethel, where did Mitzi come from?" said Harry.

"He followed me home, lost I'd think. I've been to the police station and reported it," said Ethel.

"He's not wearing a collar," said Harry.

Ethel had taken it off and hidden it, so she could keep the dog. The police station was just part of the deceit.

"I'll have to buy him a collar and a leash," said Ethel.

Harry was beginning to feel uncertain about the dog story. He didn't want a dog anyway, at least not a dog that wanted to mate with him.

Where was the wretched animal? Peeing all over the place no doubt. It wasn't a real dog anyway, clipped with curly hair. It was a lady's dog, not a man's dog.

"I wouldn't be seen dead walking down the street with the stupid dog," he thought to himself.

"Ethel," he said. "How did you know the dog's name?"

Miss Weatherspoon was taken by surprise by the question, and for a moment was lost for words. She had to think quickly.

"Pardon, Harry," she said.

Harry repeated himself.

"Aha," she said. "I'm an authority on dogs, especially French poodles. Judged at Crufts for many years. The common names for French poodles are Mitzi, Froo Froo, Di Di or Didi, or just Darling. Easy. She answered to Mitzi."

Harry thought, "A likely story."

"Where's the bloody dog now?" he wondered.

Miss Weatherspoon was beginning to feel hot, and uncomfortable with Harry's persistent questioning.

"Better change the subject quickly before I'm caught out," she thought.

"Harry, I've a little present for you, to make amends," said Ethel, handing him a tin of pipe tobacco.

She gave Brian a bar of chocolate, looked at me saying, "It's a pity you're not hungry, Derek, otherwise you'd get some chocolate."

Another stab in the back. I'll get my revenge. "Hope you're sick, Brian," I said to myself.

I was not sure if it was really good to be home again. I was hungry and sleeping in a room with Brian. I thought about the bird left behind, trying to keep warm against the chimney pots. Dad came and kissed us both goodnight, his breath smelling of strong acrid tobacco. Miss Weatherspoon came into our bedroom, and kissed Brian goodnight. She ignored me as I slid under the sheets.

"You don't like Auntie Ethel, do you, Derek?" said Brian, gloating at the attention he was getting.

"Be quiet, you slimy worm," I replied.

"I'll tell Dad what you said," came the reply.

"Please yourself," I said.

I went to sleep thinking about the lonely bird, wondering where Clare was, the nun, the lady with the parrot, and the old man who gave me the rabbit's tail. I'd forgotten all about the lucky rabbit's tail. I jumped out of bed, found it, and put it under my pillow. I was soon asleep, forgetting my problems, and my prayers.

CHAPTER 13

The Dream

"*Tell me not, in mournful numbers,*
Life is but an empty dream!
For the soul is dead that slumbers
And things are not what they seem.
Life is real! Life is earnest!
And the grave is not its goal;
Dust thou art, to dust returnest.
Was not spoken of the soul."

A Psalm of Life.
Henry Wadsworth Longfellow 1807-1882.

CHAPTER 13

I stepped onto a cotton-wool cloud, and sat down. Perched opposite me was the bird I'd seen earlier. The bird began to speak.

"I'm your guardian angel. I've been sent to look after you. Are you feeling happier? I understand you have been very unhappy. Tell me everything. I'll try to make you cheerful again."

Without my noticing the bird vanished, and in its place was a man standing in the clouds. The cotton-wool mixture was made up of many soft waxen colours, which changed their hue as puffs of slow moving mist mingled together, occasionally covering the figure. The figure reminded me of the large colourful alabaster statue of St Joseph at church. He stood erect with outstretched arms, the palms of his hands open in a welcoming gesture. He was clothed in long flowing garments of blue and gold, which changed colour with the swirling mist. The face of the man was kind, gentle and smiling. He had a neat, pointed tuft-like beard, and long hair resting on his shoulders. A blaze of bright golden light lit up his body. The bird appeared again, perched on his shoulder.

I thought perhaps I was seeing an angel, but there were no wings.

"What would make you happy, Derek?" said the figure.

"I would like to see my mother again," I said.

"That can be arranged, but we will have to go on a long journey, which takes us across the Stygian Lake. Do not be afraid, follow me. Do not lose sight of me. Have faith, Derek."

The figure moved into the mist, and almost disappeared. I stood up. We both floated into the whirling mist. Faster and faster the mist swirled round in a maelstrom. I was dragged down in turbulent confusion, and found myself stretched out, bewildered and disorientated on a black sandy volcanic beach. Black clouds hung over a stretch of water, which disappeared into the horizon. The man was sitting in a small boat at the edge of the water. The bird was still with him. He beckoned me to join him.

"We have to journey across the lake. It's dark, gloomy, and many monsters lurk there. I will have to leave you now, but I will be with you in spirit. Do not despair, Derek, have faith! I will join you when you reach the other side of the lake."

The man melted away, leaving the bird perched on the prow of the boat. We moved away from the shore line, heading into the gloom of grey, slow-moving mists, and heavy dark storm clouds. It began to get chilly. I found an old sack of sorts at the bottom of the boat, which I slipped over my shoulders. Strange disturbing noises were all around me, prolonged dull groans of agony and pain, loud harsh creaking sounds, like trees splitting and bending in the wind; sharp explosive cries, and growls of animals, high pitched squealing and squeaking, thunderous and violent winds whipping up the surf, thunder rumbling and crashing, followed by bright flashes of lightning criss-crossing the sky. High boiling foaming waves rocked the pitching boat, but it still moved forward, heading towards a distant blue cloudless calm sky.

A slimy giant green warty toad-like creature with penetrating fiery orange eyes jumped into the boat. Its mouth was wide and curved like a gigantic cucumber. It opened and shut its menacing jaws, exposing large fangs and sending out jets of fire and steam. It came towards me, making a maddening high-pitched 'brr' call. Eight stubby legs slid over the bottom of the boat, dragging a bloated belly along in a slurry of glutinous slime. I sat traumatised in fear waiting to be eaten alive. The lake was now bubbling steam from hot muddy whirlpools. To jump out of the boat to escape from the attacking toad would mean drowning and being sucked into a vortex of thick boiling mud. I froze, as the approaching toad inflated at each move, getting bigger and bigger. The bird flew towards me and perched on my shoulder, sending out a penetrating "caw, caw, caw" directed at the toad. The toad stopped in its tracks, puffed out its slippery oily chest, and slowly deflated as though releasing gas until it vanished. All that remained on the wooden planking of the boat bottom was a dried up withered patch, like desiccated autumn leaves.

The boat moved on. The bird returned to the prow of the boat, perched on its delicate thin matchstick legs as if in charge. The boat rocked and shook as it bulldozed its way through rough gyrating viscous liquid. We approached a small island with a towering volcano erupting fire and thick smoke. White hot molten lava flowed to the water's edge making it boil and bubble, steam and smoke with the intense heat. Noxious smells of sulphur and burning flesh hung heavy in the air. The fetidness became a mist the nearer our approach to the island. The vaporized air became nauseating with the stench of decay. I began to choke, unable to breathe. The bird had faded away in the low hanging haze. I felt abandoned and ready to die. The liquid around the boat was boiling and frothing like a witches' brew. A cacophony of deafening sounds came from the end of the island as we drew near. Black waves of cooled-down solidified lava ran down to the edge of the lake. Nightmarish savage obese animals with freakish human faces leaped from rock to rock caterwauling like cats on heat, breathing fire and smoke. The experience was too much for me. I passed out and went into a deep sleep.

I woke up in still clear water with the island out of sight, heading towards bluer calmer skies. The air had lost its chill and stink, becoming balmy and windless. It was quiet, tranquil and peaceful. The bird appeared again, spread out its wings and hovered over the boat in an act of thanksgiving. Gently it flew down to its original perch. I looked ahead and saw land in the distance swathed in a sunlit haze.

The bottom of the boat scraped against the shallow water's edge with a rasping sound as it reached the silver white sandy shore. Sitting on a rock was the bearded man we had left behind, before we had started our horrifying boat journey across the Stygian Lake.

"Were you afraid, Derek?" the man said.

"I was very very afraid at first, but I prayed extra hard. I thought of my Mother and knew I was going to see her. The bird looked after me, and my fears disappeared. Tell me, I'm going to see her. Please tell me," I said, anxiously.

"Yes, my child. You will. Very shortly. You are safe now, and have nothing to fear. We are nearly at the end of our journey. Follow me."

The bird gently flew alongside us. It had changed colour now, to blue, green and yellow, very much like the parrot the lady had had on the train. We floated on a carpet of cloud down an avenue of fragrantly scented trees full of blossom - in pinks, mauves, blues and untold colours. The trees went on and out of sight. They stood like guardsmen standing sentinel, waiting for our approach. Figures were moving in and out of the trees, busying about, fully occupied in some activity, which was not apparent. As soon as we approached them they disappeared. We were never able to catch up and pass them, but they were always there.

The light became brighter, and the avenue wider with gardens full of unusual colourful flowers, orchards of exotic fruits, fountains, trees, and lawns on either side. There were more people, some sitting, others walking, children running, skipping and playing. The air was balmy, and still. Birds were singing melodious tunes, and flutes echoed through the embracing moving mist. It was all at peace, and time stood still.

The man took my arm, although I was not conscious of him doing so, and led me into a walled rose garden. The blooms were blousy in full blossom. They had strong aromatic fragrances of sweet musk, fresh fruit, tea rose scent, myrrh, hints of apple and cinnamon, and unknown perfumes. Bunches of burnished red hips with clusters of large coloured flowers hung down in fragrant festoons of pure white, apricot-yellow, and orange, warm and glowing pinks, some shaded with mauve, rich velvety crimson gradually changing into rich purple hues. Each colour set amongst light and dark green leaves forming a large patchwork of intense tinctures and fragrance. Several people appeared to be collecting flower petals from each colour group.

"Your mother is picking the apricot-orange petals at the end of the garden," said the man. "Near the wall with the coppery-pink rambler hanging down."

I looked very hard but couldn't see her. We walked towards the wall, which seemed to recede at each step. We were not able to reach it. In the mist I saw someone dressed in a long flowing creamy robe. The figure looked up at me, and smiled. It was my mother. Her smiling face was warm, kind and welcoming. I smiled back unable to say anything. I moved closer, but couldn't get near. The mist drifted in, and she disappeared.

"You cannot get any closer, Derek. Your mother is now a spirit. Keep still," said the man.

The mist moved away. She stood bathed in a golden light, still smiling, and looking at me. She lifted up an arm, and slowly moved her hand in recognition. I smiled, and waved back. She disappeared in the mist again.

"Wake up, Derek! Fr Ignatius is expecting you to serve Mass at nine. Get a move on, it's eight now."

My Dad seemed to be shouting into my ear as he bent over me. I was not sure where I was, or what was happening to me. He pulled the bedclothes off the bed, and shook my shoulders.

I sat up, blinked and said, "Where am I?"

"You're home. Had a bad dream no doubt. A good cold wash will bring you back to earth," said Dad, pushing me out of bed.

"Funny," I thought. "I've been to heaven, seen my mother. Why did I have to come back home?"

I shivered and felt afraid as I remembered my dream, and journey across the Stygian Lake.

"There's a strong smell of roses, Derek. You've been farting rose smells. Wish I could," said Dad.

Brian woke up, full of life.

"Lovely smell! What is it?" said Brian, sniffing.

"Roses, Brian. Derek farts roses," Dad said.

I washed, and put on my best clothes for church.

"Weird," I thought. I could smell roses too. I looked under my pillow, and there with my rabbits tail lay twelve apricot-coloured rose petals. They were fresh and strongly perfumed. I hurriedly put the tail in my pocket, and the rose petals in a tin, and hid them under my mattress.

Well! Well! Well! What are we hiding then?"

I turned round quickly to find Miss Weatherspoon standing in the doorway with hands on hips. Her eyes came to rest on me like a fly on a piece of meat. I could not stop myself from blushing. She walked into the bedroom, lifted up the mattress, found the tin, and with great difficulty prized off the lid, cutting her finger in the process.

"Damn! Damn! Damn!" she said.

The tin was empty.

"You stupid boy! Why hide a tin with nothing in it?" she said.

"Don't know," I said.

She snapped the lid shut, and threw the tin on the bed, repeating, "You stupid boy!"

She looked at me in anger, turned round, and marched out of the bedroom, her black dress stretched tight across her broad flabby back. Suddenly she stopped in her tracks, turned round, and stared at me. I stared back in defiance.

"What were you hiding? You sinful, wicked, stupid boy," she said.

"Don't know, I mean - nothing," I said.

"Why did you put the tin under the mattress then?"

"I've nowhere else to put it," I said.

Feeling more confident I added, "You're in my bedroom, and using my cupboard."

"What's that smell?" she said, sniffing.

"Don't know," I said.

"You smell of roses. Hmmm! Wind, I expect," she said, annoyed.

She marched out of the room with her bloody finger pointing up into the air, muttering to herself, "I'll have the little bogger for mincemeat. He's lying. I'll sort him out. He's up to no good."

I made sure she was well out of the way before I rescued my tin from the bed. Inside the tin I found the rose petals, still with their strong perfume. I was mystified by their reappearance. A phenomenon, like my dream, but my dream was real. I knew it was, because I saw my mother. I'll have to talk to Fr Ignatius about my adventure.

CHAPTER 14

Church, Father Ignatius and Julie

.....*"Take, eat, this is my Body*
which is given for you:
Do this in remembrance of me.
.....*Drink ye all of this; for this is my blood*
of the New Testament, which is shed for you,
and for many for the remission of sins;
Do this, as oft as ye shall drink
it, in remembrance of me."

Book of Common Prayer.
Holy Communion Prayer of Consecration
Thomas Cranmer 1489-1556.

CHAPTER 14

"Bye, Dad," I said, banging my knee on the door jamb in my rush to get out of the house as quickly as possible, away from the Dragon. I'd nicknamed Miss Weatherspoon 'the Dragon', sometimes 'the bloody Dragon'. My knee was beginning to throb and bleed as I ran up the road on my way to church. I had to slow down to ease the pain. For some reason I ran everywhere, never walked. I looked at my knee. The blood was running down my leg into the top of my sock, which had slithered down to my ankle. I pulled my white shirt sleeve down over the top of my hand, and rubbed the blood away. It really didn't make any difference. My knee still bled.

I looked forward to Sundays, not because I went to Mass, and helped Fr Ignatius, that was a bore, but because after Mass I had breakfast with Julie, his housekeeper. Julie was Irish with a lovely broad soft gentle-sounding accent. She was the exact opposite of the coarse loud-mouthed Dragon. I was in love with Julie. She fed me with as much as I could eat, always gave me a kiss on my cheek, and a bag of sweets before I set off home.

Julie was a small slim woman, and big breasted. Her breasts seemed to be disproportionate to the rest of her body. I quite expected her to topple over with the extra weight above her waist. Her bosoms were high up on her chest, not separated. They appeared to be joined together. There was no gap, or cleavage. Unfortunately for me her dresses were buttoned right up to her neck, and finished with a high collar, which hindered any chance of looking at, or down her cleavage. Occasionally her dress buttons would be tight across her chest, which pulled the dress material apart, revealing glimpses of bare flesh, but nothing more. I always thought it was a great pity that Julie dressed in this fashion, rather than a low-cut dress revealing a cleavage, which after all is the embodiment of a woman's breasts. A copious gap provokes, and draws the eye, like a picture frame to a painting. I couldn't see Julie's cleavage, or pick out the individual shape of her breasts but it didn't seem to make any difference to me. I still found her bosoms inviting. I had a yearning to be held tightly against them.

"Bless me, Father, for I have sinned," I said, disguising my voice in an attempt to conceal my identity.

"How long is it since your last confession?" said Fr Ignatius.

"Don't know," I said, putting on an imitation Irish brogue.

"Think! Is it two, three, four, five six weeks?" said Fr Ignatius.

"Six weeks, I think, Father," I said.

A stony silence followed. Neither of us spoke. I didn't like going to confession. Telling someone your misdoings. It didn't seem a natural thing to do. I bet Fr Ignatius wouldn't tell me his sins. The problem was if I didn't go to confession I couldn't receive Holy Communion, and Fr Ignatius would want to know why. If I took Communion, Fr Ignatius would want to know why I hadn't been to confession. He seemed to know everything. "Is he God?" I thought.

I coughed, and began to pick my nose, dislodging a large dried up bogey from my left nostril. It sat balanced and prepared for action on the tip of my forefinger. I carefully transferred it to the tip of my thumb, once again ready for combat. Above the wire mesh grill separating me from Fr Ignatius was a crucifix. I flicked the bogey with as much force as I could muster at the crucifix. It missed, and disappeared. With hindsight I was pleased. Christ would not have been very pleased with me if I'd hit Him, and it may have been another sin to confess. I think Fr Ignatius must have dozed off momentarily. There was complete silence, apart from the fitful buzzing of a fly.

"Ah. Well. Hmm," Fr Ignatius muttered suddenly.

"How long did you say?"

"How long, what?" I said, not concentrating.

"Since your last confession," came the reply.

"Can't remember," I said.

"Oh well! What sins have you committed since your last confession?" said Fr Ignatius.

"Yes, Father," I said.

"Well! What are those sins? You need to tell me," came the reply.

"Missed Mass, had dirty thoughts, said 'bloody' and 'fuck' and 'shit' pinched currants, told lies, drank altar wine, wanted to feel ladies' breasts, stole a bird's egg, pee'd in my Uncle's mug of tea, spat in his bacon butty - can't remember any more, Father," I replied, out of breath, and forgetting to conceal my real identity.

"Will you repeat your sins slowly?" said Fr Ignatius.

I repeated my sins, forgetting some, and adding others.

"Why do you want to feel ladies' breasts?" said Father Ignatius.

"Don't know," I said.

"What sort of dirty thoughts do you have?"

"Don't know."

"Why did you do those horrid things to your Uncle?" questioned Fr Ignatius.

"What things?"

"Pee in his tea, and spit in his sandwich."

"He was mean, nasty, unkind and horrible to me. I hate him!" I said, with venom.

"To hate someone is a sin," said Fr Ignatius.

"I don't care. It's too hard being a Catholic. I'm going to be a Methy, or a Jew. My friends can sin as much as they like. They don't have to go to confession," I said, resentfully.

Fr Ignatius ignored my comments, saying, "My child. Are you sorry for your sins?"

"Only some of them."

I heard Fr Ignatius sigh, and through the wire grill of the confessional I saw him cross himself with the sign of the cross.

He muttered, "I give up. What do I do with him Lord? He's always the same."

Striking his breast with a clenched fist he exclaimed with each thud.

"Have mercy! Have mercy! Have mercy! Guide me with this difficult child."

Fr Ignatius blew his nose, which rattled the door of the confessional. He coughed and sneezed, sending his germs, strong tea, and stale tobacco breath through the wire mesh of the grill. A small curtain should cover the grill, but it was always pulled aside for eye contact by the priest with the confessor. I always covered my face with my hands, and wore my sunglasses when I remembered, which was seldom. Whatever precaution I took to remain incognito I'm sure Fr Ignatius recognised me.

"Do you have a sincere sorrow for your sins, and a firm purpose of amendment," said Fr Ignatius.

"Don't know," I said, not being really sure what he meant.

"Are you sorry for your sins?" came back the reply.

I was getting really irritated and just wanted to get out of the confessional box. It was all too much hassle.

"Well! Are you sorry?" grunted Fr Ignatius again.

"I've told you, Father. I'm only sorry for some of my sins," I said, feeling self-assured.

"Say five Our Father's, five Hail Mary's, and make an Act of Contrition," said a despairing Fr Ignatius.

I hurriedly said aloud without stopping to breathe.

"Oh my God. I am sorry for my sins - most of them God, because they displease You, who is infinitely good and lovable. I firmly resolve with your help to do penance for them, and never sin again, apart from the ladies' breast thing, and hating Uncle Jack."

Fr Ignatius said something in Latin, crossed himself several times. I crossed myself too.

He said, "Go in peace, say a prayer for me. Don't be late for Mass, Derek."

With difficulty I got up from the kneeling mat. The blood from my knee had stuck to it like glue. I pulled the mat away, and turned it over. I was glad to get out of the confessional. It was like being shut up in a closed wooden box.

"What an ordeal," I thought.

I felt much better in the fresh air, and knelt in a pew before the altar, crossed myself, and sank my head into my hands - more in relief than an act of prayer. I thought about the journey to see my mother who was picking rose petals.

"I must get even with the bloody Dragon," I said aloud to myself, looking up to the crucifix above the altar. Those in prayer around me, looked up from their devotions, and stared across at me.

"Mind yer business," I thought.

How can I get my own back on the Dragon?

"Help me God with my crusade," I said aloud.

Perhaps I could put a dead rat in her bed, or when she's in bed asleep cover her with dog poo, and wet concrete. I made up my mind before God to be avenged.

My thoughts turned to Julie, and the breakfast with her after Mass. I longed to see her smiling face, and heaving bosoms. I wondered if she had nipples, and wore a brassiere. Did it fasten up at the front, or the back? I hadn't seen Julie since my Mother died. I felt I needed to see her, be in her company, eat breakfast with her, sense her warmth and love. The thought of her breasts filled me with a sensation of peace and spirituality. I was in the presence of God as I conjured up a picture of her naked bosoms.

"God works in mysterious ways," I thought.

Forgetting to say my penance I got up, leaving more blood on the kneeler, and went into the sacristy to prepare for Mass. A quick gulp of altar wine made me feel positive about my future, and the fate of the Dragon.

I dressed in my black cassock, which was far too long. I had to be very careful not to trip up on the hem as it dragged on the floor as I walked. Fr Ignatius said, "You will grow into it."

My white surplice was too big as well. The sleeves were too long and wide, and it reached down to my knees. Once again Fr Ignatius maintained, "You will grow into it."

They were always too big. I prepared the altar wine, water jug, towel and bowl, and gingerly carried them to the small table in the sanctuary, ready for Mass. I lit the two candles either side of the altar, genuflected, and returned to the sacristy. Fr Ignatius was still hearing confessions. The half-full bottle of altar wine was on the table. Feeling thirsty I took another mouthful from the neck of the bottle. It warmed my inside, and made me feel good. I always felt stressed out, and under pressure after confession. I took another mouthful, gulping it down hurriedly as Fr Ignatius appeared. I nearly choked with wine dribbling down my chin. Fr Ignatius gave me a quizzical look saying, "Up to no good, Derek?"

"Yes. I mean, no, Father. Don't know," I said.

"Put the cork on the bottle, Derek. We'll talk about it later. After Mass," came the reply.

"Yes, Father," I said, looking as if butter wouldn't melt in my mouth.

"Ready, Derek?".

"Yes, Father."

They walked out of the sacristy together, Fr Ignatius in front, his hands joined, and pointing upwards in devotion. Derek reluctantly followed behind, dragging his heels, picking his nose, and repeatedly hiccupping. At the foot of the altar steps they genuflected. Fr Ignatius turned to face the congregation saying,

"In the name of the Father, and of the Son, and of the Holy Ghost."

"Amen," came the half-hearted, half-asleep, wavering response from the congregation.

"Please try to respond together," said Fr Ignatius.

The congregation shuffled about, coughed, some sneezed, blew their noses, and felt uncomfortable at being admonished. Late-comers with children disturbed those who were trying to concentrate, whilst others just wanted to get the obligatory ordeal of Mass over.

"The Lord be with you."

"All together, please," said Fr Ignatius, lifting his hands up in the air like an orchestral conductor.

"And,"

"And,"

"also,"

"so,"

"all,"

"so,"

"With you,"

"you," came the staccato response.

Fr Ignatius gave up, and carried on with the Mass eager to get it over with. It was like this every Sunday at early Mass. He thought of it as the peasant's Mass. He much preferred sung High Mass, which followed. The congregation were more composed, older, serious and dignified. Children and babies were left at home. The atmosphere had a quieter spiritual presence, compared to the peasant's Mass, with all the hullabaloo. The choir at sung Mass generally sang in unison. He had more time to think and relax, whereas at early Mass he had to concentrate. The congregation intimidated him, with children running up and down the aisle, screaming hysterically, shouting wildly, babies crying.

"Why do Catholics have so many children?" he often asked himself.

Latecomers crashed down the aisle. Some deliberately came late he felt sure. It was the same people every week. Mick Malony's - the blind man's guide-dog, would bark if the noise became too raucous. It was pandemonium at its worst.

Fr Ignatius tried to give a sermon, but after a few minutes he gave up. The bedlam became too much for him. He felt his heart racing, perspiration began to saturate his clothing and drip from his flushed face.

With arms extended he said, in a trembling voice, "Pater Noster," forgetting the Mass was now said in English. He started again. "Our Father, Who art in heaven hallowed be Thy Name."

The congregation remained silent. He stared at them as if they had been struck dumb.

"Are you with me, or not? Christ Almighty, we are supposed to be saying the Pater Noster together. What's the problem, Mrs Jowitt?" he shouted, staring at a fat lady kneeling in the front pew.

"Don't yer shout at me, Father. My Dick'll 'ave summat to say if yer shout like tha'. I'll 'ave yer know I say me prayers to me'sen," said the fat lady.

"Where's your Dick anyway?" said Fr Ignatius.

"Es at 'om wi babbies," came the reply.

Giggling was heard amongst the congregation. Fr Ignatius felt threatened. He struck his breast three times, repeating at each strike, "Christ have mercy. Christ have mercy. Lord have mercy. Can we try again and say the Pater Noster, sorry, Our Father. All together on the count of three. One, two."

At that moment a young child ran down the aisle towards the altar, stopped in front of Fr Ignatius and said, "Want a pooh-pooh. Where's lavvy?"

A lady in hot pursuit, picked up the child and dashed out of the church with the screaming infant. Fr Ignatius said the 'Our Father' quietly to himself, and continued saying Mass.

The communicants approached the altar to receive Holy Communion.

"Are they in a state of grace to receive the sacrament?" pondered Fr Ignatius.

Very few of them went to him for confession. He knew Mrs Feverfew was carrying on with Jim Stanley, and Bob Feverfew was seeing Mrs Stanley.

"A case of wife-swapping," he thought. "I must be charitable, and not jump to conclusions," he added, mentally.

The communicants knelt at the altar rail, hands joined together, fingers pointing upwards, with eyes closed in devout prayer. Paddy Mullen, still groggy and glassy-eyed from the previous night's bout of drinking, and reeking of stale alcohol, knelt with them. His hair had not seen a brush or comb, nor his face a razor, his muddy boots and flies were undone, and his loosely knotted egg-splashed tie had been cut off four inches below the knot. He knelt innocently with eyes closed, oblivious to his appearance and smell. They all received the Eucharist, much against Fr Ignatius' better judgement.

"What a shower," he thought.

He gave Derek communion, and thought of Derek's fetish for ladies' breasts. After all, breasts do *make* a woman, gives them poise, grace and presence.

"Breasts bring you into the presence of God," he thought.

"Can't imagine a woman without them."

Since hearing Derek's obsession in the confessional he had been taking a greater interest in the female figure. In particular his housekeeper, Julie.

"She has lovely bosoms," he thought. "If only I could see more of them. Why does she have to wear those old maid's dresses?"

He blinked, adjusted his spectacles, and said silently to himself. "Enough of these sinful thoughts, or are they? They're God-given. I must respect my celibacy. Why do priests have to remain chaste? It's not fair!"

Fr Ignatius turned to the congregation and said, "The Lord be with you."

They ignored him, half had left the church.

Derek mumbled, "And with yer Spirit."

Fr Ignatius, with joy and relief in his voice, exclaimed in an ear-splitting voice,

"Ite, missa est. Sorry! I mean. Go, the Mass is ended."

Before he'd finished the sentence the remaining congregation had emptied the church, apart from blind Mick Maloney, and his dog, who were striving to find their way out of the church. Paddy Mullen remained seated, fast asleep, snoring. Derek and Fr Ignatius returned to the sacristy, both relieved Mass was over.

They disrobed. Derek dashed out of the sacristy anxious to have breakfast with Julie. He had barely covered ten paces when he heard Fr Ignatius shout, "Derek, not so fast. I want a word with you."

"Yes, Father," he said, stopping in his tracks.

"Why do you drink the altar wine, Derek?"

"What wine, Father?"

"You know what wine, Derek."

"Not me, Father. Don't like the taste, Father."

"But you told me in confession that you drank the altar wine. I've seen you drink it, Derek," said Fr Ignatius, getting angry at Derek's defiance.

I was feeling very uneasy at being questioned about the altar wine. "Better stop drinking it," I thought. I fumbled in my pocket for the rabbit's tail. I needed some help.

"Please stop all these questions about the bloody altar wine," I said to myself, clutching the small piece of fur in my hand.

At that precise moment Julie appeared, saw Fr Ignatius and said, "Father! The Bishop's on the phone. He wants to speak to you urgently."

"Holy Mary! Mother of God! Don't panic! Don't panic!" garbled Fr Ignatius, terror stricken as he dashed out of the sacristy towards the house.

I was alone with Julie. Out of trouble for the moment. Saved by my lucky rabbit's tail. We looked at each other.

She smiled, saying, "Let's have some breakfast. Usual, Derek?"

She took my hand as we walked across the drive to the house, her breasts wobbling in time with each step we took. I was happy, and tingled with excitement as I felt the warmth of her hands embracing mine. Our bodies accidentally brushed against each other, sending disturbing thrills through me.

"Hope Fr Ignatius forgets about the wine," I thought.

"My God," gasped Julie. "Your knee. What have you done, Derek? It's all bloody. Does it hurt? I must clean it up. Put a bandage on't to keep it clean. You poor thing!"

She squeezed my hand tighter to comfort me.

We reached the house. I could hear Fr Ignatius on the phone.

"Sit down, Derek," said Julie.

She poured some warm water into a bowl, and added a spoonful of salt. Gently she bathed my knee. It hurt at first. The stinging sensation sent shivers through my body. I winced with discomfort.

"Sorry, Derek," she said, looking up at me from a kneeling position.

I looked into her hazel green eyes with adulation. She held the calf of my leg with both hands, which eased the stinging, and radiated warmth through my entire being. Her breasts heaved as her eyes focussed on mine.

Smiling, she said, "Is that better now, Derek? Does your knee still hurt?"

Her words comforted me.

"I'm fine now," I said.

She took her hands away, and carefully swathed a white bandage around the cut and bruised knee.

"Right! We'll have some breakfast now," she said. "Hope you're hungry."

Sitting opposite Julie at the breakfast table in her kitchen was a real treat. I would eat my bacon, eggs, tinned tomatoes with stiff fried bread, and look at her across the table. We would chat about all sorts of interesting things. Grown up things, like going to work, getting married, and having babies. I asked Julie if she would like a baby. She said she would, but needed to get married first.

"I thought you were marred to Fr Ignatius," I said.

"Oh no! Priests can't marry. I will have to find a husband, get married and then have a baby," she said.

"I'll marry you, and we can have lots of babies, " I said.

"You're too young, Derek, but thank you," she said.

"When I grown up, we'll get married," I replied.

"I'll be too old then," she said, smiling.

She asked me if I was missing my mother, and were Brian and dad alright.

"Yes, a big lot," I said, bursting into tears.

"I'm sorry, Derek," she said, getting up and giving me a tight hug. My face flattened against her warm soft bosom. What joy to be so close to her. I could detect a faint smell of lavender, which had a calming effect on me. My mother would put dried lavender between her clothes, and dresses. There was always a lavender fragrance about her.

"Sit down, Derek. Have some toast and marmalade," she said, handing me a plate of hot toast.

"Thank you," I said, staring, hypnotized by her bosoms, which seemed to swell and throb at each breath she took. I got up from the table, without thinking, and quite unwittingly reached out and touched her breasts with both hands, like metal drawn to a magnet.

"What are you doing, Derek?" said Fr Ignatius, standing in the doorway.

Simultaneously, Julie let out a cry, pressing my hands firmly into her soft breasts, letting out a gasp, more in ecstasy, rather than alarm.

"The bees!" I cried. "Look out! There they go."

Fr Ignatius and Julie were taken aback by my outcry. They both stood surprised and shocked by my outburst.

"I didn't see any bees," said Fr Ignatius.

"They were on Julie's dress. Big ones. They were going to sting her," I said.

"I saw, and heard them, Father," said Julie. "And thank you, Derek. It was very brave of you to do what you did."

I thought, "Yes, it was brave. I could have been stung by invisible bees."

"Oh! In that case never mind. Finish your breakfast, Derek. I want a word with you before you go," said Fr Ignatius.

"Yes, Father," I said, thinking to myself. "No way! You won't catch me. I'm a ginger bread man."

"Why did you do that, Derek?" said Julie.

"Don't know, just did, thought I saw a ladybird on your dress, not a bee," I said.

Julie laughed at me, reached out, and held my hand.

"You're a funny lad, Derek. We won't tell Father. It's our secret. Eh!"

"I won't. Better go home now," I said, anxious to avoid seeing Fr Ignatius.

She kissed me on my cheek, gave me a bar of chocolate, and waved, as I skipped down the road, the white bandage dropping down to my ankles. I was happy, until I thought of the Dragon. I slowed down, kicking an empty cigarette packet along the pavement. I imagined it was the Dragon's head. I kicked harder and harder, and finally stamped on it, squashing the packet flat into the pavement.

CHAPTER 15

The Bird

"*Thou wast not born for death, immortal bird!*
No hungry generations tread thee down."

Ode to a Nightingale st. 7.
John Keats 1795-1821.

CHAPTER 15

I walked through the market place passing the building where I'd seen the bird curled up to keep warm against the chimney stacks. The space was now empty. I wondered what had happened to it. Was it still lost? I thought about the bird in my dream. My guardian angel who had guided me across the Stygian Lake, and saved me from the giant satanic monster toad. Were these two birds the same? They looked identical with their plumage and yellow beaks.

In the gutter I saw a heap of ruffled feathers, a yellow beak, and two tiny staring eyes. I picked up the bundle of feathers. It was cold and stiff. The bird was dead. Gently I closed its eyes, and carefully carried it home under my jumper. I sneaked into the back garden to avoid contact with the Dragon. Mitzi, the dog, was sniffing around amongst the vegetables, and on seeing me started to bark and jump up at me. Instinctively I shouted, "Gerr off! Gerr off!" and tried to run away.

"What's going on?" came a shout from the top of the garden.

I turned round to see the Dragon, with hands on hips, glaring. She started to walk towards me. The dog was still barking. I was cornered by the two of them. My imagination came into play. I saw her as non-human - a wild witch wearing a black pointed hat, bloodshot eyes, with barbed fangs jutting from her mouth, an old face, wrinkled and ugly. Her nose was a long curled up snout of elephantine proportions, wobbling from side to side as she walked. Foam frothed from her mouth, and sparks egressed from her nostrils and ears. She wore a black cloak reaching down to her ankles. Her arms hung down loosely below her knees with crab-like pointed claws, curling and uncurling. Her feet were cloaked with large flat black slipper-like shoes, which curled up pointed at the toes. They made a slapping noise as she walked. She looked evil and menacing as she slapped towards me.

With one hand I held the bird close to my chest, and with the other found the rabbit's tail in my pocket. Holding it tightly, I mentally said, "Go away, Dragon. Leave me alone. Go away you witch."

She stopped and said, staring at me, "What's that?"

"What's what?" I said.

"In your hand. That black thing. You stupid boy," she said.

"Don't know," I said.

At that moment Dad came down the garden breaking up my confrontation with Mitzi and the Dragon.

"Come on, Mitzi. Dinner!" said the Dragon, turning on her heels, and walking back towards the house.

She smiled at Dad, saying, "The roast will be ready by one. It's roast beef. Just asking Derek if he likes Yorkshire pud. You like Yorkshire pud, don't you, Derek?"

"Yes," I said in a resentful tone.

"Be careful with your poorly knee, dear," she replied.

Looking at Dad, with Mitzi at her side, she said, "What lovely boys you have. They're a credit to you, Harry," and off she strutted back to the house.

"Piss off," thought Harry.

"Feck off," I thought.

I had decided to use the word 'feck', rather than the other 'f' word, then I wouldn't have to tell Fr Ignatius in confession. I had also got to get the altar wine problem sorted out. It was no good drinking the wine, then denying it when questioned, and admit to drinking it at confession.

I thought, "Perhaps I should stop drinking wine, but I liked it, and it made me feel assured, fearless and confident. It seemed it was only Catholics that had this problem. My friends did all sorts of wicked things and they didn't have to confess their sins. I know! I'll become a Jew and wear a skullcap like Joseph Lewin, and Jacob Mizeti at school. I didn't think I'd qualify to be a Jew though. My nose was too small, my eyes were blue, and I'd got fair hair. Joseph and Jacob had brown eyes, black curly hair, and their noses were bigger than mine. I think they have a different type of willy, too. I could be a Methy or a Protestant, like Bill and Frank. They didn't have to go to church. They stole sweets and fags from the corner shop, swore, scrumped apples, knocked on doors and ran away. They even threw stones at windows, breaking the glass, looked at dirty pictures of naked men and women. Bill once put a lighted firework through old Mr Levers' letterbox, and Bill's friend, Sam, let down Miss

Thompkins' front bicycle tyre. They're lucky. I wouldn't want to do all those naughty things, just a few."

I desperately wanted to join Doug's gang when we went back to school, which meant passing an initiation test. I might have to break a window, or put a dog turd in the teacher's desk. Sam had to write the word 'SHIT' in white paint on the playground wall to join Doug's gang.

"Wake up, Derek," said Harry, ruffling his hair. "You look half asleep. Are you alright?"

"Yes, thanks, Dad, just thinking," I said, sheepishly.

"What about, Derek?"

"Don't know," I said.

"What're yer going to do with that dead bird?" asked Dad.

"Bury it," I said.

"Well, don't be long about it. It's school tomorrow and we've got to sort your things out. Clean shoes and sort out your school clothes," said Harry, walking back to the house.

I made a hole with a stick, and used my hands as a trowel. I wrapped up the bird in a big rhubarb leaf and put the bundle in the hole. I knelt down, and joined my hands together in prayer, "Please, God, look after my guardian Angel, if it is my guardian angel. Please don't let it be my guardian angel, God. And God, I would like to see my Mother again. Please! Please! Please! God."

I pushed the damp soil back into the hole with tears rolling down my cheeks. With two sticks I made a cross, and stuck it into the mound of earth. I made the sign of the cross, and with head bowed walked slowly up the garden path.

"What yer doing, Del?" shouted Brian.

"Nothing," I shouted back.

"Saw you peeing on Dad's rhubarb," said Brian, laughing. "Tell Dad, I will."

"You're a tell tale tit, our Brian. Don't care anyway. Tell 'im what yer like for all I care," I said.

"I will! I will, our Derek. I'll tell Auntie Ethel yer licked yer finger, and put it in the sugar bowl," came back Brian's rebuttal. "And I've seen yer smoking Dad's pipe. I'll tell Dad, I will."

I was getting angry at Brian's cocky impudence. I rushed up to him and pushed him into the nettles. Brian let out a high-pitched scream, and ran crying towards the house. Miss Weatherspoon stood in the doorway, hands on hips.

"What's the matter, darling?" she said.

"Del pushed me in the nettles," shrieked Brian.

"You wicked, horrid, nasty boy. Go to your room at once," shouted Miss Weatherspoon at me.

"I haven't got a room. You've got my room," I snapped back.

"Go to Brian's room then, you horrid boy," barked Miss Weatherspoon.

"Shan't, you're not my mother. I don't take orders from you. You're only the charwoman," I said, feeling confident, and keeping well away from my antagonist.

Brian and Miss Weatherspoon were in an embrace, with Brian still crying and clinging to her. Miss Weatherspoon was patting his head.

"There, there, darling. What a nasty brother you've got. We'll get our own back on the horrid, horrid boy.

You great big bully. I'll tell your Dad about this," she said, glaring at me in anger.

I went back down the garden path anxious to get away. I opened the door of Dad's garden shed, and sat on an upturned wooden box. Perched on the shelf opposite was a bird with a yellow beak, and black feathers, looking down at me. The bird let out a chirrup, chirrup, chirrup. I held my hand out to the bird. It flew down, and landed on my palm, looked up and said, "I'm your guardian angel, don't worry. I'll be with you always."

Suddenly, as if frightened, the bird flew out of the shed and vanished.

I was now alone with only my thoughts. I felt powerless and insecure. I knew that punishment awaited me, but not now. I tried to detach myself from my body, and let my mind run free to escape from my misery. My thoughts turned to my mother, how I missed her, and how I loved her. I knew my mother loved me, and this crisis would not have happened if she'd been with us. She loved Brian and Dad too. I was feeling more and more alone, cut off, and unloved by her death. Fr Ignatius says, "God loves us." If God loves me why does He give me such heartache, and a hard time. Fr Ignatius says it was God's will my mother died, but why does it feel like betrayal. Surely, a loving God would not allow this to happen. I couldn't understand the thinking behind what Fr Ignatius said. It didn't make sense to me. Since my mother died, I had developed a knack of suspending myself from my body and allowing my spirit to run free. It was like a switch, which I could turn on, and feel liberated. I could watch myself dispassionately. The Dragon was incapable of hurting me. Perhaps it was just my daydreaming.

"Things aren't too bad," I thought. "School tomorrow. I'll be in the top class. Then big school next year. Hopefully I'll be able to join Doug's gang," I said, to myself.

"Thinking again, Derek?" laughed Harry, poking his head into the shed.

"Yes, Dad."

"Dinner's ready. Time to stop wool-gathering," said Dad.

"Coming," I said.

"What's he talking about," I wondered.

We all sat around the table as though nothing had happened. The Dragon gave me more dinner than Brian, and seconds of Yorkshire pud. Brian was very quiet, and kept scratching his legs.

"Nettle stings, serves him right," I thought, smiling to myself.

Spotted Dick with custard followed, which was yummy.

Harry yawned, stretched, gulped down the last few dregs of beer and closed his eyes. The Dragon burped, her face as heavy as dough, and yawned. Mitzi ravenously gulped down the leftovers, opened its pink mouth, and belched. He rubbed himself against the table leg, lay down and fell asleep. Brian in silence went to his room. I quietly left the table and returned to the shed to think, clutching my rabbit's tail.

CHAPTER 16

Father Ignatius - An Irish Childhood and the Bishop

"Worse than the ordinary miserable childhood is the miserable Irish Childhood, and worse yet is the miserable Irish Catholic childhood.

Angela's Ashes - A memoir of a childhood.
Frank McCourt 1931-

CHAPTER 16

Fr Ignatius and the Bishop did not hit it off. They were always at loggerheads. It was well known within the clergy of the Diocese that inwardly they hated each other, but they did try to be nice to each other in the presence of others. The Bishop was very conservative, and agreed without question with all the edicts from Rome, including the Pope's infallibility. He expected his priests to do the same. Many priests made their own judgement on these matters, which were always in the best interests of their parishioners. Fr Ignatius was one of these priests. He was very liberal and understanding, whilst others, but very few, followed the Bishop's conservative line, and obeyed the Pope's decrees.

The Bishop's phone call had put Fr Ignatius in a bad mood. He was now on his third large scotch, and had High Mass to celebrate in half an hour. The Bishop wanted to see him as soon as possible on a matter of some urgency. Fr Ignatius knew it was about his views on birth control and divorce, which seemed to crop up more often than not. The Bishop had threatened to stop him preaching, and hearing confessions, unless he kept his views to himself, and supported the Vatican's teaching.

Some of his congregation had only two or three children, whilst others had six, seven or eight children. Mrs O'Reilly had eleven, and appeared to be having another. His conscience compelled him to advise the use of some kind of birth control. The so-called rhythm method the church recommended was an insult to a married couple's intelligence. Some of Fr Ignatius' parishioners were not very perceptive. Those who'd tried the few days a month safe sex, thinking they wouldn't conceive, were very disappointed with the result. It just didn't work, wasn't reliable, and on the so-called 'safe days' sex wasn't always mutually wanted, or possible, for one reason or another. You can't plan your love-making around a few days in the month was the opinion of the better informed, and of Fr Ignatius, and of many of his priest friends.

Mrs Mullen told Fr Ignatius, when her Paddy came home from the pub rather boozed on a Friday and Saturday night, and wanted his way with her, that she had no time to consult the calendar or take her temperature. She had no option but to let him get on with it, so she could get a decent night's sleep. She already had eight children under ten. It was a great worry to Fr Ignatius to tell his parishioners to abstain from sex if they didn't want children. In the end he gave up, knowing the nature of man and woman. After all, it was unnatural to abstain. A marriage was not just for having children like shelling peas, but a loving relationship which involved intimacy as and when required. Children had to be supported, fed, clothed and housed. Having babies just couldn't go on ad infinitum.

Despite the Bishop's threat he would not change his views. In such matters his conscience had to be his guide. The Bishop, or indeed the Pope, did not live in the real world, they were idealists, not realists. Fr Ignatius had thought of giving free condoms to those he thought needed them, but he was having difficulty in deciding how best to distribute them. He knew he could get them in bulk, and very cheap. His brother-in-law manufactured them under the label, 'Buy one! Stop one!' His catholic sister only had two children, so he knew they worked. He thought he would set up a meeting with his fellow priests in the Diocese. A number of them shared his views, and he knew he would get a sympathetic hearing. Fr Flyn, who'd had an affair with his housekeeper, was under suspension from the Bishop. He was not allowed to say Mass, preach, nor hear confessions. He would certainly be an advocate for his plans, being experienced in the ways of the flesh.

Bishop Edward had never been exposed to the real world. He had been cushioned by wealth throughout his life, and had been educated at a Catholic Public School. He had been supported by his rich parents throughout his early days as a priest. He had never been put in charge of a parish, but had always managed to secure diocesan work, which had never revealed to him the needs of the parishioners in the Diocese. His wealthy parents were more than generous towards the demands of the church. It was their generosity which had bought Edward his bishopric, not his suitability for the office of a Bishop. He was now in his mid fifties, about five and a half feet in stature, and grossly overweight. His scarlet buttoned-up cassock was always stretched to bursting point. He was pot-bellied, grotesquely misshapen, and suffered with extreme attacks of gout. Bishop Edward had a propensity for rich unhealthy food, port and Madeira - the latter which he drank to excess. Small, chubby hands with fleshy, plump fingers stuck out from his sleeves like pink balls of candyfloss. His face was rosy and podgy, his head almost threadbare with just a few long strands of silver hair carefully positioned over his shiny scalp. He wore round gold-rimmed spectacles for effect, rather than for his sight. These were perched half way down his snub-nose. Silver buckled shoes and gaiters were worn, which added to his Dickensian appearance. Bishop Edward McNally was not an eccentric. He just liked to draw attention to himself.

The Bishop chose to ignore that within his Diocese, many people were out of work, and living in poverty. Some were homeless, drugs and prostitution were widespread, and crime was a means of survival for the destitute. He was a wealthy autocratic snob, not in tune with his people, nor the clergy who served under him.

Fr Ignatius on the other hand had been brought up in abject poverty in Dublin. He was one of eleven children, two of which had died within a month of their birth. His Mother had suffered ill health as a result of childbearing, had miscarried two, and had died of tuberculosis at the age of 35. His Father had never had a job which had lasted more than three or four weeks. The money earnt had been spent on drink at the expense of food and clothing for his family. They had lived in damp squalor, more often than not in one room, and sharing one bed. His Father soon followed his Mother, dying from alcoholic poisoning. The orphaned children had been cared for, and brought up by the St Vincent de Paul Society. The boys had been taught by the Christian Brothers. The girls had had no formal education, and were sent out to work at the age of ten as maids or charwomen.

Like many Irish Catholics they lived in fear of their parish priest. He was the ultimate word of God, and had to be obeyed at whatever cost. They produced endless children at the same rate as rabbits. If they took precautions against having children they were condemned to the everlasting flames of hell. It was better to be dammed, and suffer on earth, rather than in hell.

Fr Ignatius had searched his conscience in an effort to reconcile his differences with the churches' teaching on birth control and divorce. He could not justify the hard impassioned line the church embraced. Too often he had seen families break down due to low wage packets supporting large families, with depression, despair, desperate violence, crime and insecurity as a result of Catholic teaching. He felt he had a moral duty, with like-minded clergy, to make a stand against the sanctimonious Bishop. His own upbringing and poverty had made him more determined to have an influence over the fate of his own disillusioned parishioners.

At the age of 14 Fr Ignatius left Ireland for England, and at 24 was ordained a Catholic priest. He was a few years younger than the Bishop. Tall, fit, lean, with a mop of thick steel-grey wavy hair, high cheek bones, deep set hazel-green eyes, with an honest weather beaten face. He seldom wore his dark suit and clerical collar, contrary to the Bishop's mandate. He felt more comfortable and at ease in a pair of old corduroys, an open necked shirt and woolly jumper.

The Bishop and Fr Ignatius were exact opposites in their appearance, beliefs and thinking.

CHAPTER 17

Father Ignatius - Man and Priest

Actaeon aroused the wrath of the multi-breasted Artemis, (the Romans absorbed the cult of Artemis into Diana the chaste huntress) when he chanced on her bathing at Orchomenus. Enraged at being seen naked, the virgin goddess changed Actaeon into a stag, so that his own dogs tore him to pieces.

Greek and Roman Mythology.

Chapter 17

Fr Ignatius, sitting down, with a large scotch at his side was reading his office for the day. It was late evening. He was tired, and found it very difficult to concentrate. Sunday was always a tiring day - confessions, two Masses to say with sermons, and Benediction late afternoon. He felt drowsy, nodded off, and dreamt, his breviary falling to the floor.

He was walking along the river bank with Julie, holding hands. It was a very warm day. They were both hot and sweaty. Julie stopped, took off her clothes and jumped into the river.

"Come on! Jump in, Father," she shouted, splashing about.

She became the huntress, and breast goddess, buxom, with magnificent wanton powerful bosoms provoking within him a thrilling awareness of sensual pleasure.

A loud knock on his study door shook him out of his deep sleep, and broke his dream. Standing in the doorway was Julie with his bedtime drink and biscuits.

"You've been fast asleep, Father. Sorry to disturb you," said Julie.

Fr Ignatius, still half-asleep and dreaming, paused for breath, as he visualised Julie in the doorway, naked, her ample bosoms standing proud and sensuous, her naked body of Botticelli proportions, voluptuous and tantalizing. Behind her breasts, lay her romantic heart, spiritually strong and loving. If only he could embrace her. He felt he was in love.

"Are you alright, Father?" said Julie, feeling disturbed by his dazed goggle-eyed stare.

"Just thinking, Julie," said Fr Ignatius, not quite fully awake.

Julie put down the drink and biscuits, and left saying, "Good night, Father."

"Good night, and God Bless Julie," came his reply as he made the sign of the cross. He eyed her shapely blue cotton lisle-stockinged legs disappear through the door.

Fr Ignatius was torn between his thoughts, desires and his vocation. He had secret longings which could be thought of as sinful.

"What do I do about them? Do I struggle against them? Or do I satisfy them?" he thought.

His cravings and thoughts were constantly changing in the most disturbing ways. It was all Derek's fault with his fetish for breasts. He was convinced Derek had been feeling Julie's breasts earlier in the day. There were certainly no bees about. Julie didn't seem to mind either. Fr Ignatius couldn't stop thinking about her breasts whilst trying very hard to finish reading his daily office. He'd always admired Mrs Clutterbuck's bosom. Whatever the weather, summer or winter, she always wore low-cut dresses. He could not help peering down into her cleavage as she knelt at the altar rails for Communion. Each time he tried not to look, but the lure of the unknown drew his eyes to her tantalizing chest. Her redolent perfume made the experience more evocative. Mrs Clutterbuck was not the only guilty one. There were several others who provoked his carnal instincts at the Communion rail.

He put down his breviary, failing to complete his daily office. Kneeling down by his bed he prayed hard for a release from his licentious thoughts. The next day he would go and see his friend, Fr Flyn, who might be able to give him some advice. Soon he was fast asleep, swimming with Julie in the river. He was in Utopia once again.

In the morning he'd ask Julie to marry him, and tell the Bishop in no uncertain terms what he thought of him.

CHAPTER 18

Julie

===

"Love in my bosom like a bee
Doth suck his sweet;
Now with his wings he plays with me,
Now with his feet.
Within mine eyes he makes his nest.
His bed amidst my tender breast;
My kisses are his daily feast.
And yet he robs me of my rest.
Ah, wanton, will ye?"

'Love in my bosom like a bee.'
Thomas Lodge 1558-1625.

CHAPTER 18

Julie was still tingling with excitement from the embrace with Derek. She could still feel his warm face held tight against her bosoms. His small hands squashed up against her breasts as she held them tightly to her.

"It was a pity Fr Ignatius took us by surprise. Whatever did he think?" she said to herself.

She was in bed, trying to read, but her thoughts kept returning to the early morning events with Derek. They'd been talking about getting married, and having babies. Derek even thought she was married to Fr Ignatius.

"Alas, at 35 I'm still a spinster. If only I could meet someone and fall in love. I would love to get married, and have babies," she thought.

She got up, took off her nightie, and doused herself with cold water in an attempt to assuage the glowing tingle which was surging through her body. Standing in front of the wash basin, looking at herself in the mirror, she couldn't help feeling that her breasts were beautiful - perhaps a little big. She looked so chaste and untried. Julie had never thought about it before, or even looked at herself in the mirror. She filled the sink with warm water, and with soapy hands gently washed her breasts.

The smooth sensation of slippery skin against slippery skin made her bosoms and nipples feel firm and proud. Julie felt free, relaxed and in some way transported to another planet. She found herself in another dimension, and rejoiced in the innocent beauty of her breasts through the mirror. She saw herself as a fertility goddess - Mother Nature herself, as a woman to be adored, her paps to be sucked by infants. They were after all quintessential gifts from God, loved by the child in man, and child alone. She knew that men adored breasts, and women adore men for adoring them - a happy exchange.

Perhaps she should wear clothes which enhanced her femininity, rather than clothing which inhibited her appearance. For far too long she had dressed as an old maid. She needed to change her image, break out of her cocoon, and take some risks.

"I'll get some nice flesh-coloured stockings, and throw the blue lisle ones away. After all, blue is worn by maids, and servants with cloth caps and aprons," she thought, as she slowly and lovingly dried herself, splashing on lavender water.

"Some new underwear. I've got something to celebrate. My bosoms have been hidden away far too long. They deserve something better than these thick cotton supports. I'll buy some pretty coloured silky lace bras, and silky nightwear too," she said aloud to herself.

Her bedroom was warm, and the heavy buttoned-up-front high-necked winceyette nightdress did not do justice to her new-found body.

Her friend, Bridey, Fr Flyn's housekeeper, would know what to get in the way of exciting underwear and nightwear, and even dresses.

"Yes, a real sexy dress. To make heads turn," she thought. "Something to make Fr Ignatius look at me, although he does seem to stare at me sometimes," she added. "I'll need some make-up too - to complement my face, and redden my lips. Bridey will know. After all, she's changed her image. She's going to marry Fr Flyn when he's accepted into the Anglican church as a priest. Lucky Bridey! Wish Fr Ignatius would do the same, and marry me," she pondered, slipping her nightdress back on again, and climbing into bed.

Julie lay in bed, her mind on full alert, her body tingling with excitement at the thought of buying new underwear and clothes. Eventually, she fell asleep and dreamt. Fr Ignatius was trying to retrieve a bee which had found its way into the top of her dress. They both heard it buzzing, but couldn't see it. She undid the top buttons of her dress displaying her bosoms sheathed in black lace. The bee, still buzzing, eluded Fr Ignatius. He probed, pushed, slid, but to find a bee on fully closeted bosoms was beyond the bounds of possibility. Unwittingly, and in anxious haste, he unclipped the bra fasteners. Snap! The straps parted. The tension now released, surrendered two pink fleshy breasts liberated from their captivity. But no bee. It had stopped buzzing. Perhaps it was in the room somewhere, and not caught up in Julie's body. She had not felt nor seen it, only heard it.

The alarm sounded. Julie woke, hot and sweaty, and glowing from the adventure with the non-existent bees.

Like Fr Ignatius, Julie had come from a large Irish Catholic family. One of seven children, but they were not poor. They lived in comfort, and didn't want for anything. Her Father had a number of profitable chemist shops in and around Dublin. Two brothers had become priests, two sisters nuns. The other brother and sister were at Trinity College Dublin, the former studying medicine, and the latter law. Julie had drifted over to England after failing to qualify as a school teacher at 23. She had been with Fr Ignatius for 12 years now, and felt isolated, and unfulfilled. Her Irish Catholic upbringing had left her frustrated and repressed. She wanted to escape from the shackles of Roman Catholicism with all its dogma, bygone rituals, rules, and notions of the Pope's infallibility. She doubted the religious doctrines proclaimed by ecclesiastical authority to be true. her life had always been influenced, and controlled, by her Catholic upbringing. Her father was in a position to support the deprived, destitute, conveyor-belt child-producing mothers with methods of birth control, but on religious grounds he refused to advise and help. He would rather see them suffer, become exhausted, and maybe die with endless child bearing.

Her two priest brothers supported the churches' teaching on birth control, because they had been indoctrinated by the system. Her two nun sisters were in a closed order of nuns. They had not been seen by any member of the family since entering the convent. The four of them were leading unnatural, false lives. Their outlook on the world and community was selfish. They were, like many members of the church, stuck in a time warp, safely cocooned in their private worlds, oblivious to the needs of those they were supposed to be caring for.

"Surely Christ did not agonize on the cross for people to suffer too. No, this is man's doing," thought Julie.

CHAPTER 19

School

"And then the whining school-
boy, with his satchel
And shining morning-face, creeping like a snail
Unwillingly to school."

As You Like It. Act II Scene VII
William Shakespeare 1564-1616.

CHAPTER 19

"Good morning, Boys and Girls."

"Good morning, Miss," came their staccato response.

Miss Fanshaw with piercing eyes stared at each child in turn. Her hypnotic glare reduced them to a state of nervousness, and intimidation.

The cool autumn sun penetrated the windows, shooting parallel lines of orange rays across the children's desks, dazzling and disturbing their concentration. Flocks of suspended dust hovered in the coloured sunlight. Miss Fanshaw was seated in the shade, cool, calm and in control. Her desk was raised on a platform, a good eight inches from floor level. She sat with elevated arms positioned on the desk top, her long lean interlocked fingers supporting her chin. She looked down on her subordinates annihilating each child in turn, into frightened wooden puppets. In her presence the children became speechless robots.

Miss Fanshaw's face was long, with a straight Roman nose, which dominated the rest of her features. The pince-nez she wore just below the bridge of her nose gave her an owl-like image. Her deep-set crows-feet sunken green eyes added to the illusion. High cheek bones supported a hollow face which looked like old seasoned leather. Dewlap ears hung loose and long, like old men's wizened throats. Wire wool pepper and salt hair was swept back from her head, and held tightly into a large bun, which rested like a bird's nest in the nape of her neck. Miss Fanshaw always wore an ankle length black skirt, and starched high-necked white blouse, cotton in winter, and soft fine silk in summer. In each case they hung in loose folds from a rather large, and well supported, out-of-view bosom.

She was the hollow lady. *'Shape without form, shade without colour, paralysed force, gesture without motion'[1].*

The first day back at school after the summer recess was always hard. The carefree days of the school summer holiday were replaced by regimented discipline in the hands of Miss Fanshaw. At least Derek was away from the clutches of Miss Weatherspoon. These two women dominated his life with uneasiness and fear. He never felt relaxed in their presence. Even Fr Ignatius, his friend, was giving him hassle over the altar wine. Sitting in the classroom, his hands clutching his rabbit's tail, he began to drift into another world.

He was walking through the woods, with the bird perched on his shoulder. It was a warm sunny day. The damp earthy vegetation smelt sweet and fresh. Rabbits, squirrels, toads, badgers, hedgehogs, and all manner of animal life were jumping and running around. Birds, large and small, in multifarious colours and shapes, flew, and hovered in the air. The woodland path snaked

---

[1] The Hollow Men. T S Eliot 1888-1965.

through overhanging trees, dropping down to a clear water stream, which Derek crossed on stepping stones. On the opposite bank a green and yellow striped, warty-backed toad greeted Derek with a friendly croak of welcome. The bird, flying just a few paces ahead, chirruped in reply, as if in natural dialogue. The path swung round gaining height. Derek was now walking on a carpet of tiny mauve flowers, which at every step sent up bouquets of lavender fragrances, reminding him of his mother. Ahead, the clear blue sky glowed through the tree tops. Further on through a thicket of young oak trees, the setting sun dropping to the horizon, glared and dazzled Derek with its suffused orange brightness.

Ahead, in a clearing, stood a lofty tree, leaping up, and disappearing into the sky. At the tree's base was a door, which was open. Standing in the doorway was the old man Derek had met on the train.

"Hello, Derek," said the old man. "Still got yer lucky rabbit's tail?"

"Yes, thank you," said Derek.

"Would yer like to go to the tea-party?" said the old man.

"Yes, please," said Derek, politely.

"Straight down the passage. You'll see, Derek," he said, pointing ahead.

The corridor was dimly lit, the air balmy with a deep calm. Derek, with the hovering bird in front, walked gingerly along the passage to a staircase. Standing at the bottom of the stairs was the lady with the long-tailed parrot on her shoulder.

"Going to the tea-party?" she said.

"Going to the tea-party, are we, Derek, to the tea-party, to the tea-party?" squawked the parrot.

"Shut up!" said the lady.

"Sorry!" said the parrot.

"Going to the tea-party, the tea-party, are we?" said the parrot again.

Very quickly, before either the lady or the parrot could speak again, Derek said, "Yes."

"Up the stairs. Up the stairs. Up the stairs," squawked the parrot.

The lady smiled in affirmation. Derek walked hurriedly up the stairs, panting as he went. At the top stood the nun.

"This way, Derek. God bless you my child," she said, pointing towards a door which opened automatically as Derek approached.

Just inside the door stood Clare smiling, dressed in a flowing pale peach diaphanous dress. Derek looked at her lovingly, spellbound by her presence, her rounded breasts moving with each intake of breath. They were the source of Clare's strength and love. Derek wanted to be enveloped within that love. They represented the love that Derek had lost when his mother died. She smiled, and kissed him gently on both cheeks.

"Welcome to the tea-party, sit with your mother. She's expecting you," smiled Clare.

Derek could just see his mother's smiling face through a hovering mist. She lifted up both arms, held them out pointing towards him in salutation. He raced towards her holding out his arms to embrace her.

"Derek Postlethwaite, day dreaming again, are we?" came Miss Fanshaw's ear-splitting, rasping voice.

She stood up, almost six feet of her. Stepping off the dais she slowly walked between the desks towards Derek, who sat at the back of the classroom. Derek looked up, stunned and petrified. Her loud military voice shook him from his fantasizing. He was back in the classroom again. He gazed up at her as she walked slowly towards him, mesmerized by her breasts, which were almost as big as Miss Weatherspoon's. Each one moved as she came towards him. It was as if they had a life of their own, and were not attached to anything. They could have been alive and loose, each jockeying for position like two large wobbling jellies trying to get comfortable under her blouse. She stopped, her bosoms came to rest, carefully concealed. Derek lifted his face and eyes upwards from her breasts, and met her incisive stare. They eyeballed each other. Derek became transported, back into the real world.

"Well, Derek," she said.

"Don't know, Miss, I mean, yes, Miss," Derek stuttered.

"Stand up, Boy, when I speak to you," she shouted.

Derek stood up with tears swelling in his eyes.

"Have you been playing with yourself, Derek?" she said.

Derek was not sure what she meant, and remained silent. The class began to snigger in a suppressed way.

"Quiet," she shouted.

The classroom became silent, each child terror-stricken with Derek's third degree grilling.

"Your flies are undone, Derek. Why?" she said.

"Don't know, Miss," said Derek, trembling.

"Button them up, Boy," she said.

Derek tried to button up his flies, but all the fumbling wouldn't find the buttons.

"Hurry up, Boy," she said.

"Can't find the buttons, Miss," said Derek, agitated.

"Graham, do his buttons up for him," she said, looking at the boy sitting next to Derek.

"Yes, Miss," said Graham.

Graham stood up and tried to button up Derek's flies, but the buttons eluded him too.

"Can't find them, Miss," said Graham.

"Stupid boy, sit down," said Miss Fanshaw.

Please, Miss, I'll do it, Miss. Let me do up Derek's buttons, Miss. Please, Miss!" said a squeaky voice.

"Good girl, Monica," said Miss Fanshaw.

Monica moved towards Derek, gleaming all over her face. Monica was only ten, but looked and acted like a pubescent 14 year old. She was taller than Derek, and had always liked him. The thought of buttoning up his flies really excited her. She was wearing a white dress covered with small blue flowers. It was short, and tight across her chest emphasizing her rapidly growing young breasts. The top buttons were almost at bursting point under the pressure. A white bra just visible through the dress gap held her small buds tight against her. Derek cringed at the thought of Monica groping at his trouser fronts. He felt himself blushing as she fumbled inside his flies. He'd forgotten to put his underpants on, and felt her cool fingers sliding over his warm flesh. The motion of flesh against flesh tickled and stirred him. Monica couldn't feel what she was hoping to find as her fingers explored and burrowed into the depths of Derek's trousers. There were certainly no buttons.

"Hurry up, Monica. We can't spend all day playing about with Derek. Can we?" said Miss Fanshaw.

The children began to snigger again at Miss Fanshaw's implied overtones.

"Quiet," she shouted, staring at the children with fire in her belly.

"Please, Miss. There's no buttons, Miss. Honest, Miss," said Monica.

"Let's see, shall we." said Miss Fanshaw, cautiously, parting Derek's flies with two fingers.

"Hmm, no buttons. You're quite right. Sit down, Monica."

Monica gave Derek a saucy smile, and returned to her desk. Miss Fanshaw glared at Derek, who was crimson with humiliation, and said, "Does your Mother know, you've no buttons to do up your trouser fronts, Derek?"

"Don't know, Miss," muttered Derek.

"Tell your mother. Ask her to sew some buttons on your trousers, Derek. Do you understand? It's rude to come to school with your flies undone."

"Don't know, Miss," said Derek.

"Don't know what Derek?" replied Miss Fanshaw.

"My mother can't sew any buttons on, Miss," said Derek.

"Why can't she?"

"She's dead, Miss," said Derek, bursting into tears.

Miss Fanshaw was unprepared for such an announcement. She felt guilty, momentarily out of her depth, and began to think she was losing control of the situation. Her body became clammy as she slowly walked back to her desk, and sat down facing the class.

"Is this true, boys and girls?" she said, in a serious voice.

"Yes, Miss," came a united response.

"Why wasn't I told about this?" she thought. "Heads will roll," she added, to herself.

A lump came to Miss Fanshaw's throat. She looked at Derek, saying, "We'll all be very quiet for Derek, and his poor, poor, mother."

For a few minutes the classroom was calm, and silent, only a buzzing fly invaded the stillness. It, too, stopped after several seconds, and joined the class in their grief and quiet. Tears of sadness fell, hushed sobbing added to the soundlessness. Miss Fanshaw took a small white lace handkerchief, which was tucked into the cuff of her blouse, and gently dabbed her eyes.

She looked up at the children, saying, "Our Father, who art in heaven hallowed by Thy name."

Spontaneously the children joined in with Miss Fanshaw in loud and confident voices saying the Lord's prayer.

"May Almighty God give eternal rest to Derek's mother," said Miss Fanshaw.

In unison with Miss Fanshaw they boldly said, "Amen."

"Let us now sing together, boys and girls, 'All things bright and beautiful', remembering that life still goes on, even after someone we love very dearly dies, and goes to heaven to live with God. Stand up children."

The classroom, made up of an almost equal mixture of boys and girls, stood poised, confident and ready to burst into song, some still red-eyed, others with dribbling noses, and some with both. Tall boys, little boys, fat boys, thin boys. Some had tidy hair, others with unruly hair. Black, brown, blonde and ginger hair. Some were smartly dressed, others were scruffy. The girls were identical to the boys in shape, size and hair colour, but better groomed with clean neat dresses and tidy hair. Some had short fringed hair, others had long ribboned hair, some had pigtails, others had plaits, some had bows, and others had head bands. Some wore pink, blue and red, others wore mauve, yellow and green. They stood like an herbaceous border of coloured flowers waiting to explode into a chorus of blossomed sound. Earlier they had sat in fear of Miss Fanshaw, but even the immovable had been overcome with compassion. They all stood united like a ticking time-bomb waiting to be detonated. They were ready to pay tribute to Derek's mother.

Miss Fanshaw faced the children in uninterrupted silence. Her arms raised, thumb and forefingers touching, making a small circle, the remaining fingers slightly poised and her arms motionless. She looked at each child, and without speaking summoned their readiness.

"One, two," and on the command of "three", Miss Fanshaw lifted up her arms into the air, opened up her fingers - the bomb was detonated, and an explosion of unrepressed singing voices filled the noiseless classroom with,

'All things bright and beautiful,
All creatures great and small,
All things wise and wonderful,
The Lord God made them all.

Each little flower that opens,
Each little bird that sings,
He made their glowing colours,
He made their tiny wings.

The rich man in his castle,
The poor man at his gate,
God made them, high or lowly,
And order'd their estate.

The purple-headed mountain,
The river running by,
The sunset and the morning
That brightens up the sky.

The cold wind in the winter,
The pleasant summer sun,
The ripe fruits in the garden,
He made them every one.

The tall trees in the greenwood,
The meadows where we play,
The rushes by the water,
We gather every day.

He gave us eyes to see them,
And lips that we might tell,
How great is God Almighty,
Who has made all things well.

The "Amen" came as a strong broadside, building up by a gradual increase in sound to an almighty crescendo, Miss Fanshaw's arms came to rest, as they had started, with forefinger and thumb touching. The "Amen" finished, silence followed, the sound still ringing in the air. A fly buzzed around again, and it, too, stopped and joined in the stillness.

"Sit," said Miss Fanshaw.

A scraping of chairs followed, hands went up.

"Please, Miss. Want a wee, Miss."

"The toilet, Miss."

"Can't wait, Miss."

"We'll have an early playtime," said Miss Fanshaw.

More scraping of chairs, bodies shuffling, and a stampede of children followed as the word 'playtime' was mentioned.

"Order! Order! Order! Quiet!" shouted Miss Fanshaw.

The children stopped silently in their tracks waiting for the next command.

"From the front starting with Jenny, walk slowly and silently into the playground - off you go now," said Miss Fanshaw, now back to her aggressive self.

The children followed Jenny in an orderly fashion out of the classroom. In the corridor, their speed increased to an almighty rush into the playground. Once outside they became boisterous, excited, and almost savage. The noise became thunderous, discordant and shrill, like caged animals let loose into the wild again.

"Derek," Miss Fanshaw shouted. "Come here."

Derek with head bent, sore red eyes, runny nose, looking grieved, and miserable, walked towards Miss Fanshaw's desk.

"Take your trousers off, Derek. I'll sew some buttons on for you," she said.

"Can't, Miss," said Derek.

"Why not," came a sharp reply.

"I've forgotten to put me pants on," said Derek.

Miss Fanshaw went to her cupboard, took out a tin box filled with buttons, bobbins of cotton, scissors and a plethora of sewing equipment. She selected four buttons, threaded a needle with black cotton, and with hands poised for action said in a loud crisp voice.

"Trousers off, buttons, on, one, two, three."

Derek wriggled out of his trousers, tugging and stretching his shirt to hide his embarrassment. Pulling his shirt front down, lifted up his shirt tail exposing his bottom. Pulling the shirt tail down exposed his genitals. He couldn't conceal both at the same time. He stood with one hand hiding his genitals, and one hand hiding his bottom, trying to pull his shirt down at the same time. His shirt was too small anyway, and whatever he did his private parts were on public display. He felt self-conscious, and once again humiliated by Miss Fanshaw.

Without any warning Monica rushed into the classroom, and in an out-of-breath voice gasped, "Please,

Miss, Jack Trimble's hit Albert Hoskiss in the face, and made his ...."

She stopped, rooted to the spot, before finishing the sentence. Monica was riveted to the floor, staring at Derek. Derek was taken aback by Monica's dramatic entrance into the classroom. He let go of his shirt, which left his back and front completely uncovered. Derek looked at Monica. She focussed her eyes on his genitalia. Derek turned round to hide his embarrassment, which then revealed his bottom. Monica put her right hand up to her mouth to hide her giggling. Both were crimson with blushing.

"Put this round you, Derek," said Miss Fanshaw, throwing him her old woollen cardigan.

"Yes, Miss. Thank you, Miss," said Derek, trying to wrap the cardigan around his waist.

"What are you trying to tell me, Monica?" said Miss Fanshaw.

"It's Jack Trimble. He's hit Albert thingy with his fist, and knocked all his teeth out. There's blood everywhere. Honest, Miss," said Monica, rushing back into the playground, herself now embarrassed.

"Don't tell anyone, Monica," shouted Derek, after her.

"Quiet boy, and keep still," said Miss Fanshaw.

Fifteen minutes later the children sat at their desks again. Derek was wearing his buttoned up trousers. Albert Hoskiss was nursing a cut and swollen lip. Jack Trimble was standing on a chair in the corner of the classroom facing the wall in disgrace. Miss Fanshaw sat at her desk eyeballing each child in turn. A wisp of iron-grey wire hair hung over her left ear, moving up and down with her breathing. The fly buzzed again joining in with the children, who were having a drawing lesson, as their pencils scratched away at the paper in the noiseless room.

Derek skipped and jumped home, feeling very relieved that the day's schooling was over. It had not been a good day, even the rabbit's tail didn't seem to work. Nothing had gone right for him.

"Bet Monica will tell everyone she's seen my willy," he thought.

He came across a stretch of pavement made up of concrete slabs. First he tried jumping on the joins between each slab, but that got too difficult, so he then tried walking on the joins pretending he was walking across a river over a narrow bridge. His mind began to wander. The river ran through a jungle with dangerous animals. Crocodiles reared up at him out of the water with gaping jaws bearing white sharp pointed teeth. Coming towards him was Miss Weatherspoon shouting and waving a stick at him. He ducked as the stick swung to his head. It missed. Miss Weatherspoon lost her balance and fell into the river. The last he saw, or heard of her, was a cry for help as her fat grotesque body was slowly swallowed whole by an enormous crocodile. She disappeared without a trace, presumed eaten alive.

Leaving the river behind and hacking his way through the bush he faced a barrage of arrows and spears. Several hit him, but bounced off his body. He had become invincible. Cautiously he made his way further into the jungle. A tiger growled at him, as it leapt at his throat. Instinctively he drew his automatic pistol from his belt, and shot it in the head. The tiger rolled over growling, turning into a whimper as it slowly died. He smelt burning wood and heard screams. Ahead, in a clearing, he saw Indians dancing around a fire. Tied to a stake in the middle of the flames was Monica, almost naked, her dress torn, leaving her young breasts unveiled to the leaping flames. Firing his automatic from the hip he killed two Indians, and the rest fled.

Monica saw him and shouted, "Help!"

He heard and felt a crash as he keeled over onto the pavement.

"Help! Yer bleddy fool, can't yer luke wier yer gooing," said a fat toothless lady with a cigarette hanging from her mouth. She dropped her bags in an attempt to protect herself as Derek crashed into her flabby stomach. He bounced off twisting his ankle as he fell onto the pavement. Eggs, bread, bottles, apples and an assortment of shopping spilled everywhere.

Derek, still with Monica half-naked, engulfed in flames, on his mind, couldn't quite focus on what had happened to him. Was he still in the jungle? He tried to lift himself up off the ground with his hands, but his left hand slipped in a mixture of egg yolks, and tomato sauce. He lost his balance, and fell face down into a broken jar of strawberry jam.

"You'll pay fer this, yer daft bogga," said the bag lady, angrily trying to salvage her spilt shopping from the pavement.

Derek now realised where he was, and what had happened. He tried to stand up, but his ankle hurt. He toppled over again, and sat in the jam. The bag lady, now put out by being bumped into by Derek, became frenzied, and started hitting him with a cucumber.

"Yer note burra tow-rag," she said, in anger.

All Derek could do was cover his head with his hands and wait. The bag lady gave up when the spattered cucumber broke up into bits. She gave Derek a violent kick, collected the remains of her shopping, and marched off, swearing.

Derek looked up from the pavement to see the back of the Wellington-booted, shabby-coated, head-scarfed bag lady disappear down the road. She carried the remains of her shopping on each arm, one bag dripping tomato sauce, the other leaving a trail of flour in her wake.

Covered in jam, eggs and tomato sauce Derek limped home feeling very sorry for himself. The thought did cross his mind whether he should return to the jungle to rescue Monica or not.

"Perhaps not," he silently said to himself. "Another time."

CHAPTER 20

The Man in the Fawn Raincoat

"Young girls lie bedded soft or
glide in their dreams,
with rings and trousseaux,
bridesmaided by glow-worms down
the aisles of the organplaying wood.
The boys are dreaming wicked or
of the bucking ranches of
the night and the jollyrodgered sea."

Under Milk Wood.
Dylan Thomas 1914-53.

CHAPTER 20

A covert looking man walked slowly down Cuthbert Street, staring at each house in turn on both sides of the street. Curtains were pulled aside to let penetrating eyes gaze into the road. Beth and Maggi never missed out on any intrigue. They could be relied on for up-to-date information on any goings-on in Cuthbert Street. What Beth didn't know, Maggi did.

The man, around five foot ten inches, wore a brown felt trilby hat. The hat was set at a jaunty angle with the brim pulled down over his bespectacled face. A neat black toothbrush moustache complemented his thick black horn-rimmed glasses. He wore a long shabby fawn-coloured raincoat with the collar turned up, despite the warm evening. Both hands displayed brown kid-leather gloves toning well with his polished brown shoes, and fawn coat. The man looked sly, like a cunning fox. His pace was slow, and meaningful. Occasionally he would stop, take a notebook out of his pocket, and write something down. Beth thought he was a secret agent. Maggi thought he was the bailiff.

Harry had just finished his meal of pork pie and salad. Derek, now cleaned up and his ankle strapped, was playing with his friends. Miss Weatherspoon and Brian had taken Mitzi for a walk. Harry stepped out of his front door, down the garden path for the purpose of stretching his legs, and lighting his pipe. The rain-coated man walked by, and gave Harry a furtive look.

"Good evening," said Harry.

The man just nodded and walked on.

"Miserable underhanded sod," he thought.

Harry, puffing away and enjoying his pipe, leaned over the gate in an effort to keep an eye on what he perceived to be a very odd-looking character.

Beth and Maggi, together with several other nosy neighbours, were outside their houses looking down the street in the man's direction. They were in deep conversation. They saw Harry.

"Ow do," they said, in unison.

"Hello," said Harry.

"Who's that funny looking bloke, 'Arry?" said Beth.

"Insurance man, I reckon," said Harry.

"Funny looking bogger at any rate," said Maggi.

The man had walked to the bottom of the street, turned round, and started to walk back again. He stopped about 25 yards away from Harry, fumbled in his pocket, and took out a packet of cigarettes. Slowly, tapping the end of his cigarette on the packet, he walked deliberately snail-like towards Harry.

He reached him, and stopped, saying, "Good evening," as if in response to Harry's earlier 'Good evening'.

Harry said nothing, just nodded.

"Could you oblige me with a light?" said the man, putting the cigarette to his mouth.

Harry, in silence, took a box of matches from his pocket, picked out a match, and struck it. The man leant over the gate to light his cigarette. The match went out. Harry lit another, and this time cigarette and match kindled, and the deed was accomplished.

"Thanks," grunted the man.

Both men puffed away, exhaling clouds of smoke. They stared at each other but said nothing.

Coming up the street was Miss Weatherspoon with Mitzi on a lead, and Brian alongside, eating an ice cream. She saw the man, turned round, and walked back down the street, disappearing round the corner at the street end.

Beth and Maggi, leaning over their front gates, almost opposite Harry's house, were puffing away like steam engines at their cigarettes, both convulsively coughing between puffs. With ears pricked they were trying to hear any conversation between Harry and the shifty-looking man.

"If ee'd a black 'at on, ee'd be an undertaker," said Maggi.

"Yer reckon?" said Beth.

Miss Weatherspoon walked hurriedly up the street running parallel with Cuthbert Street. She dragged Mitzi, who didn't seem to want to walk at the same pace. He was more interested in sniffing at gate posts, dried up piles of dog poo, and continually stopping for a pee. Brian had to run to keep up.

"Please slow down, Auntie," said Brian.

She ignored him, and seemed to quicken her pace. Reaching the end of the street, she stopped, looked behind, and when certain she was not being followed walked slowly back. Half way down the street she took cover in an entry between two houses. This was a short cut to the back of Harry's house and garden.

The man in the fawn raincoat muttered, "Good night," and walked up the street out of sight.

Harry replied with, "Good night," and disappeared through his front door, leaving a trail of pipe smoke behind him.

"Best get our Ted's tea ready," said Beth.

"Bit late! In't 'e 'ohm yet," said Maggi.

"Wokking late," came the reply.

"Gon te booza more like," said Maggi.

"Ah! Maybe," said Beth.

"Tarrah then," Maggi said, walking up the path.

"Tarrah, see yer," replied Beth, cleaning her specs with the corner of her checked apron as she too walked up her path.

"See yer," was heard as Maggi slammed her door.

"See yer, Maggi," said Beth, disappearing into her house banging her door shut.

Derek was in the park playing with Dave, one of his school friends. Monica and Audrey were on the swings. The boys were jumping on and off the small wooden roundabout as they swung it round as fast as it would go. They looked at the two girls, and the girls looked at them. They all anxiously wished to play together, but pride held them back. Monica was the first to make a move. She caught Derek's eye, and called out, "Want a sweet, Derek."

"Yes, please," Derek yelled.

"Come and get one," Monica shouted back.

Derek jumped off the roundabout awkwardly, and fell over, grazing his knee.

"Feck," he said, under his breath.

Monica jumped off the swing, and walked over to him.

"Are you alright?" she said. "Your poor knee. It's bleeding. Let's see."

She bent down to look at his knee. Derek sat on the grass enjoying the attention from Monica, but felt rather self-conscious. Earlier in the day she'd tried to button up his flies, and seen his willy. He felt himself going red in the face, as these thoughts crossed his mind. Leaning over his bleeding knee the top of her dress fell forward, leaving a wide gap. Derek eased himself up, just enough to allow his eyes to focus directly at, and into the gap of Monica's dress. The top button had come off, and the one underneath was undone.

"Have a bull's eye, Derek," she said, spitting on her grubby white handkerchief, and gingerly wiping the blood away.

Derek didn't hear or notice what she was doing. He was still concentrating on the gap in her dress. She moved from crouching to a kneeling position, making the gap even wider. Derek now had a full view of what was previously hidden. His eyes feasted on two small suspended pubescent naked breasts. They hung like two young lemons, small, firm, succulent and juicy. The flesh was pink and soft, the rounded tips slightly darker and teasingly intense, like tiny budded cherries. Monica noticed Derek's interest. She leaned nearer towards him enjoying his attention.

Monica was very much aware of her body, and the way it was changing. She was still girlish, but rapidly leaving behind her childish naivety. Derek had always been fascinated with breasts. His mental interest had been ahead of his physical maturity, but the two were slowly catching up with each other.

"Do you want a bull's eye or not, Derek?" she said, again, taking a sticky black and white-striped boiled sweet from her pocket.

"Yes, please," said Derek.

She gave Derek the sweet, and continued with her first aid, adding more spit to the handkerchief. Derek felt her warm gentle hands against his flesh. They sent a tingling sensation through his body. Monica too felt a thrill of excitement as she dabbed at Derek's knee. She noticed his legs and thighs had a delicate coating of soft fine hairs, like the thick silky smooth down on the backs of leaves and fruits. His too small short tight trousers rode high up his plump goose-pimpled thighs. Her mind went back to the classroom as she tried to button up his flies. She noticed they were now securely fastened. They were both enjoying the moment of childish innocent contact. Their bodies electrified with a frisson of excitement as they touched.

It started to drizzle and black clouds hung heavy. In the distance lightning flashed across the sky and thunder clapped. Rain, like stair-rods, fell from the heavens. The children ran across the park. Derek arrived home, drenched and steaming.

Harry had fallen asleep in his chair reading his newspaper. His burnt out pipe loosely clasped between his teeth, rested on his chin.

Miss Weatherspoon, Mitzi and Brian were now walking back home in the rain. They were all very wet. Miss Weatherspoon kept a watchful eye for the man in the fawn raincoat, who seemed to have faded away, much to her relief.

The man in the fawn raincoat, suitably dressed for the weather, had been last seen entering the local police station. Before entering he looked up and down the street in a manner suggesting he wished to remain incognito. He furtively opened the door, went inside, making a further surveillance of the street, before the heavy oak door banged shut behind him.

"Good evening, all," he said, glancing at the police sergeant sitting at his desk.

A uniformed constable stood in the background drinking a large mug of tea.

"Cup of tea, Sir," he shouted.

"Don't mind if I do," came the reply.

The rain-coated man disappeared into a room down a dimly lit corridor.

Monica and Derek still felt inflamed by the day's events as they lay in their beds tossing and turning trying hard to sleep. Monica was sure she was in love. Derek just liked the pampering and Monica's breasts.

The day ended. The street slept peacefully, apart from Miss Weatherspoon, who had something on her mind. Mitzi too was restless, disturbed by a buzzing fly.

CHAPTER 21

The Gang

"Something nasty in the woodshed."

Cold Comfort Farm, ch. 10.
Stella Gibbons 1902-89.

CHAPTER 21

"Wud yer like te join us gang?" said Ginger.

Derek's mind was on other things, and he didn't hear him.

Six of the gang had moved into the senior school. They needed replacements quickly to keep together their own clique, which only consisted of Doug, Ginger and Terry. It wasn't generally known that only three members were left. They needed numbers to maintain and assert their authority and power amongst their equals. In order to get new members immediately they were prepared to relax the rules for joining. It was unprecedented to have a girl in the gang, but to involve Monica could be an advantage.

Monica's father kept an off-licence. If Monica joined the gang there could be a plentiful supply of cigarettes, liquor and sweets. Doug and Ginger would get Derek to join, and then get Derek to involve Monica. They knew that Monica was interested in Derek by her volunteering to button up his flies.

Ginger was a tall lad, with a mop of red curly hair, and freckles. His runny nose was always dripping, which he constantly wiped clean with the back of his hand, or by vigorous sniffing. His voice had a rubbery nasal sound, which made it difficult to understand what he was trying to say.

Doug too, was big. They were the tallest in the class and physically ahead for their years. Their birthdays just missed the deadline by a few weeks for going into the senior school. Doug's voice was getting crusty, and his upper lip sported soft black down, which had the hallmarks of a thin black moustache. Greasy thick black straight hair was sleeked back over his head with a middle parting. It was long, lustrous and lacquered, and fell loosely each side of his parting.

Terry was the opposite to Doug and Ginger, a timid, thin and pale-faced boy with blonde hair. In appearance and physique he was around two years behind his actual age, but mentally very bright. He constantly picked his nose, and chewed it. He only joined the gang to save himself being teased, and for self preservation. It was well known by his school mates that he'd eaten and swallowed a worm, which he washed down with a mug of Doug's pee, as a condition for joining the gang, but being a member had given him some status amongst his peers.

It was better to be a member of Doug's gang, rather than run the risk of being bullied.

Miss Fanshaw heard about the incident following Terry's illness. He was off school for a week with severe bouts of being sick, and stomach cramps. His condition was diagnosed by his doctor as a suspected appendicitis, but a visit to the hospital confirmed that it was something he'd eaten. Doug, Ginger and Terry swore on the Bible that the rumours that Terry had eaten worms were all lies.

Miss Fanshaw did not believe them, and took the matter up with Mr Gradgrind - the head teacher. Mr Gradgrind was seeing Mrs Bounderby - Doug's Mother, at the time, and didn't want to upset the arrangement. Mr Bounderby was a very big man, with a short fuse.

"Let sleeping dogs lie," thought Mr Gradgrind.

Ginger tapped Derek on the shoulder.

"Doug says yer cun join us gang if yer want, Del," he said nasally, with air releasing through his nose, rather than his mouth.

Derek didn't understand a word he said. "Yer what?" said Derek.

"De yer wunt te join us gang?" he repeated.

At that moment Doug arrived on the scene looking very important. He wore black long trousers, which hung over his shoes and trailed on the ground, and a black wrinkled shirt. A pair of too large black horn-rimmed sun glasses rested loosely on his nose. The bridge was held together by black adhesive tape, and one lens had a crack across it. His forefinger constantly pushed the bridge of the glasses up from the end of his nose, so it rested in the hollow below his eyes. Each time he took his finger away the glasses fell down again. Doug seemed unaware of the non-stop exercise of adjusting his sunglasses.

"Ow do, Del," said Doug.

"Eh up, Dug," said Derek, consciously adjusting his dialect to Doug's speech pattern.

"Yuh cun join us gang if yuh want, Del. What yuh say?

"Ah I wud. Wot de 'ave to do te join, Dug?"

"Seeing us yah mam's ded, we'd mak escepsons. We'd like yuh to get Mon te join too, Del. Wot yuh say?"

"Ah'll see worra cun do, Dug," said Derek.

"Le'rus know, see yuh then, Del," said Doug, turning back to be with Ginger, who'd stopped to stroke a dog.

"Cheerio then," said Derek, quickening his pace, intent on finding Monica.

Derek found Monica with another girl in the play park on the swings. He walked towards them with his eyes fixed on Monica as she swung backwards and forwards. Her legs pointing straight up in the air as she came swinging towards him. Her dress billowed and swelled with air as she climbed higher and higher, uncovering her smooth white thighs. Two buds lay hidden beneath her flattened dress. Her scarlet knickers were just visible at each forward thrust of the swing, leaving in its wake the rusty screech of chains, as they scrunched together in momentum. A shiver, like an electric current, ran through Derek's body as he watched, glued to the ground.

Slowly the swing lost its spirit, and came to rest. Monica's dress deflated against her body. The grinding rusty chains gave up. All was quiet. They looked at each other and smiled.

"Doug wants to know if you'd like to join his gang," said Derek.

"Only if you join, Derek," said Monica.

"Let's join together then," said Derek.

"What do we 'ave to do to join. I'm not eating worms, or drinking stuff like Terry," said Monica.

"Don't know! Let's go and find out, Mon," said Derek.

Monica jumped off the swing, put on her shoes, and off they both went in search of Doug. Doug, Ginger and Terry were sitting on the park bench, almost out of sight from the general public. All three were surreptitiously smoking cigarettes. Terry was puffing between bouts of uncontrollable coughing, and obviously not enjoying the experience. The other two sat like old men with cigarettes held between their fore and middle fingers, taking infrequent puffs to stem their own coughing. Doug and Ginger were red in the face, and Terry an ashen green colour. All three were red and watery eyed, and did not seem at ease with smoking.

"What do we 'av to do to join yer gang, Doug?" said Monica.

Ginger and Doug went into a huddle, started coughing again, and after a few seconds looked at Monica. Doug made the first move.

"You'll be the first gel in us gang. We want yer to keep us in fags, tuffies and booze, and we want yer to show us yer fanny. Then yer can be a member, and be in charge of any gels who join."

Monica didn't turn a hair. Derek didn't quite understand the challenge. Ginger started to giggle, and Terry was being sick in the hedgebottom. Doug eyeballed Monica with a serious look on his face. He was trying to feel superior, in control, and put Monica on the spot. Monica eyeballed Doug back, and walking towards him said,

"OK with me, Doug, but I want te see yours and Ginger's willies first, before I show yer me fanny. Yer've got te drop yer trousers and pants down te yer ankles, and lift yer shirt up, whilst I count te 50."

Doug and Ginger started to blush, looked at each other, and went into a huddle again.

"Alright then, but count te 20, not 50," said Doug.

"OK, 40," said Doug, looking at Ginger for confirmation of the arrangements.

"OK with me." said Ginger, very embarrassed, his face almost crimson.

"It's a deal, Doug," said Monica. "let's go in the woods."

They all followed Monica into the woods alongside the play park. Monica, now in control, stopped in a small clearing.

She looked at Derek and Terry, saying, "Stand at the back of me. I don't want to see *yer* willies. Doug and Ging stand next to each other in front of me. When I say ready, steady, go! Drop yer trousers and pants down to yer ankles. I'll start counting."

Doug and Ginger, looking very subdued and put down, lined themselves up and faced Monica. Monica picked up a stick, like a baton, and slapped it against her leg authoritatively. She was now in charge, ready to give orders. Doug and Ginger were on parade waiting for the command. They looked at her timidly, withdrawn and obedient. Monica on the other hand looked superior, aggressive, and manly. She slowly walked in front of them, eyes on the ground, her baton slapping against her legs. To and fro she went, occasionally looking up at them, and swishing her baton in the air. Monica was enjoying her few moments of glory. She was unchallenged as Doug and Ginger were afraid to move or speak. The suspense was too much for them. They became nervous, and started to fidget. Ginger's nose was running, but he was too frightened to wipe it. He sniffed, but was unable to control the flow, which started to gain in abundance and gather speed as gummy fluid flowed over his lips, down his chin, onto his shirt, some dripping onto the ground. He looked uncomfortable, and terrified. Monica stared at him and said, quietly but firmly, "Wipe yer nose yer mucky little boy."

Ginger wiped his nose with the back of his hand, his chin with his fingers, and then wiped his hand on the front of his shirt. Doug started to shuffle his feet about. Monica looked at him, and said, "Going somewhere, Doug."

"No, I'm waiting to drop me pants, Mon," came Doug's nervous reply.

"In good time, Doug. There's no hurry," said Monica, smiling at him. "Get ready for it. I don't start counting until yer pants are down, and yer shirt fronts are up. One, two."

They both started to make a move, their hands went for their belts.

"As you were," shouted Monica. "I haven't given the order yet."

Their arms resumed the position of hanging by their sides. They waited in trepidation for the next command. Ginger's nose started to drip again. He sniffed hard. Doug coughed. A wasp buzzed around his head attracted to his hair lacquer. Both started to twitch. Monica said nothing, just eyeballed each in turn.

Derek and Terry looked on and sniggered. They were overcome by Monica's ability to control the two school bullies. She had them eating out of her hands. Derek looked on in awe, enchanted by Monica's naked arms, the hiss of silk and cotton as her baton swished against her dress, which stretched against her thrusting thighs as she moved up and down in front of Doug and Ginger. Would they ever be able to take command of the gang again? Monica had undermined their established power over their equals. He saw Monica, like Clare, with a plunging neckline, blood red lips, and long blonde hair resting on her naked shoulders. He looked on, and wanted to be near enough to feel her body against his. Monica turned round, and looked at Derek. They looked straight into each other's eyes, and simultaneously smiled. Derek glowed with adulation at Monica. This was not just a school boy and girl friendship, but unfulfilled passion, just simmering away.

"One, two, three, go!"filled the air, as Monica boldly called out, staring closely at Doug and Ginger.

Derek mentally came out of the clouds, and fell back to earth. Monica's commanding voice shook Terry from his smoker's coughing fit. All three had their eyes glued on Doug and Ginger as they furtively fumbled with their trouser belts, braces and buttons. Their trousers dropped down to their ankles.

Monica shouted, "Pants down, hurry up!"

Ginger looked at Doug, partway pushing down his underwear, and stopping, his pants just above his knees.

"Get on wi it," Monica shouted again.

Eventually their pants reached their ankles resting on their trousers. Ginger's shirt front did not quite cover his genitals. A wrinkled-up tiny pink stub showed below his pale blue shirt. Doug's shirt fell to his knees, hiding all. They both stood motionless, staring straight in front, their eyes raised above Monica's head, their faces flushed like shiny ripe cherries.

"Well," said Monica. "Yer 've not finished, lift up yer shirt. Let's see what yer made of."

Slowly, very slowly they lifted up their shirts. Their lips, noses and eyes squeezed together as though they were trying to hide themselves from intruding eyes.

"Hurry up," Monica impatiently commanded.

Doug lifted up his shirt to reveal short sparse black pubic hairs, in which lay hidden a shrivelled, wrinkled, curled up penis, resting on a tight crazed scrotum. Monica went over to Doug and peered closely between the top of his thighs.

"One," a long silence followed.

"Two," she said.

"Come over here, Derek," she added.

Derek and Terry joined Monica, and all three looked intently at Doug's thighs. Derek and Terry giggled. Monica remained very serious.

She looked up at Doug, and said, "Three! You've got a tiny willy. Yer won't get very far with that. Four!"

Ginger stood like a stalagmite rooted to the ground. His face squeezed up, hardly breathing, lips sucked into his mouth, his nose flowing like a washerless tap. His shirt still hanging down. Ginger had not dared to lift it up. Monica looked into Ginger's eyes.

"Five," she said.

She stood back a step, and with her stick lifted up his shirt.

"Where is it?" she said. "Grab yer shirt, Ging," she added.

Ginger tightly took hold of his shirt, the bones of his fingers showing white as he squeezed his shirt tighter and tighter. Monica turned to Derek and said, "He ain't got a willy, Derek. Can you see it?"

Derek had a close look.

"Yer right, Mon. It's so small. I reckon it's shrunk into his belly."

Turning to Terry he said, "Can yer see it, Terry?"

Terry peered at Ginger's belly, and said, "It's a small 'un, Del."

"Six," Monica said.

All three burst out laughing and walked away.

Looking over her shoulder, Monica shouted, "We don't want to join yer rotten gang anyway. Yer silly boggers. Tarrah!"

They made their way back to the playground and sat on the swings, each sucking a bull's eye.

A man and woman holding hands came out of the woods into the clearing. They too burst into laughter as they saw Doug and Ginger with their trousers down, holding up their shirt fronts. They made their way into the play park, A fragment of white shirt, like squeezed out toothpaste, stuck out of the man's flies. His shirt tail hung loosely over the back of his trousers flapping freely in the evening breeze. The woman's partly undone white silk blouse blew bereft outside her skirt in harmony with the man's shirt. Both looked flushed, relaxed, and content, quite unaware of their suggestive appearance.

Humiliated, Doug and Ginger hurriedly pulled up their trousers, and ran into the woods to hide.

"I don't want te be in yuh gang no more, Dug," cried Ginger. "I hate yuh, and yuh rotten gang," he added between sobs.

"Please yer'sen. Cry baby!" said Doug, fumbling in his pocket for a cigarette.

Ginger ran off to the play park, leaving Doug in a cloud of smoke.

Monica, Derek and Terry were on the swings singing,

> *"Swing high, swing low,*
> *Doug's got a silly willy,*
> *Swing to, swing fro.*
> *Ginger's not got a willy.*
> *Up in the air,*
> *Down on the ground.*
>
> *Swing high, swing low,*
> *They've silly little willies.*
> *Swing to, swing fro.*
> *What a lot of silly willies.*
> *Up in the air,*
> *Down on the ground.*
>
> *Swing high, swing low,*
> *Pull up your trousers.*
> *Swing to, swing fro.*

And hide your willies,
Up in the air,
Down on the ground.

The sun came to rest. The singing stopped. The children went home as night moved into the play park. Only the man and woman stayed behind, sitting and cuddling on the park bench.

CHAPTER 22

Exit Miss Weatherspoon

"He had but one eye, and the
popular prejudice runs
in favour of two."

Nicholas Nickleby, ch 4 (Mr Squeers).
Charles Dickens 1812-1870.

CHAPTER 22

Harry heard a loud knock. Thud! Thud! Thud!.

"I'll get it," he shouted to Miss Weatherspoon.

Through the glass threshold he saw a tall coated, hatted figure. Harry opened the front door. The man in the fawn raincoat stood with briefcase in hand.

"Good evening, Sir," he said.

"Good evening," said Harry.

The man put his hand inside the buttoned up flap of his raincoat, and fumbled between his coat and jacket. He pulled out a small black plastic wallet. It lay flat in the palm of his hand. With his thumb he flicked the cover off. It opened at once and lay like a small flat book in his palm.

The man looked at Harry, as if to say, "Bet you can't do that."

He lifted the wallet with his thumb and forefinger, and held it up in front of Harry.

"Detective Sergeant Timothy Ironsides from New Scotland Yard. Fraud Division," he said.

Harry saw a photograph of the man with his name and signature. Before he was able to read more, the wallet was snapped shut with a pop, like a balloon bursting. It was quickly concealed again somewhere within the folds of his raincoat.

"Could I have a word, Sir. Strictly in confidence of course, somewhere private. Don't want to alarm the neighbours, do we, Sir?" said the man.

"Please come in," said Harry.

Harry took him into the front room, shut the door, saying, "Sit down."

"I prefer to stand. If you don't mind, Sir."

He opened up the briefcase, and took out a dog-eared beige folder.

Miss Weatherspoon, with one ear glued to the keyhole and bent almost doubled up, tried desperately to hear and see what was happening behind the closed door. Mitzi, by her side, was sniffing between the door gap and the floor.

The man, hearing Mitzi sniffing, conscious of being over-heard and seen, looked towards the door, screwed up his eyes and started to sniff himself.

"What's that noise?" he said, alarmed.

"Only the dog," said Harry. "I'll let him in," he added.

"Please don't," said the man. "Don't like dogs, brings me out in a rash. Starts me asthma off, can't breathe. Besides they go for me ankles, bite me you know, rather you didn't, if you don't mind, Sir. I think I'll sit down, Sir," said the man, laboriously taking gasps of air.

"Like a cup of tea?" said Harry.

"No, thank you. Perhaps a glass of water, Sir," came the reply.

Harry left the room, shutting the door carefully behind him. He saw Miss Weatherspoon disappear hurriedly into the kitchen with Mitzi chasing at her heels. Harry followed them, collected the water, turned to Miss Weatherspoon saying,

"Keep Mitzi in the kitchen, and please don't eavesdrop."

He returned to the front room to find the man somewhat agitated, both hands resting on his lap with his two thumbs rotating about each other. He looked pale and a little shaken. The man drank the water swallowing one pink and one brown tablet, which he squeezed out of a plastic strip.

"I'm allergic to cats and dogs. I'm alright now," he said.

Harry was beginning to wonder, "Why the visit? Had he done something wrong? Was Derek in some sort of trouble?"

All sorts of things went through his mind. He too, was feeling uneasy. The man just sat, said nothing, with his hands resting on the beige folder on his knee. Both thumbs started to rotate about each other again, first slowly, and then fast, and slowly again. This process repeated itself, until his thumbs came to a standstill. He took off his thick black horn-rimmed glasses, pinched the top of his nose with thumb and forefinger, and rubbed his eyes. He replaced his glasses, looked at Harry, smiled, and resumed his earlier confident persona.

"Sorry about that, Sir" he said.

"How can I help?" said Harry, anxiously.

The man opened the beige folder, took out some photographs, and gave them to Harry.

"Do you recognise the woman in the photographs?"

Harry looked at each one in turn. They were all dissimilar. Their hairstyles and hair colour were different, eyebrows, and eyes, some wore glasses, some had thick red lips, and smiling, some had thin pale pink lips and frowning, some wore high-necked collars with pearl necklaces, some wore large floppy hats, one even wore a nurse's cap. Not one photograph matched the other, apart from a few, where the closeness of the eyes suggested a common feature. Harry looked very closely, comparing each one with the other.

"Yes," he thought. "It's the eyes."

They were the same shape. The same distance from the bridge of the nose. They had the same penetrating look. The eyes were the same in each photograph.

"It's Weatherspoon," he thought. "Yes, it's bloody Weatherspoon."

"Have you seen this woman, Sir?" said the man.

"Not sure," said Harry. "The eyes look familiar."

"We know she's in the area, and we need to speak to her."

"Think it's my housekeeper," said Harry. "She's in the kitchen."

The man stood up quickly. The beige folder slipped off his lap, with all its contents of photographs, and loose papers spreading themselves on the floor.

"No time for these," said the man.

"Follow me," said Harry.

They both rushed into the kitchen, but no Miss Weatherspoon.

"Damn, she's fled," said the man.

Miss Weatherspoon could be seen running through the back garden, bag in hand with Mitzi chasing after her.

"She won't get far," said the man. "I've two plain clothes policemen blocking her exit into the road."

Miss Weatherspoon was last seen caught on the barbed wire fence at the bottom of Harry's garden. The barbed talons holding onto her sky blue directoire knickers, her glasses and hair askew, with Mitzi excitedly barking up at her.

A few minutes later she was gone, all that remained was a ragged piece of sky blue material flapping in the breeze from the barbed wire. Mitzi was hastily trotting up the garden path, as though in hot pursuit of Detective Sergeant Ironsides, who hurriedly returned to the front room with Harry following.

A loud knock came at the door.

"Tel Sergeant Ironsides we've taken the lady to the station," said the plain clothes policemen at the door.

Harry returned to the front room to find Sergeant Ironsides on all fours with his head almost glued to the carpet. He was moving about as though he'd lost something. He looked up at Harry. His left eye was completely closed with his glasses askew.

"Can I help?", said Harry. "Lost something, have you?"

"It's my bloody eye. It's dropped out. Can't see it anywhere. It's a new one. Doesn't fit properly. Cost a bloody fortune," said the Sergeant, shuffling around on his knees, but his eye still eluded him.

Harry started to move furniture. Mitzi joined in the search sniffing the carpet as if she smelt a concealed bone lying low. The presence of Mitzi in the room gave way to a fit of sneezing and short noisy gasps of breath from Sergeant Ironsides. He tried to speak, but his efforts only próduced a rasping wheezing sound. Harry realised that Mitzi had brought on an asthma attack. He picked Mitzi up, and almost flung him into the kitchen. Midway through the air Mitzi let out a belch, and disgorged what appeared to be Sergeant Ironside's glass eye. The eye caught the sunlight sending out coloured sparkles as it dropped onto the red quarry tiled floor. It went 'ping' at each bounce rolling slowly until it hit the table leg, and came to rest. Harry picked up the glass eye, wiped it on his shirt front, collected a glass of water, and went back to the front room. The eye rested in the palm of his hand. A relieved, squinting Sergeant Ironsides picked it up.

"Thanks, thanks very much," he said, fumbling with the eye trying to insert it into its rightful place. He looked up, adjusted his glasses, drank the glass of water in one gulp and coughed.

"That's better. Thank you, Sir," he said, authoritatively.

Harry and the Sergeant searched Miss Weatherspoon's room to find jewellery, including some belonging to Harry's wife, a dog collar inscribed with 'Mitzi', a phone number, and a selection of antique bric-a-brac.

"Better get back to the station, Sir. Would like you to come down at your convenience to make a statement.

No hurry, Sir! You won't be seeing the lady in question again. She's wanted for fraud, impersonation, theft, possibly murder - you name it, she's done it. Thanks for your cooperation, Sir. Good night, Sir?"

Sergeant Ironsides and Miss Weatherspoon, alias Miss Orpwoodie, Doctor Maud Frinkle, Mrs Schneida, Lady Barkley-Pipps, and Sister Mary Joseph, and many more were never seen again.

Beth and Maggi, both puffing away like chimneys at their cigarettes, chattered over their fences.

"Knew she's no good. Too lardy dah. Don't yer know," said Beth.

"It's 'Arry I feel for. Nice bloke, 'Arry," came the reply.

"I'd sew 'is buttons on any day," said Beth.

"Me an all," said Maggie.

"I'd give 'im one an all," said Beth.

"Yer bogga," said Maggi.

They both laughed and went inside.

The following evening a chauffeur-driven Rolls Royce parked outside Harry's house. A tall aristocratic lady emerged from the rear of the car, and followed the chauffeur down the path to Harry's front door. Harry opened the front door to the sound of knocking.

"I've come for Mitzi," said the lady, in a plum voice. "The police telephoned me to say you had my dog."

Mitzi came running to the front door. His mawkish, schmaltzy face looked up at the lady in recognition.

"There you are, darling," she said. "Have you missed your mummy, my precious?"

Mitzi barked, as if to say, 'No'!

She picked Mitzi up, cuddled him gently, stroking his bony head.

Mitzi looked at Harry, Derek and Brian as if to say, "Goodbye. I'll be back."

Without a further word the lady abruptly turned round, and walked back to her car. Mitzi had been reunited with its rightful owner.

"Bitch," thought Harry, as the silver Rolls moved silently down the street.

The two boys and Harry were on their own again, much to Harry's and Derek's relief. Brian was upset initially. He missed Mitzi, and the attention, sweets and pocket money from Miss Weatherspoon.

CHAPTER 23

Grammar School Scholarship

"Examinations are formidable
even to the best prepared,
for the greatest fool may ask
more than the wisest man
can answer."

Lacon (1820) vol. 1, No. 334.
Charles Caleb Colton 1780-1832.

CHAPTER 23

I had taken the entrance exam for St Thomas More's Catholic Grammar School, and eagerly waited the results. At the time I was not too keen on taking the exam, because it would mean leaving my current school friends behind. It was a boys-only school, and it would mean not seeing Monica. It had been my intention to fail the exam for Monica's sake. Fr Ignatius and Dad really wanted me to go to the Grammar School. To please them both I appeared to be enthusiastic, but secretly I'd made up my mind to fail. I wanted to go to the same school as Monica, and would intentionally flop the exam.

Another boy, a Catholic like me, Matty Liddle, took the exam at the same time. He said he couldn't answer most of the questions, and walked out after 20 minutes. I managed to stay the full one and a half hours. Sitting in front of us at the small table was Fr Bede, one of the masters at the school, a short tubby man, with a round face, bald, and wearing steel-framed spectacles. He was reading most of the time, but occasionally he would walk about the class room peering over shoulders looking at our work. If he approved he would say, "Good boy!" If he didn't approve, he'd say, "Try again, boy!"

These interruptions frustrated me to the point that I gave the exam my best, forgetting my intentions to fail. Each time he came round I covered my work up with my hands. This upset him.

"Something to hide, boy?", he'd say, and then give an empathetic smile.

In many ways I dreaded the results, because I thought I might pass. I knew the results were due during the week after Easter. My Dad would stand at the front gate waiting for the postman. Sometimes he'd walk up the street pestering him, trying to get the mail before it was due.

"Any post today?" he'd say politely.

"Sorry! Nothing today, Mr Postlethwaite."

This went on for several days. The day my Dad went to work early the brown envelope arrived. It lay on the mat in the hall - alone, looking very official. I picked it up, turned it over, and on the flap it said 'Thomas More's Grammar School', underneath was the school's coat of arms. It was addressed to my father, so I couldn't open it. I did think of steaming it open, but the last time I steamed a letter open I was found out. The ink, ran, and the paper had gone all wrinkled. I held it up to the light, but couldn't read anything. Just a piece of folded paper which held the clue to my fate. I knew I'd passed the exam, because I wanted to fail. Throwing the envelope back on the mat I rushed upstairs to get my rabbit's tail. Holding it tightly in my hand and frantically squeezing it, I said, walking all over the house, "Please let me fail, please, please."

Brian looked at me as if I was crazy. Mrs Crabtree, our new daily housekeeper, said, "Are you alright, Derek?"

"Don't know," I said politely.

"I mean, yes. I'm alright," I said.

I picked up the envelope, and hid it under the mat out of sight, hoping Dad wouldn't find it.

Later in the day Matty Liddle came up to me in the playground looking very glum.

"How'd yer gerron?" he said.

"Don't know, haven't heard," I said.

"I failed the bogger. Who'd wanna gu te tha tuffee nosed school. It's fer toffs," he said, wiping his runny nose with the back of his hand.

He walked away, kicking a stone, and obviously upset at failing. He turned round, tears in his eyes, looked at me, and said, "S'pect you've passed. Yer lucky bogger. You're a clever tit, yo are, Derek Postlethwaite."

"Don't know," I said.

When I got home after school Mrs Crabtree had laid the table for tea. The dreaded brown envelope lay on Dad's plate. Dad arrived home early, fully aware the exam results had arrived. He picked up the envelope in haste, and tore at the flap to open it. He was heavy-handed, and clumsy. Suddenly he let out a yell, with blood spurting all over the envelope from a cut to his thumb. As he had slid his fingers along the inside of the envelope the sharp brown paper flap had sliced into his thumb.

"Sod it," he said, sucking the blood from his thumb.

He hadn't opened the envelope completely. He was shaking in frustration with blood oozing from his thumb down the inside of his white shirt-sleeved arm.

What didn't soak into his sleeve dripped onto the white tablecloth. Mrs Crabtree saw the incident, and within seconds had the bloody thumb staunched and shrouded in a sterile hygienic white bandage. Dad was ready once more to open the envelope. Both hands were shaking. Nervously he completed splitting the envelope open. By now his entire body was trembling. From the envelope he took a folded white sheet of paper, and opened it up with the edges held between his shaking fingers. I could see the red, blue and gold crest on the top of the letter. I watched Dad's eyes as they moved from side to side across the page. Tears rolled down his cheeks.

He sniffed, saying aloud, "You've done it. You've done it, our Derek."

"Done what," I said. "You've got it. You've got it. You've not only passed, you've got a bloody scholarship, lad."

"What's a scholarship?" I said anxiously, thinking there may be some way out of going to the Grammar School.

"It means I don't have to pay any school fees, 'cos you're a clever lad."

"Oh!", I said.

"Mrs Crabtree," Dad shouted. "Derek's got a scholarship to St Thomas More's Grammar School."

His face radiated with tears, laughter and happiness. I was miserable, and unhappy, but tried not to show my feelings.

"Congratulations! Well done, Derek," said Mrs Crabtree.

My head and shoulders stooped down to hide my misery.

"Cheer up, Derek. You did it." Dad hugged me tightly with joy for himself, not as a proud father or out of any affection for me. He'd won the scholarship really, not me.

"You'll need a complete school uniform, new shoes, school cap, and a good leather satchel for your books. An overcoat for the winter too. Eh! Derek. I'll set you up. You deserve it lad. Can't have you looking like a ragtag."

"What's a ragtag, Dad?" I said.

"You know, ragtag and bobtail," Dad said.

"Don't know," I said.

"A ragamuffin," came the reply.

I was none the wiser and continued to sulk.

"I want you to go round to the presbytery, and show this letter to Fr Ignatius. He'll be tickled pink when he reads it. Off you go lad," said Dad, giving me the letter.

Reluctantly I dragged my feet to the presbytery which was up a very steep hill, about half a mile away. I rang the front door bell and waited. Over the front door above the lintel was a recess in the wall containing a statue of Our Lady of Sorrows, according to Fr Ignatius. It had been newly painted in gold and a deep brilliant blue. Our Lady's long flowing robes shone bright in the failing evening sun. A pigeon perched on her shoulder added further to the bird lime already covering her feet. I rang the bell again, secretly hoping the house was empty. The small front garden looked out onto the busy road. Catholics who drove by the presbytery in their cars, lorries, buses and the like always sounded their horns as they went by. It was a greeting, hello, a good morning, afternoon, or evening.

Fr Ignatius would respond by saying out loud, "Bless you. Peace be with you," and then cross himself.

The front door stammered hesitantly as it was pulled open rubbing against the carpet. It was flung ajar with Julie clinging to the door knob.

"Oh! It's you, Derek. Come in. Why didn't you come to the back door? I know, you've come to see Father, not me," she said, giving me a tight hug.

A frisson of excitement ran through me as her firm bosoms hardened against my small body. She held onto me tighter and tighter. The air was gradually being squeezed from my lungs. I was gasping when she released her hold.

"Lovely to see you. You've made my day," she said.

"I've got to see Fr Ignatius," I said.

"He's out. Back soon though. Have a jam tart whilst you're waiting," she said.

She took my hand and led me into the warm bread-smelling kitchen. I sat down at the scrubbed clean kitchen table to a plate of jam and lemon curd tarts. Julie sat down at the table opposite me with her large rounded breasts almost resting on the table top. They were not ugly big, but pleasurably big, motherly and comforting. I loved to be with Julie and enjoyed the loving attention she always gave me. I always felt at ease with her. Mrs Crabtree, our new housekeeper, was the same. She didn't have big breasts though, only small ones. Sometimes she didn't seem to have any at all.

Mrs Crabtree was kindness itself. She treated me and Brian as equals, with no favouritism either way, not like the Dragon. Julie and Mrs Crabtree could not replace my mother, who I missed all the time, every day. They were both naturally kind, loving and understanding. My mother, on the other hand, had always been there for me. The umbilical cord had never been severed. We were still inextricably joined. She was irreplaceable and the void she had left in my life could never be filled. Julie, Mrs Crabtree, and even Clare whom I met on the train, went some way towards assuaging my heartache. I even found comfort in Monica's friendship. They compensated for the Dragon's hostility, and hatred towards me, and the mysterious loss of my mother.

The front door slammed shut, the house seemed to shake.

"That'll be Father now. He's always noisy, bless him," said Julie.

Fr Ignatius came bursting into the kitchen.

"Cup of tea, please, Julie. I'm gasping," he said. "The bloody Bishop will be the death of me. He's unsympathetic, lacks humanity, doesn't understand his flock, shows no mercy, nor understanding as to how people really live. He's not in tune with the real world. Same goes for the Pope, and his entourage. The church is isolated, and inward- looking. They all live on another planet."

Fr Ignatius and Julie looked at each other with tears in their eyes.

"Let's get married, Julie, and join the Anglicans. They're not perfect, but they're more liberal, and understanding."

Fr Ignatius collapsed in a chair at the table, saw me, put his head in his hands in exasperation, and was obviously upset by his meeting with the Bishop. He remained silent, only sobbing. Julie looked at me embarrassed, and hurriedly made a pot of tea.

"Your tea, Father," she said, placing a cup of tea at his elbow.

"Thanks," he said.

"Sorry, Derek, Julie. Had a difficult meeting with his Lordship."

He sucked at his too hot tea, until only the tea leaf dregs were left. Julie poured another cup, which was drunk the same way.

Fr Ignatius got up, turned to me, saying, "Goodbye and God bless you, Derek."

He walked out of the kitchen, making the sign of the cross, giving me his blessing. I felt disturbed, and anxious, at his distress. He looked tired, and at the end of his tether.

"Father's upset and very tired. You'd better see him another day, Derek, if you don't mind," said Julie. "Can I give him a message?" she continued.

"No, thank you, nothing important," I said.

Julie gave me a kiss on the cheek, squeezed my hand, and waved me goodbye. She was trying hard to hold back her tears. I ran down the hill all the way home, breathless, red-faced and crying, to be greeted by my impatient father.

"Well! I bet Fr Ignatius was very pleased when he read the letter. What did he say, lad?"

"He wasn't in. He hasn't seen it," I said, feeling worked up by the day's events.

"That's a pity. Better go tomorrow. Let's have the letter for safe keeping," said Dad.

I went through my pockets, but couldn't find it.

"Must have lost it somewhere," I thought.

Mrs Crabtree overhead our conversation.

"Is this what you're looking for. I found it on the table," she said.

"You stupid boy," said Dad. "You never took it with you. You'd better pull your socks up when you go to Grammar School," he added, in a fierce voice.

"Not going to Grammar School," I said.

"Why not?" Dad replied, in anger.

"Don't know," I said.

Dad lifted his hand to strike me, but thought better of it.

"We'll talk about it tomorrow, eh, Derek," he said, trying to be patient and paternal.

"Don't know," I repeated.

"I give up," came an abrupt reply.

Taking his pipe and tobacco from the table he stormed off into the garden.

Miss Crabtree tried to console me.

"Walk me home, Derek. We'll have an ice cream on the way,"

She took my hand, and gave it a squeeze of affection, as if to say without speaking,

"Never mind. I love you."

We walked down the street, both licking ice creams, and laughing. I soon began to feel better.

I never saw Fr Ignatius again. He had a massive heart attack that same evening and never recovered. Julie was heartbroken. After the funeral she disappeared out of my life forever. I heard she had retuned to Ireland. I was upset because she had never said goodbye. I felt I had been betrayed again. I had lost my mentor, in Fr Ignatius, a kind and lovely man - he never did chastise me for drinking the altar wine - and Julie, who treated me as her own. Once more my world was falling apart.

"What is this God doing to me?" I thought.

I was too young to share my feelings with others. I cried late into the night, red eyed and unable to sleep.

I loved Fr Ignatius and Julie, and now they too were gone, disappearing without a trace, like fleeting clouds.

CHAPTER 24

Six Months Later St Thomas More's Grammar School

"There are no Rules in this school.
But God help you if you break them."

Anonymous.

CHAPTER 24

Clouds hung low in the morning sky with a faint mist clinging to the tops of trees and houses. The early morning created tones of purples, blues, browns and greens against the misty backdrop of buildings, distant fields and woods. Nothing seemed to be its true colour. The effect was almost surreal. A chill gust of wind rustled through the trees. The crisp air made me hold myself tight and squeezed-up in order to create more body warmth. I shivered more in apprehension of going to my new school, rather than feeling cold.

It was early September, and autumn seemed to have arrived early. On days like these my Dad would take me mushrooming. We never found many. Those we did find were full of maggot holes and uneatable.

I was with Dad at the bus stop waiting for the school bus to take me to my new school. Dad insisted, much to my chagrin, that he would escort me on my first day. Anyone would think *he* was starting school with all the fuss he was making. He even put brown shoe polish on my leather satchel to give it an extra shine. The brown polish rubbed off onto my new blazer, which didn't please him.

I was not happy all dressed-up like a coloured circus clown. I wore a maroon cap with four strands of sky blue shiny braid spiralling from the centre to the edge of the cap, with the school crest sitting central above the peak. The maroon blazer was similar, with blue braid round the cuffs and lapels, the school crest emblazoned on the breast pocket. My white shirt with school tie and socks to match completed my school uniform. I felt a freak, and envied my junior class mates who'd started at the secondary modern school a week earlier. They were able to wear anything they liked.

"Aye up, Del," shouted Mike Flannagan.

He sped down the High Street on his paper round, with his newspaper canvas bag flapping in the wind.

With head bent down cycling at full speed, he cried, "Good luck, Del."

"Thanks, Mike," I said silently.

He disappeared round a bend in the road almost colliding with an oncoming van with horns blaring. An unseen cat meowed in reply.

On each side of the high street were rows of houses. Opposite the bus stop were semis with small front gardens, others were terraces with their front doors opening directly onto the pavement. A few shops broke up the line of dwellings. Those on the bus stop side were detached and much larger. They stood well back from the High Street, with long gravel drives, tall trees, lawns, and well manicured gardens. They were well hidden from the road with high hedges and stone walls.

The dawn chorus had almost finished, apart from a few birds still singing, not wanting to miss out in their morning greetings. A dog joined in with an occasional barking.

The milkman's float hummed by with bottles ratting in its wake.

Fresh bread smells filled the air from the local bakers.

Letterbox flaps clattered as the postmen fleetingly dashed up and down, to and fro, discharging the Royal Mail.

The gold hands against the purplish face of the church clock stood at 7.30am and a single chime pierced the air.

The small town was waking, curtains drawn back, and slowly everyone was on the move, as another day came to life.

Down the street a door banged shut, shattering the stillness. A man with an umbrella and briefcase came running out of his garden and up the street to the bus stop. An unlit cigarette hung from his mouth.

"Bus gone yet?" he said, panting.

"Hope not," Dad said.

"Missed the bugger yesterday," the man said.

He was tall and lanky with greasy swept back black hair. His black horn-rimmed spectacles matched his hair, and magnified his blue eyes. A thin scraggy neck, with an enormous Adam's apple, which looked as though he had an egg stuck half-way down his throat made him look like a scarecrow.

"Rushed off me bloody feet, every morning alike," he said.

He lit his cigarette, and coughed at the first intake of smoke.

"Be the death of me, fags"! he said, fitfully coughing.

"Get up earlier, and stop smoking," Dad replied.

To which the man angrily retorted, still coughing, "Mind yer bloody business. What's it to do wi you!"

"Only trying to be helpful," Dad said.

The man, still coughing, looked at Dad and was about to say something when the bus arrived.We took our seats and remained silent.

I closed my eyes as the bus rattled along towards the unknown. My thoughts turned to Monica, who the day before had started her new school. She was going to a public boarding school for girls only, somewhere further north. She too had to get all dressed up in a new school uniform. Her colours were mid grey and pillar box red. In the winter she wore a grey felt hat with a red band, and the school crest stuck in the middle, but in the summer her hat was a boater made of straw. Monica had matured rapidly during the last six months. She was much taller than me now, and her breasts were very big. They wobbled when she moved quickly.

We were walking slowly along a path canopied with tree branches, the sun sending shafts of light through the gaps. Monica spontaneously reached out for my hand, and squeezed it quite hard. I felt excited, and offered to carry the bag containing the picnic. Bird song filled the noiseless quiet. The spicy sharp strong smell of wild garlic hung heavy in the stillness. Now and then an agitated pigeon's cry filtered through the trees. The path became narrow as we went further into the woods. Stones and twisting tree roots made the path hard and uneven, causing our feet to ache. The air became damp with the smell of earth, rotting wood, and vegetation. Small animals scurried through the undergrowth. Chinks of blue sky and sun punctured the tree cover. Whispers of air rustled overhead leaves. The further we walked the darker it became, and the tighter Monica held my hand. It was eerie.

We came out of the woods into a newly mown meadow. There was a clean smell of scented hay. The dry coarse freshly cut grass swished against our legs as we walked, making them sting, raw and red. We found a comfortable spot to sit down for our picnic of lemonade, squashed potted meat sandwiches, and chocolate sponge cake. After a short time our bottoms began to tingle and itch from the dry prickly grass. We talked about all sorts of things, Monica asking all the questions, making me blush and feel uncomfortable.

"Do you miss your mother, Derek?" she said.

"Yes."

"What happened?"

"She died."

"I'm sorry. Do you remember her?"

"Sometimes I do. Sometimes I don't. It's funny. I don't understand. I wish I could. I dream about her sometimes, and my dreams are very real and powerful. Then I wake up, and she's gone."

"That's a pity. I'm sorry, Derek. Was your mother beautiful?"

"She was beautiful for me."

"Do you want some more chocolate sponge, Derek?"

"Yes, please."

Monica gave me what was left of the cake. She held up her right hand with three fingers covered in chocolate. Slowly she put one finger into my mouth.

"Please lick the chocolate off, Derek," she said.

Unhurriedly I sucked off the thick creamy chocolate, deliberately taking my time as her finger slid in and out of my mouth like a piston driving an engine. I repeated the process on her other two chocolaty fingers.

"Let me lick your fingers, Derek," she said, pressing the fingers of my right hand into the cake's chocolate cream.

She too, licked my fingers. This physical intimate exchange gave us an understanding of each other, which was personal and privy only to us. We ate the rest of the cake between us, licking any chocolate off each other's fingers, laughing and smiling at each other in the process.

"Did your mother have nice breasts?" said Monica.

"Don't know," I said.

I wasn't going to tell Monica about my mother's beautiful breasts. They were a special memory for me. I tried sometimes to visualise being breastfed by my mother when I was a baby, but found it difficult to simulate. I often thought I would like to emulate being breastfed. Perhaps I could experiment with someone. As these thoughts went through my mind I was staring directly at Monica's bosoms. The top of her dress stretched tightly across her heaving breasts, moving up and down as she breathed - in and out. A small gap between two pearl white buttons closed and opened with each breath, unmasking naked flesh. The gap became larger as Monica's breathing intensified. Monica seemed aware of my interest. I started to blush. She remained cool. We looked into each other's eyes. She looked longingly at me. I was beginning to feel a nervous pleasurable anticipation.

"Do you think I have nice breasts, Derek?" said Monica, shuffling closer to me.

"Don't know," I said, feeling awkward by the question. "How would I know? I haven't seen them in the flesh, or felt them. If she needs my opinion she'd better put her money where her breasts are," I thought to myself.

"Would you like to see them, Derek?"

"Don't know!" I said. "Well I did know, but I couldn't tell her I was longing to see her wonderful breasts," I thought.

She unfastened all the buttons of her dress down to her midriff, slid her arms out of the short sleeves, letting the dress drop down over her shoulders to spread festooned on the mown grass. She leant back, her arms taking the weight of her body, and pushed forward her chest. Her nippled breasts sheathed in a brassiere of white silk lace stood out proud and inviting.

Looking at me intently, she said, "Would you like me to undo my bra, Derek?"

"Don't know," I said.

By this time I was hot. My forehead was red and clammy.

"Of course I wanted the bloody bra off," I thought.

Monica reached with both hands behind her back, and undid the bra strap. At last her breasts were unfettered, set free, and nakedly visible. They took on a new dimension, sensual, tumescent, powerful, fertile, temping and seductive. They hung slightly pendulous in joyous vision, their secrets revealed.

"Would you like to caress them, Derek."

"Don't know," I said.

Wow! I desperately wanted to fondle them, rub my face between them, kiss them, suck at her upright noble nipples.

By now Monica was almost facing me, and only an arm's length away. Slowly, and quite deliberately she reached out, took my hands in hers, and placed them on each of her breasts. My hands were too small to hold them in their fullness, but each breast lay nestled, cupped in my palms. I knelt before her in a gesture of God-fearing devotion, with both hands resting comfortably under her bosoms. They were warm, swollen, soft and yet firm, as my hands lingered in a frenzied thrill of excitement. Her nipples felt hard against the palms of my small hands, and almost punctured the flesh. My whole body froze, became excited, and shocked like the force on an electric current penetrating my subconscious. Monica's breathing became intense, and broke the silence as we both relished the experience, looking into each other's eyes. She leant forward, and kissed me gently with her moist plump unforgettable lips. A bird alighted on the grass for a few seconds, shook its head, defecated, and took off again.

"Wake up, Derek! Daydreaming again. You'll have to pull your socks up, lad," said Dad, stirring me from my musing.

For the moment I was not conscious of my whereabouts, or where I was going on the bus. Slowly I crawled out of my reverie, and joined the real world.

"How far have we to go, Dad?"

"Bout ten minutes now, I should think," he replied.

I lapsed into my subconscious again recalling my adventure with Monica in Turner's Wood. The experience in its isolation sharpened my thoughts of losing my mother, and discovering Monica, Julie and Clare, and the closeness we had enjoyed. The physical element of both girl and woman in some way was a necessary replacement to compensate for the loss of my mother. It was not a sexual fantasy, but a surrogate need. I needed the warmth, love and intimacy to replace my Mother, who had been my lifeblood. There seemed some sort of parallel between the living and the dead. My mother was lost forever, apart from in my fantasies. Monica, Julie and Clare had been physically with me, and although they had now disappeared out of my life, they were still alive. I was bereft again. My innocent love for Monica was thwarted by difficulties. She had disappeared to a different school. I had imagined we could be together all the time, and enjoy a happy girl and boy relationship growing up into adult life. I desperately needed a mother replacement, but everyone was deserting me, even Fr Ignatius had gone. I was unwittingly trying to retreat from the ill-fated realities of my life through my imagination. I was on my way to a new school without friends. I felt depressed and miserable. I searched in my jacket pocket for my rabbit's tail, and held it tight. The bus came to a grinding halt at the school gates.

We were met by Fr Francis, a tall, lanky man with a shiny bald head and stubbled face. He smelt of stale sweat, beer and cigarettes.

Dad left me with Fr Francis, who barked, "Follow me, boy."

He took me into a dismal room, smelling of cats, with other boys sitting at desks.

"Name, boy?" he asked, glaring at me as if I had no right to be in the room.

"Derek, Sir," I said.

"Derek what, boy? I'm a priest, not a knight of the realm. Tell me a knight from ancient history, boy".

I stood silent and frightened.

"Go on then," he shouted.

"Don't know, Sir."

"You stupid boy. You address me as 'Father'."

"Yes, Father."

"Well then, a knight from ancient history boy?"

"Don't know, Sir. Sorry! I mean Father, Father."

"Sir Walter Raleigh, boy."

"Yes, Father."

"Your name, boy."

"Derek, Father. Postlethwaite, Father. Derek Postlethwaite, I mean."

"Derek Postlethwaite what, boy?" He shouted, sending a shower of spittle over me.

"Don't know."

"You ought to bloody well know by now, boy. Derek Postlethwaite, Father. Alright boy?" he yelled.

"Yes, Father."

"Sit over there, Postlethwaite. Next to that pink fat boy, and don't talk," he bellowed, sending more spittle over me.

Nervously I sat down behind a desk next to the pink fat boy. There were 18 boys sitting at desks, each looking nervous and frightened.

Fr Francis wore a long black sleeved cassock down to his ankles. A black leather belt held the garment ruched together in the middle. One end of the belt hung from his waist, and swayed to and fro as he walked. A black cowl covered his shoulders, chest and arms, underneath dangled a wooden crucifix on a leather thong. The front of the cowl acted as a bib, collecting spilt food, dribble, and loose scales of dry, dead skin from his polished scalp. He paced up and down in front of us holding a clip board in his left hand, and swinging the end of his leather belt around in circles in his right hand. He looked at me menacingly.

"Have you seen Wormwood, boy?" he said.

I remained silent, hoping someone else would say something. Terror hung in the air. He glared at me.

"You dumb?" What's yer name, boy?"

"Derek, Sir. I mean Postlethwaite, Father."

"Where's Wormwood? Anyone seen Woodworm? He's bloody late. What a shower we've got this term."

A small stout man wearing a monocle entered the room. He was dressed the same as Fr Francis, but cleaner and much smarter.

"Good morning, Headmaster," said Fr Francis.

"Health and Benediction in the Lord, Francis," came the reply, in a gentle cultured voice.

"New boys all arrived, Francis?"

"One missing, Headmaster, by the name of Woodworm."

"He'll turn up, no doubt. Go and look for him, Francis."

"Certainly, Headmaster. Right away, Headmaster," he said, meekly disappearing, taking his overbearing attitude with him.

"Health and Benediction in the Lord, boys," said the Headmaster, smiling at us.

"Father Francis just sees to the new boys on arrival. He's not on the teaching staff. He does odd jobs and works in the kitchens. Now, boys You'll have gathered I'm the Headmaster. I also teach botany. Does anyone know what botany is?"

All remained silent.

"It is the study of plants. We'll be studying their classification, structure, physiology, ecology, and economic importance, and the biological characteristics of the plants. The Headmaster sat down at a small table, hands clasped together, his facial muscles tightly clenched holding his monocle in his left eye.

"Does anyone know what a stamen is?" he said.

A boy shouted out from the back.

"Is it a boy's willy?"

The monocle dropped from its firm hold on the eye, and hung loosely from the Head's podgy red neck.

"What's a willy, dear boy?"

"A thingy for making babies, Father Headmaster."

"What's your name, boy?"

"Tom Downhill, Father Headmaster."

"Well done, Downhill. A willy, or a thingy, is called a penis. That's its real name. It's the male organ of copulation for producing babies, and urine secretion. A stamen is the male organ of a flower, consisting of a stalk, like a filament with an anther in which pollen is produced. This is the flower's reproductive seed, like a man's seed. Don't worry about it, boys. When we have a real botany lesson we can look at it in greater detail, and I'll make it easier for you all to understand."

My mind began to wander again. I was not able to concentrate, and didn't understand what the Head was talking about. He stood over me, his podgy red monocled face looking into my eyes as I stared up at him, frightened and alone.

"What's your name, dear boy?" he said, sternly.

"Don't know," I said, in terror.

"Don't know your name, dear boy?"

"Derek Postlethwaite, Sir. I mean, Father. Sorry, I mean Headmaster. Father," I said, now feeling paralysed with fright. Unconsciously I put my hand in my jacket pocket feeling for my rabbit's tail for comfort. It wasn't there. I felt in the other pocket. It wasn't there either. I fumbled about in both pockets, but the rabbit's tail had gone. I felt doomed, and started to cry, big salty tears rolled down my cheeks, into my mouth, and down my chin, dripping onto the desk.

"Have you lost something, dear boy?" said the Headmaster.

"Don't know, Sir. Father. I mean, Headmaster," I said.

At that moment Fr Francis appeared, clipboard held at the ready. He'd been smoking. A strong smell of tobacco filled the air, forcing the Headmaster to distance himself.

"Well, Francis, any sign of Wormhole?"

"No, Headmaster. He's not turned up yet."

"I'll telephone his parents," said the Headmaster, leaving the room.

Fr Francis paced up and down the room, head bent, looking at the floor as though he had something on his mind.

He stopped in front of Derek, looked down at him and said, "Is that your dead mouse on the floor, Postleton?"

"Don't know," I said, looking down at my rabbit's tail.

Fr Francis picked it up between forefinger and thumb, holding it at arm's length.

"Who owns this dead mouse?" he said, enraged, looking at the boys in turn.

Each boy with pursed lips, eyes squinting with knitted brows, pinched noses, frowning with fear, and wrinkled fluted faces, sat mortified in unbroken silence. Fr Francis stormed out of the room, across the playground and threw the so-called dead mouse in the river.

"Anymore mice, dead or alive go straight in the river," he said.

A faint knock was heard at the door.

"Yes," shouted Fr Francis.

The knock was heard again.

"Open the bloody door, and come in," shouted Fr Francis, much louder, sending showers of spittle everywhere.

The door was gingerly opened, and a thin bespectacled, freckled-faced boy stood in the doorway.

"What do you want, boy?"

"Nothing, Father," said the boy.

"What's your name, boy?"

"Cyril, Father."

Fr Francis approached the boy to within twelve inches, bent down, and looked straight into his eyes. With thumb and index finger he pinched his left ear, and pulled him into the room. The boy let out a high shrill yelp of pain.

"Cyril what, boy?" bellowed Fr Francis, into his other ear.

"Wormwood, Father."

"So you are Woodworm. Thank you for joining us," shouted Fr Francis.

Cyril stood petrified. A wet patch appeared in the crotch of his trousers. The patch got bigger, and a slow deliberate trickle ran down the inside of both trousers legs making a small pool between his feet. Cyril stood looking at us, not realising what he'd done. He constantly pushed the bridge of his glasses with his middle finger to settle on the ridge of his nose. This was repeated time and time again.

"You dirty boy, go and sit down, Woodworm. I'll sort you out later," shouted Fr Francis.

A bell sounded.

"Stand! Walk out quietly. Fr Basil will take over after break."

We filed out silently, relieved to get into the fresh air away from the tyranny of Fr Francis.

The pink fat boy I sat next to was Barry Fry. He was overweight with a flushed podgy face, fair haired, with a faint soft down moustache. His squinting eyes, Japanese like, were almost hidden by his puffy high cheek bones. He ambled from side to side as he walked. Outside in the playground eighteen of us huddled together, frightened and intimidated by Fr Francis.

"Can we be friends?" said Fry.

"Don't know," I said. "Well 'err, yes! Don't see why not," I continued.

"Want a Mars bar, Postleton?"

"Postlethwaite's my name. Yes, please," I said.

Ali Shah, a tall boy with thick black wavy hair, big, dark, almost black, penetrating eyes, his hairy face full of ripe pustules shouted, "Anyone want a fag? Do wi one me'sen."

Two boys eagerly took one each from the proffered new shiny packet. The cellophane wrapping caught up in a wisp of air floated away. The two boys, Tim Heather-Barrow, and Jack Tarrant, lit up and nervously puffed away. Ali Shah seemed to swallow the smoke without exhaling, like a seasoned smoker, whereas Jack and Tim sucked in and out quickly, coughing between each puff.

Cyril Wormwood surreptitiously joined me and Barry. He said nothing, just listened to us talking, looking from one to the other. He repeatedly adjusted his thick round tortoiseshell spectacles to fit his lean freckled face. His brown greasy hair dangling over his forehead and eyes. He seemed oblivious to his urine soaked trousers.

Wormwood looked at us both, dumbstruck, shaking and in shock, desperately wanting to be included. Fr Francis had humiliated him in front of the other boys, and reduced him to a physical and mental wreck. We both looked at him. Tears rolled down his cheeks. He started to tremble.

"Want a Mars bar, Wormwood?" I said, feeling sorry for him.

"T 't thanks," he said.

The bell sounded to return to our classrooms. The three of us kept together as best we could, amongst a throng of unruly older boys - all trying to get through the doorway at once. In the corridor the noise stopped, and graciousness prevailed. Each boy calmly went into his classroom. We three found our classroom and sat in individual desks next to each other in the second row, with Wormwood in the middle.

Fr Basil stood in front of us smiling, showing his discoloured uneven teeth. He stood about six feet tall, possibly in his early forties. His face was scarred by pock marks, speckled in shades of purple, and crimson. His shiny pitch black hair was swept back from his forehead, and kept in place by hair grease resembling thick engine oil. He wore the same black habit as Fr Francis, only cleaner, apart from snowy white specks of dandruff covering his shoulders. He looked at us with deep cadaverous staring eyes, smiled, and said in a loud voice, "Splendid! What a terrific bunch of new boys. Super! But don't piss me around, or I'll piss you around - in circles. Eh! Know where we all stand, eh? Excellent."

Fr Basil was our form master. He spent the rest of the morning explaining the School Rules, School House system, obligatory weekly chapel and confession, social graces, punctuality, homework, sports and so on. We were then allocated to our respective Houses. By happy coincidence, Fry, Wormwood and me were assigned to the same House - St Georges. Alec Pilkington, a sixth former, was our House Captain. Pilkington, although only eighteen, looked and acted like a young man in his early twenties. His voice was a rich cultured baritone, sounding like the honeyed tones of the saxophone. A thin moustache, naturally curly hair, and blue eyes set him apart from the rest of the sixth form. Out of school uniform he could be seen often in a brown felt trilby hat, smoking a pipe, wearing a smart suit and sporting a red cravat. More often than not he'd be driving one of his father's many cars, with a pretty girl at his side.

Osbert Pilkington, Senior, was a school benefactor, and owner of a nearby brewery. In these circumstances the school had to overlook many of Pilkington Junior's indiscretions, especially a recent assignation in the cricket pavilion with a certain lady. The lady had been identified by a white lace-edged handkerchief embroidered in red with the initials L.H. Other evidence suggested that carnal passions had taken place. The teachers were all priests, with one exception - Miss Lizzie Hagswell. She took the lower school for Physical Education. Miss Hagswell was introduced to us just before the end of our first day, perhaps to encourage us to attend school the next day. Our first lesson was games. She was in her early twenties, although we thought of her as much older, and looked upon her as a mother figure.

A tall and commanding lady, well built with no superfluous fat, a nipped-in waist, wide hips, and rounded tight buttocks, enhanced by long slender well-shaped legs. She always wore colour co-ordinated shorts and T-shirts, allowing her well defined, not oversized breasts to shudder as she walked. Her long thick blonde hair, tied with matching ribbon, nestled in the nape of her neck. She was a fine handsome Epicurean woman, with big cornflower blue eyes, retrousse' nose, and bee-stung lips. Her mouth was large, revealing passion. At every opportunity she flaunted herself between staff and boys. They all loved her for it, especially the celibate priests. Heads turned as she walked by, their primal urges aroused. They glanced sideways, quickened their pace, slowed down, stopped, anything to get as near as possible to the Grecian beauty. Miss Hagswell loved the attention.

My day ended with Fr Basil reprimanding me for speaking to Wormwood.

"I'd only asked if he was alright, Father," I said.

"You don't talk in my lessons, unless I speak to you. Next time, boy, you'll get a caning. Get the message boy?" said Fr Basil.

"Yes, Father," I said.

"Stand up when you speak to me, boy," he said, angrily.

I stood up, shaking and silent.

Fr Basil addressed the class.

"For homework, write two thousand words on how you enjoyed your first day at school. I want it neat, no spelling mistakes, and written in ink by tomorrow morning. Off you go, quietly, don't talk, or I'll cane the bloody lot of you - you shower of halfwits. Splendid!" he added, feeling pleased with himself.

He lifted his cane high above his shoulders, bringing it down with a crash onto the table top. The ends split at the explosion of bamboo against oak. The long pithy stems splayed out in outrage, indignant at their treatment. Our bodies cringed as we trundled out , heads and bodies stooped, not daring to breathe. In the playground we ran amok. A happy release from the oppression of school, and the tyranny of priests.

Miss Hagswell walked across the playground. Her tall slim figure oscillating in consummate time.

Maurice Woolsack was heard to exclaim, "Wow!" in his rusty voice, followed by an inaudible sound, finishing with 'her one', Maurice was the oldest boy and most mature of the new boys. He almost had a moustache, dark brown hair with thick eyebrows meeting in the middle, like a long thick hairy caterpillar. His hands were constantly in his pockets, moving about. He was nicknamed 'Wanker'.

Miss Hagswell reached the edge of the playground, turned round, smiled teasingly and said, "Hello, boys! See you soon."

We were too stunned to respond. Even Woolsack was unable to make comment.

CHAPTER 25

The Park

"Women. *Rabbit rabbit rabbit women*
Tatter and Titter
Women prattle
Women waffle and witter ....
.............Women gossip Women giggle
Women niggle-niggle-niggle
Men Talk.
Women yatter
Women chatter ....
Women yap yap yap ....
Bossy Women Gossip
Girlish Women Giggle
Women natter, Women nag
Women niggle niggle niggle.
Men Talk" ....

Men Talk (Rap).
Liz Lockhead 1947-

CHAPTER 25

For late afternoon the sun was still warm as it moved across the sky dipping slowly towards the west, preparing to slip away quietly, and bring the day to a close. Some people were walking their dogs. Lovers were stretched out on the grass, fondling and kissing. Shoppers and workers were taking a short cut across the park to avoid the busy road. School boys and girls were having a sly smoke and experimenting with each other, glad to be free from school, and hurrying home.

"Gorra fag?" said Beth, rummaging through her large plastic handbag.

The bag was a jumble of articles, containers, anything from a corkscrew to a tin of fish paste. After several attempts she pulled out a box of matches.

"Exchange no robbery," said Beth.

"Thanks, midduck," said Maggi, striking a match, which immediately went out.

After several attempts, both puffed away contentedly between bouts of coughing.

"Bloody fags gi' me palpitations with all this bloody coughing."

"Ah! Know what yer mean, meks me eyes watter," said Beth, wiping her eyes with the back of her hand.

"Look at them dotty boggers, 'Ees gorr 'is 'and up 'er clouts. Look, Beth. The dotty bogger."

On the bank a couple were groping each other in wild abandon. Flies unbuttoned, petticoats lifted. They sank into self-indulgent raptures, kissing with animal passion.

"My dear, Rupert, not here. What are you doing?" said the girl.

They both stood up, adjusted their dress, held hands, and walked into the bushes. Their passions aroused.

"She'll be up 't spout, soon as eggs is eggs," said Maggi. "Mebbe she's a bun in 'oven o'ready at the rate them is at it," replied Beth.

Derek trudged across the park eating an ice cream. His school cap was awry, socks were down to his ankles. His knee was grazed and bleeding, with blood trickling down his ivory-skinned legs. His tie was undone, and ice cream splashes spotted his blazer. He stopped, looked around, walked over to a bench, and sat down. A bird alighted at the far end of the bench, and started to sing. Derek broke off the end of his cornet, and held it out for the bird. It hopped along the slatted bench, took the biscuit, gave out a shrill whistle in thanks, and flew off.

"Perhaps it's my guardian angel," he thought.

Derek pondered about his day, trying to come to terms with his new school. He hated it, and the masters. They were repressed sadists. The only saving grace was Miss Hagswell. The thought of her reminded him of Clare and Monica. His emotions gave way to tears. He got up, wiped his cheeks with his fingers, and slowly continued his way home.

"Is that 'Arrys lad yonder?" said Beth.

"Ah! Rekkon so," said Maggi.

'E looks posh w' is new school clothes don 'ee," said Beth.

"Dus an all. A proper toff I rekkon," said Maggi.

"Is mam wud 'av bin proud on 'im. Don't yo know," came the reply.

"Wud an all," muttered Maggi.

"Ey up Del!" shouted Maggi.

Derek, lost in his thoughts, looked up in the direction of the sound. He saw two seated figures frantically waving at him. He waved back, and walked on.

"Want a duddo, Del?" shouted Beth.

Derek pretended not to hear. He wasn't sure what a 'duddo' was.

"Possibly a sweet," he thought.

A cyclist rode by, chased by a dog.

"Gerrof yer bike, no biking in't park, yooth," yelled Maggi.

The cyclist came within a few feet of them, turned round, lifted up his two fingers in a V sign, kicked out at the dog, lost his balance, and fell off. His expletives were lost in Beth and Maggi's laughter.

"You mukki bogga!" said Beth, followed by Maggi's rebuttal.

"Yo dutti sod! Mind yo language!"

The cyclist limped off, wheeling his bike.

Beth and Maggi were silent for a few moments. Their heads were bent down in deep thought, with hands resting on their laps.

Maggi looked up and said, ""Looks black over Bill's mother's, Beth."

"Berra gerrof 'ohm before it pisses down," said Beth.

"Cud do wi a pee any rode," came the reply.

"Me too. Squee'ez yer buttucks," said Beth, making an agonizing face.

They both stood up, pulled down their dresses, adjusted their underwear - bras and pants by furtive hand movements. They slowly walked off. Beth's big bum wobbled as she walked. Whilst Maggi's stick body strutted along beside her.

The couple surreptitiously came out of the bushes looking bashful, they were dishevelled and red faced with guilt. Some loose silky garments hung flapping from the girl's handbag as they walked away, hand in hand.

"Tarrah then," said Beth.

"Tarrah, midduk," said Maggi, as they parted company.

"See yer!"

"See yer, duk!"

CHAPTER 26

Mortal Sin

"*Masturbation: the primary sexual activity of mankind. In the nineteenth century, it was a disease; in the twentieth, it's a cure.*"

The Second Sin (1973) "Sex."
Thomas Szasz 1920 –

CHAPTER 26

"Who hasn't masturbated?" said Fr Louis, the Christian Doctrine teacher.

The boys remained silent, and looked glum.

"Well then. Who's masturbated," said Fr Louis, in a louder voice.

Still no response from the class. His network of purple veins became more prominent under his pale papery skinned face.

"You at the back. The boy with the big nose and pimples. Stand up," he shouted.

All remained still and silent. Fr Louis walked between the desks to the back row. He seized a boy by his hair and lifted him to his feet. The boy yelled out in pain. Tufts of hair fell to the desk and floor as Fr Louis released his hold.

"What's yer name, boy?" he said.

"Gareth Jones, Father."

"You Welsh, boy?"

"No, Father."

"When did you last masturbate, Jones?"

Jones stood still, and silent.

"Well!" said Fr Louis, eyeballing him.

"What does 'masturbate' mean, Father?"

"Ah! We're getting somewhere. To masturbate is to stimulate your genital organs for the purpose of sexual pleasure. In other words playing with yourself, boy. Do you understand?"

"Yes, Father."

"When did you last masturbate, boy?"

"This morning, Father."

"How often do you masturbate, boy?"

"Every day, Father."

"How often everyday, boy?"

"Once or twice, Father."

"Sit down. You dirty, wicked, boy." said Fr Louis.

With flared nostrils, his slitted eyes focussed on the boys, and his purple veins pumped up like damp molehills, he roared out, "Who hasn't played with himself this week? Stand up!"

All remained silent and seated.

"So you all masturbated this week. You dirty, sex-mad shower of animal filth."

Several boys sniggered, some silently cried, some bowed their heads in their hands hoping to become invisible, whilst some sat paralysed as if turned into stone.

"You are all guilty of mortal sin, and condemned to the everlasting flames of hell. You are without grace, and have committed the sin of lust, one of the seven deadly sins." Fr Louis looked at the boys, who tried to avoid eye contact in the fear they might be accosted by him.

"You, boy!" he said, walking towards Wormwood. "Stand up, boy."

Wormwood stood up shaking, and wet himself. Fr Louis didn't seem to notice the slow dribble down his trouser legs, and the wet patch collecting at his feet. He was more intent on reducing him to a shivering, speechless wreck.

"What are the seven deadly sins, boy?"

Wormwood said nothing. He was too frightened to speak. He started to cry and twitch.

"Go and stand in the corner, you stupid boy."

Fr Louis dragged him by his blazer collar, and pushed him to the front of the class into a corner facing the wall.

"Who knows what the seven deadly sins are? Lust is one, of which you are all guilty. You dirty boys."

The class remained still, and silent.

"Pride, Covetousness, Anger, Gluttony, Envy and Sloth are the rest."

Fr Louis looked at me, saying, "You, boy, tell me the seven deadly sins."

"Stand up, boy, when I speak to you."

I stood up.

"Well then," he said.

"Don't know, Father," I said.

"I've just told you, you stupid boy."

I remained silent, my head lowered as if in shame.

"Have you masturbated today, boy."

"Don't know, Father."

"Do you play with yourself, boy?"

"Don't know, Father."

"Go and stand in the corner you idiot."

Fr Louis was obsessed with masturbation, inflicting physical and mental punishment. He maintained that slaps, use of the strap and in his case a purpose-made cane, which he called Oscar, was an article of faith in the Catholic Church, and that boys were born inclined to all kinds of evil, which had to be eradicated by strict discipline, and corporal punishment.

His use of physical violence, and sexual innuendos were tantamount to child abuse.

The bell sounded. The lesson was over. Fr Louis walked out of the classroom without as much as a farewell. The boys relaxed, and smiled, relieved to be rid of their maniacal teacher.

Fr Basil walked into the classroom for the next lesson, erect and smiling. His polished hair glinting peacock colours as the sun shone on his greasy head.

"Good morning, boys," he said.

"Good. Good, morning, morn, Sir, Father, Father," came a staccato reply.

"Splendid! Excellent!"

"Fry collect the homework, please."

"Yes, Father," said Fry, feeling pleased with himself at being given such a responsible job.

"Who hasn't done their homework? Two missing. Hands up. Come on, don't be afraid. I won't eat you," said Fr Basil.

Woolsack put his hand up. I followed, encouraged by Woolsack.

"Well, Woolsack, where's your homework?"

"The dog ate it, Father."

"What sort of dog, Woolsack?"

"A Jack Russell, Father."

"Tomorrow I want two compositions. The original and, 'Why did the dog eat my homework'?"

"You, Postlethwaite" Where's your homework?"

"Don't know, Father."

"Did you do your homework?"

"No, Father."

"Why not?"

"Don't know, Father."

"Try again, Postlethwaite. Why not?"

"I forgot, Father."

"Two compositions tomorrow. The first one and, 'Why I forgot to do my homework'. Is that clear, Woolsack and Postlethwaite?"

"Yes, Father," we both said in unison.

"Splendid! Excellent!

The rest of the lesson was uneventful. Fr Basil taught Maths, which was a complete mystery to me and Fry. Out in the playground we realised we had not understood anything he had been talking about. The theorem of Pythagoras was a conundrum which we didn't understand. We concluded that the hypotenuse was something to do with an hippopotamus - some sort of river-horse.

None of us had masturbated, although the urge had sometimes been very powerful. We decided to experiment in the secrecy and safety of our bedrooms, and report back to each other the next day. The mortal sin issue was not really a problem, because we could always go to confession.

Our last lesson of the day was P.E. with Miss Hagswell. She was, compared with most of the perverse priests, the personification of sensuality and fun. She laughed at us, and with us. She was kind, helpful, but always in control. We never took advantage of Miss Hagswell. We achieved, because we were not afraid, and we respected her. We were all very soon in love with our P.E. teacher. Woolsack and Johnson were sexually disturbed in her presence, evident by their arousals. This Miss Hagswell ignored, but she loved their display of approaching manhood, and adulation. We showered together in one large shower room. Most of us were without pubic growth, although some had wisps of black straggly hair. A few had thick black tufts, and large penises, Woolsack in particular. His slack penis hung long and thick. He soon became known as 'Penishead'.

"You want to get those little pricks exercised," said Johnson, looking at Fry and Wormwood. "You won't do any damage with them."

Woolsack joined in the laughter, adding, "Get Liz to give you some exercises in P.E."

Hurriedly I hid myself behind a towel, and dressed myself still wet, for fear of being ridiculed. My prick compared with the others was small too.

Fr Francis stood at the end of the shower room taking a great delight in seeing pink naked boys swarming about. He appeared to be moving his wet lips with sexual appetite: his resentment was trapped in the choice of celibacy as a priest. He lusted over their young innocent bodies, and that of Miss Hagswell, knowing he would die without ever tasting the delights of roused flesh. He'd given his life to God, in a moment of weakness, without knowing for sure if God even existed. If there was no God, no heaven or hell, his priesthood would have been in vain. He was not alone in lusting after Miss Hagswell. He, with others, longed to touch her, feel her warm flesh against theirs, lay naked in her softness, and bury himself deep within her dark secrets. His self abuse did not satisfy this daily passion for sins of the flesh.

"Lusting again, Francis," came a voice from just behind him. "Take a cold shower and come to confession after vespers. "It is good for the soul, Francis."

"Yes, Father Headmaster at once."

An embarrassed Fr Francis disappeared out of sight very quickly. The Headmaster took over the vigil, not to spend time in prayer, but to gratify his own craving for young boys.

CHAPTER 27

Manhood Revealed

"When I was a child, I spake
as a child, I understood
as a child, I thought as a child,
but when I became a man,
I put away childish things."

Bible 1 Corinthians ch. 13, v.1.

CHAPTER 27

I hurried tea, and started my homework. Two compositions - a tall order. It meant staying in, and not going out to play with my mates. I was hoping to get some information on masturbating. I knew it meant stimulating my prick, getting it hard, but I wasn't sure what happened. I remember getting a nice feeling when I was in Turners' Wood with Monica. Miss Hagswell made me feel excited too, warm and tense. I loved it when she showed me how to vault over the wooden horse, and climb the ropes, swinging from the gym ceiling. She spiralled up the rope like a sliding snake. Her ankles trapped the rope as it glided through her long slender legs, held tight against her body. The rope caressed her thighs and breasts as she moved silently upwards like a gliding fish. Her knuckles tensed white as her hands gripped the rope, hoisting herself to the ceiling. The entire length of her body was stretched, straining taut against the thick rope, with her loose shirt top riding high above her navel. I looked up at the exposed flesh with its midriff of fine, soft, fair-coloured hair. A small line of very fine tiny curls ran from her navel disappearing under her cotton shirt. Her legs, thighs and arms had the same fine down, conspicuous by the sun shining on her body. I was captivated by her lithe figure, excessive beauty, and quantity of fine hair. The touch of her warm hands on my body as she supported me in my efforts to climb the rope filled me with a longing to feel her warm body against mine. There was even a hint of lavender about her, reminding me of my mother.

It was with these thoughts I went to bed, much earlier than usual, which caused my father to think I was unwell. I assured him I was just tired after a day at school, and all the homework I'd done. I threw my clothes in a heap on the floor, desperate to start experimenting with myself.

I stood naked. I could just see from my waist upwards through the wall mirror. I looked down at my genitalia. Compared with Woolsack and Gilbert Cockfoster, my prick was small. It lay flaccid, asleep, and not wanting to move, like a purring kitten. I wondered if there was any sign of hair. Looking down, and fumbling at my small assemblage was difficult. I couldn't really see. I went into the bathroom for a hand mirror.

My Dad heard me and shouted, "Thought you'd gone to bed, Derek."

"Just been for a wee, Dad," I said.

"Night! God bless!"

"Night, Dad!"

Brian opened his door.

"You woke me up, Del."

"Sorry, Brian."

"Why you're naked?"

"Getting ready for bed."

"What yer want a mirror for? You've got one in yer room."

"I've got a wart on my bum, and want to look at it."

"Oh!" Brian said, shutting his door.

"Why can't he mind his bloody business," I thought, feeling very agitated.

It was turning dusk. I switched on my bedside lamp and angled the light towards my groin holding the mirror in front. After intensive exploration around my pubes I discovered some fine short hairs of a sandy colour. Some were turning brown. They were not long, but they had definitely started to grow. I felt proud and manly. I'd heard Cockfoster in the showers telling Tom Mates that rubbing Vaseline around the pubic area encouraged a quick, thick, growth of black hair.

"It's like a fertiliser," he said. "Ginseng liquid or powder is better, if you can get it."

"Another trip to the bathroom for Vaseline - damn!" I said to myself.

This time I put my pants on. I inched across the landing, quiet as a mouse, so I thought.

"Is that you, Derek?" came Dad's voice, floating up the stairs.

"Want a drink of water, Dad," I said.

"Night! God bless!" shouted Dad.

"Night," I said, having got the jar of Vaseline.

Brian stood at his door again.

"What yer want that for," he said.

"Got a boil on me bum," I said, glaring at him contemptuously.

"Thought it was a wart," he said.

"What's the bloody difference?" I said, in anger.

"Tell Dad you said bloody," he replied.

I ignored him, and banged my bedroom door shut.

I positioned a chair against the door just in case anyone tried to get in. Alone at last, sitting on the edge of the bed I rubbed the Vaseline with vigour around my genitalia, the full length of the penis, up and down, up and down. It became slightly swollen, and enlarged. I massaged lustfully, applying more Vaseline. It became stiff, and felt wonderful. My body grew tense with excitement, but nothing else happened. My hand and arm was tired with the effort, my penis raw and tender. I slowed down. It became soft, and limp, like a damp squib. I was exhausted. I rolled over into bed, worn out, and was soon fast asleep.

The rope felt rough against my naked body as I worked my way upwards. My goal was to reach Miss Hagswell who was slowly disappearing into the mist. The climbing was easier as the rope became slippery. My body glided through the vapour upwards and upwards, the greasy rope riding high through my legs. I blacked out. We were together now. I had reached my destination with only the thick lubricated rope between our bodies. We moved up and down against the rope salaciously, excited by the action, our passions inflamed. We looked into each other's eyes. The rope taut between her firm breasts and legs dropped out of sight.

"See-saw."

"Marjorie daw."

"Up and down."

"In and out."
"Jack and Jill."
"Humpty Dumpty."
"Fr Louis - dirty bastard."
"Give me a penny."
"Knit one."
"Slip one."
"Kiss me."
"Kiss me."
"Go on."
"Go on."
"Yes."
"Yes."
"Bang!"

The impact exploded, as the first blood was drawn. I could feel and hear my heart beating faster and faster. I was frightened by the tension in my body, and libidinous charge - the fleshy violence unleashed. So great was the excitement, I had experienced my first wet dream. The mental adventure left me exhausted. I slept the sleep of the just until Dad woke me the next morning.

"Wake up, Derek. Dreaming again."

"Little did he know," I thought.

The stiff dried musky patch on my pyjamas and bed sheets confirmed the realization of my fantasy. With joy I had unconsciously surrendered myself, and with conviction I was now an assured man. I had taken a quantum leap, an abrupt end from boy to man, which changed everything.

CHAPTER 28

The Surgery and The Undertaker

"You were born with your legs apart.
They'll send you to the grave in a Y-shaped
coffin."

What the Butler Saw (1969) act I.
Joe Orton 1933-1967.

CHAPTER 28

The surgery was full with fat and thin people, some short, others tall, some old, others young, some sitting, others standing, babies crying, children playing A faint odour of stale sweat hung about the room, more dense around two fat ladies, who sat with their fleshy legs prized apart, their thighs too fat to be held together for decency's sake. They both wore short coloured cotton dresses riding high up their spreading legs. One wore sky blue, the other pink elasticated directoire knickers, which tightly clung around their voluminous thighs. Their ample breasts hung low, and rested on their inflated stomachs. One constantly wiped her nose with the back of her hand, whilst the other loudly and repeatedly sniffed. The only difference between the two was their hair colour, one was black, the other a strong reddish-brown. They were twin sisters, married to twin brothers, and they both had colds.

Sitting opposite was Enoch De'Ath, the undertaker - known as 'Deathwatch'. He wore half-moon pince-nez spectacles, which helped to disguise his otherwise ghoulish features. His only interest in life was dead people, and their gold fillings. Sitting in the surgery he could be seen taking notes in his little black book, as patients came and went. His latest business venture was offering a discount on funerals paid for in advance, either in full or in monthly payments over twelve months. He was rather miffed that very few people had subscribed to his offer. As an extra incentive he was offering velvet lined English oak coffins at considerable cost to himself - so he said.

Enoch De'Ath sat next to Beth. He constantly moved along the bench pushing her sideways until their thighs touched. She moved, and he moved too. Another move would mean Beth falling off the end of the bench. She stood up.

Maggi had been in with the doctor for more than her allotted time, and the waiting patients were getting irritable. She came out of the Doctor's room adjusting her dress, and red-faced. Heads nodded, chins wagged, eyes fluttered, and hushed chatter broke out. Beth went in next. The Doctor was washing his hands.

Walking home together, Beth said, "Yo were a long time wi' doctor. What's up wi' yo then?"

"It's me itch. It's cum back, Beth."

"What itch? Dint know you'd got an itch."

"Ah well, I 'ave."

"Where's yo itch then?"

"It's, yo know, down there, in me whatsit, me thingy."

"Oh! Yer thingy. What's Doc say?"

"Our Eric got te lay off of me, leave me alone until it's gone.

"I've got some cream forr'it."

"Eric won't like that, looks forward to a bit on't Sat'dy night after the boozer, I rekkon," came Beth's reply.

"Ah!" And the rest of the week. 'Ees a bloody sex maniac."

"Anyhow what yo see Doc for?"

"It's me tit."

"What's up wi yo tits?"

"Thought one of me nipples 'ad dropped off."

"What did Doc say?"

"E said it was turned inside out or summat. Can't remember. E squeezed it out."

"Did it urt?"

"No, it was nice."

"What about yer other tit?"

"That's OK. Ted suks on that 'un," she added.

"Did yo see the twins, Maggi? What's up wi 'em yo rekkon?" said Beth.

"Summat te do wi being too fat. Not sticking te diet Doc gave 'em," said Maggi.

"They dint 'arf stink, dint wesh. The dotty boggers. They ought te put 'em int care. Made me feel sick sitting near 'em. That bleddy Deathwatch kept touching me legs, Maggi. The mukki bogger. 'E stinks too."

"You'd be so lucky. Gorra fag, Beth? Pay yer back."

They lit up and ambled down the road leaving a trail of smoke behind them.

A stray collarless dog cocked its leg up against a red pillar box at the edge of the pavement, and peed. The steamy yellow, strong-smelling liquid trickled across the pavement! Beth and Maggi slowed down, stepping over the flow.

"Dotty sod," said Beth.

"It's crapping I don't like," said Maggi.

CHAPTER 29

Five Years Later The School's Demise

"Wilt thou forgive that sin, where I begun
Which is my sin, though it were
done before?
Wilt thou forgive those sins
through which I run
And do them still, though still
I do deplore?
When thou hast done, though hast
not done -
For I have more."

A Hymn to God the Father (1623)
John Donne 1572-1631.

CHAPTER 29

I was in my final year at St Thomas More's Grammar School. The school had changed dramatically in the last five years. It was no longer run by priests of the Assumption - only Fr Basil remained. Some priests had left in disgrace or under suspicious circumstances. The school was still a Grammar School, but controlled by the County Council Education Department.

Two priests had been accused of paedophilia, and were waiting trial. Fr Louis was already in prison, accused, and convicted of mental, physical and sexual abuse of boys in his charge. Brother Michael, the tall, handsome, athletic, field sports master left in my second year to marry the pregnant Miss Hagswell. We were all very upset by Miss Hagswell's condition, having played no part in it. Lower School Physical Education was not the same anymore. The disappearance of Fr Francis was a mystery. It was thought he had committed suicide. The police visited the school, and questioned a few of the boys to try and establish when he was last seen. He was never found. Fr Cuthbert, the bursar, left under a cloud, accused of misappropriating school funds. Fr Basil was the exception and remained with the school as teacher and chaplain.

The remaining priests and the Headmaster rejoined their order in Ireland. The mood in the school changed with the advent of Catholic lay teachers.

There was no longer the ethos that the pain of confession was good for you, and we should always experience an overwhelming sense of guilt and unworthiness, which had to be eradicated by kneeling in the confessional box once a week. To say that confession is good for the soul is perhaps spiritually healthy, but to kneel before your teacher priest, or parish priest, and admit your failings is not mentally healthy. It is not rational, or natural to confess your sins to someone you know, and who knows you.

Gilbert Cockfoster confessed to Fr Louis that he'd put frogspawn in the priests' soup whilst he was on duty at lunchtime in the staff dining room. This had resulted in a chronic stomach disorder amongst some of the teaching staff. The lower school had to be shut down for three days until the staff recovered sufficiently to resume duties.

Cockfoster was expelled the next day, charged with putting frogspawn in the teachers' pea soup, despite vehemently denying the accusation. The school had no factual proof, but said they had conclusive circumstantial evidence, which was sufficient for Cockfoster's expulsion. The sin, which was, in Cockfoster's view, only a bit of fun, did not deserve expulsion, nor not being given absolution. Those who had had the soup said it was the best pea soup they'd ever had, and the stomach disorder was possibly due to other factors. The confidentiality rules of the confessional in this case were broken.

Fr Louis always disguised his voice in the confessional by wearing a gas mask, and speaking through wet blotting paper in the filter. This had the effect of him talking in a vapid empty way. Confessors in turn would try to disguise their own voices. I would suck a gob-stopper, and tie a wet handkerchief around my mouth, which didn't work.

"Stop talking gobbledegook, Postlethwaite," said Fr Louis, on one occasion. "Can't understand what you're trying to tell me."

"Yes, Father," I said.

"That was the idea you stupid priest," I said mentally.

Fry would put a peg on his nose. Our attempts to disguise our voices were futile. The priest would spy on us through a small hole purposely drilled into the partition between himself and the confessor. When not in use the hole was plugged.

"Hands joined together, boy, if you want absolution," said Fr Louis.

This prevented us from covering up his spy hole.

Confessions were compulsory each Friday afternoon, seemingly by a neutral unknown priest, but this was never the case. The priest was always one of the teachers. My Friday confession became perfunctory, without meaning, or sincerity.

"Bless me, Father, for I have sinned. It's one week since my last confession."

"Well, my child. Have you had impure thoughts."

"Yes, Father."

"What have you done to offend Almighty God?"

"I've had impure thoughts."

"What sort of thoughts, my child?"
"Don't know, Father."

"Was it about girls or boys my child?"
"Yes, Father."

"Was it about taking girl's clothes off?"

"Yes, Father."

"Did you want to feel between their breasts, child?"

"Yes, Father."

"Did you want to feel between their legs, child?"

"No, Father."

"Why not, child?"

"Don't know, Father."

"How many times have you pleasured yourself since your last confession, my child?"

"Don't know, Father."

"Do you enjoy masturbating, child?"
"Yes, Father."

"Do you masturbate every day, child?"

"Yes, Father."

"Do you do it alone, or with a friend, my child?"
"Don't know, Father."

"Have you offended Our Saviour in any other ways, child?"

"Don't know, Father."

"Have you any more sins to confess, boy?"
"No, Father."

"I absolve you from your sins, boy."

Muttering away in an inaudible voice the priest continued,

"Indulgentiam (makes the sign of the cross) absolutionem et remissionem peccatorum nostrorum, tribuat nobis omnipotens et misericors Dominus."

"Amen," I said.

"In nomine Patris, et Filii (we both make the sign of the cross) et Spiritus Sancti. Amen"

"Amen" I repeat.

"For your penance say the rosary three times, and make an act of contrition. Come and see me next Friday. Pray for me, boy. Bless you, Postlethwaite."

"I'm not praying for you, Fr Louis. I hate you," I said to myself.

My guilt of sin had been forced on me by the priest's cross-examination, and auto-suggestion, which was directed at me to satisfy his own perversions. There was no genuine forgiveness, advice or reassurance. The guilt I felt, regardless of my sins, reinforced by the priest's threat of eternal damnation, and the fires of hell, left me anxious, withdrawn, and ashamed. The repeated weekly compulsory confession and interrogation reduced me to a nervous wreck. I had to commit sins to have something to confess each week. I couldn't lie in the confessional.

The true concept of confession had been abused by a regime of authoritarian priests, who used the sacrament for their own perverted motives, rather than the forgiveness of sins, as part of God's infinite love.

The change in teaching staff, gave me, the boys, and school a change in moral values, spirit, and a new definition. It was the Renaissance for St Thomas More's Grammar School.

CHAPTER 30

Wash Day

*"Nothing grows in our garden, only washing.
And babies!"*

Under Milk Wood.
Dylan Thomas 1914-1953.

CHAPTER 30

A warm south-westerly wind blew across the gardens. The sky was blue with just a hint of cloud. A weak early morning sun shone with the prospect of a hot dry day ahead.

Maggi was trying to fix her new washing line between two posts, but one end was a few inches short. She walked up the path to her open back door, and in a thunderous voice shouted, "Eric, gerrup an fix this bleddy washen line."

She repeated the command three times before Eric appeared in a torn, grubby vest. His trousers were held up by two red braces, straps worn over his shoulders and secured by two safety pins to his trouser waistband. Half his face was covered in shaving soap. His short cropped silver hair stood on end like a hedgehog's back. A lit cigarette hung from his mouth.

"Watsupp, duk?" he said, coughing.

"The bleddy weshing line 'int long enuff," said Maggi.

"I'nt it ta bogga," said Eric, tugging at the line.

He soaked the rope in a bucket of cold water, and with great difficulty, and the help of Maggi, managed to stretch and fasten the line onto the post's steel pins. The rope held taut between the posts was now secure, but out of Maggi's reach.

"Too bledy 'igh," said Maggi. "You'll 'ave to move the bleddy posts when yo cum bak from wok."

"I'll get yo a longer line, yo daft bogga," he thought.

Eric pulled the rope down whilst Maggi, on tiptoe, hung out her washing. Her arms were straining, and armpits stretched like catgut. They both walked back into the house grumbling at each other.

"I'll be late for wok now," said Eric.

Maggi ignored him, lit a cigarette, coughed, and put the kettle on.

"Want a cuppa, Eric?" she shouted.

"Gorra ge' te wok," he shouted back.

"Plees yo sen yo silly bogga," she said, quietly to herself.

The washing wafted in a warm breeze.

The line began to weaken at one end, as it began to dry out. The metal ring at the rope end rubbed against the post's steel pin. The breeze became stronger. At each gust the rope began to loosen itself from the ring, until the strain became too much. Rope and eyelet parted with an explosive clap. The line, and washing, collapsed to the ground.

Maggi sat inside enjoying a strong cup of tea and a cigarette, with the knowledge that her washing was getting a good blow.

Eric cycled down the road to work. Beth walked up the road carrying a heavy shopping bag.

"Ay-up, Eric. 'Ow yo gooing on?" she shouted.

"Am orryte, duk," Eric shouted back, feet and pedals racing.

The boom of a jet soared overhead, disappearing into the clouds, leaving a thin chalk-white vapour trail, spreading and swelling, until it became lost in the heavens.

CHAPTER 31

School Cricket - The Herbert Sutcliffe Memorial Cricket Trophy

'There's a breathless hush in the Close tonight,
Ten to make and the match to win,
A bumping pitch and a blinding light,
An hour to play and the last man in,
And it's not for the sake of a ribboned coat,
Or the selfish hope of a season's fame,
But his Captain's hand on his shoulder smote
 "Play up! Play up! and play the game!"

Vitai Lampada (1897)
Sir Henry Newbolt 1862-1938

CHAPTER 31

For my sixteenth birthday my dad bought me a full size cricket bat. It was my pride and joy. It was a genuine bat, the same that was used by test and county players. It had a willow blade, and cane handle layered with thin strips of rubber, bound with twine, and covered with a black rubber sheath. The handle was spliced into the top of the blade. The bat always stood in the corner of my bedroom with my batting gloves draped over the handle. I would stare at it, smell the linseed oil blade with impassioned joy, handle it, caress it, lift it high above my shoulders and thwack another imagined six, as bat and ball smashed into each other. I always produced lots of runs in my bedroom, but in reality I was lucky to reach double figures until I played in the School Boy's Final at Granchester County Cricket Ground.

I only played for the school first eleven when regular players were unavailable, which was seldom. I had reasonable success playing for my house, and the second eleven, and more often than not opened the batting, but I was never happy facing a new ball.

I knew I would be more successful if I batted lower down the order - number four or five. I was confident I could get runs given the opportunity. I'd never really got over losing my lucky rabbit's tail when Fr Francis thought it was a dead mouse and threw it in the river. He'd had his comeuppance. I was not sorry. My new bat would bring me luck, and success. It was magic. I knew it.

I was twelfth man for the school playing against Granchester Grammar in the School Boy's Final. It was a foregone conclusion St Thomas More's didn't have a chance of taking the honours, and becoming holders of the Herbert Sutcliffe Memorial Cricket Trophy - a large silver bowl, engraved with the school winners. The school had yet to share the honour with Granchester Grammar, the current holders.

The big day arrived. I was replacing David Hobbs, who had a severe tummy bug. It was Saturday, the penultimate week before the end of term, and my last few days at school. There had been rain the previous day, and the wicket was slow, and possibly in drying might take spin. St Thomas More's won the toss and put Granchester in to bat.

We took to the field in crisp whites. I wore my school cricket cap, feeling important and proud to be representing my school in such a prestigious match. I fielded at square leg, my favourite position. Granchester Grammar School started slowly, until Tom Gunn came in at number four. Tom, a county prospect, was related to the late George Gunn, and cricket was in his blood. He batted with great skill and determination, and soon reached a very quick 50. He would dance down the wicket to meet any type of bowling, grinning all over his face, intimidating the bowler. Spin bowlers lost their rhythm and confidence and ceased to spin, with Tom engaged in battle at the wicket. He was a wonderful stroke player, orthodox, with perfect timing, his footwork faultless on the front or back foot. By lunch Granchester Grammar School had reached 264 for seven, with Tom Gunn on 81. Tom was greedy for runs, hypnotising and willing the bowlers to pitch the ball where he wanted it. Unless we got him out quickly we had no chance of winning the trophy.

My friend, Bob Truman, who had not bowled so far, was our last hope. He was a medium fast bowler, and could make the ball swing if conditions were right. He was suffering with a strained right shoulder, which severely slowed down his action. Bob paced out his run, moved the field around, and motioned me to deep square leg, and Bill Thorpe to fine leg, almost on the boundary. He repositioned the slips, and moved the on-side fieldsmen deeper. Bob was ready to bowl. The umpire signalled. Bob started his run, but stopped halfway. He started to swing his right arm up, down, and over.

The umpire looked at him. "What's up, lad?"

Tom Gunn shouted in frustration, "Get on wi 'it!"

Bob ignored both, took up his bowling position again, and ran up to the wicket delivering his first ball.

"No ball," shouted the umpire.

Tom halfway down the wicket, lashed out wildly with his bat. Missed! He was just back inside his crease, before the keeper instinctively had the bails flying in the air.

"Del," shouted Bob, and motioned me to go deeper almost on the boundary.

The next ball, pitched on the off, was driven through the covers, but well fielded. Both batsmen ran down the wicket, almost crashing into each other, before deciding it was unsafe and returned to their creases. No run was taken. Tom, by this time, was feeling thwarted, and threatened. He desperately wanted to reach his 100. He needed to restrain himself, and his batting, and play only the safe shots. Bob, on the other hand thought he was in control, and only had to tempt him into taking chances.

"A few loose balls may do the trick. I'll get the bogga out," he thought, winding himself up to bowl.

The next ball was short, pitching middle and leg. Tom loved these balls.

"I'll hit this one out of the ground," he said to himself.

Without appearing to rush he rocked onto his back foot just inside the line of the ball, and hooked it high into the air towards square leg boundary for six.

Both batsmen looked at the ball soaring into the air, not bothering to run, thinking it was a safe six.

I watched the ball, which seemed to be suspended above me, not moving, stationary, like a skylark hovering at great height. Moving directly underneath it I held myself in readiness to take the catch, but the ball had disappeared, hidden by the sun. Time stood still as I waited for the ball to appear, but I never saw it, until 'Thump!' it went into my cupped hands, unseen, hard, painful, the ball plummeted. The force knocked me over onto my back, hitting my head on the rock hard turf - the ball still held tightly in my grasp. The fielders cheered, shouted and clapped, Tom Gunn was out for 81. Granchester were now 264 for eight wickets. Only seven more runs were added to their score. They were all out for 271.

We had lunch in the pavilion where the county players met and dined. Our team were feeling depressed at the thought of trying to match a score of 272 to win. I heard Tom Gunn talking to his mate Colin Carter.

"It'll be all over by four. We'll he home by six, and in't flicks with Pam and Aud by seven. Back row again, Col? Eh! Bowl the buggers out. Hit that sod in't chest that caught me."

"Right, mate, see what I cun do," replied Carter.

The wicket was rolled, and the new ball taken. Granchester Grammar School took the field, and Carter bowled the first over. He was tall, lanky, red faced, with the suggestion of a thin black moustache. He bowled with a quick pace. Each time the ball left his hand he gave out a menacing grunt. Carter was able to make the ball move off the pitch, enough to beat the batsman. Within an hour we had lost two wickets, and one retired hurt for only 22 runs. The last batsman had been hit in the ribs by Carter. There was a sharp crack, and yell of pain as the ball crashed into May's chest.

"Carter's a bloody homicidal maniac. Hope he slows down when I'm at the crease," I thought.

I was beginning to feel hot and sweaty and thought, "I'd sooner be watching rather than playing."

I was in the dressing room padded up and ready for action. I slowly walked out swinging my bat to loosen up, and sat down on the bench next to Mr Dexter, our sports master.

Alec Smith was the other bowler, who was difficult to play. An accurate leg break bowler, not as lethal as Carter, but menacing and dependable. He could pitch a ball outside the leg stump, and turn it to hit off stump, such was his spin. If it turned another inch it would miss the stumps altogether. At times he was just unplayable. Spotty Hewitt went in number four. He had a reputation for staying at the crease for most of the innings, but rarely reaching double figures.

Shouts of,

"No!"

"No!"

"Go Back!"

"Go back!"

"Bloody fools!"

Another wicket lost. Pip Phillips, stumped by the keeper. Three wickets down, and one retired hurt. I was next. I stood up, bat held tightly between my arm and body.

"Postlethwaite," said Mr Dexter.

"Yes, sir."

"Play carefully. Take your time. You've got all day. Contain yourself. Control your batting. Don't take your eye off the ball. Elbow. Elbow bent! Straight bat. You can do it, boy. Fiver if you make a ton," said Mr Dexter.

"Thank you, sir," I said, forcing a smile.

Reg Potts, the Upper School Classics teacher added, in his soft cultured voice, "Benedicat vos Postlethwaite."

Mr Potts was sitting the other side of Mr Dexter.

"You're sticking your neck out, Ted. Fiver's a lot of money," said Reg.

"I'm pretty safe. He'll never make a hundred. I like to encourage them, Reg," came the reply.

I walked into the field to feeble applause from the fielders. I was tense and shaking, perspiration was building up on my brow. I felt nervous and terrified. It was like walking into a cock-fighting pit to be torn apart by frenzied impatient cocks, hungry for human flesh, and the taste of blood.

Shouts from the spectators.

"Go for it, Postlethwaite."

"Good Luck!"

"Give it some welly, Postlethwaite."

"The cheers and clapping came to an abrupt end. I stood alone at the crease, taking guard.

"Middle, please," I said.

"Te leg a bit," said the umpire.

I moved my bat a fraction.

"Bit more! Centre! Bang on, lad!" said the umpire.

Mentally I was trying to take control of the situation. I had a new bat. I was leaving school. I was going to see Monica in the school holidays. I hadn't cut myself shaving with Dad's old blunt razor he'd given me. Mr Dexter was going to give me a fiver for 100 runs.

"I'll do it. I'll bloody do it. Sod Carter. I'll hit him, and his mates all over the field. I bloody will," I thought in a dream.

The umpire moved down the wicket towards me.

"You alright, lad?" he said.

"Fine! Never felt better," I said.

"We're waiting fo' thee," he said.

"Sorry," I said.

"Keep the buggers waiting," I thought.

I looked up towards the bowler, my bat held firmly. I moved it up and down a few inches jabbing it into the ground. Thud it went each time, dry dust blew up. My feet shuffled in anticipation. The adrenalin started to feed and pump away, like a wild rat scrambling inside my stomach.

"Tactics," I thought.

The umpire signalled. Carter ran up to bowl. I held my bat up in the air. The umpire threw his arm aside to signal the bowler to stop. Carter slowed down, and came to a halt half way down the wicket. I nonchalantly moved down the wicket a few paces, picked up a fictional piece of loose turf, and patted the spot with the toe of my bat. I resumed my position at the crease, took my time inspecting the field placing, and signalled to the umpire my readiness to bat. The umpire shouted to me, somewhat in anger, "Sure yer ready, lad? Ain't got all day."

I smiled back in agreement. The umpire signalled. Carter ran at an almighty pace with fury written all over his flaming red face. He let the ball go with a grunt. It sped towards me like a bullet.

"No ball," shouted the umpire.

I had nothing to lose, everything to gain. Without attempting to rush I let my bat take over. The meat of the bat connected with the ball, went 'chop', disappearing over the bowler's head for an easy six.

"Well hit."

"Great shot, Postlethwaite."

"Well played," came a chorus of shouts.

"Keep it up," shouted Mr Dexter.

The next ball was more controlled. A straight bat, with elbows angled, sent it back to the bowler. Two more balls played safely and contained, finished the over, and no more runs were made. The score now stood at 73 for four wickets. We needed 199 runs to win. The next over conceded two runs made by Spotty Hewitt.

My turn next. The first ball I hit through the covers for four. The second ball, a bouncer, I hooked for six to the leg boundary. The remainder of the over was played defensively with no more runs added. The next over Spotty Hewitt was caught on the boundary from one of Alec Smith's cleverly disguised slower balls.

Ted Butcher came in at number six. A well-built lad, who could hit the ball with accuracy once he'd got his eye in, but he was not very fast between the wickets. We conferred mid-wicket. Ted was to play defensively, take no risks, whilst I went for the runs. Our strategy worked well. Within the next hour I had reached 51 runs, and our score stood at 164 for five. With only two more runs added, Ted was run out. The score was now 166 for six, 106 runs to win with myself, and three more to bat.

Tea was taken, laid out in the members' room. A long trestle table was set with huge plates of sandwiches, cream cakes, jelly and ice cream. Cups of tea were poured from a large silver urn, inscribed with the names of batsmen who had scored 100 runs not out at the ground. The urn had been given to the County Club by Lord Trenchingham-Smythe - a benefactor of the club.

Fry and Wormwood came up to me just before play resumed.

"Well played, Postlethwaite. That six of yours was a beautiful shot," said Fry.

Wormwood, stuttering, said, "A real sm sm smash, smasher! Good sh sh show, Postlethwaite."

"Well done," said Mr Dexter, patting me on the back.

"Keep it up, boy."

"Benedicat vos," added Mr Potts, not to be left out.

"Yes, sir," I said confidently.

A few words from Ahmed, our Captain, made me resolved to save the match, and make a century.

"I could do with a fiver to take Monica somewhere nice," I thought. "With my magic bat I'll do it. I'll bloody do it."

"Go for it, Postlethwaite, we've still got a sporting chance. You're our only hope now," said Ahmed, giving me a gentle friendly nudge with his clenched fist.

I walked back to the wicket with Pete Giles, number eight batsman. I took guard again, marked out the crease. The sinking sun was strong, and partially blocked out my view of the bowler. I had the white side-screen moved directly behind the bowler, and sent for my cap, adjusted the straps on my pads, looked intently at the field placing, and nodded to the umpire. I was ready.

Carter was bowling again. He looked agitated and annoyed because I'd kept him waiting. The grunting ball came whistling down wide on the leg side. I left it alone. The wicket keeper missed it, deep fine leg dived for it, and missed. The ball made the boundary. 170 for six. Exactly the same thing happened with the next ball, wide on the leg side and four more wides … The next ball was slower, pitching six inches outside the leg stump, a bat's length in front of the crease. My left foot met the ball as it pitched, with ball, foot and bat simultaneously following each other. The ball sped along almost singeing the grass in its wake. Two fielders dived for the ball, but the red bullet had a mind of its own, one destination to reach. It crashed into the advertising boards with an almighty explosion. The wood split at the impact. The umpire signalled four.

"Good shot, Postlethwaite."

"Well hit, Del."

"Bloody good shot," shouted an enthusiastic onlooker.

Clapping and shouting erupted. The next two balls flew through cover point two inches above the grass, and ripped into the hoardings. The last ball of Carter's over, a late cut, gave way for another four. Carter was not very popular, eight wides and 16 runs.

Peter Giles faced the next over from Alec Smith. His first ball nearly took the off stump out of the ground. The second ball was loose, and out of control. Giles left it well alone. Smith beckoned the fielders to close in on Giles. Smith bowled, this time a bouncer hitting Giles on the chin and drawing blood. Giles had to retire with a split chin requiring four stitches. George Goff, number nine, was next in. He played the next three balls defensively without scoring. The end of the over.

Carter took the next over feeling very frustrated. He licked his lips furiously, rubbing the ball relentlessly in his trousered groin, moved the field deeper, and increased his run up by half as much again. He handed his sweater to the umpire. He was ready to bowl. His delaying tactics were intimidating.

"Two can play at that game," I thought.

The umpire signalled to play. Carter was in position to send down his first delivery. I raised my bat, took off my sweater, and gave it to the umpire at square leg. I took guard again, and patted the turf with the toe of my bat to remove any unseen lumps.

" 'ave yer quite finished, lad?" said the umpire.

I nodded agreement.

"Play," shouted the umpire.

Carter, now exasperated, came down like a thunderbolt.

"Wide," yelled the umpire.

The keeper missed the ball, and it rocketed to the boundary for four. The next ball I hooked to the leg side boundary for six. The over finished with me adding a further 12 runs. 60 runs left to win. I now stood at 78.

The next over with Goff facing Smith was tense. Smith moved the field closer, and slowed down his pace. Goff blocked each ball, keeping a straight bat, but misjudged the last ball, and was out to a brilliant third slip catch.

Last man, Ian Cotham, was our best spin bowler, but a hopeless bat. The game was up.

"No it wasn't," I thought.

I want my ton, and we only need 60 to win. I conferred with Ian.

"Only run for two, never one or three, unless it's the last ball of the over. I'll get those bloody runs."

"Do your bit, and I'll do mine. We're going to win this match between us."

"OK, Del," said Ian, not very confidently.

The strategy worked well. We added a further 20 runs. I was on 98, and we needed 40 runs to win. But Cotham now faced the bowling.

Mike Foster, Granchester captain, had the ball. He was throwing it slowly from one hand to the other. He moved the field close, intimidating Cotham. Foster was going to bowl, left arm round the wicket. He took a short run, and discharged a slow ball, which seemed to hang in the air, and drop suddenly. Cotham hit out and it soared into the air. He ran, I ran, but it was safely caught. Cotham was out. My aspirations were dashed. The enemy applauded. Gasps and sighs joined in. We were finished.

"Two bloody runs off my 100," I thought. "Sod it."

"Sorry, Del, got carried away," said Cotham, as we started our walk back to the pavilion.

"Stay where you are, Postlethwaite," shouted Ahmed, our captain from the pavilion.

"May and Giles to bat yet."

"The walking injured going to bat," I thought, with the adrenalin beginning to surge through my body again.

Pete May walked to the crease, ribs strapped, took guard and faced Foster's delivery. The ball went high in a wide arc, and dropped at the toe of May's bat and stopped. May edged it away a few inches and lent on his bat as though in pain. The next four balls were exactly the same, donkey drops, no more runs were added. Carter was given a rest having conceded 34 runs in two overs.

I faced Viv Vaughan, their off-spinner. He was very slow and deliberate. The first ball almost stopped mid-air for a breather, so much so, my timing went, and I missed the ball in toto. By the end of the over I'd adjusted to the slow pace, and took one run off the last ball to face the bowling again.

I reached my 100 with a four, which I drove through the covers. The ball ploughed through the spellbound fielders tearing them apart, and crashed into a bunch of spectators. My first 100 runs with my new bat. The fielders clapped, a few made unenthusiastic remarks, hardly audible.

"Well done."

"Well played," and some,

"Get the bugger out," could be heard.

Their comments were eclipsed by our own team and school supporters. They waved, clapped, shouted and roared. I raised my bat, took off my cap, and waved back.

Donkey-drop Foster conceded four boundaries, and two sixes - 28 runs. My score stood at 127, and we needed 11 runs to win.

"If only I still faced the bowling," I thought.

May now confronted the bowling. It was Alec Smith again. May was in too much pain to lift his bat. He just stood there and hoped for the best. The last ball, pitched middle and leg, turned, clipping the off stump just sufficient to dislodge the bails. May was out, relieved to be walking back to the pavilion.

The last man, Giles, came to the crease. His chin was stitched, and a plaster edged with blood covered his lower jaw. He looked uncomfortable, and terrified. I had a word with him.

"I'll knock these few runs off this over," I said, confidently.

"Hope so," he stuttered hesitantly.

Carter took the next over, and deepened the field. Off came his sweater and cap. When he'd finished I put my sweater on, but left my cap off.

"Anything to upset grunting Carter," I thought.

Carter measured his run up again, hammering his boot into the turf like a bull pounding its hoof in fury.

"Can we start, bowler?" shouted the umpire.

"OK with me," said Carter.

Carter ran towards me, but misjudged his run up. The ball left his fist as he grunted.

"No ball," yelled the umpire.

I danced down the wicket to meet the ball and hit it high and straight over the boundary for six. Five runs to win. The next ball was more accurate. I played it safely, and sent it swiftly over the turf back to Carter. Carter picked it up, walked slowly back to the start of his run up, rubbing the ball methodically into his groin. He turned to face me, spat on the ball, polishing the spit vigorously into it. He kneaded the ball against his trousers once more, and ran towards me. The umpire stopped him.

"What yer doing, laddy? Haven't signalled yet. Get back. Wait till I give the green light."

"Sorry," said Carter, taken aback.

The umpire signalled. Carter, this time more disciplined, sent down a slower ball. I didn't wait for it to pitch, but took two controlled paces down the wicket, and punched it hard through mid off to the boundary. The spectators yelled and cheered. We were level pegging now at 271. One run to win. Carter's next ball was deadly accurate. It pitched short, and hit me in the chest.

"Ow's that?" shouted Carter.

" 'E's out!" yelled the wicket keeper. "The umpire's got his hand up. Leg before wicket," he added.

"Not out. Don't push your luck, bowler," he shouted, with arm raised in a gesture of warning.

"Don't appeal unless yer sure. What de yer tak me for, a bloody novice, lad?"

"Sorry, sir," said Carter, feeling put down.

His next ball zoomed through the air right on target, but pitched short again. I swiftly, and with perfect timing, hooked it for six. We had won by five runs. The spectators cheered and yelled themselves hoarse. Shouts of,

"Well done!"

"Bravo!"

"Good show."

"Great knock, Postlethwaite!"

The fielders clapped, but without passion. They were too distressed at losing. Granchester's Captain shook hands with me, saying, "Damn good knock old fruit. You beat us fair and square. Well Done!"

Carter ignored me. Far too upset at being hit all over the field.

I walked back to the pavilion to cheers and deafening applause, and shouts of, "He's a jolly good fellow."

It was my day of glory. We had won the Herbert Sutcliffe Memorial Trophy for the first time. I was named 'Man of the Match', receiving a miniature replica of the cup, and a crisp £5 note as my prize. Mr Dexter gave me the fiver he promised. Mr Potts had bet Mr Dexter £1

I wouldn't make a century. He gave me the £1, saying "Benedicat vos Postlethwaite," patting me on the back at the same time.

In the dressing room I hugged my bat, and cried. Together we'd made 143 not out, and won the match, and the Trophy. Through my tears I saw my mother in a cloud of mist. She lifted her arm, and held out her hand to greet me. I walked towards her, my hand held out to touch her. She receded into the mist, and vanished. She too, had shared my moment of glory.

"Are you alright, Del?" said Ahmed, walking towards me. "Looks like you've seen a ghost," he added.

"I've just seen my mother," I said.

The team cheered, and took me shoulder high around the cricket field, singing, 'For he's a jolly good fellow'.

CHAPTER 32

Prize Giving and Leaving School

"Lord, dismiss us with Thy blessing,
Thanks for mercies past receive;
Pardon all, their faults confessing;
Time that's lost may all retrieve;
May Thy children
Ne'er again Thy Spirit grieve."

Hymn for end of term.
H J Buckoll 1803-1871.
Hymns Ancient and Modern.

CHAPTER 32

"Derek James Albert Postlethwaite," reverberated through the hall.

"Cricketer of the year," said the Deputy Head.

Cheers broke out from the school and parents. The seated staff slapped their hands on the long trestle table. The Deputy Head raised his arm to silence the excitement.

"Postlethwaite, almost single handed, saved the match, and secured for St Thomas More's School the Herbert Sutcliffe Memorial Trophy."

Once more the brouhaha erupted. The school, the parents and guests, stood up, clapped, cheered, applauded, feet stamped, shouts of 'Hoorah', 'Hoorah' as I walked up the carpeted steps to receive my prize. At that precise moment I felt a sudden urge to go to the toilet. I clenched my buttocks together, and just hoped the lavatorial sensation would disappear. The School Governors, Headmaster, and teaching staff sat together, looking glum, and feebly joined in with the applause.

The Head stood up to greet me, and said in a bored voice, "Well done, Postlethwaite. You've done better in the field than in the classroom."

Lord Trenchingham-Smyth, eccentric Chairman of the Governors, stood next to the Head to hand out the prizes. He was tall, red-haired, turning grey, ruddy-faced, wearing a loud tweed jacket, and yellow corseted waistcoat, straining at the buttons sending out fans of creases across his pot belly. His big wide-awake eyes and jolly face shone with pleasure, as he vigorously shook my hands, handing me a book, silver cup and brown envelope.

"Good show, young man, sooner be a damn good shot than a highbrow bore meself."

His walrus moustache moved in a jerky spasmodic way as he spoke.

"Ha! Ha! What! What! Damn good show, young man," still shaking my hands.

"Fancy joining the Army, young man? Need chaps like you - with a good eye. Think about it. Eh!"

My book, held insecurely in my left hand, dropped to the floor.

"Off you go, Postlethwaite. Pick it up. Next please!" said the Head.

Lord Trenchingham-Smythe turned to the Head and said, "Fine young man that. Bloody good eye. What! Good officer material. What! What!"

"Lousy scholar, though," replied the Head.

I returned to my seat to more applause, overhearing the comments whilst picking up my book from the floor. I still had to collect my school leaving certificate, which was only a poor pass. My scholastic achievements were abysmal during my five years at the school. I did not obtain good enough marks to reach matriculation standard.

Throughout my five years at St Thomas More's my progress had been unsatisfactory according to my mentors. My teachers, and my father, were in despair at my slow rate of progress, and unwillingness to work. I did try in my last year to do some school work, but my mind was always on other things.

I never had a school report which pleased my father. He didn't really encourage me to do better, only chastised me for my current poor performance, exemplified by my reports each term. My term results were always better than my exam results, due to help from Fry and Wormwood with my homework. Sometimes I just copied their work. From my first year to my last year the comments against most subjects would read,

'More effort required'.

'Untidy work'.

'Fair'.

'Could do better if applied himself'.

'Satisfactory. Should pay more attention in class'.

'A daydreamer. A don't knower'.

'Greater application needed'.

'Disappointing. Must improve'.

'No apparent effort, or improvement'.

'Weak. Lacks application'.

'Improvement spoilt by talking in lessons'.

'Work spoilt by bad attention, and silliness'.

'Keen at times. Does not seem to like learning given homework'.

'Better class and homework needed'.

'Needs to curb certain independence of spirit'.

'Good at sports. Won his final in the House Boxing Championships'.

'Good at cricket and rugby. Plays for his House and School'.

My penultimate school report to leaving school had an additional comment from the Headmaster. We had a mutual dislike for each other, so his remarks were not surprising.

"Could have worked better this term. He is still too talkative, and lacking in self-control. His line of defence is still "Don't Know." Can't imagine what sort of job Derek will get on leaving school, but I wish him luck. He will need it."

These comments really upset my father. He thought I needed army discipline to sort me out, but I was too young, otherwise he would have sent me to the nearest army recruiting office. Compared with Brian, I was an odd ball. It never occurred to him that there could have been an underlying reason for my behaviour. The love which nurtured me before my mother died was missing. It could not be replaced by my father, simply because he was male. I'd lost a mother - of female gender. Male and female are not synonymous - physically or mentally. One cannot replace one with the other. My father was not capable of making good my loss. Perhaps I was seeking attention in my subconscious, but couldn't quite find it whilst at school.

I remember my first day at St Thomas More's, and now I am facing my last day. No more school after today. The first day was painful, shared with Fry and Wormwood. We were left alone in strange surroundings, subject to the whims of freaky priests. I remember Fry, and poor Wormwood, peeing himself in fright. Other first year boys were like little old men, looking for companionship, seeking love to assuage their fears, but none came. My father said I was lucky winning a scholarship to the Grammar School. He put it down to luck, not my ability to achieve.

Sitting with the other boys, waiting my turn to walk up again onto the platform to receive my school certificate, I wondered what my father was thinking.

Was he pleased with me?

I kept my cricket success to myself, not giving much away when questioned. I looked behind me, and saw my father a few rows back, sitting next to a lady. They were deep in conversation. She was smiling up at him as he spoke. She saw me, smiled, and waved. I smiled back, lifting my hand in recognition. I thought I smelt lavender - my mother's fragrance. It was quite faint, subtle, and made me feel happy. For a short time I was transported by the evocation of lavender, and lost with my thoughts.

"Postlethwaite. Postlethwaite. Where's Postlethwaite?" shouted Mr Pogson, the Deputy Head.

Fry nudged me. I came to, walked up the steps again, by the Deputy Head, who glared at me saying, "Day dreaming again, Postlethwaite?"

"Sorry, sir," I said.

Lord Trenchingham-Smythe shook hands with me again, gave me my certificate, saying, "Bloody good knock of yours, Postlethwaite. Fine innings young man. Keep it up. Well done. Ha! Ha! Ha! Good show."

"Thank you, sir," I said.

He turned to the Head, saying, "Good eye, that boy. Good officer material don't you know."

The Head, gimlet-eyed, gave me a resentful look as if to say, "Clear off. Don't dare come back. Don't want to see you, again. Had enough of you. Feck off, Postlethwaite."

Returning to my seat, I thought to myself, "Feck off yerself, you old fart."

On the way home from prize giving we had fish and chips. They tasted good.

"Who was that lady sitting next to you, Dad?" I said.

"I was sitting between Mr and Mrs Blewitt."

"Funny," I thought, "sitting next to Barmy Blewitt's Ma and Pa."

"Who'd you think I was sitting next to," Dad said.

"Don't know."

It was no good telling Dad my mother was at the prize giving.

"What's in the envelope, Derek?"

"Don't know."

"Well aren't you going to open it, lad?"

"In good time, Dad. When I get home."

I was feeling more confident. My school days were over. I was now six feet tall and starting to shave. I had hairy legs and arms, and masses of black pubic hair.

"I might be able to grow a moustache given the Vaseline treatment," I thought.

In two weeks time I was starting to work at the Provincial Bank, not my choice, but at least I'd have some independence. I'd already opened the envelope. It contained a crisp £5 note from the school governors for bringing honour to the school, and defeating Granchester Grammar School. For the past five years St Thomas More's had suffered humiliating defeat. There was great rivalry between the two schools, academically and on the sports field. Both schools' governors were continually at each other's throats vying for their own importance, and their school's excellence.

I was feeling rich, with £15 to my name.

"Buy myself a decent pipe, now," I thought, "rather than smoke Grandad's old cherry wood pipe."

It ought to have been buried with him when he died. It tasted foul, and smelt of dog shit. I had to secure the stem with adhesive tape to hold it together. It was not very satisfactory, and was always bending, and coming apart. The herb tobacco I smoked in it smelt like burning bonfire garden rubbish when I got it going, and it made me feel sick.

I lay in bed content and happy. I'd seen my mother, and was seeing Monica at the weekend. My school days were over. I'd left, redeeming myself somewhat. At least in the eyes of some.

A full moon filled a clear starlit sky with light. Cats meowed and fought for domination in the stillness. Night moved in the streets.

CHAPTER 33

Port and Lemon

"O plump head-waiter at The Cock,
To which I most resort
How goes the time?
Tis five o'clock.
Go fetch a pint of port."

'Will Waterproof's Lyrical Monologue'.
Alfred Lord Tennyson 1808-1892.

CHAPTER 33

"Another port and lemon, Beth?" said Maggi, getting up from her seat, and making for 'The Feather's Bar'.

"Don't mind if I do," said Beth. "Oh! And bring me sum fags an' crisps," she added. "Right oh, duk," said Maggi.

They both sat puffing cigarettes, eating crisps, and drinking.

"Did you 'ear about yung Derik Postlethwing, Maggi?" said Beth.

"Worra about 'im?" said Maggi.

"E's gorra lot of runs atta cricket match for 'is school. 'E wun a cup for 'is school an all. It worr in the papers," said Beth.

"Our Eric said summat about it," replied Maggi.

"Nice lad. Grewed up real nice," said Beth.

"Ah! 'E 's an all," said Maggi.

"Must be all of six foot," said Beth.

"An more, I rekkon," said Maggi.

"E's a gud luking lad now 'es grewed up, don't yer know," said Beth, scratching her armpit.

"E's an all," said Maggi.

"E's left school yo know," said Beth.

"Ah! So I 'eard," said Maggi, picking her nose.

"Our Ted says 'es gorra job in't bank," said Beth.

"No dairn t'pit, or muck-cartin 'ont farm for our Derek," said Maggi.

"E's ad gud edification, yo know, said Beth.

"E 'as an all," said Maggi, chewing a crisp.

"Is poor Mam wud 'av bin rate proud on 'im," said Beth.

"She wud, an all," replied Maggi.

"In't a bogga," said Maggi.

"Warr is?" said Beth.

"Me porr 'an lemun's all gon," said Maggi, draining her glass.

"Tis an all," said Beth, drinking her last drop.

"Gerr us sum more, duk," said Maggi.

Beth eased herself up, pushing down on the table with her flat hands until she could stand upright.. She pulled down her dress which had worked its way up her thighs. Her large wobbly fleshy bosoms, like over ripe melons, were visible as she bent over the table.

"Am bleddy stiff, Maggi," she said.

She shuffled to the bar, holding onto the chairs and tables, swaying unsteadily as she went.

"You sit down, me duk. I'll bring 'em over for thee," said the barman.

"Thanks, mate."

"Thanks, duk." They said simultaneously.

They lit another cigarette and sat silently, apart from belching occasionally.

Ted and Eric turned up just before closing time to take them home. Beth and Maggi repeatedly hiccupped as they clung to their husbands, barely able to stand.

"They'll be no bleddy use tonit," said Ted.

"Not bother me. Gone rite off of it since she's ad that bleddy itch," said Eric.

"Aint it cleared up yet?" said Ted.

"She says not," said Eric.

CHAPTER 34

The Bank

"*The pride of the peacock is the glory of God.*
The lust of the goat is the bounty of God.
The wrath of the lion is the wisdom of God.
The nakedness of woman is the work of God."

The marriage of Heaven and Hell (1790-
1793) 'Proverbs of Hell'
William Blake 1757-1827.

CHAPTER 34

I walked into the chilled emptiness of the Provincial Bank on King Street. It looked forbidding, like a colossal Greek temple with its tall Doric columns. This experience was far removed from my real urge to be a farmer.

Dad said, "You'll have a good salary, and pension, good prospects if you pass your banking exams. You may even make manager one day. Play your cards right, and you've a job for life."

I only got the job because Dad was friendly with the Manager. His firm banked with the Provincial, and Dad went to the bank most days. Mr Brittlebank, the Manager, was more interested in my cricket and tennis ability, rather than a potential aptitude for banking.

In the marble chill of the bank, dressed in my new grey suit, white shirt, blue tie and well polished black shoes, I felt like a waxwork. Everyone seemed to be looking at me. The uniformed doorman, sitting at a Victorian upright desk, his face ashen, and monolithic, said, his eyes and lips only moving, "Can I help you, Sir?"

"I'm starting work in the bank today," I said.

"Sit down, Sir," he said, his eyes focussing towards a row of chairs against a wood-panelled wall. He picked up his telephone, and spoke to an invisible man.

"Mr Titlark will be with you shortly," he said.

He continued to stare into space with a vacant look on his face, drumming his fingers on the polished oak desk top. He matched the lack of any human feeling or light in the bank. It was like a mausoleum. Dark oil portraits of previous bank managers hung above the chairs, intimidating both customers and staff.

I didn't intend to stay in the bank. It was only as a temporary measure to please my Father, and confound my critics, that I reluctantly joined. Not that I had much choice.

The irony was I was hopeless at maths. I hadn't any idea about figures, percentages or banking, although I could add up accurately. I had only passed my maths in school certificate because I had copied from Cyril Wormwood. We had done a deal before the exam. Cyril had become good at maths and very quick. He surreptitiously passed me his paper to copy during the exam. In turn I was to give him £1, and introduce him to Monica's friend, Sally Stoffer. The ruse worked, but Sally didn't like Cyril. He had too many spots, and always smelt of carbolic soap.

Mr Titlark was the accountant and responsible for the staff and their training. There were six male cashiers who manned the tills, and dealt with customers in the main entrance hall. Four male clerks dealt with the clerical work behind the tills. A bevy of young girls working as typists, telephonists, accounting, and comptometer machine operators. The girls were under the supervision of Hazel Fraser. The Manager, Mr Brittlebank, had his own secretary, Louisa Latimer. I was introduced to all the staff as the new Junior. I was known as Junior, and called Junior, which I hated. I was assigned to the existing Junior, Billy Tate. My duties were opening the post each morning for the Manager, making the tea when required, writing the post book up, posting the mail, and filing customer's paid cheques, doing errands, and any odd jobs. Some days the Manager sent me to his house to help his wife clean the silver, and cut the lawn. On one occasion I was sent for the purpose of helping Mrs Brittlebank clean the house. She had not been well, and they were expecting visitors in the evening. I reluctantly arrived at the house to find the front door wide open. I rang the bell, but no reply. Looking through the window I saw Mrs Brittlebank lying on the chaise-longue, scantily clad, with an empty bottle resting between her legs. I walked into the room.

"Good morning, Mrs Brittlebank," I said.

She gave no response, just snorted as she continued sleeping. She was wearing only a pair of very loose French knickers, and a bra. She was totally non compos mentis. I'd never seen an almost naked woman before. I'd seen bare breasts, but nothing so visual and tactile as this head-to-toe loose-bodiced splendour in the form of Mrs Brittlebank. She was like an apparition, appearing quite unexpectedly.

"Was she real?" I asked myself, "or is this a dream?"

I looked at her from all angles trying to get the best possible view of her nakedness.

"Much better than being in the bank," I thought, smiling.

As though she heard my thoughts she opened her eyes, and looked up at me.

"Where am I? I feel awful. Oh! It's you, Derek."

She tried to ease herself up, but fell back, and went to sleep again. I shut my eyes, not believing what I was seeing.

"Get me some water, please."

I opened my eyes. Mrs Brittlebank was looking at me through her dishevelled blonde hair. One leg was lying aslant overhanging the flat part of the chaise-longue, displaying her pale smooth skinned thigh. Unveiled were tufts of curly brown bushy hair where her knickers had stretched with the tension of her hanging leg. For the moment I was speechless, intently ogling her exciting, unprotected body.

"Please get me some water, Derek," she said, in a whisper."Thank you, Derek. You are a sweet boy," she said, trying to sit up.

"Pass me some cushions for my back. Thanks!"

I placed two cushions behind her back to support her shoulders against the back of the chaise-longue. As she lifted her arms I could see wisps of fair hair in her armpits, adding to her sensuous tantalizing body,. She shuffled her bottom to gain a sitting posture. The way she was sitting caused her breasts to bulge forward provocatively.

"That's better," she said.

"It's a good job you came along. I might have slept for the rest of the day. Nigel wouldn't be too pleased to come home, and see me like this."

She suddenly became aware of her nakedness and me looking at her, but did not seem at all embarrassed or put out. She had been fiddling with her bra straps. Eventually she slid them both over her round shoulders. Her breasts sprang forward, yielding and plump, with rosy nipples, pricked-up like pink rose buds. I was hypnotized by their symmetry and loveliness. We both caught each other's eyes. She smiled. I smiled.

"Go on, have a feel!" she said.

I was gob smacked.

"Should I, or shouldn't I?"

Decisions, decisions! Panic, panic!

"What should I do?" raced through my mind.

I went weak at the knees, and red as a beetroot. I said nothing. We both remained silent. I was spellbound, and in a state of shock.

"Oh well! Too late!" she said, trying unsuccessfully to fasten her bra at her back.

"Er. Er. Well. Yes. Don't know," I stuttered, with a longing to feel her breasts, but it was now too late.

"Derek, be a dear and fasten my bra for me. It's a bit awkward like this for me."

She leant forward, her breasts taking on a pear shape posture. She arranged her breasts so they took the shape of the bra cup.

"Ah! That's better," she said.

"Now just put the hook into the eye. Not too tight. Wow! Your hands are cold, Derek."

"Sorry, Mrs Brittlebank."

I took my hands away, breathed on them to warm them up.

"Please call me Betty."

"Yes, thank you, Mrs Brittlebank, I mean, Betty" I said, feeling very uncomfortable, and getting hotter.

My face was flushed, and burning, with beads of perspiration breaking out all over my body. The bra squeezed her breasts together forming a deep sensuous cleavage. All at once I felt sexually excited, and wanted to touch her. My eyes rested longingly on her half-reclining body. I was captivated by her scantily-dressed nudity.

"If only I could …."

"Are you alright, Derek?" she said, waking me up from my fantasy.

I looked the other way in my embarrassment.

"Oh! Er. Er. Don't know," I said, feeling very awkward.

"Derek, dear! Would you be so kind and make me a cup of black coffee. Everything's in the cupboard over the fridge. One heaped spoon of coffee. The continental, not the original. You know where the kitchen is? You are a sweetie. What would I do without you? Oh! Take this bottle. Where the hell is it?"

"It's on the floor," I said, picking it up. It read 'London Gin'.

"Half fill it with water. No! About a third, and put it in the cupboard by the French windows.

"Before you go, pass me a cigarette from the silver box on the table. Thank you, Derek. Light it for me, please."

Cigarette smoking did not suit me. I'd tried it at school in the silk-worm shed, and killed most of them with the smoke. I was violently sick at the time, almost coughing up my lungs and brains. I lit the cigarette and gave it to her. Her slender hands with bright red nails caressed the black and gold paper cylindrical tube. She drew deeply on it, raised her chin and fixed her eyes on me, blowing the smoke sideways.

"How old are you, Derek?" she said, smiling.

"Sixteen," I said.

"You look older. Have you got a girlfriend?"

"Sort of. Nothing serious. We're just good friends," I said.

"Do you like working at the bank?" she said, still smiling.

"Don't know," I said, adding, "I'll make the coffee."

I went to the kitchen with the empty gin bottle. I didn't like the cross examination, and wondered how I might escape.

Handing her the coffee, she said, "Thank you, darling. Do you think I'm attractive?"

"Well. Er. Er! I don't know," I said, feeling uncomfortable.

"Put it another way, Derek. Do you fancy me?"

I didn't know what to say. I liked her, especially in her bra and knickers, but I couldn't really say so. The door bell rang.

"Please see who it is, Derek. I'm not in to anybody."

A tall man with drooping shoulders, late fifties, stood at the door. He wore a shiny dark grey pinstripe suit with baggy trousers, white shirt with winged collar and tie. His black shoes were clean, but had a dull matt finish. Thin greying hair, swept back over his bald head was held down by a glossy lustrous grease. A fine tracery of ruptured blood-vessels purpled his large nose on which sat a half-moon pince-nez, supported by his puffy cheeks. He carried a black homburg hat in one hand, with an umbrella hooked by its handle in the crook of his arm. In his other hand he held a thin black brief case.

"Good morning," he said.

"Good morning," I replied.

"Is Mrs Brittlebank in, may I ask?"

"Well yes, and no. She's not well, and can't see anybody today," I said.

"Oh dear! I am sorry. You must be young Mr Brittlebank."

For some reason, I said, "Yes!"

"I'm sorry she's unwell. Please give her my card."

"Thank you," I said, peering at the card in my hand.

"Good day to you, Master Brittlebank."

He turned round, clicked his heels, put his hat on, and went down the drive, crunching the gravel as he walked with his oversized feet.

I read the black-edged card he'd given me.

MORTICIANS UNLIMITED

OBSEQUIES. INTERNMENTS. ENTOMBMENTS. CREMATIONS

MONUMENTAL MASONRY. GILDING. FLORAL TRIBUTES

CHAPEL OF REST. WOODLAND BURIALS. HORSE-DRAWN FUNERALS

PRE-PAY-PLAN YOUR FUNERAL NOW FOR GENEROUS DISCOUNTS

DIGNITY WITH CARE

AFFILIATED TO FUNERAL OMBUDSMAN SCHEME

PRESENTED BY ENOCH DE'ATH. DIP.F.D. M.B.I.E.

Tel. 71395

Mrs Brittlebank was asleep again when I returned. I put the empty gin bottle in the cupboard without adding any water, and left the visiting card on a small table next to the chaise-longue. Giving her further impassioned close examination, I crept quietly out of the room.

"Is that you, Derek?"

I stood still waiting to hear more, but could only hear the wall clock ticking in the stillness, and Mrs Brittlebank's gentle murmuring as she slept. I returned to the bank, relieved to be out of the house.

It had been raining and the roads were all glossy and shimmering in the wet. A musky scent of damp rotting vegetation filled the air.

I was never sent to help Mrs Brittlebank again, much to my chagrin. The Bank Manager never questioned me about the last visit. I did wonder if Mrs Brittlebank had said anything to discredit me.

CHAPTER 35

Hazel

"Go, lovely rose!
Tell her, that wastes her time and me,
That now she knows,
When I resemble her to thee,
How sweet and fair she seems to be."
'Go, lovely rose!'

Edmund Waller 1606-1687.

CHAPTER 35

Hazel was the supervisor in charge of all the bank's female staff, in particular the young girls who worked the comptometers. She was around 40, tallish and slim with rich brown hair swept back from her olive-skinned oval face, and tied in a small pony tail resting in the nape of her neck. Her laughing bright hazel eyes slanted over high cheek bones. Her mouth was round and generous with a line of pink soft skin, where her wet lips met.

Mr Titlark introduced me to her on my first day at the bank, as he did most of the staff. Immediately there was empathy between us. It was as if we had known each other before. She wore a very mild lavender fragrance, reminding me of my Mother. Whenever our paths crossed she would slightly lift her head in recognition, and smile. Her smile was infectious, leaving me feeling content, relaxed and glowing with happiness. I purposely looked for her in the bank, especially first thing in the morning. My clandestine motives were an innocent reassurance of my ego. I seemed to have found a romantic life force, which became a necessary need I had to satisfy. It was not a sexual need, but a comforting requisite.

Hazel seemed to be replacing a memory. I felt reawakened. I looked forward to going to the bank each day. My father even remarked on my appearance and change in attitude. I would wear a clean shirt each day, use expensive after shave, have my hair cut when it really didn't need it, clean my shoes daily, which I rarely did. I even borrowed my father's ties, so I could wear a different one each day, matched to a silk handkerchief which I tucked into my jacket breast pocket, letting it loosely drape a few inches.

Each morning I hurried to work feeling excited at the prospect of seeing Hazel. The weekends were miserable. I longed for Monday to arrive. After a few weeks I became disillusioned and frustrated. My chance encounters with Hazel were not achieving anything. I didn't know what I was looking for, or wanted, but I did know I needed to be with her, talk to her, and get to know her. The relationship had to be pursued for me to find why I was so drawn to Hazel. I suppose I was looking for a loving relationship. Sex, per se, was not yet on my agenda. I did not see Hazel as a sex object, but more as a mother figure. Certainly Hazel was very beautiful and desirable. I could think of nothing better than feeling her warm body held tightly to mine. She generated a closeness, and intimacy, which only exists in special relationships. I had missed out, and only experienced the pain, and empty void of not knowing the close bond of a mother's love, and the essential nurturing relationship between mother and son.

My feelings for Hazel were unlike my attraction for Betty Brittlebank which was nothing more than lustful pleasure. Her nakedness *did* stimulate an appetite for licentiousness, which due to my naivety was not fulfilled, despite her enthusiasm.

Hazel was the missing jigsaw piece I needed to make good my loss. She had become important to me. How could I achieve this?

Late one afternoon at the end of my fifth week in the bank I went my usual late afternoon errand to the Post Office, carrying the mail in a large brown leather Gladstone bag. I was generally the last to leave, the caretaker locking up after me. I always tried to leave at the same time as Hazel, so our leaving would be simultaneous, but the strategy never seemed to work. We would miss each other sometimes by only minutes. I would usually see her disappearing down the road as I tried to catch her up. It had to be a chance meeting so I could pursue some kind of rapport without being too obvious.

It was Friday afternoon and beginning to rain. The streets were busy with traffic.

Office and factory workers were rushing home for the weekend. I hurried with the mail to avoid getting wet.

"Derek! Derek!"

I heard my name repeated twice. I looked towards the sound, turned, and in that moment we found each other. Hazel was standing in a shop doorway. Our eyes met, and in an instant our relationship was complete. Her warm gaze and innocent smile filled me with absolute joy. She was tall in stature, and slim. Her bosoms were emphasized by her-close fitting clothes, leaving a discreet cleavage, covered by a diaphanous silk scarf she wore about her neck. We walked towards each other. She held out her hands to greet me. They were warm against my cold wet flesh. She held my free hand firmly with tenderness. We walked to the Post Office saying little, Hazel's arm linked through mine. We huddled together, sharing the umbrella between us, as the rain became more determined.

"I've been waiting for you, Derek. I've so wanted to talk to you. Each day I've tried to catch you, and missed you. But not today. Our lucky day."

At this, she squeezed my arm against hers as a sign of achieving her quest.

"I've been trying to meet you, too," I said.

"I know. I've seen you trying to catch my eye. It's difficult in the bank. You've only got to be seen talking to someone more than once, and you're having an affair," she said, squeezing my arm again.

"Yes, the cashiers seem a funny lot. I've noticed how they make rude comments about customers and bank staff."

We posted the mail, leaving the bag, which I always collected the next day on my way to the bank from the Post Office. A black Ford Consul splashed through a puddle showering me with water as it pulled up outside the Post Office. The doors remained closed. No-one got out. The engine was still running and the wiper blades seesawing across the windscreen. Steam rose from the bonnet, and mingled in with the steady drizzle. Mr Brittlebank sat at the wheel, with his secretary, Louisa Lattimer, sitting in the passenger seat. They were in a deep embrace, oblivious to passers-by. In no time the inside of the car was steamed up. We had caught them in flagrante delicto. Moving on quickly, and not wishing to be seen by them, we made our way towards the rose gardens walking closely together, our bodies rubbing as we shared the umbrella. A faint hint of lavender hung in the air.

"They're lovers," said Hazel, in her gentle rasping cultured voice.

I thought of my involvement with Mrs Brittlebank.

"Go on, have a feel." With hindsight I wished I had.

I often thought about her remark, and would fantasize about fondling, and nuzzling in between her swollen breasts. Her loose-bodiced unsupported tactile bosoms haunted me daily. Several times I'd been on the edge of asking Mr Brittlebank if he needed his lawn cutting.

"You've gone all quiet, Derek. Are you alright?" said Hazel.

"Yes, just thinking. Sorry!" I said.

"Penny for them, Derek."

"Not worth a penny," I said, feeling guilty, not wishing to discuss my experience.

I began to like Mrs Brittlebank the more I thought about her. She seemed a lovely lady, without children, whose husband preferred his secretary. She was obviously very lonely.

I did get on well with Mr Brittlebank. He was jolly, a good cricketer, and always included me in the County Bank's team. He would often invite me to play for his club at the weekends. We always ended the day's play with a visit to the local pub, 'The Bat and Ball', after the match. It was on one of these occasions I tasted my first beer. I would feel like a real man holding a jar of beer in my fist, more so if I'd had a good day playing cricket. I soon got the taste for beer. It seemed to be part of cricket, and with my pipe smouldering away, I was in my element. Working in the bank was not so bad after all.

"You're day dreaming, Derek. Do I have this effect on you?" said Hazel.

"No, sorry! I'm so pleased we met up," I said, feeling confident and without inhibitions.

We reached the park. Spicy, musky scented roses invaded the damp air from the recent rain. The drizzle had stopped, and the benches were almost dry. We sat and talked for nearly two hours, and arranged to meet after work the next day to see 'Brighton Rock' starring Richard Attenborough, and Sheila Sim at the new cinema - The Ritz.

As we parted, Hazel gave me a kiss on the cheek and squeezed my hand. She walked down the street, leaving me tingling with excitement. At the corner, before disappearing round the bend, she turned and waved. I hadn't moved, and waved back. I caught the bus home, reflecting on my sudden happiness. It was a state which existed because of our meeting, and being together.

"Did Hazel feel the same?" I wondered.

I could still smell the spicy-scented roses as the bus trundled up the hill out of town.

CHAPTER 36

One year later The Robbery

"Grief is the price, we pay for Love."

Queen Elizabeth II.

CHAPTER 36

Two gun shots rang out, reverberating through the empty streets. It was early morning around eight o'clock, with few people about. There was a damp chill in the misty air. The sun was trying hard to burn through the hanging clouds. I was walking from the bus station on my way to the Bank.

Within what seemed only seconds after the gun shots, a car, at breakneck speed, appeared from nowhere, out of control, and crashed into a shop's plate glass window, which displayed ladies' bridal gowns. I was about 20 yards away. Two police cars, sirens blasting, pulled up outside the shop. An ambulance arrived shortly afterwards. Two bodies were carried out on stretchers. One completely covered with a red blanket. The other stocking-faced and bloody. The ambulance pulled away slowly at first, and, gathering speed, it went full pelt like a rocket, up the road, with horns blaring like orchestral trumpets at full blast.

The commotion drew inquisitive onlookers to the scene, including myself. More police arrived, and the accident scene was roped off with blue and white police tape. I overheard a policeman say there had been a break-in at the Provincial Bank. I rushed to the Bank to find police cars, motor cyclists, an ambulance and fire engine, with policemen dashing about, keeping onlookers back. On the pavement lay a stretcher covered up with a red blanket. A man carrying a small doctor's bag was talking to Mr Brittlebank, and what seemed to be a high ranking policeman. A crowd had gathered, including several bank staff. I looked around for Hazel, but there was no sign of her. Mr Brittlebank saw me and beckoned me over to him.

"Bad news, Postlethwaite, I'm afraid. Go into my office. I'll join you as soon as I can."

"Yes, sir," I said.

I sat alone in his office terrified something dreadful had happened, and waited for what seemed an age, although it must have been no more than two or three minutes. Mr Brittlebank appeared with a policewoman and the doctor. I stood up as they entered the office.

"Sit down, Derek," said Mr Brittlebank.

"Thank you, Sir," I said, sitting down again.

"Brace yourself, Derek. I've some terrible news. I know you and Hazel Fraser were very good friends. I'm afraid to say she was shot in the head by one of the robbers, and died instantly."

I sat speechless. My mental process for understanding what had happened to Hazel was blocked out. I didn't understand the implications of what had been said to me.

"Yes, Sir," I said.

All three looked at me.

The policewoman sat down next to me saying, "Hazel is dead, Derek. Do you understand? She was shot in the head and died immediately. She didn't suffer at all. Are you alright, Derek?"

She draped her arm on my shoulders to comfort me. By this time I realised that Hazel had been killed.

I stood up, bowed my head, saying, "I understand. Can I go?"

"Of course, Derek. I'm so very sorry. Please go home. The Bank will be shut today and resume normal business tomorrow. Only come to work when you feel ready. I'll understand."

I walked from the Bank to the rose garden in the park, sat on the same bench where I'd sat with Hazel, and cried, and cried. I sobbed my heart out for most of the day, and went home red-eyed and distraught. My love for Hazel was not aroused by passion, but by feelings of happiness, being wanted, and contentment. Our love was not an emotional love per se. It was an innocent love devoid of intrigue, romance and affaire de coeur. Our hearts were at peace with each other, calm and untroubled by emotional constraints.

Once more I was reduced to the status quo. The jigsaw piece was lost again. The picture was destroyed.

My life now lacked the loving relationship I had experienced with Hazel, which in part had replaced my mother's love. Without warning or preparation it had all been destroyed by the quirk of man. I became a prisoner in my own cell again, back in solitary confinement. My thoughts, dreams, and aspirations were once more ebbing away like the retreating sea.

We had both enjoyed a tender, warm relationship which had replaced our own personal loss. Hazel had lost her husband and seven year old son in a car crash nine years earlier. They had died instantly in a head-on collision. The other driver was drunk, and driving on the wrong side of the road. He too, was killed. Hazel was the only child of a retired army colonel who had served in the Indian Army most of his service life, and latterly with the Raj. He was knighted for his services to the British Government in India. Sir Anthony Fraser married an Indian princess, the daughter of a Rajah.

Sir Anthony and Lady Savita were delightful people, young in heart and spirit, despite being in their eighties. On occasions Hazel had taken me to visit them at their country home in Scotland. We would walk the mountains, salmon fish in the Tay, and eat the catch for supper, washed down with Sir Anthony's finest Chablis. Hazel was educated at Roedean. She was a refined and cultured lady with artistic tastes. Our various weekend trips to London always included a concert at the Royal Albert Hall with Sir Thomas Beecham, or Sir Adrian Boult conducting, or a visit to the theatre. Hazel stimulated my love for music, theatre, art, and reading.

I was now without my mentor, counsellor, guru, soul mate, and surrogate mother - alone again. I still saw Monica when she was home from boarding school, but that was a girlfriend affair, something quite different from my maternalistic relationship with Hazel.

The fatal accident was a quantum leap from a happy existence, which had been organised and loving. My life had now become unsettled, and everything changed.

After Hazel's death my attitude to life took on a different meaning. My faith as a Catholic collapsed.

What was God doing when all this happened. We had been abandoned - Hazel, me, her parents, friends, and all who knew her. I could not come to terms with the loss of Hazel, and the way she died. It was so unnecessary. Her life, and those close to her, were governed by chance and random change. She was the victim of a surprisingly cruel and savage fate, and we were the losers, the no-hopers, who didn't know anything for certain, who were unable to determine or control events. Our lives were in the hands of probability, dictated by luck or fate. God had nothing to do with it. I began to question if there was such a person. If there was, He had taken my mother, and now Hazel, without any explanation. God works in mysterious ways is *no* explanation, but it is the Church's answer to many cruel happenings. Who are the losers? The victims, or those left behind. My parish priest had no answer.

"Have faith," he said.

"Faith in what?"

I was left once again in a situation with which I was unable to understand, nor reconcile. My Faith had no answer. God had let me down. In the meantime I was alive although even being alive was hard. My thoughts, dreams and aspirations had once more turned to stone.

CHAPTER 37

Ted and Eric

"Meine Ruh' ist hin,
Mein Herz ist schwer."
"My peace is gone,
My heart is heavy."

'Faust' pt 1 (1808)
Johann Wolfgang von Goethe 1749-1832.

CHAPTER 37

"Ay-up then, Eric", said Ted, wiping his dripping nose with the back of his hand.

"Ow-do, mate," said Eric, fumbling about in his trouser pocket.

"Ow's your Maggi?" said Ted, now wiping his hand on his jacket.

"Orryte," said Eric.

" 'As er itch gorn yet?" said Ted.

"Ah! It went, then it cum bak, bleddy nuisance. If it ain't 'eddake, its un itch. Ain't 'ad oat for nai ont week," said Eric. "Ow's your Beth's tits now?" he added.

"Orryte, but 'er nipples gorn," said Ted.

"Funny job that," said Eric, still fumbling in his trouser pocket.

"Ay yo gorra'n itch?" said Ted, now picking his nose.

"Rekkon 'av summat, Ted," said Eric, frantically. Scratching his head with the other hand.

"Rum job at Bank. That gel yung Postlething's walking out wi' gorr 'ersen shot," said Ted.

"Ah! She was ode enuff to be is Mam an all," said Eric.

"Is Dad reckons they wer just gud mates," said Ted.

"Pull t'other one," said Eric.

"Both robbers killed an all, one died in 'ospital," said Ted.

"It's a rum job, any rode," said Eric.

"Fancy arff ut Feathers?" said Ted.

"Ah! I'll 'av 'arff wi yo, mate," said Eric.

They both walked slowly down the road towards 'The Feathers'. Ted's trousers were floating a good eight inches above his ankles, and Eric's trousers were torn behind both knees. Their flies were undone. Eric's trousers were pinned up with red braces, whilst Ted's were tied at the waist with a piece of string. They swayed, walking down the road, as it they'd already been drinking. They slowed down to speak to Derek Postlethwaite who approached them from the opposite direction.

Derek politely touched his hat, saying, "Good evening, Mr Brown, Mr Smith. How are you both?"

"Orryte, serri," came their reply, in unison.

Derek walked on towards home. His black tie in sharp contrast to his crisp white shirt, black polished shoes, and suit.

A week later the Bank was back to some resemblance of normality, but for Derek the Bank, and his life, would never be the same. He'd made up his mind to leave the Bank and join the Army as soon as he was old enough. He felt unsettled, walking down the garden path to the front door. It was turning cool, and he was glad to be home. He picked up the evening paper, and read the headlines.

"Bank robbery went disastrously wrong!

Bank official. Two raiders killed.
Coroners Inquest Verdict."

Derek went to his room with heavy heart, shedding more tears.

CHAPTER 38

The Funeral

"For dust you are
And to dust you shall return."

The Bible
Genesis 3. v 19.

CHAPTER 38

Since the Bank tragedy I was not sleeping at all well, waking up with horrific dreams in the early hours of the morning, and not being able to get back to sleep. By lunchtime I became unreliable and felt like a zombie. On the eve of Hazel's funeral I went to bed late in the hope I would have a good night's sleep. I woke at 2am and slept fitfully, disturbed by footsteps outside my bedroom window. I lay rigid, not moving, and quiet, wondering if there were intruders prowling about outside.

"Did Dad lock and bolt all the doors? Shut the downstairs windows?" I thought, as I lay contemplating my next move.

The footsteps seemed to have ceased, but then I heard a noise, like a vase crashing onto a stone floor. I crawled out of bed, and quietly went down the stairs, almost bent double in fright. I crawled through the house, and crouched down in the kitchen. Outside the window I heard muffled voices, and footsteps walking away. Two gunshots echoed in the stillness, followed by the sound of a car starting up, and the engine revving, and accelerating away for all its worth. I went outside and found two cigarette butts, smoking and glowing in the garden. An all-powerful bang followed. The impact of metal against flesh shook me out of my deep sleep. I woke up, recoiled in bed, letting out a cry of fright. My pyjamas and body were soaked in perspiration. My heart raced, and my head throbbed. It was not quite 4am. My nightmare was still pumping away in my head. I was awake, but trying to finish my dream.

"Was I hurt? Who was with me? Was I in the car? Where was Hazel?"

"Bastards!" I cried out. "Stop them. Police. Why so many police cars?"

Slowly I realised I was fully awake, but very disturbed with the nightmare still racing through my mind. I got up, dowsed myself with cold water, made a cup of tea, and sat in Dad's armchair. I was soon asleep again.

I woke with the sun shining through the' window, and the cloudless sky a pale blue. I began to wonder what was going to happen. I'd never been to a funeral before, having been excluded from my mother's on the grounds I was too young, and wouldn't understand. I felt uncertain. I wanted some meaning. Some reason for the day's events. I wondered where my life was going to go after the funeral.

Looking through the window I saw a bird perched on the fence. He cocked his head up, his yellow beak hungrily pointing towards me. He was still, and silent, his tiny brown beady eyes staring at me, as if in recognition. I stared back in empathy. Suddenly he let out a melodic song, as if to welcome the new day. He sang his heart out, and flew off.

He seemed to saying, "I've done my best, now go and do yours."

Silence followed. I was alone again.

It was 7am and time to get up.

The stillness was broken with Dad shouting to Brian, "You'll miss your bus for school if you don't get a move on."

Thank God I'd finished with St Thomas More's. Brian was bright, and doing well. Always top of the class, but hopeless at sport. I was the opposite, not so good in the classroom but I could hit a cricket ball to the boundary. Brian couldn't. He couldn't even hold the bat correctly. He had become a swot, always with his head in a school book. Good at maths, rather like Cyril Wormwood. Brian looked a bit like Cyril, with specs and spots. We rarely spoke to each other now, he was always too busy reading. Another shout from Dad shook me out of my reverie. I felt crestfallen at the prospect of the day ahead. I just wanted to be swallowed up in my grief, and left alone to fade away.

The Bank was closed in the morning out of consideration for Hazel, and to allow the staff to pay their respects. The funeral was at St John's Catholic Church, with Requiem Mass at 9.30am. I sat at the front with Sir Anthony and Lady Savita Fraser, at their request. I felt very conspicuous, but couldn't refuse them. I was the only person they knew. My Dad came, but he was sitting almost at the back of the church. A strong musky smell of incense hung in the air, causing a dense milky mist to float down the aisle. The coffin was carried into the church by four pall bearers, and placed in front of the altar. The priest in black and gold vestments intoned, 'The De Profundis'.

> *"Out of the depths have I cried unto Thee, O Lord,*
> *Lord hear my voice."*

He speeded up the prayer in a soft inaudible voice, chanting with a gradual increase in volume, intoning.

> *"The bones that have been humbled shall rejoice in*
> *the Lord.*
> *Amen."*

The hymn 'Now thank we all our God', followed before the onset of Mass. A dissonant congregation, coughing, sneezing and crying, were accompanied by a tuneless organ - all making an atonal noise.

After the hymn the priest had the effrontery to say, "Please put more effort into the next hymn for the sake of the deceased."

"Hazel deserves better than this," I thought. "He didn't appear to know her name." The Mass ended with the final hymn.

> *."O love that wilt not let me go,*
> *I rest my weary soul in thee."*

Once again only a buzzing drone was heard. The priest did not even join in with the congregation in their unhappy efforts to sing. The priest then recited, 'The Prayer for a Happy Death'.

> *"Oh God, Who had doomed all men to die ....*
> *.......Through the same Christ, Our Lord. Amen."*

"What meaningless platitudes," I thought. "Archaic! Said for the sake of established custom."

"How can you have a happy death? Who's happy? The victim, or those left to mourn, and pick up the pieces?

Hazel would be amused by the behind the times ritual, I felt sure. We often discussed Catholicism with its outmoded concepts, and attitudes written in stone.

There was no blessing. Today of all days we needed God's blessing, another whim of the Church. The coffin was carried down the aisle in silence led by the priest. Sir Anthony, Lady Savita, both sobbing silently, myself choking back my grief, followed the coffin out of the church to the waiting hearse. Mrs Brittlebank who was wearing a large, black, wide-brimmed hat with half-veil, smiled, and notionally pursed her shiny, red lip-sticked lips at me. I smiled back in recognition. Mr Brittlebank nodded, and grimaced as we walked by. Louisa Latimer, standing next to Mr Brittlebank, with head bent, wiped a tear from her cheek as we passed. The church was full, with friends, and bank staff, wearing black, black ties and armbands. The congregation followed us out, and stood crestfallen as the cortege moved away for the cemetery.

Few people stopped, or noticed the funeral procession. Most were too preoccupied with their own business to recognize what was happening. Some hats, and caps were removed, and signs of the cross made. More policemen were on duty than usual, but not required. They stood with bowed heads as the cortege drove slowly through the sleepy town. The hearse arrived at the cemetery, followed by two cars with the principal mourners. The pall-bearers shouldered the coffin to the graveside. We followed, standing around the cold, damp, empty grave as the coffin was slowly lowered to its resting place. And then she was gone, soon to be forgotten. Her body, love, beauty, intellect and life to be ravished by time, and the elements, leaving only a memory as a reminder of a person we loved.

The priest began more prayers with,

> *"I am the resurrection and the life, sayeth the Lord,*
> *He that believe in me, though he were dead, yet shall he live, and who so ever liveth and believeth in me shall never die."*

A bird flew down, and perching on a nearby headstone sang a lament. He looked at me.

A voice within me said, "Be brave. Your turn now."

I recited Psalm 23.

> *"The Lord is my shepherd: therefore can I lack nothing.*
> *He shall feed me in a green pasture: and lead me forth beside the waters of comfort.*
> *He shall convert my soul: and bring me forth in the paths of righteousness, for his Name's sake.*

*Yea, though I walk through the valley of the
shadow of death.
I will feel no evil: for thou art with me;
Thy rod and thy staff they comfort me."*

I momentarily stopped for breath, to hold back my emotions. I was almost choking with grief. Tears rolled down my cheeks, falling onto the white paper sheet I was reading. I looked up at the mourners, who, with eyes closed were silently weeping. Our grief was united, and complete. I continued, confident and with renewed passion.

*"Thou shalt prepare a table before me against them
that trouble me;
Thou hast anointed my head with oil, and my cup
shall be full.
But thy loving-kindness and mercy shall follow me
all the days of my life:
And I will dwell in the house of the Lord for ever."*

I felt grown up, strong and proud that Sir Anthony had asked me to make a contribution of prayer for Hazel. Mentally I included my mother in my offering. Despite my grief I felt a calm and controlled contentment.

"Well done, Derek," came a quiet voice a few paces behind me.

I turned and saw my father. We both smiled, perhaps in recognition of our own personal loss. The mourners joined in with the priest reciting 'The Lord's Prayer'. Before leaving the graveside we each took a handful of red earth, and let the grains patter down on the coffin. Unhurried, and in the silence, the mourners left the graveside. I was left with Sir Anthony and Lady Savita. We stood in silence with tears flooding our cheeks. After a few minutes we left, their frail bodies leaning heavily on each of my arms, to a waiting car.

Refreshments of sandwiches, tea and cakes were served in 'The George Hotel' for the mourners. It was an unhappy occasion, with people talking in small groups in very soft voices - not wishing to be heard.

Mr Charles Bonzi of Wagstaff, Wagstaff and Wagstaff, Solicitors, took me to one side, and told me that Hazel had left me £10,000. He would be in touch with me shortly. He shook my hand, went purple in the face, and sneezed with surprising ferocity before turning his back on me and leaving.

I said goodbye to Sir Anthony and Lady Savita. They made me promise to keep in touch, and visit them in Scotland. Sir Anthony told me I had given Hazel a fresh stimulus for life after the loss of her husband and son. She had loved me dearly, and accepted me as her own. Once more, tears swelled up in my eyes. Her love and sentiments were lovingly returned. I too, felt we had shared a relationship which could only be found between mother and son.

I walked down the street, the sun still shining in a blue sky. I looked at my watch - a birthday present from Hazel. It was too early for my meeting. I felt more relaxed now in the fresh air, and went to the rose garden in the park. I sat down on the same wooden bench, which we had both sat on - Hazel and me, at our first meeting.

I was aware of her presence, and a closeness to her. The smell of lavender lingered in the air.

> *I am sitting, waiting for time to pass.*
> *Waiting for what?*
> *Waiting for my future - whatever it is going to be.*
> *I didn't know.*
> *I didn't really care.*
> *It was so uncertain.*
> *But so is my life.*
> *Life is unpredictable, illogical, and frail,*
> *As was Hazel's.*
> *She was killed, because fate dictated it.*
> *What was the justification for her death?*
> *I want an answer, an explanation.*
> *Can God give me an explanation?*
> *No! He hasn't got a rational answer.*
> *Too many shifting sands.*
> *I give up!*

These questions and answers flashed through my mind, as I sat, waiting for time to pass. I tried to stop thinking. I had to be positive. If Hazel was still alive would my life be any different. I don't know. All I'm left with are memories, and thoughts of what might have been. What I do know is that I loved Hazel, as I did my mother, which was infinite, like no other love. It was inexhaustible and special. Only memories are left to be cherished for all time.

A bird flew down and rested on the arm of the wooden bench. It gave out a few chirrups and tweets, defecated, and flew off, perhaps to remind me of the time. I looked at my watch. It was time to go. I took off my black tie, held it to my lips, folded it up, and put it in my pocket. I got up from the bench, and walked slowly into the town.

Inside 'The Beehive Café', we kissed each other in greeting, had a cup of tea and left.

I walked back up the street towards the park again, clutching Monica's hand. We looked at each other, smiled, our hands locked together.

"Life's not too bad, after all," I thought. "Perhaps this is my future."

A hint of lavender hung in the air.

FINI

ABOUT THE AUTHOR

John Lalor was born in Nottingham. After leaving school he joined Lloyds Bank. He spent two years National Service in the Army, spending most of his service in Germany. On demob he joined a firm of Dyers and Finishers, before starting his own textile company exporting to Eastern Europe. He is married with six children. Graduated with a BA honours degree in English Studies. Other work has included management of a professional orchestra, teaching, postman, citizens advice bureau and accountancy. He is a committed Christian, defecting from Roman Catholicism to the Anglican Church. Rock climbing, mountaineering, long distance walking, music and reading have been his main interests. He is currently writing a sequel to his first novel.

ABOUT THE BOOK

An unpredicatable socio-comic novel with serious overtones and implications, set in middle England.

Current contentious issues within the Catholic Church are addressed.

Derek Poslethwaite, a dreamy, imaginative nine year old Catholic boy, who has to cope with his mother's death, puberty and his erotic fantasies. A subconscious part of him still thirsts for maternal comforts, which represent the love he has lost…

The novel's colourful characters encroach frequently into the most unlikely events of his young life, which sometimes leave him agonised and embarrassed.

0845 600 55 55

Printed in the United Kingdom
by Lightning Source UK Ltd.
107747UKS00001BA/1-3